How could Elizabeth say no? It would have been a terrible insult, especially from an officer's wife.

Not that she wanted to say no. Not really. She had kept herself out of his way the whole evening, all the while very aware of his presence. All the while wondering what it would be like to have *his* arm around *her* waist.

Now she would find out.

At first, she kept her smile cool and polite and counted her steps to herself, though she didn't need to for she was a good dancer. But it was a lovely tune, and she relaxed and lost herself in the music.

Michael Burke was as good on the dance floor as he was on horseback, she thought. She could feel his gloved hand against the small of her back, and the warmth it created seemed to be spreading up her spine. It frightened her, the effect that physical closeness with the man had on her. It seemed to create sensations she had never experienced before. She could put no name to them, but somehow they were dangerous. Elizabeth shivered.

"Are ye cold, Mrs. Woolcott?" Michael asked.

Desert Hearts

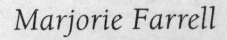

Marjorie Farrell

A TOPAZ BOOK

TOPAZ
Published by the Penguin Group
Penguin Books USA Inc., 375 Hudson Street,
New York, New York 10014, U.S.A.
Penguin Books Ltd, 27 Wrights Lane,
London W8 5TZ, England
Penguin Books Australia Ltd, Ringwood,
Victoria, Australia
Penguin Books Canada Ltd, 10 Alcorn Avenue,
Toronto, Ontario, Canada M4V 3B2
Penguin Books (N.Z.) Ltd, 182–190 Wairau Road,
Auckland 10, New Zealand

Penguin Books Ltd, Registered Offices:
Harmondsworth, Middlesex, England

First published by Topaz, an imprint of Dutton Signet,
a division of Penguin Books USA Inc.

First Printing, May, 1996
10 9 8 7 6 5 4 3 2 1

 REGISTERED TRADEMARK—MARCA REGISTRADA

Printed in the United States of America

This book is for my mother, Marjorie Powers Farrell, who, remembering Irish history, kept her heart open to all the dispossessed.

Author's Note

Transforming historical fact into fiction is never easy. This time, my additional challenge was presenting another people's history and culture accurately and with respect.

Each Navajo is given several names. The "war name," thought of as the person's real name, was never used directly and was known only to her family. Another name, a descriptive one, (like "Blue Mule") was used when talking about others but never in direct address. In introducing oneself one would do so by relationship and clan name.

I wanted to be accurate and respectful, yet not confuse my readers, so I chose a compromise. The Diné were given names by the Mexicans. Barboncito, Manuelito, and Delgadito are all historical figures. Later on, Anglo names like John or Mary were given. These names would be used in direct address in the non-Navajo world. Since I was writing at the time of Spanish usage, I decided to give my main Navajo characters Spanish names that Anglos could use in addressing them. Serena and Antonio and the other Diné in my story only address each other relationally. I am thankful to Barre Toelken's essay "The Demands of Harmony" for guidance. Any inaccuracies are my own.

I have read several versions of the Navajo Creation

Myth. This book would never had been written, however, had I not read Paul Zolbrod's *Dine Bahane* ten years ago. It is his version that I heavily depended upon in telling the story of *Asdzaa nadleehe,* or Changing Woman.

The *kinaalda* ceremony is detailed in Charlotte Frisbie's book *Kinaalda.* I hope the "presence" of many *bilagaana* readers at the parts I describe will not offend.

Almost all of the incidents in the book, including the story of the horse race, are true and in historical sequence. I am greatly indebted to *Bury My Heart at Wounded Knee, The Long Walk,* and *The Book of the Navajo.* I took some liberties; for instance, Michael is stationed at a fictional composite of Fort Defiance and Fort Wingate.

For a general sense of what army life was like for women, I am thankful to *Army Letters from an Officer's Wife* by Frances Roe. It was her grandmother who said to her: "It is a dreadful thing not to become a woman when one ceases to be a girl."

I want to thank Elaine Weintraub, a former student of mine, who showed me a newspaper clipping about the Choctaw contribution of $700 to the Irish during the Famine. This story is at the heart of this book, for I believe with Irish President Mary Robinson that the best commemoration of those who suffered and died in the past is to take their suffering "into the present with us, to help others who now suffer in a similar way," wherever that may be.

Prologue

"Do you have a few pennies, Grandfather?"

The old man looked down at his granddaughter. "If it is for white man's candy, no," he said firmly, but with a smile that softened his words.

"No, Grandfather, I know how you feel about that. 'White man's candy rots your teeth,' she chanted in the singsong voice that their white teacher used when she was teaching them something.

"You are most disrespectful to your elders," her grandfather said, once again a twinkle in his eye belying his tone. She was his favorite grandchild. "Now what is this money for?"

"Pushmataha told the council about some people, Grandfather. They are starving the way the Choctaw and Cherokee starved years ago when we were made to come here."

The old man stiffened. "That was before you were born, Little Bird. You were lucky not to be alive yet, for most likely you would have died. Many of the children did."

"Mothers and children are dying in this other place, Pushmataha says. He is raising money to help them."

The old man had a faraway look in his eyes. He wasn't seeing the dried-out, poor acres that he had been struggling to farm for the last fifteen years. He wasn't even thinking of how much cash money they would need to help them get through the winter after the summer's drought. He was looking back to the bad time when half of their people had died. He was remembering the white woman who had been watching them pass by, who had seen his wife stumble and fall against him. She had taken the shawl off her shoulders, cold as it was, and put it around his wife's. She had said something in English and patted his arm awkwardly and then run back into her house. The shawl hadn't saved his wife. She lay dead in his arms the next morning when he awoke. But it had saved something in him, something that kept him human. A strange woman and a poor one, from the look of her, had shown him that all people had hearts, not just the Choctaw. Up until then he had only seen the way whites let their own people go poor and hungry; only seen their greed for land. But that white woman, in revealing her heart, had kept his alive.

He got out of his chair and went to the stove. Opening the tin can that stood on the shelf above, he pulled out a silver coin.

"Grandfather, that is a lot of money!"

"We will still have enough, Little Bird. More than these people have, it seems. Where did Pushmataha say they were from?"

"Across the ocean. They belong to England."

"Hunhh," grunted the old man. "That explains a lot. Now you bring that to school tomorrow mornin'. People who have suffered and survived need to keep their hearts open to others, Little Bird."

The old man closed the canister. It would be a hard winter, but they had shelter and food. Some of their own people had become fairly prosperous. His nephew could help them if money and food ran out. And maybe one of these starving people from across the ocean would keep his heart soft and alive within him for a day when another's need was greater than his own.

County Mayo, June 1848

"They look good, don't they, Da?"

"They do, Michael, thanks be to God."

Joseph Burke looked over at his son. The boy was not

much more than a walking skeleton. But then, neither was he or any of his neighbors. The miracle was they were alive atall, any of them, after the last two years of famine and fever and eviction.

Whenever he thought of it, he could feel his heart beating harder in his hollow chest as anger gave him a few moments of life and strength. He had been one of the most prosperous men in their village. Had owned a cow and two donkeys. Had never failed the rent, even in '46. But the fever had felled him. Taken him down for months, and then taken his wife and their two youngest for good. And then the rest of them were thrown out of their cottage and forced to rent just a small piece of land. But it made him light-headed and dizzy to think of it, so think of it he wouldn't.

The small potato patch was white with blossoms. It would provide barely enough to get them through the winter, but if they could make it one year with a decent crop, why then things could change. He was hardworking and so was his son Michael. His hand dropped to the boy's head. He had Mary's hair, Michael did, thick and black and springy. There were times when he would see the back of the boy's head and thought he would die of the pain of never being able to run his fingers through Mary's curls again or tease her about the gray strands threading through it. It comforted him, though, sometimes, to put his hand gently on Michael's head, like now, and imagine that he could, by touching her son's hair, somehow touch her, letting her know that they were still here.

"Let's tell Caitlin, Da! It will be cheering her up and she'll maybe sit up today from hearing it."

Caitlin had her da's hair, fine and brown, but it was plastered to her skull and tangled from her tossing with fever. She was the oldest, and had taken care of the rest of them when Mary died. She had been the longest recovering from the fever, thought Joseph. He had wondered, some nights, would she survive. Would any of them, with no broth to nourish them, only a few oats and rotten cabbage leaves to make "soup" out of. The Indian corn from the relief committee had gone long ago.

God had kept them alive. Joseph knew that. For it wasn't themselves who could do it and it most certainly wasn't the damn British.

"Cait, Cait, the praties are bloomin'," said Michael. "Do you think you could sit up for that news and for a bit of cabbage broth?" he added in a teasing tone.

Cait smiled up at him and pulled herself up on one elbow, although even that small effort made her break out into a fine sheen of sweat. "How is this, Mickey Joe?"

Only Caitlin called him Mickey Joe, like his mother had done. And she hadn't teased him like that for a long time. She must be feeling better. The Blessed Mother and his *own* mother Mary must have heard his prayers. He helped his sister pull herself up further against the wall.

"The crop will be a fine one, Cait, and we will have colcannon again."

She smiled because she knew he needed her to. But she wasn't very hungry and couldn't even remember now what colcannon tasted like. But she did manage to swallow a little of the broth Michael spooned into her.

Three weeks later, Michael awoke to the sound of keening. It was odd. For the first year, keening and wailing had become so commonplace you hardly paid attention to it at all. Someone else had died; someone was grieving. It was happening every day, everywhere. But by the time of the fever, most of the older women who were so good at the keening were gone and those that were left had no spirit for it.

This keening was low, thought Michael, who was not quite fully awake. It seemed to come from very deep, almost as if the man—for it was a man—was keening for the earth, for Ireland herself. It is Da! Not Caitlin, he prayed as he stumbled over to where his sister lay on the floor. No, she was still breathing. He stooped his head to get out of the scalpeen, and there was his da, covered in black putrid slime, smelling like ... oh, sweet Savior, smelling like '46. The white and the green were gone. All that was left in their small patch was blackened and withered. His da was rocking and keening. It was a terrible sound. His da never cried, not even when his ma had died. Now his da was bringing up sobs so deep he was wrenching his guts and vomiting as he cried.

"Da, Da!"

"What is it we have done, sweet Jesus, Mary, Mother of God? Haven't we worked hard enough? Haven't we paid them, year after year, their damn blood money? Haven't we lost enough? Our homes, our land? Our sons to their armies? Our daughters to starvation? And haven't we been faithful to you through it all? This blight is blistering the very soul of Ireland. Who will be left of us?"

Michael thought they both would die from it, right there. His da from his heart giving out and himself shaking to death in the rain and the cold and the rot.

His da became silent at last and then stumbled up. He had cried so much that even if it hadn't been raining, he would be soaking wet. The rags clung to his ribs and Michael could see his very heart beating.

"I will not have us all die," Joseph Burke said fiercely, his voice hoarse from his keening. "I might go, and Cait, but not Michael. Not Mary's Mickey Joe."

He turned to his son and pulled him close. Michael thought he would smother in the embrace, the smell of the blight was so strong. His father let him go at last and looked into his eyes. "You must get out, Michael. One of us must live. We will get you to Galway, to a ship bound for America."

"No, Da, no. I can't leave you. It will get better, I know it will. Maybe it is just our potatoes."

"It is all of us, Michael. And no one gives a bloody damn. We are lice to them, as we have been since Cromwell. But by God, one of my nits shall live," he said, laughing as hard as he had been crying just before. "And Mary's hair shall not be buried with her," he added, almost to himself as he pressed his boy to his chest again.

There was nothing to pack. There was nothing in the scalpeen but one cookpot, one cup, and a cracked bowl.

Whatever clothes they were wearing was all they had. There was only one blanket, which had been torn in half. Half for Michael and his father and half for Caitlin. She made Michael take it. "You'll be freezin' yourself to death on the sea otherwise, Mickey Joe," she said, putting it around his shoulders. She could hardly stand, but there she was, shaking in her shift, giving him the old blanket that would hardly keep a babby warm, much less him.

"No, Cait."

"Yes, Mickey. I don't want to be worrying about you."

"Come, Michael," his da called. "Sweeney is ready to go."

His da couldn't come with him. He had to say good-bye here. He gently folded Caitlin in his arms and kissed the top of her head. "I will send for ye when I make my fortune in New York, Cait."

"No, ye will make your fortune and then come home to us, Mickey Joe. Promise me that you will come home."

"I will, Cait."

He said good-bye and stepped outside.

He wouldn't have left them starving. He couldn't have; he would have starved and died with them. But it was as if God knew he would need help to go, and a week after his da made the decision the relief committee announced a small miracle. Money had come in from America. From Boston and New York and, the parish priest added, even from the wild Indians. Even the Indians way out West had heard of the famine and collected money for Ireland. If even the wild Indians on their horses had heard of their trouble and reached out to help, then surely the English would be shamed into it, said Father O'Connor.

Now Cait was stronger and his da looked more alive than Michael had seen him in a year. So he was off to America with one and a half pounds of Indian corn and a few coins in his pocket.

Once upon a time, Bridget McBride's nephew had sent a book home to her. She'd read it over and over and passed it around the village. It was a book about the Wild West and it had a picture of an Indian on it, his legs wrapped around a piebald horse. Michael had never forgotten it. He had thumbed the worn little book when it came to their house and sat astride their old donkey, his back straight, his toes dragging, imagining a lance in his hand and eagle feathers on his head.

It was hard to imagine someone going out West and telling that Indian about the poor, starving Irish. He tried to picture that handsome warrior reaching into a pouch and drawing out some coins. He was going to America because of that Indian. His da and his sister might live because of that Indian. Someday, please God, if he made it to America, he would go see some wild Indians, before he came home to Ireland.

Santa Fe Trail, northern New Mexico, 1854

"Oh, where is the girl who will go out West with me?
We'll live in some desired place and happy we will be.
We'll build a little cabin with a ground for a floor
And a distance for the window and a plank for the door.
Will you go out West, will you go out West, will you
go out West with me? Will you go out West, will you go
out West, oh, sa-ay will you go out West with me."

Her father looked over at Elizabeth Jane while he was singing the song and slapping the reins on the horses' backs. He had a fine baritone voice, but he had been singing the song since they left Boston. And humming it. And whistling it. Mostly he sang it to their mother, with what she called "that come hither look" in his eye.

Her father must have been wanting to leave Boston for a long time, Elizabeth Jane thought. Why else would he be so happy about being ruined and bankrupted and shamed and disgraced. He hadn't acted shamed and disgraced. He had acted relieved, even when Grandfather Eliot got on him. He had taken Grandfather's stake money quite cheerfully and when it was suggested he leave the state, he'd nodded and said, "Indeed, that is just what I plan to do." Grandfather had only meant for him to move to Connecticut or New Hampshire, Elizabeth Jane was sure. But Papa bought all five of them tickets for the train and then a steamboat to Missouri that very week.

Elizabeth Jane had been furious. She was just entering her third year at Mrs. Compton's Academy for Young Ladies. She could read Latin and French and play the piano. And best of all, she was the star pupil in drawing and painting.

"I will stay here, Papa," she had said quite calmly and properly. All the young ladies at Mrs. Compton's were calm and proper. "You and Mama and Jonathan can go."

That was when Papa had started singing the song. "Oh, where is the girl who will go out West with me . . . ?" He sang it to her mother, but Elizabeth Jane also knew that she would have to go with her family, will she or nill she.

"I need another woman with me, Elizabeth Jane," Mother had said to her. "Someone to talk to. Someone who will help keep this family civilized. I know how much you love school, but the truth is we don't have the money for you to stay, even if I could be persuaded to leave you behind."

So here she was, many long weeks later, on the last part of their journey, listening to her father sing his song again, watching him trying to coax a little enthusiasm from her.

"I swear, Helen, the child acts like she's never left civilization," she'd heard him say one night. "The only thing that seems to bring her enjoyment is her paintbox."

"She's scared, David. And she is not a child still, nor yet a woman. She is just holding on as long as she can to what is familiar to her."

"I thought I'd have more trouble with you, Helen," her father said, "but you've taken to the trail like a mountain man!" Then there was whispering and soft laughter and Elizabeth Jane knew that they had slipped away to do whatever it was married folk do.

Was she scared? And wasn't she already a young lady? She knew how to walk and talk like one. Her breasts were swelling quite nicely and filling out her dresses. Maybe her mother thought there was still more swelling to go?

Now that would be too bad. What there was was sufficient enough, thank you.

They had separated from the other wagons after Raton.
The wagon scout had warned David Rush, but he was too
impatient to hold to the pace of fourteen wagons when he
could get there faster on his own. The scout had shook his
head and waved them good-bye with a worried frown on
his face.

"Are you sure this is the right thing to do, David?"

"We are through the worst of the mountains. And we
are only a week or so out of Santa Fe. The weather should
hold."

"It isn't the weather, David. What about Indians?"

"Most of them are settled Indians, Helen. They live in
towns. Not like the Sioux or Cheyenne. We'll be safe.
And besides, I'm a good shot."

Elizabeth Jane was glad to say good-bye to the wagon
train. All of the girls her age had been rough-and-tumble
tomboys, none of them with much schooling. There were
even two Irish families on the train, a fact that appalled
her. Mrs. Compton had always warned her girls against
the Irish children in Boston. "They are of an inferior
race," she had explained. "Dirty, lice-ridden,"—here she
had lowered her voice—"and they are in thrall to their
papist superstitions."

If the truth be told, Elizabeth Jane had felt a little
lonely having to keep away from Kathy Kelly and her
friend Mary. They were less hoydenish than the other
girls and in the beginning had wanted her to be friends.
She had held back out of fear of their difference, and
soon all the girls on the train were calling her a stuck-up
snob.

It hurt, though she didn't let them know. She didn't
think she was a snob. She just didn't want to leave Miss
Elizabeth Jane Rush behind in Boston. She didn't want to
leave her home behind, and she didn't know how else to
hold on to it.

"This looks like a likely spot to camp tonight," her father announced, pulling the horses up.

They were down out of the mountains, but not out of sight of them, and there were still trees around and water and grass.

"Elizabeth Jane, will you get us some water from the creek," her mother asked, handing her the wooden bucket.

"Can't Jonathan do it, Mama? I hate the way the water slops all over my dress."

"Elizabeth Jane Rush, do as your mother says," said her father sternly. "You are a big girl of fourteen and Jonathan is only seven."

"Yes, Papa." When her father sounded like that, which was rare, you obeyed him. Jonathan stuck his tongue out at her as she walked by and without thinking, she stuck hers back, forgetting that she was a young lady.

"Lizzie stuck her tongue at me, Mama," cried Jonathan, moving off to where their mother was unpacking the pots and pans.

"Lizzie" indeed. She hated it when he called her that and he knew it and she was almost ready to turn back and box his ears for telling, but she was almost down the hill to the creek by now.

It was a lovely warm evening and the creek ran happily over the rocks. Elizabeth Jane pulled off her stockings and waded in. She had to admit that squishing her hot toes in cool red mud felt good and was something you couldn't do in Boston.

All was still except for the creek running and the sound of her father's voice.

"Oh, sa-ay, will you go out West wi—"

Elizabeth Jane heard a sharp crack at the same time her father stopped singing. Had he snapped a branch for the fire? Then she heard Jonathan scream. And then her mother. She stood paralyzed in the cold running water. Jonathan was yelling, "Mama, Papa! Let me go!" Mama was crying and saying, "No, please, no."

Elizabeth Jane put the bucket down very carefully at the edge of the creek and, lying flat on her stomach, crawled up the bank. Papa was lying near the fire and a red stain had blossomed on his white shirt like a great rose. There were six or seven of them. They weren't Indians, they were white men. Maybe some were Spanish, thought Elizabeth Jane, registering black hair and knee breeches. She could smell them from here, or maybe that was her imagination. She could smell the whiskey. That was not her imagination. They were passing a jug around, three of them. Another was tying Jonathan to the back of a mule. He was very still, but surely he was still alive if they were bothering to take him? Then she saw Mama and wished she hadn't. The other three men had her on the ground and were doing something to her. Her skirts were up and at first she screamed, "No, no" as each man got on top of her and did whatever he was doing to her. Then one of the others came over and shot her through the head. "That'll shut her up," he said.

Mama lay there staring up at the sky, her skirts around her waist, her most private parts exposed. Elizabeth Jane slid a few feet back down the hill and lay there trembling and nauseous. If they came for water, they would see her and tie her to a mule. Or maybe, since she was almost a woman, they would do to her what they had done to Mama.

She heard them going through the pots and pans and tins in the wagon. Looking for jewelry and money, she guessed. She heard one cursing, "Goddamn pins and needles," and pictured him opening Mama's sewing box. That seemed more of a violation than anything. With her eyes closed, she could see the small rosewood box, silk threads carefully laid out, pins in the small blue velvet pin cushion and needles in the oblong tin needle case.

She lay still for a long time. She had to relieve herself very badly, but couldn't even squirm to distract herself. Finally she had to let go and could feel her legs go warm with her own water, and then cold.

Even after she heard them leave, she lay there. What if one of them had stayed behind and was watching? Finally she had to get up. It was getting dark, but at least the moon would be full in a day or so, and as it rose, it gave her enough light to make her way to the wagon.

She didn't look at her father or mother. Instead, she crawled into the ransacked wagon and pulled a quilt around her. She couldn't stop shaking for hours, and slept only fitfully in the last hours before dawn. When she awoke, she was disoriented. She could smell coffee as usual, but it was close and strong, not wafting in from the campfire where Mama was cooking breakfast. Then she realized the smell was coming from the bed of the wagon, where coffee, sugar, and beans were all spilled together.

"Mama, Papa," she whispered, and climbed down.

It was a beautiful morning. Cool, as it always was before the sun was fully up, and the greens of the sage and grass and cottonwoods by the creek were lit from the inside by the clear light of morning. Everything shone pure. It was like waking up to the first morning of the world.

Until she looked over at her father. The rose on his chest was no longer crimson, but brown and black. Both her parents' eyes were open, and that was wrong. Elizabeth Jane knew someone should smooth their eyes closed. She looked around, as if to ask for help, but of course she was the only someone there. She walked to her father first and drew her hand over his eyes. When she turned to her mother, she realized Helen Rush's thighs were smeared with reddish brown blood and Elizabeth Jane pulled her mother's skirts down quickly before she brushed gently at her face.

Then she stood there and let the sun come up. What else could she do? She tried to stop it. She closed her eyes and willed it to stay low in the sky, willed time to stop. The sun had no business rising and bathing everything in its clear light. The sun had no right to make such a morning. How could it rise on such horror?

She was very thirsty and she stumbled down the hill to the creek, picking up the wooden bucket from the bank. What if Mama had given in to her? Would Jonathan be alive? And she tied to the back of a mule? She splashed water on her face and on her legs, which were sticky from wetting herself, and then climbed up the hill again.

She had nothing to do. She had nowhere to go. So she just sat against the wagon wheel and watched the sun climb higher in the sky and listened as the flies began to buzz around her parents' bodies.

A day later the soldiers found her. It took them a few minutes to get through the buzzing, for the flies seemed to have moved inside her head and were all she could hear.

"This one's alive, Lieutenant."

Lieutenant Thomas Woolcott dismounted and walked over to kneel beside the girl. Her eyes opened when he touched her arm. She seemed to be looking at him, but he wasn't sure if she was *seeing* him.

"Are you hurt anywhere, miss," he asked gently.

The girl seemed to be listening the way she was looking: she was there and not there at the same time.

"She's in shock, Lieutenant. I've seen it before after an Indian raid."

"This wasn't no Indians," said their scout, who was walking around carefully. "Boots, not moccasins, for one thing. And we're too far from the Navajo, and the Jicarilla haven't done any raiding for the past year. Comancheros, from the look of things. Worse than any tribe I know."

Elizabeth Jane started shivering when she saw one of the soldiers approach her mother's body. Lieutenant Woolcott moved himself in front of her and rubbed her back rhythmically. "Get me something to put over her," he whispered to the trooper standing closest to him.

The man found a wool shawl in the wagon and Woolcott draped it over Elizabeth Jane's shoulders.

It was Mama's best shawl and it smelled like her: a combination of milled soap and rosewater cologne. It was the scent of roses that did it. It brought her mother to life and Elizabeth Jane could hear her voice, see her dabbing the cologne behind her ears. Great wrenching sobs racked her and the lieutenant wrapped his arms around her.

"That's the way, miss. Just let it all out."

She cried until she had no more tears and then she slept. By the time she awoke, it was dark and the fire was lit. She looked around for her father and then remembered: her parents were dead, her brother gone, and the soldiers were here to keep her safe.

The bodies were gone, she realized. She saw the lieutenant studying the fire, a cup of coffee in his hand, and she pulled herself up and went over to him.

"You are awake then, miss," he said kindly.

"Yes, sir. My name is Rush. Elizabeth Jane Rush."

"Well, Elizabeth Jane Rush, you have had a hard time of it. Where was your family headed? Do you have any relatives in the territory?"

"We left everyone behind, Captain. We were headed for Arizona by way of Santa Fe."

"Only 'Lieutenant,' " he corrected her with a smile. "Lieutenant Thomas Woolcott. Where are you from, Miss Rush?"

"Boston."

"And do you have family there?"

"Only my grandfather."

"Then we will see you safe into Santa Fe and make sure you get back home."

"Oh, no, I don't want to go back to Grandfather's," she said immediately. "He wouldn't know what to do with me. And he wasn't very happy with Papa when we left."

"Hmmmm." Thomas Woolcott looked down at the girl by his side. She was over the initial shock, he could tell, and seemed to know what she *didn't* want to do. "But where will you go, Miss Rush? You are only a girl."

"I am fourteen, Lieutenant. Really almost a young lady."

"Santa Fe is hardly the place for a young lady from back East."

"Isn't there some school where I could work? Or seamstressing? I can sew very well, Lieutenant."

She was almost grown, thought Thomas Woolcott, having felt her soft curves when he had pulled her to his side to comfort her. He was ashamed of himself for even thinking about a fourteen-year-old that way, but there was something about the way she had composed herself and was trying to deal calmly with the horror that life had handed her that drew him.

"I have a sister in Santa Fe, Miss Rush. She is a widow with three small children and from what I've seen of them, could use some help. I could see if Nellie could take you in and you could try it out for a while. Then, if you change your mind, I can see that you get back to Boston."

Elizabeth Jane turned to him, her eyes full of relief and gratitude. "Thank you very much, Lieutenant Woolcott. If your sister is willing, I would like to stay with her."

The next morning at dawn, he found her standing by the two mounds that were her parents' graves.

"I think Papa went quickly," she whispered.

"It seemed so."

"But Mama . . ." He could feel her whole body tremble as her voice died away.

"Don't think about it, Miss Rush. Your mama is at peace now."

"And Jonathan? Will you be able to find him?"

The lieutenant hesitated. "I only have a few men with me and I need them all to get you to Santa Fe. I can't go after those bast . . . excuse me, those villains. But I will send someone out as soon as I report back to the fort." Not that they'll be likely to find him, he thought. He'll be some Mexican family's slave by then, and impossible to find.

"He is only seven. What would they want with him?"

Thomas Woolcott cleared his throat. "There's raiding back and forth between Indians and New Mexicans for slaves, Miss Rush. Likely the Comancheros will sell him to some household where he'll be set to hauling water and chopping wood and such. He'll work hard, but he'll stay alive."

The girl was very still and when Woolcott looked down he knew she was crying again, this time noiselessly. "I . . . the last thing I said . . . I stuck my tongue out at him and we wrangled like we always do . . ." Her voice broke. "But he is only a little boy, Lieutenant."

"I know, miss, I know." He waited until her tears had stopped. "It is time to say good-bye, Miss Rush."

Elizabeth Jane knelt down and said a short prayer. He

could hear her whispering a good-bye to her mother and father and then one to her brother. He wanted to run his hand over her hair as she knelt there, but restrained himself. This was surely too hard a country to live in, he thought to himself, and not for the first time.

Chapter One

Michael dismounted slowly and stiffly. After a month in the saddle even he, an experienced cavalryman, was happy to be almost at his destination.

"We are here, boyo, or almost," he added as he loosened the girths on Trooper and Frost.

At first he had thought that the green meadows in the distance must be a new kind of mirage. Certainly he'd seen enough "water" not to be fooled again. But the meadow was at the mouth of a canyon and Fort Defiance had been built near Cañon Bonito to take advantage of the water and grass. So it was real. No mirage.

When they smelled the water, the two horses picked up their heads and Trooper nudged Michael between the shoulders, as if to say, "Come on yerself, boyo, all that green grass is waiting." And when they reached the first canyon spring, Michael was on his hands and knees, about to drink with his horses, when he saw them: the prayer sticks with feathers and the pieces of turquoise at the bottom of the clear pool.

Pulling himself away was almost as hard as getting his horses to move, but he cursed them in a friendly way and pulled them further downstream. The spring was obviously a shrine of some sort and he didn't want to disturb it.

"Will I see Indians, sor, if I join the cavalry?" he had asked the recruiting sergeant with open-eyed eagerness.

The sergeant had laughed. "You'll see Indians, son, I

promise you that. And you'd better pray that you see them before they see you. Now put your 'X' right here, Paddy."

"My name isn't Paddy, sor, it is Michael Joseph Burke," he had said slowly and with dignity. "And I can write me own name."

"Oh, 'tis an eddicated mick? Well, Mickey Joe, you are in the U.S. Army now," said the sergeant, folding up the enlistment papers.

Michael winced at "Mickey Joe." Only Cait had called him that. But he would not think of Cait or Da or any of them now. He was going West and he would see Indians.

He had seen them, of course. More at the end of his rifle than he'd wanted or expected to. He had been so young. Believed that joining the cavalry meant helping to protect the rights of both natives and settlers. Meant being a peacekeeper. Instead, more often than not, he'd been a war starter. But he'd seen and come to know many Indians since then: Sioux, Cheyenne, Crow. And now, here he was in the New Mexico Territory, about to meet Navajo. Or more than likely, he thought cynically, about to fight Navajo.

The descending trill of a canyon wren brought him back to the present. His horses had drunk their fill and were munching grass contentedly. He was dressed in his greasy buckskins and filthy shirt less than an hour from his new post. He stripped quickly and plunged into the stream, wading up canyon toward the next pool, where he was going to enjoy a long and thorough soak.

Elizabeth was going to try again. For two years she had been walking out from the fort to the mouth of the canyon, attempting to capture the color of the sandstone cliffs. But the color changed from day to day, moment to moment. It seemed that she could dip her brush in ochre and look up and see that the canyon walls were just a little bit lighter, or had a tinge of coral that she had missed. And so they pulled her back, again and again, frustrating and satisfying her at the same time.

She passed the shrine, curious as always about the

sticks and stone piles around it. She walked slowly, loving the feel of the warm pink sand under her shoes and smiling when a lizard flickered across her path. She was not paying close attention to anything but the path when she heard a loud splash and, startled, jumped behind the nearest sagebrush and crouched down, her heart gone wild in her chest.

It had been quiet around the fort for months, so she didn't think she was in any danger from hostiles. And anyway, no Navajo would make that much noise? She finally got the courage to stick her head out from behind the bush. A man was sitting there in the pool a little ways ahead of her, stark naked, splashing away as casually as though he were in his own bath, she thought. It didn't look like anyone she knew from the fort, but then, she thought, she had never seen anyone from the fort but her husband in the bath. And this man looked nothing like her husband from behind: he had thick black hair and muscular shoulders and, oh my God, he was standing up, a very white behind. He looked like a piebald, with his brown neck, tan torso, and white legs covered with more black hair. She made herself close her eyes. What on earth was she doing, ogling a man's body? She was a virtuous, married woman and had never desired anyone but her husband. No, she thought with familiar sadness, that wasn't really true. She had never desired even her husband.

She didn't desire this man either, that was the truth. But as an artist, she did appreciate natural beauty, and despite the odd distribution of suntan, she could see that this man had a body that someone like Michelangelo would have loved to sculpt or paint. It was unfortunate that she would have to sneak away ... that she could not just sit down and sketch.

She backed away carefully, praying fervently that he wouldn't turn and see her. She shivered with sudden fear. She had been so intent on the abstract, physical beauty of his body that she only now was worrying about what that body could do to her. At the fort, she was Mrs. Woolcott, wife to Lieutenant Thomas Woolcott and protected by her position. Here, alone, she was no one. With his dark hair, he might be a Comanchero . . . She took a deep breath. Calm yourself, Elizabeth Jane Woolcott, she scolded. He has not seen you. He is no doubt passing through. And you are not in danger, not so close to the fort, or your husband wouldn't allow you outside the gates.

It was usually a half-hour walk, but she made it in twenty minutes, flushed and dripping with perspiration. When the sentry asked if she was all right, she just nodded and said quickly that the sun had felt too hot today to stay any longer.

A half hour later, she looked up from the sketches she was making and crumpling, sketches of a strong back and solid curved buttocks. There was a stir outside and she stuffed the papers in the kitchen stove and went to her door to see what was going on.

A trooper was walking by, on his way to the enlisted men's barracks. A tall man, his curly black hair slicked down. Mrs. Taggert moved from her front door over to Elizabeth's. "That's the new master sergeant, Mrs. Woolcott. Come all the way from Utah. Sergeant Burke."

As though he had heard his name, the new man looked up and flashed a smile at the ladies. His eyes, a startling blue in his tan face, seemed to be saying, "Aren't I the handsome charming devil that all the ladies love."

"Oh, another Irishman," said Elizabeth dismissively and loud enough for Michael to hear. "Full of himself, no doubt, and full of whiskey on payday."

Michael flushed with embarrassment and anger as he continued walking. He hadn't heard those tones in a long time: the fine eastern lady, the damned English prejudice no matter how American they considered themselves. He couldn't help smiling at women. It was so good to see one out here. Especially a pretty one like her. But she was one pretty one he would be happy to avoid. And since she was clearly an officer's daughter or sister, it would be easy enough.

"Did you find some time for your sketching today, Elizabeth?"

"I did, Thomas," said Elizabeth as she poured him a second cup of coffee.

"And did the cliffs stay the same color for you?" he asked with a smile, as he did almost every night.

"No, Thomas, they are most amazing that way."

The words sometimes varied, but their general conversation did not. She would inquire about his day, he would report briefly and then ask about hers. Even after six years of marriage, Elizabeth found the predictability of their routine comforting. Thomas was the same competent, protective man he had been when he had found her nine years ago. His hair had grown gray, of course, and his face more wrinkled from both age and sun. His belly hung over his belt a little and he tired earlier at night. But he was never too tired to ask about her day and her drawing.

"I hear the new sergeant arrived while I was out on patrol," said Thomas, leaning back in his chair and loosening his belt.

Elizabeth could feel her cheeks flush. "Yes, Milly and I saw him walk by."

"I hear he is an experienced Indian fighter and good scout. We need someone like that."

"Do you think it will come to fighting, Thomas?" Elizabeth asked, happy to change the subject and banish from her mind Sergeant Michael Burke and his blue eyes.

"I hope not, but I fear it will."

Elizabeth hated the thought of her husband in danger. They had been at Fort Defiance for three years and during that time the intervals of peace had become shorter and the campaigns against the Navajo longer. When he was away, she felt as though the bedrock upon which her sense of security rested became quicksand.

"I hate the thought of it," she said passionately.

"I know, my dear. But I'm an old cavalryman who's survived many a skirmish and will survive many more. I'll always come back to you, Elizabeth," he said reassuringly.

Elizabeth put her arms around his shoulders from behind and pulled his head close to her.

* * *

Later that evening, Thomas sat on the edge of their
bed, pulling his boots off.

"I wonder how this new man will get along with Lieutenant Cooper. Now this is between you and me, Elizabeth, but Cooper is a prideful ignoramus and like all
officers just out of West Point, thinks he knows it all because he's studied war in a classroom."

He also thinks he knows it all about women, thought
Elizabeth. She had noticed that the lieutenant kept his
eyes on her when he thought she wasn't looking and was
his most charming to her when the officers and their
wives got together for dinner.

"He's only been here a few months, Thomas. He'll
learn."

"He'd better and damn quick," said her husband, turning down the lamp next to their bed and crawling in beside her. "Are you . . . um . . . tired from your walk
today?"

"Not really. Are you recovered from your patrol?"

"Oh, I think I could stay awake a little longer," said
Thomas, pulling her closer and turning her face to his for
a kiss.

She liked his kisses. She always had, and that part of
their lovemaking always felt right to her. But Thomas
wasn't a man given to kissing for longer than a few minutes. He got right down to business and that was the part
when Elizabeth just left. Oh, her body stayed and she
made sure her body felt welcoming and she made noises
that she imagined conveyed pleasure, but she herself
watched from the corner of the ceiling.

Thomas never seemed to know this, for which she was
profoundly grateful, for she did love him even though she
didn't desire him. She owed him everything: her life, her
time with Nellie, and her marriage. She would never have
married, she knew that now, if he hadn't asked her. Only
Thomas could she allow to touch her in this intimate way.
She had had a few offers in Santa Fe. Not many, because
most considered her stuck-up and standoffish. But those
few offers she had graciously turned down, having re-

signed herself to spinsterhood. When Thomas finally spoke, so nervously and apologetically because of their age difference, she had accepted him with great affection, and she had admitted to herself, great relief. She would have a place in the world as a married woman and at the same time she did not have to let go of the familiar. Over the years, Thomas had become like family and now she would never have to lose family again.

"Master Sergeant Michael Joseph Burke reporting, sir." Michael snapped off a crisp salute and stood at attention.

"Michael Joseph Burke, is it now," said the lieutenant in a stage Irish brogue.

Día, not one of those, thought Michael.

"Well, we have a few of your countrymen here at Fort Defiance," said Cooper, turning and looking out the window, leaving Michael standing at attention.

Lieutenant Cooper was tall and slim, with bright yellow hair dulled a little by the brilliantine he had slicked it down with. His uniform looked as if it had been poured on his body, it was so free of wrinkles. Michael was thankful that he had followed his instincts and kept his uniform carefully wrapped in his saddlebags, although he should have been traveling in it. He glanced down quickly: his boots were old, but they had been spit-shined. He was no disgrace to the army, thank God.

"You came from Camp Supply in Utah?"

"Yes, sir."

"And what were your duties there, Master Sergeant Burke?"

"Training the new recruits, sir. And tracking, whenever they needed an extra scout."

Cooper turned from the window and sat down.

The bastard was going to keep him at attention, thought Michael as the lieutenant slowly sifted through the papers on his desk.

"Well, we don't have brand-new men here, Sergeant. And we have a professional scout," he added with a patronizing smile. "Oh, at ease, Sergeant."

"Thank you, sir." The crick in his shoulders smoothed out.

Cooper looked him up and down. "At least you don't look like you lived with your pigs, Sergeant. I compliment you on your professional appearance."

"Thank you, sir." Michael could feel the heat of anger staining his cheeks. The last five years he had received only respect from the officers under whom he'd served, and a few of them had actually been Irish, so there was understanding as well as respect. But in his early years in the cavalry, when he was a green recruit, and had had more of a brogue, he had learned the hard way to keep his temper with men like Cooper. He was a little out of practice, it would seem, however, given the impulse that arose to reach out and grab the skinny shite by the throat and throttle him.

Cooper shuffled a few more papers and then said, "Well, it seems as though we need someone to lead the wood detail, Sergeant. You will be in charge of four men and make sure we are kept well supplied."

It was damned insulting and Cooper well knew it, thought Michael. To use an experienced, seasoned man as himself on such a task. Collecting wood, indeed!

"Yes, sir. Thank you, sir. Will that be all, sir?" It took everything he had to keep his voice from shaking with anger, but he wouldn't give the effete bastard the satisfaction that he had gotten Michael's goat.

"Yes, Sergeant. You are dismissed."

Michael came to attention and saluted, receiving a very lackadaisical lift of the hand in return. Just as he was halfway out the door, the lieutenant said, "Oh, and, Sergeant . . ."

"Yes, sir."

"I noticed your horses. One is the army's and the other . . . ?"

"My own, sir."

"That is unusual for a sergeant."

"But not at all against regulations, sir."

"She is an unusual-looking animal."

"She is, sir."

"And where did you get her?"

"I won her, sir, in a horse race at Fort Kearney."

"An odd thing, surely, to take the losing horse?"

"No, sir. I beat her owner on another mount and chose Frost from his string."

"We have races here from time to time, Sergeant," said Cooper casually. "When things are quiet, as they have been, the Navajo come in for them. I have a gelding who would probably beat yours, given that it's a mare. He has beaten several Indian ponies so far."

"I congratulate you, sir."

"Well, I may see you out there someday then, Sergeant."

"Yes, sir."

Michael's jaw was sore from clenching it. When he reached his quarters he was tempted to rip off his uniform, saddle up Frost, and head back to Utah.

"Goddamn his bloody soul to hell," he spat out. He unbuttoned his good smock and folded it carefully, placing it in the small trunk at the foot of his cot. His old uniform would do very well for wood gathering, thank you!

Chapter Two

Mother of God, what a pitiful crew, he thought as he viewed the four men assigned to him. Two were at least ten years older than he was and the other two merely boys.

He called the roll and had them line up as though for parade inspection. One of the older men was as tall as Michael, the other about a foot shorter and many pounds heavier. Of the two boys, one was tall and skinny and the other short and stocky. Lined up, they looked ridiculous, almost as ridiculous as he must, he thought, commanding such an oddly assorted troop.

"Private Fisk."

"Yes, *sir*." The barrel-shaped one with grizzled hair stepped forward.

"Private *Ma*honey."

"Ma*ho*ney, sir." The short and stocky boy stepped forward.

He has balls, correcting my pronunciation, thought Michael. The boy looked sullen and stubborn.

"Well, now, me apologies, Private Ma*ho*ney," said Michael, his soft brogue becoming more pronounced. "In the west of Ireland where I come from, we pronounce it differently."

"In New York, where I come from, it is Ma*ho*ney. Sir," he added, almost as an afterthought.

"I will try to remember that," said Michael pleasantly. "But I hope, if I forget once in a while, you will know to whom I am giving orders?" Michael's voice was mild, but the boy heard the undertones.

"Yes, sir."

"Private Spratt."

The tall, skinny boy stepped forward. It was all Michael could do to keep from laughing aloud.

"I don't suppose your Christian name is John, Private?"

The boy flushed and stammered, "No. No, sir. Paul."

"Thanks be to your wise mother, Private. And how long have you been in the army?"

"Six months, sir."

"Mahoney?"

"A year, sir."

"Private Elwell."

Now this is a man I can trust, though Michael as he looked Elwell over. He seemed to be close in age to Fisk, in his forties, but in much better shape. No stomach to speak of. He had no beard, but a drooping salt and pepper mustache, which he probably grew, thought Michael, to offset the receding hairline. He was an average-looking man, but there was something about him, an energy despite his age and experience, that drew Michael to him.

"And how long have you been in the army, Elwell?"

"Twenty-three years, sir."

Twenty-three years, obviously intelligent, and still a private? Well, some men weren't made for command, thought Michael, no matter how competent.

"I am Master Sergeant Michael Burke, as you already know. I am new to the fort. Indeed, new to the territory. Not new to the army, however," he added. "Now, I have been assigned to wood detail, and so have you."

Michael could almost hear a collective groan, which they would, no doubt, release when they were away from him.

"It is not the most glamorous task, but then, me boys, there aren't many glamorous tasks in the U.S. Army, are there? We will assemble tomorrow morning on the parade ground after general inspection for a daily drill. For now, you are dismissed."

* * *

"Daily drill!" Mahoney spat in front of him after Michael walked away. "Daily drill for the wood detail?"

Fisk just shrugged his shoulders and walked away.

"I don't know, Jim, I kind of liked him," said Spratt.

"Oh, Spratt, you'd like anyone, you poor skinny bastard."

Elwell put his hands on both their shoulders. "Come now, younguns, let's enjoy our last day of relaxation before the sergeant whips us into shape."

And whip them into shape Michael intended to do. When they lined up before him after breakfast, he had them fetch their rifles, and he put them through a good twenty minutes of rifle drill before he released them, informing them that he would meet them at the corral at 9:30 sharp.

Fisk could be brought back into shape, he thought, though he'll never be as sharp as Elwell, who put as much energy into the drill as a young recruit. He didn't even seem to be trying to impress him either, thought Michael. He would guess Elwell to be one of those men who did everything as well as he could for the sake of it.

Despite his sullen air, Mahoney was also sharp. Or could be, thought Michael with a grin, if he lost his obvious belief that if he gave his all to his work, he was giving himself away. It was hard in the army, Michael reflected as he drank his coffee and looked around the mess hall curiously at all the men who were to be his companions. Especially hard on the enlisted men. There was a balance you could find between slavish obsequiousness or outright rebellion against the harshness of the army hierarchy. You *could* remain your own man and follow orders. He believed he had, and he thought Elwell had. Mahoney was obviously struggling. The only way for him now to make a statement—that he was still a man, even though a lowly private subordinate to everyone—was to hold back. And Spratt? Only time would tell. He looked like the sort who could be easily cowed. But that could change, Michael knew. At any rate, he could help toughen the boy up.

* * *

Michael went to the stables first, to bring a piece of apple to Trooper and Frost. The big bay nuzzled him and nibbled at his suspenders. "That's all for you, me boy," he said and moved on to the mare's stall. The horse's rump was facing him, and the mare turned her head curiously.

"Oho, 'tis the cold shoulder ye're givin' me, Frost? Well, no apple for ye this morning." Michael turned his back as though he were about to leave and stood there for a minute. Then he felt Frost's warm breath against his neck and the horse tipped his cap off, a trick that gave the two of them much pleasure.

"So, I won't get away with it, will I?" Michael teased, and grasping the mare's halter, breathed a few breaths into her nose.

"I've seen Indians do that, Sergeant," said a voice behind him. It was Elwell, come to saddle his mount.

" 'Tis a way of talking, I suppose. Anyhow, it lets her know I'm both her boss and her friend."

"More a friend, I would say, sir," said Elwell with a twinkle in his eye.

"Em, yes," admitted Michael.

"Mules this morning, sir?"

"That's what I've been told, Private Elwell. The wood detail rides them and leads them. Even me."

Elwell shook his head in disgust. "I know why I'm on this detail, sir. But you have a fine reputation as a drill sergeant and scout."

"In the army, you follow orders, Private, you know that," said Michael noncommittally.

"I've been following orders for twenty-four years and look what it's gotten me," grumbled Elwell as he turned away. "On the back of a damned mule!"

Fort Defiance was located in a wide valley, which was mainly grasslands formerly used by the Navajo for grazing and now by the army. Wood supplies for the fort had to be gathered from a few miles away. Those on the wood detail were in for a long, hot day.

Michael looked around him curiously as they rode out.

New Mexico seemed to be as dry as Utah, but somehow easier to take in. There were the same red cliffs crumbling away in slow motion, but they were not as high or as awesome. There was something homey about the place, he realized by the end of his first week and then smiled to himself. How could the desert ever feel like home to someone who came from a green island and who had grown up with the scent of the sea in his nostrils? Who had emigrated to another island, this one a city, but with the comfort of water around him. The West had thrilled him, and terrified him and awed him, but never before had he thought to call it home.

Three weeks after his arrival, it was known all over the fort that Master Sergeant Michael Joseph Burke was someone to keep an eye on. The wood detail set out regularly, their shoulders as straight on muleback as they were during their daily drill. Where other men had been teased about riding shavetails, these men let no openings and actually were beginning to look proud of themselves.

"And why shouldn't ye be," Michael had said after the first few days. "Without wood, the fort cannot function. Let those who are laughin' at ye boys go without breakfast some morning and we won't hear them laughin' anymore."

The men took it in. Not immediately, but little by little they began to realize that they were performing an important job, no matter how lowly it had been made to look. Even Mahoney lost his sullen look from time to time, though he made sure to find it again whenever Michael was looking at him.

"I hear that new sergeant has whipped those men into good shape, Elizabeth," said Thomas one morning at breakfast.

Elizabeth had her back to him as she stood frying bacon at the stove. Her face was flushed with the heat, she told herself, not at the sudden memory of her first sight of Sergeant Burke.

She slid the bacon onto her husband's plate and a few

strips onto her own. She poured him his coffee and herself tea. Drinking tea reminded her of Boston and civilization and Mrs. Compton's Academy for Young Ladies. "I was surprised when Cooper assigned him wood detail," continued Thomas. "He's reported to be a very competent man. You'd have thought Cooper would have put him in charge of a platoon."

"I am not surprised, Thomas. After all, he's an Irishman. So many of them are prone to heavy drinking. I am sure Mr. Cooper wanted to see what the sergeant was like before giving him any major responsibility."

Thomas watched his wife drinking her tea. She was a loving and good wife to him. And most generous to anyone in need. But she had never let go of some ideas and habits that she had brought with her from the East. He suspected that she held on to to them mainly to keep some connection with her past. When someone's world has been shaken, she will cling to anything she can, he had realized. He had seen it years ago with his mother, when his father died.

"The Irish have supplied some fine officers for the U.S. Army, Elizabeth," Thomas responded mildly.

"I am sure they have. But Sergeant Michael Burke isn't one of them."

After Thomas left, Elizabeth washed the dishes and wiped the table, muttering to herself. "Michael Burke, Michael Burke. That is all the women are talking about too." She had seen the way some of the laundresses had looked at him. And the officers' wives were almost as bad. Many of them were much older than she was and sometimes when they were laughing and joking about their . . . well, their intimacies with their husbands, she felt very young. And when they started joking about young Sergeant Burke and his black wavy hair and bright blue eyes she couldn't help seeing his beautiful curves rising from the creek. She wanted to banish that memory, for it made her feel something very unfamiliar and disturbing.

Chapter Three

Michael had had to take the men a full four miles to the west to find wood one morning and the gathering took a long time since their source was small, scattered juniper trees. They were all hot and tired riding back and even Michael couldn't keep his shoulders as straight as usual. As they got closer to the fort he was half dozing in his saddle and it took him a few minutes to make sense of what he was seeing in front of him. Someone was walking slowly, leading a lame horse. A woman. What in blue blazes was a woman doing out here all alone, he thought, rolling his shoulders to loosen them and kicking his mule into a trot.

When she heard the mule, Elizabeth turned around fearfully. The setting sun was in her eyes and at first she couldn't see who was bearing down on her. If it was a hostile, there was nowhere to run, she thought, for she was in the middle of the valley. Then she could see the army blue and waved happily to the rider. She stopped smiling, however, when she saw who it was. Wasn't it just her luck to encounter Sergeant Burke!

"Good afternoon, Miss Woolcott," said Michael, pulling up his mule. "I see your mare has gone lame." Michael lifted his cap. "Sergeant Michael Burke, ma'am."

"It is *Mrs.* Woolcott, Sergeant," Elizabeth replied coolly.

This lovely young woman was the lieutenant's wife? Michael kept his face blank. "I beg your pardon, Mrs. Woolcott. Let me take a look at your mare's leg."

Michael dismounted and ran his hand gently and expertly over the mare's left foreleg. " 'Tis a bit hot and swollen, but I think she'll recover easily, ma'am."

"She stumbled in a gopher hole, but luckily it was only at a walk," Elizabeth explained.

"Then you and she are lucky indeed. She could have broken her leg and you your neck. Now then, we are still more than a mile from the fort. I'll have to take you up behind me. I am glad you wear a sensible skirt and use a trooper's saddle, ma'am," he said with a smile. "Sidesaddles always seem ridiculous to me out here in the wilderness."

Elizabeth looked around as though some other solution might present itself. The four privates had caught up with them. She was certainly not going to ride behind one of them. And the extra mules were loaded with wood.

"I'm afraid it's me mule or shank's mare, Mrs. Woolcott," said Michael with an exaggerated brogue.

"Thank you, Sergeant," said Elizabeth.

Michael mounted in one graceful movement and then reached down for her hand. "Here, and use my stirrup to get up and over."

Elizabeth settled herself behind his saddle.

"This won't be the most comfortable ride, ma'am," he said, "but 'tis better than walking." He gathered up his reins and turned back to his men.

"You lads go ahead. Me mule will be slower, carrying two of us." As the men filed in front of them, Michael turned to Elizabeth. "You'll be needing to put your hands around me waist, Mrs. Woolcott, just to make sure you don't go sliding off. Don't be shy about it. I'll never even notice."

Elizabeth looked for someplace, anyplace else to put her hands. Michael kicked the mule and it gave a little buck and he reached behind him to hold her on. As she began to slide sideways, she automatically grabbed at his waist, and he said, "Now that's a sensible girl," and off they went.

At one point Michael looked down at her hands, which were pressed very pleasantly against his waist. Her left hand seemed to be stained with shades of red, but her right hand was clean. At first he was worried she was hurt, but then he realized the stains were paint, not blood.

"Are you an artist, then, Mrs. Woolcott," he asked, patting her left hand with his right. "And is that why you were off so far on your own?"

"Not that far, Sergeant. And yes, I paint. Although I don't know that I am good enough to call myself an artist."

"This is certainly the place to become one then. With the light changin' from minute to minute and the cliffs goin' from crimson to coral to pink in no time atall. And the red earth and the green sage. 'Tis a beautiful wild place."

There was a rhythm and poetry in Michael's softly accented speech, thought Elizabeth, surprised that a man from such an ignorant race like Mrs. Compton had said the Irish were would even notice the colors, much less be able to describe them so eloquently. She was suddenly very conscious of the muscles under the rough wool of his uniform. She lowered her eyes, which was a mistake, for then she was looking at that wonderfully shaped bottom, which was swaying with every step of the mule. Oh dear, what was wrong with her, that she was having such thoughts. She squeezed her eyes shut and tried to picture her husband's kind face and familiar, slightly overweight body.

"But do you think it is wise to be out here alone, ma'am?" Michael continued. It was none of his business, but if he hadn't come upon her, anything might have happened.

Elizabeth stiffened. "I have been walking and riding out and painting for three years now, Sergeant Burke. I assure you, my husband is convinced of the safety of it or he would never let me go. Nor would the post commander."

The implication was "Mind your own business, you low-class noncom," and so Michael decided he would, rather than risk another "I am an officer's wife" rebuke.

The rest of the trip was made in silence and Michael

was all proper formality when he lifted her down in front
of the stables. Her husband had seen them coming in and
hurried over.

"Elizabeth! Are you all right?"

"I am fine, Thomas," she said reassuringly, patting his
arm. Eagle stumbled in a gopher hole and lamed herself."

"You weren't thrown?"

"No, and I was very lucky that Sergeant Burke and his
detail were on their way back to the fort."

Woolcott turned to Michael, who was busying himself
with his saddle while husband and wife greeted each
other.

"Sergeant Burke."

"Yes, sir," said Michael with a salute.

"At ease, man. I just wanted to say thank you for res-
cuing Mrs. Woolcott."

"It was my pleasure, Lieutenant, Mrs. Woolcott." Michael pulled his heels together and gave them a slight
bow. "And now I must make sure my men are taking
good care of the mules." He turned and walked off into
the darkness of the stables.

Of course his men were taking good care of their
mules. They knew damn well he would be on them like a
tick on a dog if they didn't. But for some reason he didn't
want to stay and watch the lieutenant and his wife. He felt
disappointed, but there was no logical reason why. Firstly,
had Elizabeth Woolcott been the lieutenant's daughter or
sister she wouldn't have been available to him anyway, if
he was attracted to her. Which he was not. He had had
enough of eastern snobbery, thank you, to last him a life-
time and she had that ladylike air about her. Though she
certainly *was* pretty, with her dark blond hair and hazel
eyes. Now just when did ye notice the color of those eyes,
Mickey Joe, he teased himself. Because secondly, she was
a married woman. But thirdly, she was married to a man
a good many years older. And why would she have done
that? he wondered. Mr. Woolcott seemed nice enough, but
what a waste . . .

Fisk, Spratt, and Mahoney were gone, having unsaddled and brushed their mules, but Elwell was still there, wiping his mule down as though it were a well-bred race-horse.

Michael did not yet have a friend at the fort, and there was something about Elwell that made him think he would make a good one. The difference in rank made it harder, of course, but that might be leveled out by the difference in age and experience.

As though Elwell knew what he was thinking he looked up and grinned.

"So you thought Mrs. Woolcott was his sister or daughter?"

Michael leaned against the stable door. "I did. 'Tis not surprising, given the difference in their ages. Is there a story behind it?"

Elwell kept on smoothing the mule's withers with his cloth. "I've heard something about him finding her after her parents were massacred. She is supposed to have lived with his sister till she came of age."

"So she married him out of gratitude?"

Elwell shrugged. "They seem to have a real affection for one another."

"Well, 'tis an interesting story." Michael paused. "And what is yours, Elwell? An obviously competent and experienced man like yerself and still a private?"

"A little matter of the wrong woman," said Elwell, putting down his cloth and turning to face Michael.

Michael looked at him questioningly.

"I was a sergeant a few months ago, Burke. And I have been quite, uh, friendly with one of the laundresses, the Widow Casey."

Michael grinned.

"Oh, she *is* a widow, one of the few real ones over there. Anyway we were friendly, like I said. And one night I came upon Mr. Cooper with her. Forcing her." Elwell's voice was hoarse with suppressed fury. "I knocked him down. Blacked one of his blue eyes and bruised his jaw. He didn't appreciate it, the vain bastard that he is. So he demoted me. He could have court-martialed me, of course, but he knew Mrs. Casey would have testified in my defense. So here I am."

"And Mrs. Casey?"

"We are still very friendly," said Elwell with a grin. "And there are quite a few girls back there who would be friendly to you, Sergeant Burke."

"Call me Michael when we're off duty."

"What about coming over for a cup of coffee tonight at the widow's then, Michael."

"I just might," Michael replied with a twinkle in his eye.

He had never been one to be constantly chasing after the women, whether dance hall girls or laundresses. But neither was he an archangel, like his patron saint. He had a body. And his body had needs. And a woman would take his mind off the feeling of Elizabeth Woolcott's arms around his waist.

The rest of the week passed very slowly for Elizabeth. She walked a short ways into the valley on Wednesday and did some sketches of rabbit brush and needle grass. Usually such detailed work relaxed her, but that day she found herself pulling apart stem after stem of needle grass in order to collect the distinctive seed heads. She had drawn them before, the sharp "needles" that blew away on the more fragile "threads" and spiraled themselves into the ground. This time she just sat there with a bunch of them in her skirt. She picked one up and winced as it pricked her finger. She couldn't imagine why she was feeling so restless. Finally, she shook out her skirt, gathered her things together, and walked slowly back to the fort. Part of her was listening for the sound of hoofbeats. But it was too early for the wood detail to be returning and why would she be interested in them anyway!

That Sunday, the fort took on a festive air. Things had been very peaceful for the last few months, and every few weeks the Navajo would drift in to trade blankets and to join the horse racing.

"Do you think Sergeant Burke is going to race that

odd-colored horse of his?" her husband wondered aloud as they walked home from the morning service. "I hear he won the horse way up in Nebraska. If he does, I may just wager on him. Although Manuelito's nephew has come in first a few times."

"The race depends not just on the horse but on the rider," replied Elizabeth. "I wouldn't put my money on Sergeant Burke until I saw him on something other than a mule, Thomas."

"And then there's Cooper," continued Thomas. "He's won almost every time he's gone out."

Elizabeth could see that the horse race fever that took over the fort in good weather had gotten to her husband. Well, if the truth be told, she was excited too. Entertainments were few and far between at Fort Defiance. She enjoyed the race days almost as much as her husband, particularly when the Indians participated. Usually the women came along and she loved looking at the patterns on their blanket dresses as well as the weavings they brought to trade.

"Are you racing today, Sergeant?" Privates Spratt and Fisk asked Michael after they had finished their daily drill.

"I'll be watchin' the horses along with you, me boys," he answered in the exaggerated brogue he used when he was teasing. "Sure, and me and me old mule need to get a look at the competition first."

"We thought you might be entering your painted mare," said Sprat.

"Ye did, did ya? And ye were planning to drop a few coins on me, were ye?"

"In support of our sergeant, we just might," said Fisk.

"I see. 'Tis loyal ye are, me boys. And ye wouldn't mind atall if I lost them?"

"We wouldn't mind seeing Mr. Cooper lose," said Mahoney, who had been standing behind the other two, tinkering with his rifle as though he were completely indifferent to Michael's intentions.

"Mr. Cooper is our commanding officer, *Ma*honey," replied Michael, "and I can brook no disrespect for him, Private."

"Yes, *sir,* Sergeant," said Mahoney, his face flushed.

Michael didn't blame the man for his opinion of Cooper. After all, he shared it. But you couldn't allow even a hint of insubordination from your men, especially one like Mahoney, who was teetering on a thin edge. He could become a very good soldier, could Mahoney. Or get himself court-martialed. Michael was always struggling to handle him just right, but sometimes the boy drove him crazy, like now, as he stomped off with that sullen look on his face.

While Fisk and Spratt went ahead to breakfast, Elwell walked along with Michael.

"So you'll just watch this time?"

"Maybe. I'll watch the shorter races, that's sure, since Frost's strength is her endurance. And I'm curious to see how these Navajo ride."

Chapter Four

The hogan door faced east, as was the custom, and when Serena pushed the blanket aside, she had to lift her hand to shade her eyes as she went from the cool, dark interior to the bright light of the sun.

For the first time in three years she was greeting the morning with feelings of joy and expectation. Her happiness was not pure. It was mixed with a deep and lingering sorrow, for never again would she hear her daughter's voice or see her slim body racing one of the sheepdogs.

Serena sometimes thought it would have been easier if her child had died. Then they would have left the hogan and all memories of her behind. But to know that she was alive somewhere, maybe in Cubero or Abiquiu, working in some Mexican household, crying for her mother, eventually forgetting her mother, never to have her *kinaalda* . . . Serena took a deep breath. She had promised not to torment herself. Three years was enough, both for her and her husband.

She could see Antonio at the corral, getting the horses ready, and she went back into the hogan to pack their food and the blankets she was bringing to the fort. It was only in the last year she had started weaving anything but what they needed for every day. She had several small pieces that she was proud of and she wondered if any of the *bilagaana* would even notice the subtle differences she had begun to introduce into the usual patterns.

When she finished packing, she wandered over to the

corral, where Antonio was running his hand down the blood bay gelding's leg.

"Is he ready to race today?"

"I don't know. The leg feels cool and the injury was very slight to begin with. I'll see how he is when we get to the fort."

"I would enjoy watching you beat that yellow-haired *bilagaana*. And Armijo too, who walks around puffed up like a toad after winning a race," she added with a smile.

"It's good to be able to bring you with me. Things have been quiet for a while. I'm hoping they stay that way. If no *ladrones*, Diné, or Mexicans disturb the peace," he added bitterly.

His wife reached out and placed her hand gently on her husband's shoulder. "You can't be responsible for everyone in Dinetah, husband."

"And well I know it," he answered. "But the *bilagaana* seem to think we can control even men who live hundreds of miles away."

"They are very stupid, the *bilagaana*."

"Yes, and also very dangerous." He sighed. "But enough of such talk," he added, dropping a kiss on the top of her head. "Today is a day to let go of our worries and show them again why they cannot hope to match the horses and riders of the Diné!"

During his time on the plains and in Utah, Michael had gotten used to the paradox of being in the army of the West. Over the years, he had come to know many Indians well. He had traded with them, raced them, and a few times had been privileged to enter one of their homes as a welcome guest. Many cavalrymen did this, of course, but Michael's Lakota and Crow friends intuited a certain openness and sympathy that went beyond his fellow soldiers'. He was truly interested in who they were as a people. He had never forgotten that it was money collected from Indian people that had saved his family. He had never discovered what nation it was that had reached out to another suffering people, but that only made his sympathy broader.

Being in the army had brought him what he had dreamed of years ago when he had enlisted. But it also meant that after months of getting to know some of the Lakota or Crow well, a fragile peace would once again be destroyed and he would find himself riding out after people who may well have been friends and acquaintances. He hated the fighting, although he was good at it, and thank God he had never been involved in an all-out war, only in isolated skirmishes.

He was looking forward to meeting the Navajo today. All he knew of them was that they were cousins to the Apache. They had vast herds of sheep and horses and had been warring for years with the Mexicans. Who were now *New* Mexicans and citizens of the United States. Which was why Fort Defiance was here. To protect the New Mexicans from the raiding and slave-taking of the Navajo.

Anyone who was looking for war-bonneted warriors trailing eagle feathers down their backs would have been disappointed, thought Michael as he watched the Navajo ride in. The men wore buckskin knee breeches studded with silver conchos and blankets around their shoulders and only a feather or two stuck in the bandannas that covered their foreheads. Silver hoop earrings were their only other ornaments. The women wore blanket dresses gathered at the waist with a woven sash. At first glance, they were not impressive. But Michael wasn't looking for beads and war bonnets, although he couldn't deny that his first sight of the Lakota and Crow warriors had thrilled him, for they matched the image he had carried in his head since he was a child. Today, he was watching how these people rode, and looking closely at their faces.

Although they were coming in slowly, every now and then a young man would ride ahead and then, pulling his horse in a tight circle, would gallop back to the main band. These riders looked like part of their horses, and their mounts responded as though they were indeed one creature. And as the people got closer, Michael began to notice distinctive decorations: silver disks flashing from breeches and belts, and the distinctive blanket patterns on both men and women.

One horse and rider caught his eye. The horse was a blood bay and smaller than Frost or Trooper. His coat burned in the sun and he seemed to carry the sun's energy inside him as his rider held him down to a fast walk. The rider himself looked to be only a few years older than himself, thought Michael. His face was still except when he turned to say something to the woman at his side, obviously his wife. Then it came alive.

"Tell me, do ye know who that man is, Elwell," Michael asked.

"That's Antonio, Manuelito's nephew."

"Manuelito?"

"One of the headmen who's been trying to keep his people to the treaties he signs. He and his nephew are *muy rico*—they own many sheep and horses."

"Good horses, by the look of that bay."

Elwell grinned. "Do I hear a little competitive interest, Sergeant?"

"I'm still planning to watch for a while, Private. But I must admit I'm feeling a wee bit restless, watching that bay prance by."

The racing took place in the valley north of the fort, where distances of half, three-quarters, and a mile and a quarter had been measured off. While the riders rode out to the starting points for the first races, the Navajo women spread their blankets in front of them, hoping to trade for *bilagaana* trinkets like mirrors, brushes, buttons, needles and thread, and foodstuffs like coffee and "sweet salt," as they called sugar.

Elizabeth loved it when the women came in. They sat with great dignity, surrounded by striped weavings of red and black and white and yellow. The geometric designs drew her eye, and she had a few months ago traded for a small blanket which she had hung on their wall. Today she walked slowly, her eyes down on what was spread before her, until she reached one of the women near the end. Here was a weaving different from all the others. Not radically so, but original enough to speak the word "fellow artist" to Elizabeth's soul. She knelt down and examined the zigzags and diamonds, running her hand lightly over the wool. She had a pocketful of silver buttons with her and two books of needles, but it seemed insulting to offer those in return for the beautiful piece in front of her.

She looked up into the face of the weaver, her eyes beaming her appreciation.

"You like it?" said the Navajo woman.

"You speak English!" said Elizabeth, without thinking to keep the surprise out of her voice.

"You speak Diné?" the woman asked with dry humor.

"Why, no," Elizabeth replied with a blush.

Serena was ashamed of her impoliteness. "My husband's uncle has had dealings with the *bilagaana* for years. He speaks both Spanish and English and taught his nephew and his nephew taught me."

"I don't think I have seen you here before."

There was an awkward silence and Elizabeth fingered the buttons in her pocket. "All of the blankets I've seen today are well made and beautiful," she said hesitantly, "but this one is special."

Serena's face softened with the pleasure of having her work recognized.

"I have the usual things to trade with," Elizabeth continued, "but somehow they don't seem enough."

Serena just sat there in silence.

Elizabeth cleared her throat. "You have painted a design with wool. I am also a painter. Will you keep the blanket for me? I have something back at my quarters ..."

Serena nodded. She wondered what the *bilagaana* woman was going to offer her. Perhaps a fancy mirror? A hairbrush? She had to admit that while she had no use for a mirror and in fact felt very uncomfortable gazing into one, she liked the *bilagaana* brushes.

Elizabeth was back, slightly out of breath and holding a rolled-up piece of paper in her hands. She knelt down and unrolled it in front of Serena.

"Since your blanket is a work of art, it seemed only right to offer you a piece of mine in return."

The paper had colors on it. After a few minutes of looking at it, Serena realized what it was: a representation of the cliffs near the Ojo del Gallo. The *bilagaana* woman had almost captured the colors of the rock . . . but who could ever capture the colors of those rocks? It was interesting, though, and even a little shocking. Presumably this was a part of a ceremony and here the little *bilagaana* was trading it?

She remained silent as she looked at the painting.

It was hard for Elizabeth not to receive a reaction and she rushed into the quiet between them. "I go out as often as possible to paint the cliffs." The Navajo woman had a frown on her face. Maybe she didn't like the painting? Elizabeth rushed in again to apologize. "I know I haven't gotten the colors right . . . or the blue of the sky."

"You do this often? It is an everyday thing, not part of a ceremony?"

Elizabeth was puzzled for a moment. And then she remembered something the post commander's wife had told her. The Navajo had medicine men who painted with sand as part of their curing ceremonies.

"Oh no, this is nothing very special. Well, it is special to me, but not religious. Although"—Elizabeth hesitated—"I never thought of this before, but I do feel closer to God out by the cliffs than I do at services sometimes."

Serena knew a bit about what the *bilagaana* called religion. They seemed to be a very odd people, these "new People." They had one God and they only thought about him, it seemed, on one day of the week. And here was one of their women, who had considerable power if she could capture the cliffs as well as she had. And yet she seemed to have no sense of this power. But she felt very good about what the *bilagaana* woman had done: she had regarded her weaving in a way no other *bilagaana* had: as work done by an equal.

"I would like you to have the blanket as a gift," she said.

"Oh, no, I couldn't do that," Elizabeth protested.

Serena pulled back into herself. Really, these people were like children, impulsive and impolite.

Elizabeth felt the distance between them instantly. She knelt there quietly and rolled up her painting.

"I would like to accept your gift," she said after a moment.

Serena smiled at her and folding the blanket carefully, handed it to Elizabeth.

"And I would like to give you a gift," Elizabeth said, praying that she was doing the right thing. "I would like you to have this, if you like it. From one artist to another?"

Serena nodded and placed the rolled-up painting in her carrying bag. "Thank you."

"My name is Elizabeth Woolcott. Mrs. Woolcott," said Elizabeth, holding out her hand.

The first and most important thing to know about a person for the Diné was the name of her clan. With a Diné woman, Serena would have shared that. But she knew that to the *bilagaana*, names were important, and so she gave the name she had been called by Mexicans. "And I am Serena," she said with a smile. "I am married to Manuelito's nephew." She did not reach out her hand, so Elizabeth just let her own fall to her side.

"Does your husband race today?" Serena asked.

"Oh no, he is a little too old for horse racing. There he is, over there."

Serena saw a gray-haired, heavy-set officer. She was surprised and felt sorry for the young woman. She was probably considered pretty by the *bilagaana*, and here she was, married to a man much older. It happened among the Diné sometimes, it was true, but she had always felt sorry for those women.

"Is your husband racing?" asked Elizabeth.

"Yes, and I think it is getting close to the time for the first race," said Serena. She seemed to be waiting for Elizabeth to do something, although she sat there quietly enough. Then Elizabeth realized she was waiting for her to leave, to join the other women of the fort so that Serena could stand on the sidelines with the Navajo. It seemed strange to go off without her, for she had felt very close for those few moments, but she only uttered a quick good-bye and hurried off.

Chapter Five

Antonio was not in the first two races, which were only a half mile. He knew that the bay did best with distance, although he still wondered if the leg would hold up. He had kept the bay to a slow trot on the ride out along the valley, and the fetlock was still cool, so he hoped he had nothing to worry about.

Manuelito was in the first race, riding his chestnut mare. Lieutenant Greasy Hair, who was riding in that race too, kept glancing over at the headman. He hadn't been able to beat him yet, although several times he had come close. Antonio didn't think that Lieutenant Greasy Hair was going to win today, either. Antonio smiled to himself. He enjoyed coming up with insulting names for the lieutenant, for whom he had no respect. Although he had to admit the man was a good horseman, and presumably a competent warrior.

When they started off, he could see that the race would be close, but from a distance it was hard to tell who had won, especially since they looked nose-to-nose. But he could not see a mass of *bilagaana* soldiers milling around the lieutenant's buckskin, so he was sure that Manuelito had beaten Lieutenant Bony-Ass again.

One more half-mile race and then it was his turn. He turned the bay to ride out to the three-quarter-mile mark. There wasn't much competition from the soldiers in this race. But he was a little worried about Haastiin Ntl'aai. He had a new gelding, a black who looked pretty fast.

And the man was a reckless rider, willing to risk his neck to win.

Antonio decided to hold his horse back a little. He was in the longer race because of the bay's endurance, after all. Let Haastiin Ntl'aai whip his horse up to full speed for the first quarter mile. Antonio suspected that his clansman had chosen the wrong distance.

As indeed he had. As they neared the fort, Antonio could hear the soldiers shouting. Those who had bet on the black were sure they were going to have heavy pockets that night. But in the last quarter mile, the horse began to fall behind, and Antonio called on the bay's reserves.

Michael had made no bets. He wasn't stupid: he was too new to the horses and riders to know who was likely to win. But his eye had been caught by that blood bay and he wasn't surprised when he found himself screaming as loud as the men who had their money on him. He came from a good three lengths behind, his rider settled down with the reins slack, just letting the horse bring him in. He overtook the black three hundred yards from the finish and passed him as if he were standing still. The Navajo were silent, but the soldiers went wild.

"Did you see that, Sergeant?" said Spratt, who was pounding Fisk on the back. Even Mahoney had lost his air of indifference and was tossing his hat up in the air.

Michael grinned. "Next time I'll put a little of me own money on that bay," he said.

"How about putting up more than money, mick," said a voice behind him. It was Lieutenant Cooper. Mahoney grabbed his hat up and jammed it on his head as they all stood to attention.

"At ease, men. My horse was too tired to take his race after patrol yesterday," said Cooper, "but I'd like it if some trooper beat one of these little savages."

Día, the man couldn't admit that the Navajo's horse was better, thought Michael.

"You are always grooming that wild-eyed gray of yours, Burke. You obviously think she has something. I want you to prove it. Or have you gotten too used to riding mules?"

"I hadn't thought to race today, sir, just to watch," Michael answered quietly.

"And if I ordered you to, mick?"

"Then of course I would ride, Mr. Cooper."

"Consider yourself ordered then."

"Yes, sir." Michael saluted and was off to the stables. There was one more three-quarter-mile race, which he wouldn't make, so that meant he was in the mile. It was Frost's distance, it was true, but he hadn't had the time to do any training these past few weeks. And the damned lieutenant would probably put money on him and then keep him on wood detail for the rest of his career if he lost!

Elizabeth had been standing with the other officers' wives for the shorter races. She had been thrilled to watch Serena's husband come from behind and win. How proud his wife must be, she thought as she tried to find her in the small knot of Navajo women gathered near the finish line.

When the colonel's striker brought out a pitcher of lemonade for the ladies, Elizabeth drank two glasses greedily. Standing still in the heat and dust dried her out even more than her walking and riding did.

"Oh, look, it is that handsome new Sergeant Burke," said Mrs. Gray, the colonel's wife. He must be riding in the mile."

"My, he is a handsome man, isn't he," commented the doctor's wife. "And look at him, he is riding like an Indian."

Elizabeth didn't want to look. She wanted to ignore him and forget how it felt to have had her arms around his waist. But her eyes were drawn to him, as indeed all the women's were, and as he rode by, he took off his cap and waved to them before riding down the valley.

"He's a charmer too, that one," said Mrs. Gray.

Elizabeth watched him trot down the valley. He rode only with an old saddle blanket and girth. And she was almost sure it was a hackamore, not a bridle he was using. His oddly colored gray must be well trained indeed. She looked like a quiet and steady mount, but did she have both the stamina and speed for this race?

"Good afternoon, ladies," said a voice behind them. It was Mr. Cooper. "I see you all have your eyes on my sergeant. We'll see if the mick and his mare are any good today. He's up against Antonio in this one."

Mrs. Compton used to call them micks and Elizabeth had sometimes had the phrase "dirty little micks" run through her mind when she would see a bunch of ill-dressed, boisterous Irish children on Boston Common. And she didn't trust Sergeant Michael Burke's Irish charm. She was sure it was all on the surface. But she also did not like Mr. Cooper, whose own brand of charm was ... well, oily and less charming. Right away, she felt herself shift into a defense of Sergeant Burke. "I would assume that the sergeant has confidence in himself and his horse if he is entering the last race of the day, Mr. Cooper."

"Oh, he wasn't intending to race today, Mrs. Woolcott. He is in the race because I ordered him to ride. I've lost to Manuelito too many times, and Burke won that horse of his in a race. I have a hunch we'll beat the Navajo in this one."

Her Thomas would never have abused his power that way, thought Elizabeth proudly. He might only be a second lieutenant under this West Point bantam rooster, she thought angrily, but at least he was someone to be proud of.

"In that case, Mr. Cooper," she said with cool politeness, "I hope Sergeant Burke and his mare come through for you."

Michael was halfway out to the starting point when the next-to-the-last race began. He watched the four men gallop by. He could hardly see them with all the dust they were raising, but he was pretty sure the blood bay was not among them. Two races in a row would be too much, he thought as he rode on. But the gelding might be in this last one.

Indeed, and so he is, Michael thought, and only one other and him nothing to worry about atall. The blood bay was not quite the bundle of unspent energy as he had been when he entered the fort, but Michael could tell that his first race had merely acted as a warmup. The other horse was one ridden by a second lieutenant whom he knew by sight. The officer's horse was high-strung and looked fast, but Michael could tell by looking at his narrow chest and long legs that he was not made for distance.

He smiled and nodded at the other two riders and dismounted. He walked around Frost, picking up and examining each hoof carefully, keeping up a quiet conversation with her. He stood in front and putting his hand on either side of the mare's cheeks, he breathed into her nostrils and then remounted.

The second lieutenant snorted. "Do you think that sort of hocus-pocus will win a race, Sergeant?"

Antonio only looked curiously at both men and mounted his bay in one graceful movement. The dust had settled ahead of them and he knew that the starter would flash the signal any minute.

When the mirror flashed, Michael let the other two take the lead. Luckily he had thought to tie his handkerchief around his neck and he pulled it up to keep from choking on the dust. He let Frost sit right behind the blood bay while the second lieutenant kept a lead of two lengths for the first half mile.

Shortly after that, however, the chestnut began to slow. It was almost imperceptible, but by the three-quarter mark the bay had overtaken him and Michael was alongside of him. With one-quarter mile to go, the lieutenant was definitely out of the race and it would be between Frost and the blood bay.

Frost hung right where Michael wanted her, now a half length behind the bay. They knew each other very well, the mare and he, and Michael knew he had no worries about Frost's ability to finish the race and finish strong.

But the bay was showing no signs of tiring, so it would all come down to the last eighth of a mile and who had a last burst of speed left. Michael was sure Frost did, but did the bay?

He let Frost narrow the distance until they were alongside. The post was going wild, but to Michael it seemed as though the screaming was way in the distance, so hard was he concentrating on Frost's responses.

"All right, me girl, run!" he shouted, and he could feel the power in the mare's hind legs as she pulled up nose to nose with the bay. They were almost at the finish line and Michael knew it could be a tie, depending on the bay's responses. He gave one last wild shout and Frost pulled in front by a nose as they crossed the line.

"Did you *see* that! Did you see that!" Mahoney was hoarse from shouting. "Did you see our sergeant?" The boy was pounding Spratt on the back so hard he almost knocked him over.

Elwell heard him and the grin that split his face became even wider. Our sergeant, indeed. And tomorrow he'll go back to being the stubborn little bastard he is! But by God, the boy was right to be proud. Master Sergeant Michael Joseph Burke was one hell of a rider.

When Michael dismounted, he was immediately surrounded by soldiers clapping him on the shoulder and thanking him for keeping their pay in their pockets. When he finally was able to break away, he looked around for the other two riders. The second lieutenant had dismounted and was leading his obviously blown horse down to the stables. Michael waved and shouted, "Good riding, sir. Your horse would have been the winner in a shorter race." The officer grimaced, but gave him a wave back.

Michael looked around for the blood bay. He was being led away by a young boy while his rider walked next to him, watching his front leg carefully. He motioned the boy to stop and knelt down to examine the bay's left leg.

Michael gave Frost's reins to Elwell, who had just broken through the crowd. "Josh . . . Private Elwell, could ye hold my horse for me? I'll be right back."

"The leg's a little warm, is it?" he asked when he reached the Navajo, not knowing whether the man spoke English or not.

The man looked up. "A little. His leg was swollen last week and I am worried I pushed him too soon."

"Then maybe I was lucky," said Michael with a friendly smile. "With a completely sound leg, your bay might have beat us."

"I make no excuses, soldier. Your mare is a very good horse," Antonio replied quietly.

"She is, isn't she," said Michael with an infectious smile.

The *bilagaana* was not bragging, thought Antonio. He was just naturally rejoicing in a fine mount. This man knew how to win without being offensive. "She is a very interesting-looking mare. What do you call her?"

"Frost."

Antonio nodded his approval. "A good name for a horse that color. Where did you find her?"

"She is an Appaloosa . . . a horse of the Palouse River. Bred by the Nez Percés."

"An Indian horse then? Won in battle?"

"Of a sort. I won her in another horse race, in Nebraska. But not from a Nez Percé. From a soldier who traded for her."

"I don't suppose you would be interested in a trade?" Antonio asked with a smile.

"Trade Frost? She's too much me friend. Even if she were slower, I'd not trade." Michael hesitated. "Em, me name is Michael. Sergeant Michael Burke."

Antonio knew that the *bilagaana* custom was to give your name to strangers. Since Antonio wasn't his war name, but only a name given him by the Mexicans, he didn't mind telling it, but he identified himself first by relationship, in the Diné way. "I am Manuelito's nephew. Antonio."

"You are the headman's nephew then? That is why you speak English so well."

"Not so well," Antonio said modestly.

"Very well," insisted Michael. "I hope we will meet again. Not just in a race."

"I would be interested in getting to know a *bilagaana* soldier who takes care not to disturb a Diné shrine."

It took Michael a moment to realize what Antonio was talking about. "You mean to say, there I was, washing meself with not a care in the world and all the while I was being watched? And how did ye know it was me?"

"The Diné keep a close watch on the soldiers. And your horse is distinctive, as we've just agreed," Antonio added with a grin.

Antonio was amused to see the *bilagaana* soldier flush. " 'Tis glad I am it was me horses ye were paying attention to and not me arse!"

There had been another observer, Antonio remembered. But he wouldn't embarrass the man further by telling him that one of the officers' wives had seen him too!

Chapter Six

On race days, there was always a dance in the evening so that winners could celebrate and losers commiserate. This one was open to all the noncommissioned officers and their wives as well, while the enlisted men caroused in the mess hall.

"You look lovely tonight, Elizabeth," said Thomas to his wife when she emerged from the bedroom. She was wearing her second-best dress, a dark blue lawn shirtwaist with a white lace collar and pearl buttons up the front.

Elizabeth blushed. She usually did not spend much time in front of the mirror, but tonight for some reason she found herself experimenting with her hair, trying it up on top of her head, then loose with a dark blue velvet ribbon, before she finally just twisted it into her usual knot at the base of her neck.

Thomas put his arms around her waist and pulled her up to him for a kiss, which she returned eagerly. The smell of his bay rum and the familiar taste of cigar and coffee were reassuring. She didn't know where her restlessness was coming from, but she felt a wave of affection and gratitude for the steady love and security Thomas had been offering her for years.

"Now you be sure I get to waltz with you, Lizzie," he teased her as he placed her shawl over her shoulders.

She reached up and patted him on the cheek. "As if you didn't always get a waltz, Thomas!"

* * *

There hadn't been many respectable women at Camp Supply and Michael hadn't been to a dance in over a year. He certainly hoped he would remember the steps, he worried as he pulled on his gloves and smoothed his jacket.

When he arrived the music had already started and he was surprised to see Joshua Elwell with the musicians. So Elwell was a fiddler, was he, thought Michael. And a good one too. He would have to hum a few tunes to the man and see if he could teach him a couple of reels.

Although it was a mixed dance, Michael noticed that the noncommissioned officers and their wives were clustered together and only Lieutenant Thomas Woolcott was dancing with a master sergeant's wife. Michael offered his hand to the quartermaster's daughter, who ducked her head and blushed, but put her hand in his nevertheless. Miss Mary Baker was only seventeen and was very aware that she had just been asked to dance by one of the handsomest men in the room. It took her halfway through the *schottische* to recover her composure and show Michael that she was a fine dancer.

"Thank you very much, Miss Baker," he said when he returned her to her parents. "I was a lucky man indeed to capture you before a stampede starts over here," he added, smiling down at her. "But sure, with such a fine-looking mother, it will be hard to tell who they're stampeding after." He winked at the quartermaster and his wife.

"Go along with ye, Sergeant Burke," said Mrs. Baker, who was originally from Kerry. "That fine Irish tongue will not get you anywhere with me!"

Michael heard the musicians striking up a waltz and gazed around the room. He wasn't about to waltz with an impressionable young girl. He wasn't full of himself, mind you, but was quite conscious of his ability to charm women and didn't need to raise the hopes of a seventeen-year-old by dancing with her twice in a row. He realized that the commander's wife was chatting with one of her friends while her husband was off in the corner deep in conversation with two officers. He bowed to the Bakers and strolled over.

He would probably be made a fool of, he thought as he approached her. The dance might be mixed, but he would be willing to bet what he'd won that day that not too many sergeants asked the colonel's wife to dance. Well, he would and be damned. She could only say no, and since she was a gracious woman from all he'd heard, she would at least say it nicely.

"A lovely lady like yourself shouldn't be sitting out a waltz, Mrs. Gray. May I have this dance?"

Janet Gray looked up into Michael's blue eyes. He said the words easily and with just the right combination of respect and charm but she knew that a refusal on her part to any noncom would hurt and humiliate. And why should she refuse, she thought as she smiled up at him. He was a good-looking young man and she was going to enjoy her waltz with him. And her Charles was off with his cronies in the corner.

"Thank you, Sergeant Burke," she said with a smile and offered him her hand.

Michael moved as gracefully and expertly as she thought he would and when she saw Charles looking over at her with his eyebrows raised, she only gave him a little smile and went on chatting with Michael.

"You rode a very exciting race today, Sergeant. I declare, you had all us ladies having palpitations at the finish line, it was so close."

"Somehow I don't think ye're the sort of woman for palpitations, Mrs. Gray," he said, smiling down at her. "Not the wife of Colonel Charles Gray who's been stationed in the territory for five years."

"You are right, Sergeant," she admitted. "I was making a poor attempt to flirt with you, but I suppose I am too old for that anyway," she added with mock sadness.

"And now ye are just trying to pull a compliment out of me, ma'am," he replied with a twinkle in his eye. "But ye need no compliments from me, Mrs. Gray. Ye're a very handsome woman."

"And you are a very bold young man, Sergeant Burke!"

"Sure and ye wouldn't be dancin' with me otherwise, had I not summoned up me boldness and courage."

"You are incorrigible, but very enjoyable. And a very good rider," she added more seriously. "It was clear to see that you and your mare have a real partnership."

"Thank ye, ma'am."

"I heard a rumor that you were ordered to race, Sergeant Burke. I am sorry if that were true and Lieutenant Cooper abused his authority over you."

Michael remained silent.

"I see you are a discreet soldier, Sergeant Burke. Well, that is only to your credit."

When the waltz was over, Michael returned Mrs. Gray to her friends. The musicians were taking a break and he walked over to Elwell.

"That was fine music ye were makin', Joshua. I'm going to have to teach ye a few jigs and reels."

"I only know one Irish tune besides the 'Garry Owen,' Michael, a slow air," said Joshua, picking up his fiddle and beginning to play softly.

Michael remembered the tune well, and if he closed his eyes he would be home again, listening to his sister Cait hummin' it with a faraway look in her eye. She'd been sixteen and Michael had teased her unmercifully, for she had fallen in love with young Donnelly to that tune at one of the *ceilidhs*. That was just before the hard times. Just before young Donnelly died, the week after their ma.

The music was sweet and slow and sad and reached down into Michael's soul, waking all the memories he'd held at bay for years. He wasn't ready for them and he lapsed into his broadest brogue when he interrupted Elwell's playing.

"Josh, me boy, I'll have to teach ye a few lively chunes, I can see. 'Tis too sad ye're makin me," he said as he covered his eyes dramatically.

Elwell laughed, but when he looked up he was surprised to see that Michael's cheek was wet and that he was quickly wiping it even as he teased. Elwell stood up and joked back, not wanting to embarrass the man. "Let me cheer you up, Sergeant. I hear the punch has been treated by Dr. Osborne. For medicinal purposes, of course, but I need to treat your sudden melancholy."

Michael wasn't much of a drinker, but one glass of punch enabled him to push down the memories and focus on the here and now. And when the music started up again, he danced almost every set.

When the last dance was announced, he looked around. He had been a paragon of courtesy and partnered almost every lady there. Except Mrs. Woolcott. There she was, only a few feet away. He didn't think she liked him very much but damn it, he could show her an Irishman could be as light on his feet as any Mr. Cooper, who had been her last partner.

He walked over and gave her his most formal bow. "May I have this waltz, Mrs. Woolcott?"

How could she say no? It would have been a terrible insult, especially from an officer's wife.

Not that she wanted to say no. Not really. She had kept herself out of his way the whole evening, all the while very aware of his presence. All the while wondering what it would be like to have *his* arms around *her* waist.

Now she would find out.

At first, she wouldn't let herself feel it. She kept her smile cool and polite and counted her steps to herself, though she didn't need to, for she was a good dancer.

But it was a lovely tune and the fiddle was carrying it and she let go of her control and lost herself in the music.

Michael Burke was as good on the dance floor as he was on horseback, she thought. She could feel his gloved hand against the small of her back and the warmth it created seemed to be spreading up her spine. It frightened her, the effect that physical closeness with the man had on her. It seemed to create sensations she had never experienced before. She could put no name to them, but somehow she knew they were dangerous. Surely they were sensations a wife should feel only with her husband. She shivered.

"Are ye cold, Mrs. Woolcott," Michael asked. Someone had opened the doors and the night air had made her shiver, he thought.

"No. Well, perhaps a little, Sergeant Burke."

She was very quiet, little Mrs. Woolcott, he thought. He couldn't tell if it was shyness or distaste. He couldn't guess what she was feeling, but for himself . . . well, he had to keep reminding himself that she was someone's wife, for the feeling of having her in his arms was very sweet. Perhaps it had been Elwell's playing that tune, perhaps it was the glass of punch, but Michael's emotions were closer to the surface than usual. And she had such a small waist, Mrs. Woolcott. And her head barely came to his shoulder.

He couldn't think of a charming, teasing thing to say for the life of him to break the tension or whatever it was that was thick between them. Here he could chatter all night to the colonel's lady, and a second lieutenant's wife had him terrified.

Her dark blond hair, shining with reddish glints, was swept softly over her ears and pulled back in a knot. There was a hint of jasmine in the air. He liked it, that she used scent sparingly. He hated it when women doused themselves with perfume. He looked down at her hand in his and grinned. The paint stains he had noticed before were faint, but still noticeable. He guessed it was the usual condition and he liked her all the more for having something in her life that was important enough to get a little dirty for.

When the music stopped, he walked her over to where her husband was standing with a few other officers.

"Thank you very much, Mrs. Woolcott," he said with another very formal bow.

"You are quite welcome, Sergeant. I enjoyed our waltz," she replied with equal formality and turned to her husband.

The officers and their wives left first and when the last of the couples were gone, Michael walked over to Elwell.

"Ye did tell me, Josh, that Mrs. Casey had, em, a friend."

Josh grinned at him. "She does. Mary Ann."

"Are ye visiting Mrs. Casey tonight, Josh, and do ye think she might introduce me to Mary Ann?"

Michael was very pleased to find out that Mary Ann was a buxom woman and obviously experienced, whether she was a widow or not. A night enjoying her company was just what he needed. It would, he hoped, chase every picture of Mrs. Woolcott right out of his head. He might be a long way from Ireland and his upbringing, but he had no intention of allowing his thoughts to wander to a very married woman, no matter how odd a partnership he thought it was.

Chapter Seven

The wood detail was wandering further and further in their search for fuel. Two days after the horse race, Michael led them north and they passed by the small canyon where he had bathed in the creek.

"There's probably a good supply of wood in there, Sergeant," said Fisk as they rode by.

"Could be, Private Fisk, but we'll save it for the cold weather when we won't want to be riding that far out from the fort," Michael answered, telling a partial truth. His reasoning made sense to the men, however, and they rode on cheerfully as he hung a little behind them, remembering the shrine he had found and the pleasure of bathing in that canyon stream. He couldn't explain it to himself, much less to his men, but he had a strong feeling about the place and he didn't want to be riding the mules in and worrying about the men disturbing the shrine.

They gathered their wood a few miles northwest and after the mules were loaded, Michael gave them a short break. His four soldiers pulled out their mess kits and canteens and took shelter from the sun under a small juniper. Just as Michael was pulling his own canteen from the mule, Spratt jumped up and fumbled at his holster, calling, "Sergeant, Sergeant, Indians!"

"Sit yerself down again, Private Spratt. And don't be so quick to draw your revolver."

"But, Sergeant . . ."

"Private Spratt," Michael barked in his best drill sergeant's voice.

"Yes, sir. Sorry, sir." Spratt knelt down next to Mahoney, who was strung tight as an overstretched piece of wire, thought Michael. Thank God for Elwell and Fisk, who were still eating and drinking as though they hadn't a worry in the world, although Michael knew they would respond in a minute if he needed them.

He hoped he didn't.

The riders were coming from the southwest and the sun was almost directly in Michael's eyes as he tried to make them out. There were six of them and he was sure they were Navajo. "Sure, and who else would they be, boyo," he chided himself.

As they drew closer, he relaxed, for the lead horse was very familiar. It was the blood bay that he had raced and presumably his rider was Antonio. He moved away from the shelter of his mule and walked toward the approaching riders.

It *was* Antonio, he saw and then he fully relaxed. No matter how calm he had appeared on the outside, he was not ashamed to admit that he didn't like being so far from the fort with only four men. If they did meet any hostiles, they would have a poor chance of making it back.

"It *is* you, Sergeant," said Antonio. "I see you are not riding your mare today?" he continued in a gently teasing tone.

Michael assumed an expression of wounded pride. "Sure and ye're not insultin' me mount, are ye, Antonio? Why, I bet me mule could take yer bay quite easily."

Antonio laughed aloud and dismounted.

"It's good to see you again, Sergeant."

"And I was very glad to see it was you, Antonio."

"You have little to fear, Sergeant. The Diné have kept their word." Antonio's face had become serious. Michael had not meant to insult him, but from what he had heard, things had been in a constant state of flux between peace and war these last ten years.

"I don't question Manuelito's word," he responded with equal seriousness. "But I know from experience how hard it is to control every member of a spread-out people.

And how hard it is to convince the army that you cannot be responsible for individual renegades."

Antonio's face relaxed. "You are indeed a rare *bilagaana* if you understand that, Sergeant."

"I was just about to have me 'afternoon tea,' " Michael said and then realized from Antonio's expression that the phrase was too idiomatic to convey humor. "We are having a late lunch," he added, handing his canteen to the warrior.

Antonio gestured his men down and they sat silently opposite the cavalrymen, their faces set and unsmiling. Elwell offered one a piece of bread and he took it without a word.

Antonio went back to his horse and pulling down a buckskin pouch, slung it over his shoulder and joined Michael.

He accepted some cheese from Michael, and then placing the pouch in front of him drew out a handful of what looked like dried ears and extended his hand.

Michael had never seen anything like them before and he kept his face expressionless as he said thank you and took one. He automatically brought it up to his nose and exclaimed, without thinking, "Why, it smells just like peaches!"

"Why shouldn't it?" said Antonio, chewing on one. "It is a dried peach."

"I've only seen dried apples meself, and not too many of those," said Michael, savoring the chewy, sweet morsel.

"We have thousands of peach trees north of here in Canyon de Chelly. My uncle has an orchard and always keeps my family supplied." He paused and then looked over at Michael with a glint in his eye. "What did you think it was, Sergeant?"

Michael grinned. "The thought did flit through me mind, but only for a moment, mind ye, that it resembled an ear."

Antonio laughed and the men under the juniper, both troopers and Navajo, smiled at one another, despite their ignorance of the joke. They were all very happy that their sergeant and Antonio were clearly friendly.

"You were willing to taste it anyway, *bilagaana*?"

" 'Tis the polite thing to do, you understand," said Michael with a twinkle in his eye, broadening his brogue. "And at one time in me life, I learned to eat anything," he added more seriously.

"When you speak like that, you sound different from the other *bilagaana*," Antonio remarked.

Michael paused. "I come from a small green island, Antonio. To get there, you would have to travel many weeks to the east and then cross the ocean."

Antonio frowned. "I've heard of the ocean before, but to the west."

"That is the Pacific. I came from over the Atlantic. Anyway, I left home when I was young because of a great famine. I've been here for many years, but I have never lost me brogue completely."

"It has a soft sound, this 'brogue.' I like it."

"Thank you, Antonio."

Both men were silent for a moment, sensing that the first and fragile threads of friendship were now between them.

Michael broke the silence first. "You are Manuelito's nephew. That means you must know a little about the situation here. Do you think it is likely to remain peaceful?"

Antonio scooped up a handful of pink sand. He held it out in front of him, almost openhanded. "There are many Diné and when they are held loosely like this, Sergeant, only a few of them slip away." He closed his hand tightly and small pink streams of sand slid through his fingers. "The tighter the people are held by the *bilagaana* and their own headmen, the faster they slip away." He waved his hand, letting the sand fall in an arc. "This is Dinetah. The Holy Place. It is bounded by four mountains. We only ask to live here, within them. But we are being pushed further west by every piece of paper we sign."

"But you *have* signed them?"

"Yes. Manuelito and Armijo and Barboncito and the others have signed. They have given their word. For themselves, this means the treaty will not be broken. But there are always the *ladrones,* Sergeant. Amongst all people," he added bitterly. "Yet it is only the Diné the army punishes."

"I want to ask one more question," Michael asked carefully. "I wish to better understand the Diné and I ask it respectfully."

Antonio nodded, giving him room to speak.

"There has been sheep stealing and killing and slave taking, Antonio. That is why the army is here."

Antonio frowned and was quiet for so long that Michael was afraid he had just broken the threads of their beginning friendship.

"I am so filled with anger at this that it is hard to speak," said Antonio with controlled passion in his voice.

"I am sorry for asking then," said Michael, beginning to apologize.

"No. It is only by talking that anything can be understood. It's just that I have heard my uncle say this *many* times and he has never been heard."

Michael waited patiently, still fearful that he had caused an irretrievable break.

"But I think you want to learn. You didn't drink at our spring. You didn't gloat over your winning, like Stringy-Ass Cooper does."

Michael had to smile at that.

"Listen, *bilagaana,*"—Antonio was talking softly, but with pent-up anger and frustration—"we have been at war for hundreds of years with the Mexicans. We steal their sheep and their children. They steal ours. But at least when we steal children, it is not to make them slaves. Stolen Diné children are made to work for their whole lives. We make Mexican children part of our families. You *bilagaana,* you New Men, were also at war with the Mexicans. You should have welcomed us as allies. Instead, when you make peace with them, you make them your friends and us your enemies. Why should only Diné return stolen sheep and children? Why is it that only the Mexicans are believed? Why must we deliver up the *ladrones* amongst us? It is something we cannot understand.

My uncle and the other headmen have asked these questions many times and never got an answer. But the headmen realize how much power the *bilagaana* have. So they see the necessity of making treaties. But the reasons are hard to explain to the Diné, especially when you know they are right."

Michael had to agree with him. He knew only a little history of the territory, but he had seen the same pattern over and over again in Nebraska and Dakota: an agreement made and then broken by a few renegades. Many perished for the transgressions of a few. And the constant pushing, pushing of the tribes west, by both army and settlers.

"I have seen the same thing before, farther north," he admitted quietly.

"This year has been a prosperous one for the Diné. There has been no need for raiding. And Haastiin Keshgoli—you call him Sandoval—seems to have been quiet," he added bitterly.

"Haastiin Keshgoli?" Michael struggled to pronounce it correctly.

"We call him an enemy because he takes part in the trading of his people."

"There are men like that everywhere," said Michael. "In Ireland, we had the *gombeen* men."

"*Gombeen*?"

"They were the men who took advantage of bad times and loaned money for food at very high interest." Antonio still looked puzzled. How could one explain the concept of charging interest for borrowing money needed to stay alive to someone whose people believed in taking care of their poor and hungry?

"It is a foreign custom, Antonio. Hard for me to explain, because it is hard for me to understand too. For the most part, my people had a tradition of sharing and hospitality. They were not pushed away from their own country," continued Michael. "Pushing us too far west would have meant pushing us into the ocean. We stayed, but paid with our blood and sweat and children to work the land that had once been ours. And even then, we starved and died."

"So, maybe that is why you can hear me, Sergeant."

"My name is Michael, Antonio. Michael Joseph Burke."

Antonio was silent for a long time. Michael had found it hard over the years to get used to native peoples' silences, for he came from such a talkative people. But he had tried to respect it and found, after a while, his own chattering mind calmed down.

When Antonio resumed the conversation, it was only to trade joking insults and challenges about their respective mounts. "I have a Spanish burro that could beat your mule," he claimed.

"You think so?" said Michael. "Just you be sure to bring him in on the next race day and we'll see whose arse gets over the finish line first!"

They both laughed and Antonio unfolded himself from the ground. "I must go. I've been away for three days and my wife will be getting worried about me. You have a wife, Sergeant?"

"I haven't found the right woman, yet, Antonio," said Michael with a smile.

"You'd better find one soon, before you get too old, or don't you want children?"

Michael's face softened. "I do want them."

Antonio gestured to his companions and they all mounted their horses. "I look forward to the next race, *bilagaana*," he called to Michael as they rode off.

Michael turned to his men. "Private Spratt."

"Yes, sir," said Sprat, jumping to attention.

"Did ye really want to start the next Indian war?"

"No, sir."

"I didn't think so. Next time, ye'll know to wait till your sergeant tells you when to draw your revolver."

"Yes, sir."

"In my own experience," Michael continued, "when less than ten Indians ride right up to you, they usually have no hostile intentions. It is when you *don't* see them that ye have to worry. Mount up, men."

Michael could hear Mahoney and Spratt talking away behind him. No doubt Mahoney was giving Spratt his considered opinion on Michael's judgment. Well, the boy could grouse all he liked, thought Michael, as long as he kept his fingers off his holster.

"I haven't met the right one yet." His response to Antonio's question popped into his mind. He had met many women who had attracted him over the years. Bridget McNamara, for one, who'd been the kitchen maid for the stable owner he had worked for in New York. He had stolen his first kiss from her sweet lips. But he had been sixteen and she fifteen and soon after that he had joined the army. There had been Sally, a laundress he had visited regularly while he was stationed in Wyoming, but she was not someone to be considering for a wife, however fond he had become of her. And Miss Samantha Plummer, daughter of his captain at Fort Kearney. He had fallen head over heels in love with her, he supposed. But it was a hopeless thing, which he'd known from the start, for he had only been a corporal and she an officer's daughter, the apple of her father's eye. She had eventually gone back East to marry an old friend of the family and for a while, Michael had thought his heart was broken. But when he hadn't died from it, he realized it had only been a young man's dream: beautiful, but not realistic. These last few years he had accepted the fact that he was unlikely to meet the right woman anytime soon, and had let himself enjoy the casual liaisons available to him. As he was now enjoying his evenings with Mary Ann. But he did have to wonder, he admitted to himself, why, when Antonio had asked him, Mrs. Elizabeth Woolcott had come to mind.

Chapter Eight

Elizabeth hated it when it was her husband's turn to act as officer of the guard. It meant that every third day he had to spend twenty-four hours at the guardhouse and she only saw him for a few minutes when he was allowed to come home for very rushed meals. When he was younger, it hadn't taken much out of him, but now it was obvious to her that the loss of sleep affected her husband. And, truth be told, herself. They never spoke about it directly, but Thomas knew that she slept very little when he was away. Ever since he had found her, she had had a hard time being anywhere alone at night. When she was living with his sister, she had felt safe. And when she married him, she felt she had come home.

When he was away for any extended period of time, he made sure she had company, usually arranging for one of the strikers to camp out in their extra room, which served as a storeroom. But for guard duty, Elizabeth would have felt foolish asking for company. "You don't need to pamper me, Thomas," she had told him. But it took both of them a few days to recover from their lack of sleep when he was on guard rotation.

Two weeks after the dance, Thomas's rotation came up and Elizabeth's good-bye on that morning was longer than usual.

"Now, Lizzie."

She wrinkled up her nose in distaste. She hated it when he called her that.

"Now, Elizabeth," he started over, in mock genteel tones. "You know I could get Bruner to stay with you."

"Now, Thomas," she intoned back at him, "you know I will be fine. And I will see you at lunch and dinner."

He leaned down and kissed her lightly on the cheek and she surprised both of them by pulling his face down again and giving him a lingering kiss on the lips.

"I'll be looking forward to tomorrow night in my own bed," he told her.

"If you don't fall asleep over dinner," she teased.

"No chance of that if I have this waiting for me."

She watched him walk down the line and disappear around the corner and then turned to busy herself with household chores to keep her anxiety at bay.

After lunch and a hurried visit from Thomas, she pulled out her pile of mending. But within an hour she was too restless to concentrate and so she changed into her riding skirt and jacket and walked down to the stables.

It took a few minutes for Private Stack to respond to her call and when he finally emerged from one of the stalls, he had his sleeves rolled up to his elbows and was wiping his hands on his trousers.

"I'm sorry to keep you waiting, ma'am, but I have been with Mr. Cooper's bitch. She's just about to deliver her pups. I'll saddle your mare directly."

Once she was outside the fort, Elizabeth gave her mare her head and had a satisfying long canter down the valley. The feeling of the wind on her face and the rhythmic movement of her horse under her was relaxing and when she returned to the fort her restless, nervous feeling was gone.

Private Stack was there to meet her when she dismounted. As he took the reins of her mare to lead her in, Elizabeth remembered Mr. Cooper's greyhound.

"Has Misty become a mother yet, Private?"

"Gave birth to three fine pups. Not that Mr. Cooper thinks so," he added under his breath.

"May I see them?"

"Yes, ma'am. Although this may be your only chance."

Elizabeth couldn't puzzle out what he meant, but when she made her way down toward the stall, she could hear Cooper's voice. "Goddamn you, Stack. I ought to cashier you for letting her out when the Navajo were here. It's clear that some filthy little mongrel mounted her before you got her back in. And here I thought the mating with Major Wheeler's dog was successful! Drown them all."

"Oh no," said Elizabeth without thinking, as she came up behind him.

Cooper turned. "I beg your pardon, Mrs. Woolcott. You shouldn't have been exposed to such language. But there is nothing else to do with the little mutts."

The stall door was open and Elizabeth went inside. Misty was lying there, her head curved toward three blind and squirming little creatures, alternately licking them and nudging them to nurse. Two appeared to be purebred greyhounds, brindled and fine-boned like their dam, albeit with longer hair than one would expect and broader faces. But the third was a fuzzy black-and-white ball of fur, clearly resembling his sheepdog sire. Elizabeth fell in love with him instantly.

Private Stack came into the stall with a burlap sack.

"Oh no, you can't just take them from her!"

"It is easier this way," said the private apologetically.

"I'll not have her wasting her time nursing these little mutts, Mrs. Woolcott. I intend to breed her with the major's dog and I want it done as soon as possible."

Private Stack scooped the two brindled puppies up and dropped them into the sack while Misty was busy licking the black-and-white one. She growled as he picked up the fuzzy baby and started to get up, but Cooper quieted her with a sharp "Down!"

"May I hold him, Private Stack?"

The private handed her the black-and-white puppy, and she bent her head over him protectively.

"May I have this one, Mr. Cooper?" she asked without thinking. It was awful enough to think about the other two being drowned, but not this little piebald.

"Why, Mrs. Woolcott, I would be more than happy to

promise you a puppy from the next litter. You deserve
better than this little mongrel. And how would you take
care of him?"

Elizabeth hated herself for doing it, but if it would save
the puppy, she would swallow her pride. Mr. Cooper was
attracted to her, she was sure of that. She hadn't liked him
much before, with his arrogance and veiled contempt for
field officers like her husband. He consistently treated
Thomas as though he were lacking. He always treated her
as though she had something that he wanted and would
have been sure to obtain, were she not married. She liked
him even less now. His arrogance extended to everything
in his vicinity, even his dog. He was willing to kill three
innocent puppies and deprive his dog just because they
weren't purebred.

So she would use that against him and set out to charm
and flatter him.

"I don't know much about dogs, Mr. Cooper." For the
life of her she could *not* bat her eyelashes at him, but
she did gaze up into his face as though he were every bit
the blond god he thought himself. "I can understand your
disappointment. After all, Misty is a splendid greyhound
and of course you want her pups to be just like her. It was
a sad accident, and no reflection on you." Of course, that
was exactly what he thought it was, the arrogant . . . Elizabeth could not quite bring herself to swear, even in her
thoughts.

Cooper's face softened as he took in her flattery. Not
that he recognized it as such, she thought. *He* considered
it only the truth and his due.

"I was wondering . . ."

"Yes, Mrs. Woolcott?"

"Well, I do not know much about keeping such a
young puppy alive. Might we reach a compromise? If you
gave your permission for him to stay with his mother until his eyes opened, I am sure I could take care of him after that. He would have a better start and it would only be
a few weeks that his mother was nursing him."

Cooper hesitated. He didn't want to waste any time on

the pup. But there was the delicious Mrs. Woolcott, gazing up at him with such pleading in her eyes. . . .

"I could wait a few weeks, I suppose . . ."

"Oh, thank you, Mr. Cooper," Elizabeth gushed.

"Private Stack, take the others and drown them in the trough. You can leave this one with its mother." The lieutenant gave Elizabeth his most charming smile, bowed, and strode off.

"Here you are, baby, back with your mother," she crooned softly as she placed him against a teat. She stroked him gently with her finger while he nursed and his mother, after a low growl, let her, as though she realized she would have had no baby at all, were it not for Elizabeth.

When the wood detail returned later that afternoon, Michael walked by the stall and peered in.

"Only one puppy, I see, Private. And him not looking much like a greyhound," he added, trying not to smile at the thought of Cooper's reaction.

"Actually, she had three, Sergeant, but the lieutenant had me drown the other two. Would have had me drown them all, were it not for that nice Mrs. Woolcott."

"Mrs. Woolcott?"

"She came back from her ride just as I was popping them into the sack. Charmed the lieutenant in two minutes, the lady did. Convinced him to save this pup for her and to leave him with his mother for a few weeks. Of course, it's clear that the lieutenant was enjoying being charmed by her," said Private Stack with a knowing wink.

"Mrs. Woolcott never struck me as a lady who would be drawn to anything that wasn't well bred," observed Michael.

"She is a bit prim and proper, Sergeant. Of course, she comes from the East," he added, as though that explained everything. "But I could tell she was sweet on the pup right away, and if those eyes of hers had looked up at you, they would charm the bejesus out of you too, Sergeant!"

Michael knelt down on the straw murmuring soothing

noises to Misty. The puppy was asleep, a furry little bundle with his belly tight as a drum from nursing.

"He'll thrive, this one, if he's the only one. I wonder if he'll grow up wanting to chase rabbits or herd sheep," added Michael with a grin as he got up.

"He certainly takes after his sire," said Private Stack with a smile.

"If he inherits even some of his dam's speed, he'll be a fine fellow. Mrs. Woolcott made a good choice."

"Well, she'll have some work ahead of her, for the lieutenant has only given her a few weeks before he's to leave his mother. He's a real . . ."

"Private Stack." Michael agreed with whatever the man was about to say. But encouraging his criticism would only cause trouble.

"Yes, sir. But I'm sure you know what I mean, sir."

Aye, I do, boyo, thought Michael as he walked down to his quarters. Lieutenant Cooper was an oily, stringy-arsed bastard. But Mrs. Woolcott? Now there was a puzzlin' woman. Looking down her small nose at him for being Irish. So refined and genteel. Yet willing to fight for a misbegotten mongrel like that little fellow in there.

"I have a confession to make, Thomas," Elizabeth said to her husband that night as they got ready for bed.

"What awful thing could you have done, Elizabeth?" he asked as he got under the covers. "Come on, sit next to me."

Elizabeth finished plaiting her hair and sat next to him.

"I flirted with Lieutenant Cooper, Thomas." She lowered her head as though she was a fallen woman but when he put his finger under her chin and lifted her face, he saw that her eyes were dancing.

"Lieutenant Cooper, Lizzie? I thought you detested the man? Now, if you had said anyone else . . . Sergeant Burke, for instance, then I'd be jealous," he joked.

Elizabeth had been pretending her penitence, but when she heard Sergeant Burke's name, her face colored for a moment.

"I am sure the sergeant has plenty of female attention

directed at him, Thomas. The likes of Mrs. Casey always find these Irishmen charming."

"He's a competent soldier, Lizzie, and seems a fine man to me. And for the men who aren't lucky enough to be married . . . well, you know as well as I do that we're lucky to have the laundresses, er, available," said Thomas mildly. His wife was clearly determined to dislike Burke, but there was no reason to make him out as worse than anyone else at the fort.

"Thomas, you would speak well of the devil," said his wife. "And anyway, it is Mr. Cooper we were talking about."

"Ah, yes, you were flirting with him."

"Yes, but it was for a good purpose, Thomas. Not that he thought it was for any reason but his own irresistible self!"

"Now, Lizzie, he is an officer and a gentleman."

"I am not so sure about the gentleman part."

"He has never done anything to you, has he, Elizabeth," asked Thomas, turning serious and putting his arm around her protectively.

"Oh no, Thomas." Though I think he would like to, she thought with an involuntary shiver. "I just meant that a true gentleman is not so arrogant and full of himself that a helpless little puppy could affect his self-consequence."

"A puppy?" Thomas was completely lost. "What has a puppy got to do with Cooper?"

"Everything." All the indignation that Elizabeth had suppressed in the stable was rising now. "His greyhound gave birth to three puppies today."

"Misty? He's been looking forward to that for days. He has high expectations for those pups, being sired by the major's Major."

Their eyes met and they smiled at the dog's name, which was a source of humor for everyone on the post.

"Evidently Misty was too free with her favors before she met Major, Thomas," said Elizabeth demurely.

Thomas's face creased into a smile. "No!"

"Yes. And an Indian dog at that. Or so it would seem."

Thomas's shoulders shook with silent laughter. "But we still haven't gotten to the flirtation part, my dear."

Elizabeth became serious again. "He had Private Stack drown the other two, Thomas. He was going to drown the third but I convinced him to leave the puppy with his mother."

"That's my Lizzie."

"Um, for a few weeks, Thomas. Then he is mine to care for. I hope you don't mind?"

"Of course not," he said, giving her a hug. "A dog is just what we need around here. And such a dog too: a good mix of purebred East and the Wild West! He'll be good company and then good protection for you when I am away." He did not add, And a good substitute for the child we never had, though he thought it.

"You are too good to me, Thomas," she said as she turned to kiss him on the mouth. It was rare that she initiated their lovemaking and the weariness of the past few days fell away as he responded. Their mating was gentle and sweet as always and he fell asleep satisfied, believing that he had satisfied her.

Which he had, thought Elizabeth as she lay awake beside him. He always satisfied her need to be held and loved and kissed. She had guessed a long time ago, from the other women's conversations, that there were other ways a woman might be satisfied, but if it pleased her to please him, if it felt good to hold him while he shuddered and poured himself into her, then she didn't mind what else she might be missing.

As she drifted off this evening, however, she felt something she couldn't put a name to. It was as though she had been left behind somewhere. But that was foolishness. Thomas was a most considerate lover, never just turning away from her to go to sleep, but cuddling her to him and making her feel she had given him something back for all he had given her. She had never wanted to know what other women seemed to know: the almost out-of-control loving they intimated they received and even gave back. For her, loving Thomas and being loved by Thomas was all she needed. Anything else might have reminded her too much of the day before he found her.

Chapter Nine

By the time of the next race day, the puppy's eyes had opened and Elizabeth had charmed Cooper out of one more week with the puppy's mother. Whenever she had time to spare, she visited the stables and had even started feeding the puppy with milk from a makeshift bottle. "Just so he'll be used to it when he comes to us," she told Private Stack.

She had been looking forward to seeing Serena again and telling her about the new "addition" to their family. She was very disappointed when she couldn't immediately find her among the women who were showing their blankets. She was sure she had seen Antonio ride in today, but perhaps he had not brought his wife with him. She was just about to join the other officers' wives when she saw Serena standing quietly by herself, watching the men getting ready to race.

Elizabeth hurried over to her. "Serena, I am so glad you came today."

The *bilagaana* woman's face was open and smiling and Serena looked at her warmly.

"You didn't bring any weaving?"

"I have no great need of trade goods, so I only do it occasionally," said Serena. "Today I am just here to enjoy myself and watch my husband beat the *bilagaana* soldier. The one whose horse looks like it has been sprinkled with 'sweet salt.' "

"Sweet salt? Oh, sugar! Yes, the mare does look like that. It was a close race last time," acknowledged Elizabeth. "I hope your husband does win. Sergeant Burke needs to be taken down a peg or two."

Serena frowned. She didn't understand the expression, but she understood Elizabeth's tone well enough. "You don't like this sergeant? My husband thinks he is very unusual for a *bilagaana* and counts him as a friend."

Elizabeth didn't want to insult Antonio's taste in friends, so she only explained, apologetically, "He is Irish, a people I was taught were dirty and ignorant."

The Navajo woman just raised her eyebrows and said nothing.

"But I don't want to waste our time talking about Sergeant Burke," said Elizabeth. "I wanted to show you something," she said with a touching eagerness that Serena's heart responded to instantly. She guessed she was only a few years older than this Mrs. Woolcott, but somehow she felt very motherly toward her.

"I am sure we can get back before your husband races," Elizabeth reassured her friend.

Elizabeth led her through the gates and toward the stable. Serena had not been inside the fort, although Antonio and the headmen had. It was an interesting place, something like the Zuni town. She could not imagine living so squeezed together, but obviously some people didn't mind.

She wondered what there was in the stable. A new horse, perhaps?

"Look at him. Isn't he a handsome puppy?"

The maternal crooning was irresistible as was a woman's instant pull toward babies of whatever species and Serena was as entranced as Elizabeth with the black-and-white puppy.

"He doesn't look much like his mother," Serena said with a smile.

Elizabeth grinned at her. "No, he is a Navajo dog."

"Diné," Serena corrected her.

"Diné," Elizabeth repeated. "Mr. Cooper was going to drown him, but I convinced him to give him to me. I'll be taking him home later this week."

"Mr. Cooper?" The name sounded familiar to Serena.

Without thinking, Elizabeth said, "He is the yellow-haired lieutenant who always struts like a rooster after he wins a race."

Serena's eyes twinkled. "Oh, he is the one my husband calls 'Stringy-Ass.' "

Elizabeth laughed out loud. "He doesn't really fill out his trousers behind very well, does he?"

"Not like that Sergeant Burke," said the Navajo woman appreciatively. Elizabeth had managed to banish the memory of Michael Burke's muscled bottom from her mind, but Serena's humorous comment brought it back and she blushed.

"We are both married, Serena," she said. "Surely we shouldn't be thinking of any other men's bottoms, skinny or firm!"

"Surely being married does not make us blind!" Serena joked. "A man who fills his breeches is something to appreciate. My husband has nothing to fear, for he fills his leggings, both front and rear very well!"

Elizabeth blushed again. Her Thomas had a good round behind. But he also had a good round belly. And the rest of him—well, she didn't spend any time looking when they made love.

She put the puppy down on the straw and watched him make his way on trembling legs to his mother. Watching him nurse brought a smile to her face and took her mind off older males of her own species.

"You do not have any children," said Serena. It was not a question.

"Why, no. We have been married almost seven years and I have never conceived."

Serena heard the pain in Elizabeth's voice. "Sometimes with an older man it can happen that way," said the Navajo woman sympathetically.

"Thomas has been a wonderful husband to me," responded Elizabeth. "He would have made a good father."

"I am sure. Perhaps it is why you married him?"

The question carried a double meaning, Elizabeth realized. Serena could have been saying, "You married him because he would be a good father to your children." Or perhaps she was suggesting that Thomas was somewhat fatherly to her, Elizabeth? "I married Thomas because I couldn't live without him. He saved my life," she said simply.

Serena looked at her questioningly and Elizabeth haltingly continued her story. "I . . . my family . . . we were traveling alone, just out of Colorado. We were attacked by Comancheros. My father was shot and my mother . . . set upon while I watched. My little brother was taken for a slave."

Serena was silent, but the sympathy emanating from her was almost palpable.

"Thomas found me and took me to his sister in Santa Fe. He would visit whenever he got leave. I could never have married anyone else."

"How old were you?"

"When he married me? Almost eighteen."

"No, when you lost your family."

"Fourteen."

Serena was horrified, though she didn't let her face show it. A girl just about to become a woman and her introduction to womanhood was watching her mother brutalized? She knew of the Comancheros and could imagine the scene very well. No wonder Elizabeth, although a married woman, felt so much like a girl to her. Her own coming to womanhood had been so different. How rich her life had been, despite her own great loss, compared to this *bilagaana* woman. She did not offer words of comfort, however. They would be poor things, under the circumstances.

"My coming of age was very different." It was not the words, but the feeling behind them that made Elizabeth feel enfolded in a sympathy even greater than Serena's, as though there were a feminine presence in them.

"We have a ceremony for it," Serena continued. *"Kinaalda."*

"Kinaalda," Elizabeth repeated carefully.

"The young woman who is *kinaalda* becomes Changing Woman for the Diné. It's a great gift for the people."

"Changing Woman?"

"I will tell you about her someday. But now I think it must be time for the racing. I want to watch my husband's bay beat that Stringy-Ass Cooper!"

Elizabeth laughed and they both hurried out.

When they reached the crowds, Serena nodded a good-bye and made her way to the group of Navajo women on the other side of the finish line. Elizabeth stood there for a minute, made very conscious of the fact that she was forging a friendship with a woman not of her own people. She would not really be welcome with the Navajo women. And Serena would not be able to join her with the officers' wives. Some were sympathetic with the Indians' plight, but most looked down upon them as dirty, filthy savages. Much like Mrs. Compton had taught her to look down on the Irish. She hadn't quite thought of it like that before, she realized.

She couldn't blame some of the white women, for some had seen their men off to the fighting for years. They had seen the suffering caused by massacres.

But her suffering had been caused by white men who could hardly have been matched in viciousness by any Indian "savage." She had never spent any time questioning her own attitudes toward people. The Irish were ignorant, from a backward country. They were also superstitious papists. She had taken that for granted. There had been no Indians in Boston, but the educated men and women there tended to be sympathetic to them and speak on their behalf. She herself feared Mexicans more than Indians, because there had been Mexicans amongst the Comancheros. She supposed it was partly a person's education and experiences that determined her attitudes. This was such a new thought that she stood there right at the finish line for a few moments before Mrs. Taggert called to her.

"Elizabeth, you'd better get yourself over here before you get stampeded!"

She laughed and, picking up her skirts, ran over to join the officers' wives.

When she had squeezed herself in next to Mrs. Taggert, the captain's wife turned to her and said with a wide

smile, "We have an unscheduled race to watch first, before Mr. Cooper rides." She pointed down the track.

A small burro was trotting toward the quarter-mile
starting point with a Navajo on his back. Right behind
him was an army mule with a soldier riding. With Sergeant Burke riding, Elizabeth realized as she recognized
his straight back.

The troopers were digging into their pockets, laying
bets with each other and any Navajo who were willing to
wager. Elizabeth could hear them shouting reckless bets
at one another and at Sergeant Burke's retreating back.
"Two bits says the burro doesn't make it to the finish line
before sunset!"

"Whatever is going on, Emily," she asked Mrs.
Taggert. It was hard to keep a smile from her own face.

"Evidently Sergeant Burke and Manuelito's nephew
met up a few days ago and challenged each other to this
'match race.' Would you care to wager something, Elizabeth?"

"Isn't that Lightning Jack that Sergeant Burke is riding?"

"Yes, and he is supposed to be one of the fastest mules
we have," said Mrs. Taggert, giggling like a schoolgirl.

"He is also the stubbornest son of a ..." said a voice
behind them. Elizabeth turned and there was Private
Elwell, his face red with embarrassment. "Pardon me, ladies," he said bowing slightly. "But the outcome of this
race is by no means sure," he added with a mischievous
grin. "I myself have put my money down on the burro!"

"Then so will I, Private Elwell. Emily, I will bet you
two loaves of bread that the burro wins. I have always
preferred burros to mules myself; they are so much
sweeter."

"Done," said the captain's wife.

Sweeter, my ass, thought Elwell as he watched the riders turn toward the fort. A burro can match a mule for
stubbornness any day, but trust a lady to go for something
small and sweet-looking.

The signal flashed and the race began. Or the onlookers
presumed it had. The burro was small and distant and it

was hard to tell if his legs were moving. And Sergeant Burke seemed to be turning the mule in circles.

"This way, Sergeant, this way," shouted the troopers as Michael struggled to get the mule pointed in the right direction.

Antonio's legs were already sore from keeping his toes from dragging in the dust. He hadn't ridden a burro since he was little. He had forgotten what bony backs they had and what a jarring trot. His wife would be lucky if his private parts survived the bouncing around! What with holding his legs up and trying to protect his balls, he must look like some rider. But at least he was going in the right direction, he thought as he watched Michael struggle with the mule.

Michael was cursing Lightning Jack in both Irish and English. He could not get the damned shavetail pointed in the right direction and so he finally gave in to the animal and reined him backward.

"Ye don't want to turn, do ye? Well then, ye'll cross the finish line arse first."

Antonio had gone only a few hundred yards when he saw Michael backing the mule past him. He almost fell off the burro laughing as Michael gave him a cocky grin and waved his hand.

"The *bilagaana* might beat us after all," he said to his little mount. "I just wish he'd hurry up about it."

The mule seemed quite content to be moving backward and Michael was about ready to compliment him. After all, he was demonstrating, albeit in a very annoying way, his good training! When reined backward, he backed up. They were more than halfway there and he could hear the men shouting. Antonio was fifty feet behind him, or in front of him, depending upon how you looked at it! He turned to wave to his men and at that moment the mule dug his heels in, lowered his head, and bucked him off his back.

A collective groan went up from the spectators. Michael lay there in the dust, watching the mule take off.

"Ye're running fast enough now in the right direction, ye bastard," he yelled, shaking his fist at him.

Antonio's burro trotted by, little legs moving in a steady trot. Antonio's face was set in a serious expression and he mockingly urged his mount in Navajo.

"Ye don't need to be rubbing it in, boyo," Michael called after him, standing up and brushing the dust off his clothes.

When he reached the finish line, the Navajo were clustered around Antonio with wide grins on their faces. Some of the troopers had tears rolling down their cheeks and Michael knew they weren't from their lost wages but from helpless laughter. Two of them were still rolling around in the dust, clutching their stomachs, unable to stop laughing.

"Did you see him go flying off? He's lucky he didn't end up in a cactus!"

"I told you Lightning Jack was one stubborn mule."

Michael bowed his head with mock humility and said, "I did me best, lads," as they cheered and jeered him at the same time.

He strolled over to Antonio, who was standing next to the burro.

"You were right, boyo. Yer burro's a fine animal. Are ye hoping to enter him against Cooper in the half mile?"

Antonio grinned. "I am going to give my ... legs a rest," he said. "That burro's back is as bony as the lieutenant's ass."

"I was trying to give ye a chance, ye know, ridin' backwards like that," said Michael sadly. "That's the last time I'll do a favor for a friend."

"You were lucky to get that mule moving in any direction!"

"I was, wasn't I," said Michael, starting to laugh as he realized what he must have looked like. Antonio was bending his knees to loosen them and Michael remembered what he looked like, legs out in front of him, backside bouncing on the burro, and he laughed even harder.

"Ye should have seen yerself, Antonio," he sputtered. "I'm surprised ye can still walk."

Antonio's face, which had been open and smiling, suddenly changed, and Michael wondered for a split second if he had somehow unwittingly insulted him when he heard a hated voice behind him.

"Sergeant Burke."

"Yes, *sir*," he said, whipping around to face Cooper.

"Are you satisfied, having thoroughly humiliated yourself and the U.S. Army?"

Would "Yes, sir" or "No, sir" be the proper response? wondered Michael, having a hard time keeping his face straight and his laughter under control. He decided the safest thing was to stay silent and at attention.

"Get back over to your mare, Sergeant, and get ready for the next race," Cooper ordered, giving a disdainful look to Antonio and the men who surrounded him. Their faces were closed and humorless and Antonio felt anger rising in him. He wondered how much trouble his friend was in, but as Michael walked away, he turned and gave Antonio a quick wink.

One of Antonio's men came up to remind him that he was riding soon, and shaking out his legs again, he went off to prepare the bay.

Chapter Ten

Lieutenant Cooper won his own race, although not against Antonio, who had chosen the three-quarter-mile again. Cooper beat two Navajo ponies and Captain Taggert's chestnut, and Elizabeth had a hard time keeping her face straight as she watched him strut about, accepting the congratulations of his men. Every time he opened his mouth she expected to hear him crow. And when his back was to her—well, she couldn't help noticing how loose and wrinkled his trousers were. No bottom at all, she thought, and laughed to herself.

She didn't laugh, however, when she saw one of the Navajo dogs trotting by. It was a black-and-white sheepdog, alert and curious and intent on finding someone, it seemed. Lieutenant Cooper saw the dog at the same moment as she did and went after it with a scowl on his face. Elizabeth watched in horror as he followed the dog to his owner and started arguing with a tall, distinguished-looking Navajo.

"Whatever is the lieutenant doing," exclaimed Mrs. Gray.

"I think that dog is the sire of Misty's puppies," said Elizabeth. "Isn't that Manuelito, one of the headmen?" she added, her voice full of concern. The last months had been peaceful, but the relationship between the Navajo and the soldiers was precarious, and what seemed like a small thing could tip the balance and destroy weeks of good feeling.

"Where is that husband of mine," said Mrs. Gray, looking around in desperation. When she finally spied the colonel, it was on the other side of the course, obviously intent on his conversation with Major Wheeler.

Mrs. Gray looked around and her eyes lighted on Private Mahoney, who was slouched against the fence. "Private!"

"Private Mahoney, ma'am, at your service," he said as he stood at attention.

"Get my husband over here as quickly as possible."

"Yes, ma'am." Mahoney hadn't seen anything, but he could tell something important was up. He ran across to the colonel, and Elizabeth could see him pointing back at Mrs. Gray.

"Charles, your Mr. Cooper is going to have us all massacred if you don't stop him," she said fiercely but quietly when the colonel reached her side. "It is too long to explain, but get him away from Manuelito!"

It was obvious to Elizabeth that the colonel and his wife understood one another perfectly. They had been on the frontier for twenty years together and had formed a partnership in which Mrs. Gray's judgment was trusted instantly. She wondered if she would have had the self-confidence to summon Thomas under similar circumstances. His work had always been *his* work, and her realm the household. She felt a sudden stab of envy. Mrs. Gray had always been motherly to Elizabeth, offering her care and support to her and the other officers' wives, always with a warm smile for the rawest of recruits, encouraging them as though they were her sons. But today Elizabeth had seen another side of her, the strong woman who understood very well the delicacy of her husband's position and the importance of everyday dealings with the Navajo.

Antonio and Michael had just begun the three-quarter-mile race when Cooper spied Manuelito's dog. There were five in the race, but by the end it was down to Frost and the blood bay. The bay was fresh and completely recovered from his injury and Michael was a few seconds off in calling on his mare for a last burst of speed. Those few seconds were enough to lose him the race by a head.

"Ye ran a fine race, boyo," he said to Antonio with a wide smile. "I'm blamin' meself and not me mare on this one. We would have had you if I'd called on her earlier!"

Michael's appreciation of the bay and his rider were spontaneous and genuine and Antonio knew that the sergeant was not idly boasting or making excuses. Both horses and riders were different, but evenly matched. He suspected that each time they raced there might be a different outcome depending upon the length of the course and the split-second decisions a rider had to make.

"Then I'm lucky that you didn't, *bilagaana*," Antonio said with a stern face, but a smile in his eyes. He turned to look for his wife and when he found her in the crowd, he saw her gesture to him with a look of concern on her face. He turned in the direction she pointed and saw a small knot of men, Navajo and white, around Manuelito and some soldier. When he recognized Cooper, he muttered a quick, guttural curse and started over.

Colonel Gray had gotten there before him, however, and clearly had things in hand. He was speaking respectfully and apologetically to the headman and at one point reached down to pat Manuelito's dog. Cooper was standing at attention, his shoulders pulled back so far that his blouse was wrinkled and loose, like his pants. His face was very red and Antonio figured it was either from anger or embarrassment. Or maybe both.

As he approached, Manuelito gave him a quick, reassuring look, and Antonio relaxed. Whatever had happened was almost over and it seemed the headman and the colonel had resolved it between them. He stayed back until the colonel walked away, with the lieutenant striding stiffly at his side.

"What was that all about, uncle?"

"That skinny, yellow-haired, two-stripe *bilagaana* soldier . . . !" Manuelito spat on the ground. "He says to me, to *me*, 'Keep your mongrel away from the fort. He's mounted my bitch and I had to drown the little Navajo mongrels.' "

"That was what this was about!" Antonio felt a combination of rage and despair rising in him. Manuelito, Armijo, and all the headmen had worked so hard to get the Diné to agree to the treaty. To hold the Diné in loosely. But always, always a few young men went raiding sheep and horses. And always the Mexicans exaggerated what had been stolen. These new men were powerful and more and more of them every day arrived at the boundaries of Dinetah, enraging the younger warriors. And then, along comes a *bilagaana* like Cooper, willing to alienate a headman and cause a war over the breeding of a few puppies!

"He should be honored that his bitch was found pleasing to your dog," said Antonio, trying for humor, but not quite succeeding. "These hunting dogs of the *bilagaana* have speed, but a little Diné wisdom would not hurt them."

"Colonel Gray took care of the lieutenant, nephew. Very quickly and quietly, but I think," said Manuelito, "that it won't be so quiet when he gets him inside."

Michael had seen the quick interchange between Antonio and his wife and watched him walk toward the agitated gathering of soldiers and Navajo warriors. He saw Elwell out of the corner of his eye and pulling Frost behind him, hurried over.

"What in sweet Christ is going on, Joshua?"

"I'm not exactly sure, sir. It's something about Mr. Cooper and that greyhound bitch of his. I think he's after the headman's dog as the sire."

"Jesus, Mary, and Joseph," intoned Michael. "Has the man no brain in his head atall."

"The colonel's gone over, so I think he'll take care of it. And to answer your question, sir, and begging pardon for the insubordination, the man's head is so full of himself he has no room for a brain."

"I didn't hear that, Private Elwell. And you didn't hear me say I agree with you! It's a hopeless job, we have, Joshua," continued Michael. This 'peace-keeping.' I tell you, in all my years on the frontier I have never seen a treaty broken deliberately by the Indians. It is always some fool settler or a Mexican with his sheep or a hot-headed young warrior. Or some stupid fool like Cooper, full of his own importance. The whole bloody story of it is all knots and impossible to untangle to the point of this one is right and that one wrong. Except for maybe one thing . . ." Michael hesitated.

"One thing?"

"That it is *their* country, Joshua, and we just keep pushing them back the way the bloody English pushed the Irish. I tell you, sometimes I am ready to give up the whole thing. But where else would I go, Private, an ignorant mick like me? My choice was to stay a stable lad till I died or join the army."

Elwell hadn't questioned much, for all his time in the army. And although he shared Michael's disdain for men like Cooper, he wasn't about to damn the whole enterprise.

"Wait for me, Josh. And hold me mare, will ye?"

Michael thrust the reins into his private's hands and hurried over to where Antonio was readying himself and his wife to leave.

Antonio looked at him questioningly, almost coldly, and Michael wasn't sure what to say. He couldn't blame the man for pulling back. Why should he trust a soldier? But he liked Antonio and he would be damned if he'd give up the chance of a friendship, no matter how difficult the circumstances.

He said rather formally, "I trust the colonel was able to help out with Manuelito's problem?"

"Both the colonel and my uncle agreed that while the buzzings of a gnat are annoying, they are not enough to break the peace over," said Antonio with restrained anger.

"Or, I hope a new friendship?" Michael was still speaking formally, for he didn't want to embarrass himself or Antonio. If the Navajo still wanted to pull back, so be it.

There was a long silence and Michael's heart dropped. Then Antonio reached out and grasped Michael's arm. "I don't know what the future holds for this friendship, *bilagaana*, but the Diné live in the present. Today, I am your friend."

Michael felt great relief and great joy, but he reined in his natural effusiveness and made himself respond quietly. It was an important moment for both of them. They were choosing to trust in an invisible thread of connection, choosing to create a fragile bridge, and he wanted the right words, but wasn't sure he could find them. "Let's live in today then," he finally answered. It was so little to say, but seemed to be enough for Antonio, who smiled, gave Michael's arm a squeeze, and then mounted his bay.

Antonio was unusually quiet on their ride home and Serena knew her husband well enough to let him alone with his thoughts. He would tell her what was in his mind eventually.

When they reached their hogan, Antonio went off to take care of the horses and Serena began to prepare dinner. There was a mutton stew she had made yesterday, which only had to be heated up and some stale dry bread that could be crumbled into it. When Antonio returned, he ate it quickly and, nodding his thanks, went outside again. Serena cleaned up and wrapping a shawl around her head, went out to find her husband.

He was sitting against an old, twisted juniper and when she sat down next to him, he reached out his arm and pulled her close. It was getting dark earlier now and the sky was beginning to become bright with stars. They sat quietly and watched the constellations reveal themselves until it was completely dark and it seemed as if someone had sprinkled mica across a piece of black velvet.

"Look, husband," said his wife, pointing out a shooting star.

Antonio turned toward her and brushed her lips with his. Serena put her hand on his cheek and he drew closer, this time teasing her mouth open. When she responded eagerly, he eased her down onto the old blanket he was sitting on and began to kiss her more thoroughly and passionately.

Serena loved every inch of her husband's body. He was a small man compared to most of the *bilagaana,* but most satisfyingly proportioned. As she cupped his buttocks with her hands to guide him into her, she thought fleetingly of her conversation with Mrs. Woolcott and chuckled deep in her throat. Antonio heard it as a signal to drive deeper and harder, and in a second, her legs were around his hips and she was letting him ride her while she rose to meet him in a rhythm that matched his own. After he had taken his pleasure, he rolled over on his back and pulled her on top. Using his fingers, he brought her to her own climax. She cried out and clung to him, rubbing herself against him as though she wanted to exchange skins.

After a moment, he rose on his elbow and reaching out, pulled her shawl around both their shoulders and they lay back, blissful, tired and spent, to gaze at the stars.

Serena shivered as the desert night grew colder.

"Do you want to go in?" her husband whispered.

"Let's stay out a little bit longer," she said. "It will be getting too cold to do this soon."

He hugged her closer and after a moment gave a long sigh.

"What is it, husband? Is it that stupid *bilagaana* Cooper?"

"Sometimes, when I watch the stars come out, I think of the *bilagaana.*"

"How can you think of something so ugly while looking at something so beautiful?"

"Look at the night sky. As darkness falls, only a few stars arrive, one here and one there. There seems to be plenty of space for all, doesn't there? And then, little by little, the sky gets darker and fills with more and more stars until it seems like there will be no room for another one. It is like when these new men arrived. Maybe that was our twilight. At first, there weren't so many. But it seems to be getting darker and darker for us, while they shine brighter and brighter and fill up Dinetah."

"Do you really think it is getting that dark for the Diné?" Serena asked softly. "The peace seems to be holding and they haven't asked for anything else. This year has been a very good one for our crops and sheep. You can't let fools like Cooper pull your mind out of balance."

"*Hozhro?* I feel it when I am with you, wife. And when I am out in Dinetah. But the *bilagaana* are throwing things out of harmony. There are too many of them. And too many of them are like Cooper. Not enough like Sergeant Burke."

"You like him."

"I do. It seems very strange to me to be liking a *bilagaana* soldier right now, but there is something there between us."

"I can understand. I like Mrs. Woolcott."

"That small woman who gave you her paper with the canyon walls on it?"

"Yes."

"She must have some power of her own, that woman, to be able to capture the colors of the rock."

"I think so, but I don't think she knows it."

"Well, wife, who knows whether we can keep these friends. But I told Burke today that the Diné live in the present. I suppose I lied if I am so worried about tomorrow."

"You are Manuelito's nephew. You could be headman someday. You worry because you care and I love you for it. But I hope you are wrong about this, my dear husband."

"So do I." He stroked her cheek with his finger. "Perhaps tonight will bring us a son or daughter."

Serena's eyes filled with tears.

"We will never forget our little one, wife."

Serena swallowed her tears. "I know. And perhaps it is a good time to have hope for a new life."

Chapter Eleven

Three days after the races was when Elizabeth had promised to bring the puppy home. She had managed to get him almost four weeks with his mother and the fact that he was the only puppy nursing showed. Although his legs were a little shaky, he looked at least a week older than he was, and Elizabeth was sure he would do well, especially since he was used to the nursing bottle.

"And probably ready to start lapping milk from a bowl, aren't you," she crooned as she picked him up and pressed her face to his.

She didn't hear the step behind her and she jumped and nearly dropped the puppy when she heard Michael's voice.

"Sure and is that the wee creature that almost started a war, Mrs. Woolcott?"

Without thinking, Elizabeth responded tartly, "No, Sergeant Burke, it was that 'craytur' of your lieutenant. This pup is a fine little fellow and I am taking him home with me today." Immediately after she spoke she blushed. She had committed one of the cardinal sins of the army: she had criticized a superior officer to one of his men.

"I shouldn't have said that, Sergeant Burke. Mr. Cooper is a fine officer," she said in her most proper voice, "and he is being most kind to let me have this puppy."

Michael lowered his voice. "Mr. Cooper is a proper ass, so full of himself that he nearly got us all killed on Sunday. You know that and I know it, ma'am. And don't worry, I won't be corrupted by yer lapse in etiquette," he added, his eyes laughing down at her. He reached his hand over the stall door and stroked the puppy's head. "Sure and he seems a fine dog. I have always thought meself that purebreds can sometimes be too high-strung and sensitive. A mixed breed often gets the strength of both parents without the weaknesses."

Elizabeth was holding the puppy against her breast and as Michael's finger continued stroking, he became aware of a very strong desire to be following her curves with his finger. He gave the little dog a quick pat and opened the stall door.

"Why don't ye take him now, Mrs. Woolcott, while I stay here and keep Misty from following. She might be a wee upset at losing her baby."

"Thank you, Sergeant. That is very kind of you. And it would be even kinder of you to forget what I said about Mr. Cooper."

Michael gave her a quick bow and a smile, and said, "Yes, ma'am. And may I say, Mrs. Woolcott, that wee fat fellow there is lucky to be going' home with ye. I heard his brothers were drowned."

Elizabeth made some sort of flustered thank you and good-bye and hurried off, leaving Michael leaning over the stall door, watching her go. He heard a low whine behind him and felt the greyhound bitch press against his leg. "Oh, I know ye'd like me to let ye out of here, Misty, to go off after yer baby. But he'll be fine," said Michael, scratching behind her ears. "And I'm sure yer master'll be breedin' ye again and this time ye'll get to keep all yer babbies." He opened the stall door and slipped out, closing it quickly behind him. As he walked toward his quarters to clean up for dinner, he couldn't stop thinking of how sweet and desirable the prim and proper Mrs. Woolcott had looked cuddling her puppy. "Sweet Mary, Mother of God, keep me from thinking such a thought," he prayed desperately. "She's a married woman, Michael Joseph Burke, and not for the likes of ye anyway." He decided that a visit to Mary Ann's would be a good idea tonight. Fornication might be a mortal sin, but surely God would forgive a poor Irishman who had no chance in hell of getting married for a while. And surely it was better to go to Mary Ann occasionally than be lettin' himself be wondering what Mrs. Woolcott's breast would feel like under his fingers.

"Are ye going to Mrs. Casey's tonight, then, Josh," Michael asked as he slipped onto the bench next to Elwell in the mess hall.

Elwell grinned. "I was thinking about it."

"Well, I think I'd like to come along and see if Mary Ann is free. Would ye mind the company?"

"Not at all, Sergeant, I would enjoy it, and I'm sure the women would. I'll meet you after supper."

Mrs. Casey had been a laundress for five years and her "seniority" had gained her a nice room and a half. The four of them squeezed into her sitting room and Elwell pulled a pint of whiskey out of his jacket.

"Here, Ginny," he said as Mrs. Casey offered her glass. "And Mary Ann. And, Michael, will you join us tonight?"

"Just a wee drop," said Michael as always. He never had had any problem with whiskey and he never intended to. He'd seen too many Irishmen on the streets of New York who had drunk their lives away.

"Cheers," said Elwell, lifting his glass.

"*Slainte,*" said Michael.

The others finished the bottle quickly and Elwell and Mrs. Casey were soon wrapped around each other and clearly ready to retire into her bedroom.

Mary Ann tugged on Michael's sleeve. "Come, Michael, we'll go next door and give them their privacy."

"I doubt they'll notice whether we're here or not," said Michael with a grin as he let himself be led next door.

Mary Ann lit the kerosene lamp by her bed. She kept her small quarters very clean and neat, something that Michael liked and admired in her. It was hard enough to keep the sand and dust out when you were an officer's wife with a striker to help you. And although her bedspread was worn, it was brightened by a homemade afghan.

The lamp shone on Mary Ann as she stretched herself out on her bed and brought out the red highlights in her dark brown hair. She was at least five years older than Michael and he suspected that the red came from henna, but he didn't care. She was an attractive woman, was Mary Ann, whatever her age. He sat on the edge of the bed and slowly unbuttoned his blouse while she lay there watching him.

"You looked fine on Sunday, Michael, riding your mare. I'm sorry you lost. I thought you had the race till the last few minutes."

"The blood bay and Frost are well matched, and I just might be taking turns winning."

When he turned to her after pulling off his boots and trousers, her skirts were lifted and she was reaching down to loosen her garters.

"Can I help you with those, Mary Ann," he whispered.

"Thank you, Michael."

He peeled the stockings off her slowly and then reached up under her skirts to trace her thighs with his fingers. He pulled himself up next to her and rested on one elbow while he unbuttoned her blouse and lifted her shift over her head. She was a plump woman and her breasts were round and firm and spilled over his hand when he went to cup one.

He lowered his head and teased one nipple with his tongue and she pulled his head closer with one hand and reached down with the other to feel him through his skivvies.

He shivered as she touched him and she whispered, "Do you need me right away?"

"I'll try to wait, but I'm not sure I can be promising anything." Dear God, but he had been feeling like he was going to burst since he walked into her bedroom. Or to be honest with himself, all afternoon. But he banished the thought of a smaller, daintier woman and pulling down his underwear, let himself spring free. When she rubbed her hand along him, he groaned and pulled himself on top of her. His hands reached up to knead her breast and then he was up and thrusting into her, hoping she was ready enough for him. But she was slick and wet and he came very quickly and then collapsed on top of her.

She lay still for a moment and then taking his hand, guided it down between her legs. He began to kiss her again and she came almost as quickly as he had. He was glad, for he liked women in general and Mary Ann in particular and liked giving her pleasure. And tonight he had not exactly been an ideal lover.

"That was a wee bit quicker than usual," he whispered. "I don't know what came over me."

"I don't mind when someone has to have me quick because he's wanting me so much," she whispered back. "And you took good care of me, too, Michael. Perhaps we'll go slower in the morning."

And indeed, when they awoke before dawn, Michael took her slowly and carefully. She was a hardworking woman with a hard life, Mary Ann was, and she deserved to have someone thinking of her once in a while, even if she was doing it for a little extra money. But although he had no trouble, he did feel a little removed from her and himself. He liked Mary Ann and he needed her, but he didn't love her nor did she love him. Not that he expected it or even wanted it between them, but it just left him with a lonely feeling as they lay together for a while before he had to go.

Chapter Twelve

Elizabeth got very little sleep for the next week. At first the puppy merely whimpered outside the door, but when that didn't bring him any company, he started crying in earnest. Thomas was tired enough from his day's work to turn over and go back to sleep, but Elizabeth couldn't stand the heartbroken yowling and she would get up several times a night and sit the pup down on her lap and pet him until he went back to sleep. Then she would lay him down gently in the old basket that was his bed and they'd both sleep for an hour or so before he started again.

After a night or two she snuck him into bed with them, but when Thomas saw him in the morning, he put his foot down.

"Absolutely not, Lizzie."

"But, Thomas, at least he slept last night." And so did I, she added to herself. She daren't complain about him, since he was her idea.

"It is a bad habit to develop, my dear. I guarantee, you will not want him in our bed when he is full grown and has been rolling around with the other dogs."

So she continued to get up and thought she was going to die of exhaustion until, finally, Mrs. Taggert from next door gave her some advice.

"Wrap a hot water bottle in a towel, Mrs. Woolcott, and put it in his basket with him and he will do fine."

It worked, thank God, and finally things were back to normal in the Woolcott household. More or less. For as the puppy got bigger, he set out to explore everything and chew everything, including Thomas's favorite sheepskin slippers.

Thomas was furious when he found the puppy worrying at them, but when he pulled the slippers away and started to yell at the little dog, both the puppy and his wife gave him such pleading looks that he could only laugh.

"Take it then, you little monster. This one is ruined anyway," he said ruefully.

"Thank you, Thomas, for not making me get rid of him," his wife said later as they curled up in bed together. "He is very bright, and as he gets older, he'll understand things better, I am sure."

But Elizabeth was a pushover for the puppy's apologetic looks. When she would chastise him gently, he would sink down on his fat little stomach and wag his tail and look at her beseechingly, as though to say, "I know, and I'll *never* do it again."

As he got older, he grew more out of control, but Elizabeth was not yet willing to admit she had a problem with him, although the whole fort was by now aware of what havoc the little dog was creating in the Woolcott household. The enlisted men were now betting as to when the lieutenant would shoot the little bugger, and those that had bet sooner rather than later were greatly optimistic when he came to parade one morning with a hole chewed out of his best hat.

"I don't know what to do," Thomas confessed to his commanding officer one afternoon. "He is a charmer, I have to admit. And she is crazy about him. But she hasn't the least idea how to discipline him and then when I try, she looks at me as if I were a monster."

"I've seen women like that with their children."

"But you can't drown children, sir, and I hate to say it, but I am ready to take the little bastard and drown him in the horse trough where his brothers died!"

"How soon were you thinking of doing this," asked the colonel with a big smile.

"Oh God, they're betting on it!" groaned Thomas.

"A few, here and there."

Thomas gave a disgusted groan and stalked out. To-night he was going to lay down the law: either she was firm with the little dog, or else.

It was unfortunate, then, that the puppy chose that very afternoon to pull Thomas's best blouse down from the laundry line and start chewing off the brass buttons. When Elizabeth looked out the kitchen window and saw him, she felt her heart sink. This would be the last straw, and she wouldn't blame Thomas if he came home and wrung the puppy's neck as he had threatened to do.

She walked out the back door slowly, a crumbled piece of bacon in her hand. "Here, puppy, here you are." The little dog stopped worrying at the buttons and cocked his head. Wagging his tail, he started to prance over to get his favorite treat. Elizabeth sprinkled some bacon in front of him and darted for the shirt. He saw her out of the corner of his eye and reached it before she did. He ran off, drag-ging the blouse through the dust, with Elizabeth after him. At first she crooned to him in a sweet, low voice, the voice she usually used with him. He would turn around and come close and she would think she had him and just as she'd reach for the shirt, he would scamper out of the way, his eyes dancing.

She had left the kitchen door open, and she grabbed desperately for him as he ran through the house and out the front door, dragging Thomas's blouse and looking back at her over his shoulder as though to say, "There's much more room to play this game out here."

Elizabeth lost her composure. Here was this damned little dog she had saved from certain death and there he was, gleefully making a fool of her.

"Come back here, you little devil," she screeched, run-ning after him.

He tore off down the line with the usually prim-and-proper Mrs. Woolcott screaming after him. Officers' wives opened their doors at the noise and looked at each other and laughed. They had been wondering how long it would take for Mrs. Woolcott to break.

Luckily most of the men were out on patrol, but the

wood detail was just returning as the puppy ran toward the stable, Elizabeth red-faced and shouting behind him.

The four men and Michael were dumbfounded at first at the sight of a lieutenant's wife running with her skirts hiked up, and screaming like a *bean sighe,* thought Michael. Then Fisk started to laugh and the rest were almost falling off their mules when Michael turned to them. "That's enough, men," he ordered. It took all his self-control to hold back his own laughter, but he couldn't let his detail be disrespectful to an officer's wife. "Private Elwell, have the men lead the mules into the corral and unsaddle them there."

"Yes, sir," said Elwell, struggling not to smile.

Michael dismounted and handed his reins to Elwell.

"And take my mule, would ye, Josh."

"Yes, sir."

The puppy was headed straight for him, head turned, watching to see if his mistress was still part of this glorious game and Michael had no problem scooping him up. He pried the pup's jaws open with his fingers and made him drop the shirt, just as Elizabeth rounded the corner.

"Come back, you little bastard." She was crying now, tears of anger and frustration and at first she only saw that her husband's shirt was lying there on the ground. In front of some soldier's boots. In front of Master Sergeant Michael Burke's boots. She stopped, her hand flying to her mouth, and realized what she must look like. What she must have sounded like.

"I'd say the wee 'bastard' has been thriving under your care, Mrs. Woolcott. He's certainly grown since the last time I saw him."

Elizabeth stood there, still holding her skirts up in her hand, until she noticed the sergeant's quick and appreciative look at her ankles. She dropped them instantly and nervously smoothed them and tried to straighten her hair and regain some sense of dignity.

Why did it have to be the goddamned Irishman seeing her out of control like this? And where was such language coming from, Elizabeth Jane Woolcott. A young lady from Mrs. Compton's would not be using words like 'damn' and 'bastard'!

"Give me that damned puppy, Sergeant Burke," she blurted out.

Michael's eyes twinkled, but he managed to keep his face straight.

"Don't ye want the lieutenant's blouse first, ma'am?"

He reached down and shook some of the dust off before he handed it to her. It was filthy with dust and dried manure and missing two buttons.

It was the shirt that did it. She buried her face in it and began to cry. "I should have let Mr. Cooper drown him," she sobbed.

"Drown this fine little fellow? No, no, ye did the right thing then. But ye've been goin' wrong somewhere, Mrs. Woolcott. Here, come into the stable with me and we'll pop this wee devil into a stall for a minute and talk about it."

Michael had to grab her hand to get her moving, but he wanted her inside and not exposed to the ridicule of whoever might come along.

He dropped the puppy into the nearest empty stall and turned back to Elizabeth.

"Here, sit down, ma'am," he said, guiding her to a bale of hay.

She let him push her down. Looking up at him, her chin quivering, she held out the blouse. "Look at this, Sergeant. Ruined. Like Thomas's slippers. And my best bonnet."

"And there was also that wee bite out of Mr. Woolcott's hat, don't forget," teased Michael gently.

He had hoped she would laugh, but instead, the tears poured down. "Thomas will kill me," she sobbed.

"Mr. Woolcott has always seemed an understanding and devoted husband," said Michael, comforting her as best he could.

"You are right. He is the best of men. He'll kill the puppy!"

And Mahoney and Fiske will be richer by a week's pay, thought Michael.

"And I will help Thomas," she added, anger mixed with the despair in her voice. "I am a complete failure with the dog."

"Now, now, Mrs. Woolcott, ye still have time."

"But I don't know what to do," she wailed. "I've told and told him that he is a 'bad dog' when he does something wrong, but it doesn't seem to work."

"Puppies . . . all animals, need to know who is the master or mistress, as the case may be, ma'am. They are not very intelligent, after all, and need our guidance."

"He is a very smart dog, I'll have you know, Sergeant!"

Michael smiled at her instant defense of the little 'bastard.'

"I am sure he is, ma'am. Smart enough to know how to wheedle his way around you. But not smart enough to know how to stop on his own. You need to be firm, Mrs. Woolcott."

"I'm ready to be firm, now, Sergeant, I can tell you," she said, the anger taking over again.

"Em, surely there is something in between 'bad dog' and 'ye little bastard'?" Michael did an excellent imitation of Elizabeth's most proper tones and her screeching, and she didn't know whether to laugh or be angry. It was safer to be angry.

"A gentleman would not remind a lady of her unfortunate lapse into vulgarity, Sergeant."

"Ah, but I am neither an officer nor a gentleman, am I, Mrs. Woolcott? Just a dirty, ignorant Irishman," said Michael, stung into replying with anger too. Here he was, trying to help the damn woman and she went right back to her eastern snobbery.

Elizabeth heard the anger, and also the pain behind it. Had she actually called him that to his face? She was sure not, but had thought it often enough about him and others at the fort. Yet what had Sergeant Burke ever done but be helpful to her? He was neither dirty or ignorant, but a good-looking man and a respected noncommissioned officer. He was known to be a talented scout, yet he had taken on the wood detail with great dignity and commanded his small troop of four as though they were a company. Most at the fort respected and liked him and here she was holding on to phrases that had been taught to her years ago. It was hard to let go of them, she realized as she struggled to make her perceptions fit the stereotype that had been handed to her. Something deep inside her had shaken loose and she felt like she had drifted away from a mooring. If all the Irish weren't dirty or ignorant, then what of all the other things she had learned and held on to over the years?

"I am sorry, Sergeant Burke," she said in a low, shaking voice. "You have never acted anything but the gentleman with me. It is just that I was taught to be a lady and my language and behavior were certainly not ladylike. I felt utterly humiliated and took it out on you."

Michael had felt annoyed by Mrs. Woolcott and very attracted to her, but he hadn't really liked her, he realized, until that moment. She could have continued to take refuge in rank and background. But she had chosen to make herself more vulnerable and he respected her for that.

"Only a real lady would have the courage to admit her weakness, Mrs. Woolcott. I appreciate and accept your apology," Michael responded formally.

"Thank you, Sergeant Burke." Elizabeth looked up at him and felt that inner shift again. He was looking at her with warmth and appreciation. It was different from Thomas's loving glances. Thomas made her feel cared for and protected. It was also different from Mr. Cooper's appraising gaze. From him she felt only a kind of hunger and no acknowledgment of her individuality at all. But Sergeant Burke was looking at her as a human being who had done something worthy of his respect. It felt strange, but also very good, to receive that from a man.

As Michael looked down at her, he had to put his hands behind his back to keep from reaching out and pushing a strand of hair away from her face. He cleared his throat and said, "Now, Mrs. Woolcott, you must decide if you are going to keep this little terror. . . ."

"I am, Sergeant," said Elizabeth with a hint of defiance in her voice.

"Let me finish. Keep this little terror in line," he added. "He is in the army too, ye know, and has to learn to follow orders."

"Yes, Sergeant. I understand, Sergeant," said Elizabeth in a good imitation of a young recruit.

"First of all, does the wee bugger have a name?"

"I haven't been able to think of one that feels right. Although Satan is beginning to seem very appropriate," she added with a smile.

"We have to give him a name to live up to," said Michael. "A name to be proud of. Now, his mama is a hunting dog. What do you think of Orion?"

"Orion the Hunter." Elizabeth thought about it for a minute. "It seems like a very big name for such a small troublemaker."

"Sure and it is a name he'll have to grow into, but that's precisely my point."

"I think I like it, Sergeant."

Michael chuckled.

"What is so funny, Sergeant Burke?"

"When I first got to New York, I only knew the names of the constellations in Irish. The first time I heard of Orion the Hunter I thought to meself: now isn't that marvelous, to be namin' a constellation after an Irishman."

"An Irishman, Sergeant?"

"Sure and I thought it was O'Ryan, Mrs. Woolcott," he explained as he spelled it out.

Elizabeth laughed. "It is funny, isn't it, how we can hear and read things. I remember once when I was in school and someone spilled hot soup all over the lunch table. I said, in my most sophisticated voice—I was so proud to be able to use the word in conversation—What a *cat*astrophe! Instead of what a ca*tas*trophe. And I wondered why the teacher laughed."

"You must teach him his name right away," said Michael. "And what have ye been doin' to him when he misbehaves?"

"Talking to him. Rather gently, until today!"

"There must be truth and consequences for him, Mrs. Woolcott. If he gets into mischief, out he goes. Does he have a leash or a pen?"

"No, I wanted him to have his freedom."

"He'll have more freedom in the long run if he also has a little discipline. Ye can say all the sweet things you want to him when he does something right. But when he disobeys, then you must speak sharply and put him outside. And don't be telling him the same thing over and over without making him do it. If ye want him to sit, ye just press that little bottom of his down while ye're saying it."

"That is just what Thomas has been telling me," Elizabeth admitted. "And what he does with the dog himself. I am the one who has been spoiling him."

"He's not spoiled yet. I am sure you will do a fine job with him. Think of it as forming a partnership with him."

Michael walked over to the stall and, opening the door, lifted the puppy out. "He's tired himself out, creating such a brouhaha," said Michael with a grin. "He'll sleep tonight."

"You are a devil," Elizabeth said to the puppy, "but a sweet little devil." The little dog had sunk so affectionately against her shoulder that she couldn't resist dropping a kiss on the top of his head.

Michael cleared his throat.

"Oh, yes, Orion, I am taking you home." She giggled. "It sounds so formal, Sergeant."

Michael had a hard time resisting the impulse to drop a kiss on Mrs. Woolcott's head. Her giggle had made her sound like a carefree young girl instead of the reserved officer's wife he had encountered up until now. He remembered the story he had heard about her family. Maybe her primness was as much a result of that tragedy as of her schooling in the East. Maybe she hadn't had much chance to be a carefree young girl before becoming a woman.

"He'll grow into it, ma'am." They were at the stable

door and Michael stepped back to let Elizabeth through. She turned and gave him a grateful smile.

"Thank you very much for your help, Sergeant Burke."

"Don't ye forget the lieutenant's blouse," said Michael, handing it to her.

Elizabeth wrinkled her nose. "I hope I can get the smell out of it."

"Ye'll do a fine job on the shirt and the dog, ma'am," said Michael, and he gave her a quick bow and walked off to the corral.

When Thomas got home that night, the puppy was nowhere to be seen and his wife was sitting by the sitting room lamp, sewing buttons on his best blouse.

"I heard there was a little problem with the puppy today, Lizzie."

Elizabeth lifted her face and said with tart humor, "I am sure the whole fort was aware of it, Thomas."

He couldn't help grinning. "And where is the little troublemaker?"

"He is outside on a line, Thomas. And he will stay there tonight."

"A line?"

"Yes, I had Private Stack help me rig one up near the back door. Orion must learn that certain things are off limits to him."

"Orion?" Thomas was tempted to laugh, but his wife looked so delightfully responsible and serious that he controlled himself.

"Sergeant Burke convinced me that he needed a name to inspire him. He was very helpful to me today, Thomas. The line was his idea."

"Sergeant Burke is a very competent man," Thomas agreed. Whatever Burke had said, he was grateful. Maybe their little household would be peaceful and sane again.

It didn't happen overnight, but within a month Elizabeth and Orion had both learned who was to be in charge. The dog responded to his name, he would sit and stay on command, and the next thing she was determined to do was to teach him to heel when she was walking with him and to keep a safe distance from her horse when she went out riding. When the dog was old enough, it would be wonderful to have him around for protection and would enable her to ride out a little farther from the fort.

Chapter Thirteen

Antonio and Serena had not been to the fort the last few weeks, and Elizabeth was hoping that this coming Sunday she would see her friend again. It surprised her a little how close she felt to the Navajo woman. She got along well with the other officers' wives, but she had never allowed them to get too close, with the exception of the colonel's wife.

One reason was that in the army, people were coming and going all the time. She had been reluctant to form a close friendship, only to have it broken by a transfer to another post. Thomas was the constant in her life, and the person she was most willing to share herself with.

Serena's weaving had drawn her first. Then, as they both began to trust one another, she realized that she liked the Navajo woman very much. She tried to tell herself that it was foolishness: she and Thomas could be reassigned at any time, the peace between their people was very fragile, and even if it weren't, the differences between them were too great. But she was drawn to the combination of Serena's dignity and salty humor.

There were no races this Sunday, but quite a few Navajo came in to trade anyway. Elizabeth was happy to see Serena among the women and walked over with Orion on his leash by her side. Or almost by her side. The dog was curious about everything, and Elizabeth could tell he would have liked nothing better than to grab one of the women's blankets and chew it to pieces. But she spoke to him firmly and sat him down when he wandered away and finally made it to where her friend was sitting.

"I see you have been taking good care of that little dog," said Serena.

"Well, I am not sure who is leading whom today but he is growing big and fat, isn't he? I am glad to see you, Serena. I missed you these past few weeks."

"We were visiting with my uncle near Chinle. We always go at peach harvest time."

"Peaches!" Elizabeth's mouth watered. She hadn't had fresh fruit in she didn't know how long.

"I brought you some," said Serena with a smile. "They are newly dried, so there is still a little juice in them." Serena handed Elizabeth a soft buckskin bag fastened by a bone bead and decorated with fringe. Elizabeth reached in and pulled out a dried peach. It was still a little plump, and while she chewed she could imagine the juices it would have held when it was fresh-picked. "Oh, this is just too good," she said with a delighted smile as she handed the bag back.

"No, no, those are for you and your husband."

"All these peaches?"

"There are hundreds of trees," said Serena with a smile.

"Then I'll have to wrap them in my scarf." She started to untie it from around her neck, when Serena stopped her.

"The bag is yours also."

"Oh, I can't take it. It is too lovely!"

The Navajo woman frowned. "I made it for you." Really, the *bilagaana* were hard to understand. They were always taking, taking. But try to give them something and they acted like you had handed them a scorpion!

Elizabeth realized that once again she was on the verge of an insult. "Thank you, Serena. It is beautiful and I will use it when I go riding."

Her friend nodded and then suddenly turned her attention to the sutler's wife, who was fingering one of her blankets.

Elizabeth stood there, not sure whether she should stay

or go. When Mrs. Grant had completed her trade and left, Elizabeth said quietly, "I am sorry, my friend. It is a habit among us to protest a gift. And it is hard for me to accept something that lovely, with nothing to give you."

"Do all gifts have to be like trade?" Serena asked with great curiosity.

"No, we do have special occasions like birthdays or Christmas, when gift-giving is customary." Serena was quiet, but it was a friendly silence, and Elizabeth sat down next to her and pulled Orion onto her lap.

The Navajo woman reached out and tugged at the dog's ears, and he licked her fingers.

"You know," said Elizabeth thoughtfully, "if it is hard to understand just one small different way of doing things, then I don't wonder that the Diné and the whites are always fighting."

"But we have taken the time to understand."

"Yes, but we are women. Do you think women making the treaties might make a difference?" Elizabeth said it jokingly, but found herself wondering if indeed women might be more successful.

"Here is my husband. Why don't you ask him?"

Elizabeth hadn't noticed Antonio approaching and she jumped up, forgetting she had Orion on her lap. He yipped as she spilled him on the ground and looked at her with such a hurt expression on his face that all three of them laughed.

"I am Mrs. Woolcott," said Elizabeth.

"I have heard of you from my wife," said Antonio, scooping the dog up. "And I have heard about this little dog. I think the lieutenant was right. Manuelito's dog was certainly this one's sire."

"Well, then, Orion has a fine lineage."

"Sure and he does indeed," said Michael as he strolled over.

The four of them stood there, quiet for a moment, attention focused on the wriggling dog in Antonio's arms. All were very aware of each other: a sergeant in the U.S. cavalry, who was a friend of a Navajo headman's nephew; the wife of an army officer who was forming a friendship with that nephew's wife; all of them surrounded by people, Navajo and white, who had never crossed such boundaries. Oh yes, there was a group of enlisted men gambling with a group of warriors. And the army wives stopped and fingered blankets and paid compliments to the women. But most Navajo did not speak English. And none of the *bilagaana* spoke Navajo.

Michael broke their silence first. "And is the dog behaving himself, Mrs. Woolcott?"

Elizabeth nodded. "I think receiving a name was a big help, Sergeant Burke. And also your advice on training him. I'll be able to let him off the leash soon and take him riding with me."

"Antonio, I was wondering if ye could come with me for a moment," said Michael, turning to his friend. "The colonel wanted to ask ye about something."

Antonio frowned. "It is not another lie from a New Mexican, is it?"

"I don't know anything more than that there was supposedly a raid on thirty miles from here two days ago."

Serena sighed as the men moved off. "It is those enemy Diné from the mountains." She almost spat the last two words out. My husband and the headmen try so hard but it is impossible to control all the Diné." She hesitated. "But let us not talk of worrisome things. What do you think of that fine-looking sergeant? His hair is almost as black as my husband's. If it weren't for those light eyes of his, he would make a fine Diné. His skin is dark enough."

"Only on his face and neck," said Elizabeth without thinking.

"Oho, and what do you know of the rest of him?"

Elizabeth was blushing furiously.

"I have never understood why they call us 'redskin,' " said Serena with a grin, "when surely you are the red-skinned ones!"

"Oh dear, I suppose I'll have to confess. Do you know the little canyon north of the fort? I was out there painting on the day Sergeant Burke arrived at the fort. I came upon him, uh, bathing."

Serena giggled.

"He doesn't know, Serena. It would be terribly embarrassing if he did! Anyway, he is very white under his uniform," Elizabeth said primly.

"Oh, what a shame," Serena teased.

"Well, he is quite good-looking for all he is not a Diné warrior!"

"There is a shrine in that canyon," said Serena more seriously.

"Is that what all the feathered sticks are there for?"

"Yes."

"It is a very beautiful place and I certainly feel as close to God there as I do in a church. Perhaps even closer," said Elizabeth, thinking of some of the long, boring sermons she had heard over the years.

"You *bilagaana* are very puzzling," said Serena, patting the spot next to her. Elizabeth sat down again, letting Orion run about on his leash. "It seems very important you have this one God, but then everyone fights over owning him. The Mexicans, the Mormons. And this God is a man."

"Yes," Elizabeth responded thoughtfully. "That is, Jesus, His son, was a man. But also God."

"So there is a father and a son. No mother?"

"Of course, Jesus had a mother. But only the papists worship her," said Elizabeth.

"What are these papists?"

"Roman Catholics. The Mexicans are papists." Elizabeth hesitated. "Sergeant Burke is a papist . . . a Catholic."

"You sound like you don't like them."

"I was brought up to think that they were ignorant and superstitious. You see, we think . . ."

"Who is we? The *bilagaana*?"

"Er, no. I am . . . was a Congregationalist."

"And what are they? What do they believe?"

"In one God, also. And Jesus."

"Not in his mother, though?"

"Well, we believe he had a mother, of course. But that

she can't be worshiped. Have you ever been inside a Spanish church, Serena?"

"Yes, some are quite beautiful, though I have never understood why they want to close their gods up in a building."

"Have you seen the statues and pictures?"

"Yes."

"Well, some are of Mary, Jesus' mother, and we Protestants feel they give a devotion to a woman which only belongs to God."

"Protestants? Is this another group of *bilagaana*?" Serena's head was spinning trying to keep track of all the variations.

"Oh dear." Elizabeth had not thought much about the history of Christianity before and never tried to explain it. She had never had to. In Boston, it was just *understood* that Congregationalism was the purest form of belief. But that any Protestant was better than a Catholic. From a Navajo perspective it must sound very confusing. Actually, she realized, it *was* very confusing.

Serena sighed. "There are too many differences to remember."

"One thing is true, though. All Christians believe in Jesus' teachings."

"And what did this Jesus teach?"

"He taught us to love one another, as he had loved us enough to become one of us."

"One of the *bilagaana*. So ... *bilagaana* are only to love other *bilagaana*?"

"No, no. I think he meant everyone. And I guess you would call him a *bilagaana*, but he was born into a tribe that was enslaved. He was born a Jew. They were a people not too different from the Diné, actually," said Elizabeth with a smile. "They were a desert people too, and they lived not too differently, raising sheep and cattle. Fighting with neighboring tribes. Then they were conquered by the Romans. I guess, for the Jews, the Romans were the *bilagaana*," Elizabeth said thoughtfully.

"So your God was born to a people like the Diné?"

Eilzabeth smiled and then started to giggle. "I am

sorry, Serena. It suddenly seems very funny to me, like things have been twisted inside out over the years. I never really tried to explain it before, and I never saw how far from the beginning of things we have come."

"I am glad you see how puzzling it is! Of course, one of the most puzzling things is that your God can only be a man. And that his mother can't be important. Except to the Mexicans. I am beginning to have a little more respect for them," Serena said thoughtfully.

"Is your God a woman?"

"We don't have one god. There are long stories of how we came here to Dinetah. And there are three women who are very important to us: Changing Woman, White Shell Woman, and Spider Woman. But to tell the stories would take a long time."

"Changing Woman? Didn't you tell me once that she was connected to the celebration for a young girl who becomes a woman?"

"*Kinaalda.*" Serena smiled. "You remembered."

"It is one of the few words I know in Navajo, I am ashamed to say. But I did remember."

"Perhaps ..." Serena looked thoughtful.

"Perhaps what?"

"Perhaps the next time there is a ceremony you would like to come?"

Elizabeth was so moved by the offer that she couldn't say anything at first. Such an invitation was a rare gift and she hardly felt she deserved it.

"Perhaps you wouldn't," the Navajo woman said matter-of-factly as she began to fold up her blankets.

Elizabeth put her hand on Serena's arm. "I would very much like to. I am *honored* that you would invite me."

Serena nodded and then said thoughtfully, "Some families would not want a *bilagaana* woman at a ceremony. But my sister's daughter is the right age. She should be close to her *kinaalda* ..." She looked over at Elizabeth and smiled. "It is a four-day ceremony. The last day would be the best for you to see. I will let you know when the time comes."

* * *

As Antonio and Serena rode away from the fort, she turned in the saddle and asked her husband what the colonel had wanted.

"To tell me that a raid had occurred and two Mexicans were killed and three thousand sheep taken."

"Three thousand!"

Antonio gave a sarcastic laugh. "The Diné become better and better thieves whenever something like this happens. Can you imagine a small raiding party handling three thousand sheep?"

"It is Haastin Keshgoli again?"

"Probably. Or some of his young men. We are supposed to send word to all the Diné to keep an eye out for fugitives. To 'turn them in,' as the *bilagaana* says," said Antonio, going from Navajo to English and then back again. "To betray them. They still do not understand this is something we cannot, will not do."

"Mrs. Woolcott and I were wondering today if we women could do any better."

Antonio laughed. "I have seen some very fierce *bilagaana* women. And what about Rainbow Walker? Do you think *she* would not fight the new men if she were younger?"

Serena smiled. "Maybe you're right. I only know that the lieutenant's wife listens and tries to understand." She paused. "I have invited her to a *kinaalda*."

Antonio lifted his eyebrows but said nothing.

"My niece should be ready for her ceremony soon. I think my sister would not mind. And it would only be for part of the fourth day and the next morning. It felt like a good thing to do, although some of the women may be angry with me."

"And scared. A cavalry officer's wife? She'll come with a full escort. What were you thinking, wife?"

"Maybe she can ride to the canyon with Sergeant Burke and maybe you can send some men there to escort them both."

"Hmmm." Antonio considered the idea for a minute. "If Mrs. Woolcott can convince the colonel, I suppose it will be all right. But two *bilagaana* at a ceremony . . . ?"

"I know. But I was thinking with my heart. There is something about the lieutenant's wife. If she were Diné, I would think that she missed her *kinaalda*. She feels something like a girl to me, even though we are not that far apart in age. And if the *bilagaana* are here to stay," she added with a tinge of bitterness, "surely it's a good idea to make friends with some of them. To help them understand the Diné?"

"It is funny that we both have found a friend amongst them."

"Yes, and yours is such a good-looking one," Serena teased. "He fills his uniform in a very satisfying manner."

"Oh, and I don't look satisfying to you anymore, wife," Antonio said, as though he were insulted.

"I still prefer you to a *bilagaana* soldier, husband, don't worry. But I am sorry that Mrs. Woolcott has to live with an older husband and not someone like Sergeant Burke. But she seems to love the lieutenant, even with his gray hair."

"Well, love is a strange thing. It made me choose a woman with a sharp tongue when I could have had someone quiet in my hogan."

"If you wanted someone quiet in your hogan, husband, you surely did choose the wrong woman!"

"I chose the woman I wanted," said Antonio, pulling his horse close to hers and slipping his arm around her waist for a moment and stealing a kiss before they continued on.

Elizabeth spoke that night to Thomas after they went to bed.

"Well, on one hand, it is a great honor to have been asked," he admitted.

"I know."

"On the other, it presents some concern for your safety. But if you *must* go . . ." he added with humor in his voice.

"I would really like to go, Thomas. Although they will understand if I don't, it feels important to our friendship."

"Some of the women will think you are strange to be having a friendship with a Navajo."

"I know, Thomas. Mrs. Taggert particularly hates the Navajo. Or any Indian, for that matter."

"And for all your eastern ways, you don't, Lizzie. I've always wondered at that."

"Part of it is being married to you, Thomas. You've been an Indian fighter for years, but you do it as your duty, not out of hate. And Mrs. Taggert has a reason for her feelings: she lost a brother and his family to a Ute massacre. What the women don't understand is that I've seen how brutal white men can be," Elizabeth continued, her voice tight and strained. Thomas put his arm around her. "The Indians have no monopoly on cruelty, Thomas. You and I know that. And I like Serena very much."

"I'll ask the colonel when the time comes. If he can spare the men as an escort, he'll likely let you go, seeing as how it will help relations with the Navajo."

"Thank you, Thomas. You are such a good husband to me."

"You are very easy to be good to, Elizabeth," he said, pulling her closer. "You have made me very happy these past six years. You know that, don't you?"

Elizabeth wrapped her arms around him. "Oh, Thomas, I hope I have been a good wife to you," she whispered, her voice quivering.

"I could not have asked for a better," he said. "It was you I was waiting for, all those years of bachelorhood, I guess," he added, stroking her hair gently.

Chapter Fourteen

Supplies were brought to the fort once a month from Albuquerque. A troop from the fort always met the quartermaster's wagons part of the way and escorted them the last forty miles.

Thomas had been assigned escort duty six months after they had arrived and Elizabeth had always dreaded it since it kept him away for days at a time. The last few months had been easier, though, with Orion to keep her company. But with the recent reports of Navajo raids, Elizabeth felt an anxiety that went beyond her usual dislike of being alone.

On the morning of Thomas's next scheduled departure, she tried to keep it from him as she bustled around, making the coffee and heating up the skillet for his bacon and eggs. She was so distracted, however, that the bowl in which she was scrambling the eggs slipped out of her hands and shattered on the floor.

"No, Orion, no," she yelled as the dog started to lap up the frothy mess. "Thomas, hold him please. He'll cut his tongue on the slivers from the bowl."

Thomas was used to Elizabeth's mood on these mornings, but her voice was more strained than usual. After he had pulled Orion away and put him on his line, he placed his hand on his wife's shoulder. "Get up, Elizabeth, and let me clean that."

"I've almost got it all, Thomas. But that was the last egg," she moaned.

"Just fry me up some bacon and I'll be fine."

"Don't get egg on your trousers, Thomas," she said sharply as he carried the pieces of pottery over to the scrap bucket.

Thomas grinned. She sure was in a flurry this morning. He hated to leave her in this state, but there was nothing he could do about it.

"Damnation!"

If he hadn't been so concerned, he would have laughed out loud, for his wife *never* swore.

"What is it, Lizzie?"

"You know I hate it when you call me that, Thomas. I just got my sleeve caught on the skillet handle and almost pulled it off the stove."

"But you didn't," he said reassuringly.

"No, I didn't," she said sharply, irritated by his patience.

"Why don't you sit down and let me cook," he offered.

"The least I can do before you start out on such a long ride is cook your breakfast, Thomas. I promise you, I'll have it on the table in a moment. Unless you're in too much of a hurry to wait?"

"No, Elizabeth, I am in no hurry," he said calmly and sat down at the table.

Elizabeth's eyes stung with grease smoke and tears as she flipped the bacon. Whatever was *wrong* with her? Thomas had made many of these trips. They were routine. Why was she as jumpy as those drops of bacon grease that kept spitting up at her?

She took a deep breath as she arranged his plate, buttering a third slice of corn bread hot from the oven. It seemed a scanty breakfast without the eggs.

"Here you are, Thomas," she said, sitting down next to him, and thinking she had herself under control when he looked over at her and she burst into tears.

"Elizabeth!"

"Oh, Thomas, I don't want you to go this time."

"It is the same boring detail, my dear, forty miles out and forty back."

"But you have been doing it while things were peaceful, Thomas. This last raid was only a day's ride from here."

"Elizabeth," he said reassuringly, "the Navajo have never attacked a supply train and they aren't going to start now. Not with a full troop of men meeting it. I'll only be gone a few days and I want you to promise me you'll not just sit here and fret yourself."

Elizabeth wiped her face with her napkin. "You are right, Thomas. I am being silly. It is just that . . . I know I always hate it when you go, but this feels different."

"It is perfectly understandable you'd be upset. But Orion will be here to keep you company and you'll have tea with Mrs. Gray and you'll be fine."

Thomas spoke to her in the tone he always used: quiet, reassuring, almost fatherly. It had always calmed her fears before and made her feel protected by his strength. This morning, however, it was only adding to her irritability. She knew she was being irrational, for he was only being the Thomas she had loved and relied on all these years. But she didn't want his quiet tolerance of her fear. She didn't want him soothing her like a fearful child. She wanted . . . she didn't know *what* she wanted from him, she realized.

She was annoyed at herself for her extreme reaction and annoyed at him for not seeing that it really *wasn't* extreme. Any woman would be worried about her husband going on such a patrol. And just because she was feeling vulnerable didn't mean she was going to fall apart.

Thomas pushed himself away from the table, saying, "It is time I must be going, Elizabeth."

"I know, Thomas. I will be fine. Truly I will," she reassured him. She followed him to the door and held his jacket for him as she had so many times before.

"Elizabeth, you feed me too well. You'll have to let this jacket out when I come home," he joked as he struggled with the buttons.

Elizabeth put her hands on his chest and he pulled her into his arms.

"Don't worry, Elizabeth. I'll be home safe and sound as always."

"I know, Thomas. I'm just being silly. Now go, before your men start wondering where you are."

He ran down the steps and she watched him quick march down the line. Just as he was about to turn the corner, he turned back and waved to her. She blew him a kiss and then went back inside. She had dishes to wash, bread to bake, and a stack of mending that should keep her busy. If she could get through today, she thought, she would be all right.

Two days before the supply escort was to leave, Michael had been summoned to Lieutenant Cooper's quarters.

"Colonel Gray has informed me that two of Mr. Woolcott's men are down with dysentery. He requested you be assigned to the lieutenant with a man of your choice," said Cooper coolly.

"Yes, sir."

"Whom will you choose, Burke?"

"Em, Mahoney has the potential for becoming a fine soldier, sir, but he could use a little seasoning."

"All right then, Sergeant, inform Private Mahoney. And, Burke . . ."

"Yes, sir?"

"You'll be back on wood detail as soon as this is over."

"Yes, sir."

Michael had decided to ride Frost. The mare was restless in the cool morning air and Michael had to keep her on a tight rein as they headed out of the fort.

"That mare looks ready for another race, sir." Mahoney grinned. He was riding next to Michael and his gelding was merely plodding along.

" 'Tis the cooler weather that makes her full of fire," replied Michael.

"She's a fine animal."

"That she is, Mahoney."

Frost settled down soon enough and their first day's ride was a fairly easy one. They would meet the supply wagons by morning and had seen no sign of anyone, Navajo or New Mexican.

They reached the rendezvous point, a small group of cottonwoods by a stream, early the next day and the lieutenant let them dismount and relax. When two hours went by, however, with no sign of the supply wagons, Lieutenant Woolcott called Michael over to him.

"Sergeant Burke, I'm worried about the supply train. The quartermaster is always on time, within a quarter hour."

Michael nodded. "What are ye thinking, sir?"

"I'm thinking it could be as simple as an axle breaking or a mule going lame . . ." Thomas's voice trailed off.

" 'Tis possible."

"Or they could have been attacked. It has never happened before, but with a band of renegades on the loose . . ." Thomas took a deep breath. "You have the reputation for being a good scout, Burke. I'm glad you rode that big horse of yours. She's fast and strong, from what I've seen at the races," Thomas said with a smile.

"She is that, sir."

"I'd like you to scout ahead for me." Thomas hesitated. "Ride about an hour and see if you come upon any sign of the wagons. If you don't, then turn around and come back."

"And if I do catch up with them?"

"Report back in any case, Sergeant Burke."

"Yes, sir."

"And watch out for yourself, Sergeant."

"Yes, sir. Thank you, sir."

Michael set out at a slow, steady canter. He had always enjoyed his scouting, because it gave him a chance to be alone, and that was a rare treat in the army. After fifteen minutes, he walked Frost and then kicked her into a ground-eating trot. The mare would be able to keep the pace up for about a half hour.

It was only fifteen minutes later that he saw them. One wagon was overturned and the other three had been drawn into a semicircle next to it.

"*Día,*" he whispered and pulled the mare to a walk. He

couldn't see any signs of life. He walked the mare slowly, his reins in one hand, his rifle in the other.

He heard a low, constant moaning and, dismounting carefully, he led Frost over to the wagons.

There were two enlisted men lying there. They were dead, one with an arrow through his throat, the other shot in the chest. The moaning was coming from behind one of the wagons, and Michael walked over carefully. The Diné usually took their wounded with them, but he wasn't taking any chances.

But it was a soldier, propped up against a wheel, his hand holding a cocked pistol balanced on his knee.

"Easy, boyo," said Michael as the man turned at the sound of his feet.

Blood was puddled under the boy's outstretched leg and as he shifted to face Michael, he let out a loud groan.

Michael knelt down next to him and saw that he had been shot through the knee with a rifle. Shattered, he thought. This lad won't be riding again. He'll be lucky if he doesn't lose the leg.

"What happened, lad?"

The hand holding the pistol relaxed. "It was a good-sized band, about twenty or so. On their way back from a raid. They had two women with them. I don't think they planned to attack us, just took advantage of the opportunity."

"Where are the rest of your party?"

"The master sergeant headed back to Albuquerque for help."

"You are a brave lad, then, to be guarding the wagons on your own."

The boy licked his cracked lips. "Do you have any water, sir?"

"Sure, and what have I been thinking, chatting away like I'm at a tea party," Michael joked. "I'll be right back."

He got his canteen and kneeling down again beside the boy, gave him a few sips.

"More," the boy pleaded, his hands reaching for Michael's.

"In a minute, lad."

After a few more swallows, the boy closed his eyes and relaxed his head back against the wheel.

"I am going to have to leave you, Private."

The boy's eyes flew open and he started to protest.

"I'd take you with me, was it your arm shattered. But you shouldn't be moved with that leg. But I'll leave ye my canteen. Ye must promise to drink sparingly, for ye'll have to hold out till I come back with the escort or your sergeant brings help."

"Yes, sir."

Michael patted him gently on the arm. "Ye'll be fine, lad. They'll not come back. Ye've got some water and ye're in the shadow of the wagon, at least."

"Yes, sir, I'll be fine sir," said the boy, as if repeating Michael's words would make them be true.

"Well, then, I must be leavin' ye."

He mounted Frost and headed back toward Lieutenant Woolcott. He had seen no sign of the Diné. Of course, they were very good at keeping out of sight. But if they turned south at all they would run right into the escort.

Frost was eager to get away from the smell of blood and the flies buzzing around the dead bodies. "No ye don't, darlin'," he said, holding her back. "I'm as eager as ye are but we can't be stupid either."

It seemed to take forever to reach the little grove of cottonwoods and when he finally got there, it was to find only half the detail.

"Where is Mr. Woolcott," he demanded as he slid off his horse.

"A band of them savages passed right by us. They were as surprised to see us as we were to see them," the trooper added, nodding his satisfaction. "They took off like bats out of hell and the lieutenant took off after them. One of them was wearing a cavalry cap and leading two army shavetails loaded with supplies. We figured they'd gotten the wagons and maybe even you."

"And the lieutenant's orders?"

"To wait here until evening and if he wasn't back, to return to the fort."

Michael looked around. "Did Mahoney go with him?"

"The mick kid? Yup, he volunteered."

Lieutenant Woolcott had only half the men the Diné had, thought Michael. But maybe the Diné would just run. Maybe they would do their usual disappearing act. Maybe the lieutenant would just turn back. Goddamn all renegades to hell, thought Michael as he led Frost down to the little stream.

It was close to sundown when he saw the dust of the approaching riders. There were nine horses, not ten, and Michael could see that one was carrying double. Please God, 'tisn't Mahoney down, he found himself praying, surprised at how much he would miss the lad.

It wasn't Mahoney down, he saw, but Mahoney in the lead with the lieutenant slumped in front of him. The boy's eyes widened with relief when he saw Michael.

"He's been gut-shot, Sergeant Burke. I think he's still alive, but just barely."

"Over here," barked Michael to one of the men. "Help me with him."

Thomas Woolcott was a heavy man and it was hard taking him down gently. Michael barked orders, "Spread a few blankets out. Fill a canteen," as he carried the lieutenant to the most level spot he could find.

Mahoney had ripped apart Woolcott's jacket and bound him with it. It was soaked in blood, but Michael was afraid to loosen it. Tell the truth, boyo, ye're afraid to look. He had seen men on the battlefield with their guts hanging out. He had even watched an army surgeon fold them back in again and sew a man up. He had been ordered to hold the lantern and it was lucky the tent didn't go up in flames when he'd fainted.

He laid Woolcott on top of one of the blankets and spread the other over him. He pulled off his own neckerchief and, soaking it in water, cleaned the lieutenant's face off.

"Is he all right, sir. He saved our lives," Mahoney choked out.

"What happened, lad?"

"The Indians turned into a small canyon. He insisted on taking Private Black and going in first. Some of the Indians had stayed behind in ambush and started shooting from the rocks. We went in after him, but Black was already dead and the lieutenant wounded."

"How did ye get him out?"

Mahoney dropped his head. "I had the men cover me," he said in a low voice, "and I rode in after him. I couldn't leave him there."

Michael patted his arm. "No, you couldn't leave him there. Ye've turned into a fine soldier."

Thomas groaned and Michael lifted his head.

"Water," he whispered.

"I don't think ye should be drinking, sir," said Michael. He poured more water on his neckerchief and lifted it to Thomas's lips. "Here, sir, this will keep ye from dryin' out."

"That's Burke, isn't it? The wagons?"

"Whist, Mr. Woolcott. Ye mustn't be talking. Some of the supplies gone and two men dead, sir. Their sergeant turned back to Albuquerque for help. I guess he was afraid to follow the Navajo."

"Mahoney?" whispered Thomas.

"Right here, sir."

"You are a good soldier, Private Mahoney. Be sure you recommend him to the colonel, Burke."

"Sure and ye'll be recommending him yerself."

Thomas shook his head and attempted a smile, which turned into a grimace as a wave of pain hit him.

Michael wet his lips again.

"Burke . . ."

"Yes, sir."

"Elizabeth . . ."

"Yes, sir?" Dear Mother Mary, the man couldn't die, not like this. Not and leave her alone again.

"Tell her . . . she's made me very happy . . . very happy. And, Burke?"

Thomas's voice was so weak that Michael had to put his head down next to his lips.

"Tell her I died fast and easy."

Michael reached out and took Thomas's hand. He squeezed it gently and said, "I will, sir."

"Thank you, Burke. You are a good man. I always said so."

Chapter Fifteen

Thomas Woolcott did not die slowly or easily. The only blessing, thought Michael, was that he lost consciousness around midnight.

"You need some sleep, Sergeant Burke," said Mahoney as they sat with him. "I can stay with him for a while."

"No, lad, ye get yerself some sleep." Michael kept his vigil, regularly moistening Thomas's lips with his makeshift sponge. Even unconscious, the man's mouth sought the water eagerly, and he knew that he was giving the dying man the only small comfort he could.

It was just before dawn that he slipped away. Michael had just brushed his lips again, but instead of sucking at the cloth they relaxed open and with one sigh, Thomas Wood was released into death.

Michael ran his hand down Thomas's face to close his eyes and pulled the blanket over him. He stood up slowly, stiff and aching from the long night. The sun was coming up, lighting the ocher and pink rocks around them with the clear light so characteristic of the country. It was going to be a beautiful day, he thought: crisp, cool, and clear, but Mr. Woolcott would not be seein' it. He crossed himself and murmured a Hail Mary. "And pray for us sinners, now and at the hour of our death, Amen."

Mahoney stumbled over, barely awake. The boy took in the lieutenant's shrouded body.

"When did he die, Sergeant Burke?"

"Just a little while ago, Mahoney."

Mahoney wiped his eyes with the back of his hand. "It

should have been me lying there, sir. If he hadn't gone first into that ambush ... He saved our lives."

"It shouldn't be anyone at all down there, lad," said Michael, putting his arm around Mahoney's shoulders. "Ye went after him."

"But he is dead, sir."

"Had he only been wounded in the shoulder, he would have lived because of you, Mahoney. Don't be forgetting that."

"Thank you, sir," the boy whispered.

Michael stood silently for a few minutes. He had a handful of men, a dead officer, and a wounded boy back at the wagons. He wanted to bring the lieutenant back himself, he wanted to be the one to break the news to Elizabeth, to be there for her. But he couldn't send anyone else back to the wagons. He had promised that boy someone would be back for him.

"Mahoney, I'm putting half the men under your command. Ye'll take the lieutenant's body back to the fort."

"You're not going after them?" the boy protested.

"No, but there is a lad close to your age lying by the wagons and the rest of the supplies with him. I have to get them to the fort."

They wrapped Thomas's body in another blanket, tied it with rawhide, and slung it over one of the horses. "Two of ye ride double, lads," ordered Michael.

"Yes, sir."

Michael put his hand on Mahoney's knee when the boy was mounted. "*Ma*honey," he said. "I promised Mr. Woolcott something and ye'll have to help me keep my promise."

"Sir?"

"Tell Mrs. Woolcott he died quickly and with very little suffering."

Mahoney frowned. " 'Twas his last wish," Michael said persuasively.

"All right, sir."

Michael patted his knee. "Good lad."

Michael saw them off and then, mounting Frost, he waved the rest of the men to follow him.

When they got to the supply wagons, there was no sign of the Navajo's return. The young private was unconscious, Michael's canteen lying empty next to him.

"He was lucky to pass out. Get him into one of the wagons, Private Stanton. Gently now, be careful of that leg."

There were only six mules left, so Michael consolidated what was left of the supplies into one wagon and onto the backs of two mules.

"We've got about everything, sir," said Private Stanton.

"Move them out then, men."

It was after dark when they reached the fort, but they were obviously awaited, for the gates swung open as they approached. The colonel was standing in front of his headquarters and waved a summons to Michael, who walked Frost over to the railing and started to dismount.

"You must be exhausted, Burke. And your horse, too. Get yourself some food and settle your mount and then I'll hear your report."

"Yes, sir."

Michael turned Frost and walked her slowly down the line toward the stables. He couldn't help turning his head as he passed the Woolcotts' quarters. The lanterns were lit in the parlor and also in what he assumed was their bedroom and he could see a woman's silhouette walking back and forth.

When he got to the stables, he rubbed Frost down slowly and carefully and after watering and feeding her, settled her down with a fervent "Thank you for gettin' me back safely."

He presented himself at the colonel's half an hour later.

"Come in, Sergeant Burke, come in. Sit down, man. You must be tired."

"A wee bit, sir," Michael admitted as he sank gratefully into a chair.

"Tell me what happened, Sergeant."

"We camped at the rendezvous, sir. In the morning, after waiting two hours past their expected time, Mr. Woolcott sent me ahead. I found the wagons had been attacked and two men dead. And a wounded lad, sir. How is he?" Michael asked.

"Will lose his leg, the surgeon thinks. But otherwise fine, thanks to you."

Michael shook his head. "I thought he might. His knee was shattered. Poor lad."

"He's young and healthy. He'll adjust." The colonel poured himself a glass of brandy and offered some to Michael, who shook his head.

"I'd likely fall asleep on ye, sir," he said with a smile.

"What are your thoughts on the attack, Sergeant?"

"The lad told me there were about twenty in the band, with two women captives. It didn't sound like it was planned. More like they came upon the wagons and took the opportunity offered them. And their behavior when they came upon the lieutenant suggests the same thing. They lit out as soon as they saw our men, according to Mahoney."

"And the lieutenant?"

"He had to follow, sir, seeing as how they had captives and were leading an army mule loaded with supplies."

"Yes, he did," said the colonel sadly. "He was a good man, Thomas Woolcott, and an expert soldier. A great loss, a great loss," he murmured, "both to the army and his wife."

Michael kept his voice even as he asked, "And how is Mrs. Woolcott, sir?"

The colonel shook his head. "My wife has been with her since she received the news. She can't get her to sleep or even lie down. She hasn't even cried yet. I believe it is all too sudden for her. You know her story?"

"A little, sir."

"Thomas Woolcott was the one who rescued her when she was a girl. She depended upon him, I believe, perhaps more than most wives."

"I have a message for her from her husband, Colonel Gray. It may comfort her a little."

"You should deliver it yourself, Burke, but get yourself some well-deserved rest and see her in the morning. You did well, Burke. As did Mahoney," said the colonel with a kind smile. "I promoted him to corporal."

Michael grinned. "He deserves it, sir. And Lieutenant Woolcott would have approved."

"I am happy to have the two of you back safely."

"Thank you, sir."

Michael slept through reveille the next morning and when he finally awoke and saw that the barracks were empty, he groaned.

" 'Tis busted to private I'll be for this," he said aloud as he got himself washed and dressed.

The mess was almost empty, but he spotted Elwell in the corner and sat down next to him.

"The colonel told the officer of the day to let you sleep, Michael. I see you did. It was bad, I hear."

"Not for me, for I didn't even see them."

"No, but you were with the boy and Mr. Woolcott. I hear he went quickly?"

God bless Mahoney, thought Michael. "He did."

"Why is it that we lose all the good officers and the ones like Cooper live to old age, ripe like cheese and stinking too, with their own self-importance," said Elwell bitterly.

"God knows, Josh. Have ye heard anything about Mrs. Woolcott?"

"Only that she is taking it very hard."

"I am going to call on her," said Michael, sliding off the bench. "I have a message from her husband."

"I don't envy you, Michael. I'd rather face a howling savage than a grieving woman."

Mrs. Gray greeted him warmly when she opened the door and saw him standing there, cap in hand.

"May I speak with Mrs. Woolcott, ma'am?"

"The colonel told me you have a message from her husband?"

"Yes, ma'am."

"I don't know if she'll even hear you, Sergeant, but come in."

Michael stood in the parlor, waiting. He could hear Elizabeth pacing back and forth, back and forth, and Mrs. Gray's soft murmur. After a few minutes, Mrs. Gray led her out.

There is no life in her at all, thought Michael, and his heart ached for her. She stood there, her face white, her eyes wide and staring, and just looked through him.

"There is Sergeant Burke, my dear, as I told you."

Elizabeth extended her hand as though he were a stranger. "Sergeant Burke, yes, how kind of you to come."

"If you would sit down, dear, the sergeant could too. He is quite worn out, you know," said Mrs. Gray, deliberately appealing to Elizabeth's feeling for another's need. There was no sense in appealing to her for her own.

"Oh, yes." Elizabeth perched herself on the sofa and Michael sat next to her.

Mrs. Gray gave a small sigh of relief. It was the first time Elizabeth had sat since receiving the news.

"I will get you both some tea," she announced and hurried into the kitchen.

"I wanted to express my deepest sympathy, Mrs. Woolcott."

Elizabeth gave him a quick, polite smile. "Thank you, Sergeant Burke. So very kind of you."

It was as though they had never met before. As though he'd never danced with her, or argued with her. Or laughed with her over that foolish puppy.

He cleared his throat. "Em, I was with the lieutenant when he died, ma'am."

A slight shiver went through her.

"It was a quick and easy death, I understand?"

"Yes, ma'am. But the lieutenant was conscious for a short while." Well, that was the truth, at least. "He gave me a message for you, ma'am. Would you like me to deliver it now, or would you rather wait," Michael asked gently.

Elizabeth folded her hands together slowly and carefully placed them on her lap. She turned a little to face Michael.

"You may tell me now, Sergeant."

"Em, the lieutenant asked me to tell you . . . he said it very strongly, Mrs. Woolcott . . ." Michael felt his own throat tighten with emotion. He felt that Thomas Woolcott was speaking through him somehow, telling his wife something it was important for her to hear, that he wanted her to hear, although it took almost his last conscious breath to say it. "He said, 'You made me very happy, Elizabeth, very happy.'" Michael's voice broke as though he were saying his own farewell to a beloved wife.

Elizabeth sat very still. At first Michael thought she hadn't taken in the words at all, but then she began to shake. A low moan, which seemed to come from the depths of her soul, made Michael reach out to her, but she flinched at his touch. "Oh God, Thomas." The words were torn from her throat and she was looking down at her hands, clasped so tight that her knuckles went white. Before Michael could stop her, they loosened and flew up, hitting her forehead again and again and then raking her arms with her fingernails. It was as though she were trying to reach the pain, to make herself feel it even more.

"Elizabeth," said Michael softly, trying to hold her hands still, "ye'll be hurting yerself."

"He didn't deserve to die like that," she cried out, and hearing her, Mrs. Gray rushed in.

Harsh wracking sobs were being torn out of her. And words. "Oh, Thomas, was I really a good wife to you?"

"Whist, whist," whispered Michael, putting his arm around her shoulder. "His last words were of how happy you had made him."

Elizabeth rocked back and forth, tears pouring down her face. Her crying reminded Michael of the keening women at home in Ireland.

Mrs. Gray waved him away and he stood up, letting her take his place. She pulled Elizabeth against her breast and held her like a child. "There, there, dear, let it all out."

Michael stood there awkwardly and then became conscious of a whining and barking from the back.

"Should I let the dog in, ma'am," he asked. "He might comfort her a little."

Mrs. Gray nodded as she went on rocking.

Orion almost knocked Michael down in his eagerness to get to his mistress, but once he entered the parlor, he only pressed up against her, crooning low in his throat as he thrust his nose into her hand.

"I'd better go then, Mrs. Gray," said Michael, feeling terribly awkward. He had no real place here, much as he wanted it.

Mrs. Gray nodded and he bowed and left.

Chapter Sixteen

Elizabeth was lost in a pain that was inarticulable. It felt like the only way to release it was through her body: she wanted to beat her head, she wanted to open a vein, she wanted to bite through to her very marrow. Her sobs went so deep that in a few minutes she was retching, though she had eaten nothing since she had heard of Thomas's death. Losing Thomas meant losing the person who had stood between her and the loss of her family. He had taken their place immediately, before she had had time to grieve for them. Now that he was gone, so were they, all over again. She didn't think she would live through it.

Mrs. Gray stayed with her, letting her grieve and only holding her back from hurting herself. When at least the worst paroxysms of grief were over, Elizabeth knelt by the sofa, her head against it, her face swollen and her dress soaked with tears. Orion was pressed up against her and for the first time since he had come in she was conscious of his presence and reached out to pull him closer.

"Come, my dear, you are exhausted," Mrs. Gray said, gently pulling her up. "Let me get you into bed."

Elizabeth let herself be led into the bedroom. She curled up on the bed and was asleep almost instantly. Mrs. Gray pulled a quilt up over her and, pushing her tangled hair back from her face, murmured, "Poor lamb."

When she left, she almost tripped over Orion, who had lain down in the bedroom doorway.

"I have some things to do at my own home, Orion. Will you guard your mistress for me?"

Orion gave her a measured look, as though to say, "Don't worry, she is in good hands with me, ma'am."

Elizabeth slept most of the day away. When she finally awoke, the sun was almost down and the room was in shadows. She lay there for a minute, trying to remember why she felt so exhausted, why she only desired unconsciousness. Then she saw Thomas's second-best blouse hanging over the chair. His left epaulet had begun to pull off and she had intended to mend that as well as strengthen the buttons. She would never have the chance to do that small wifely duty. She would never be able to do anything for Thomas again.

The tears started again, but this time her grief was easier to handle. This time she cried only for Thomas, not for her family or herself, but for the kind man who had taken a young girl under his protection. Who had never done anything to make her unhappy. "Oh, Thomas," she whispered brokenly. She was back standing on the porch, watching him turn to give her one last wave. If only she had run after him, if only she had flung herself in his arms and kissed him and said she was sorry for her mood that morning.

She had to use the privy and swung her legs over the side of the bed. She had eaten nothing for twenty-four hours and felt a little dizzy. She almost tripped over Orion.

"I almost stepped on you, you foolish dog," she said, her voice hoarse from all the crying.

The dog scrambled up and pressed close to her skirt. It almost seemed to her that he was trying to take Thomas's place as her support. His last puppy mannerisms had dropped away overnight, or so it seemed, and he stood there as calmly and steadily as a grown dog.

When she got back from the privy, Mrs. Gray was just coming in the door, followed by her striker carrying a covered pot.

"I am glad to see you up, my dear." And looking more yourself, she thought. The blank, trancelike look was gone, thank God.

Elizabeth nodded.

"Private, put the soup in the kitchen and take these rolls and cakes," said the colonel's wife, handing him the basket she had been carrying. "Just a little something from the officers' wives, my dear. Now come, let me help you wash up and we'll sit down together for a bowl of that soup."

Elizabeth hadn't thought she could even look at food, much less taste it, but her appetite surprised her. She finished a bowl of soup, two pieces of corn bread, and felt better.

"Charles and I want you to come and stay with us for a while," said Mrs. Gray after they had finished.

"Oh, no, I can't inconvenience you and the colonel like that, Mrs. Gray," Elizabeth protested. "And I need to get used to being on my own."

Being on your own is one thing, thought Mrs. Gray. Being homeless is another. Clearly in her grief, Elizabeth had forgotten that army widows gave up their quarters almost immediately. Once a husband died, the wife of any man was out of the army and on her way home as soon as she was able to travel. Except that Elizabeth had no home. A fact Mrs. Gray didn't want to remind her of.

"Why don't we talk it over in the morning, then," was all she said.

Elizabeth agreed.

"You will be all right for tonight, my dear?"

"Yes, Mrs. Gray. You have done so much already. And please thank everyone for the food."

Elizabeth walked her to the door, her hand resting on Orion's head. After Mrs. Gray left, she sat down on the sofa. She would often sit here of an evening, doing her mending or knitting while Thomas took the chair opposite and read. She had always felt so comfortable and safe in her marriage. Presumably Thomas had too. She had loved Thomas, of that she had no doubt. She had expressed it in a variety of ways. He must have experienced it, for he had said she had made him happy. . . .

Was that all a good wife did, she wondered. Make a home for her husband. Cook his meals, darn his socks, entertain their friends? Put up with the rigors of army life with grace and humor? She had done all that, so she supposed that made her a good wife.

Shouldn't there have been something more she was giving him? Surely love shouldn't have felt so safe, so much a habit? Had she ever risked anything for Thomas? Oh, from a civilian perspective, she supposed it would look as though she risked some danger. But she had relied on him so completely to take care of her that she had hardly been conscious of the dangers.

Had she really made him happy, giving him only a part of herself? The tears started again and the sense of her own shortcomings. If only she could *know* that what she had given had been enough for him. Had he meant what he had said to Michael Burke? She had to talk with him, had to know exactly how Thomas had looked and sounded his last moments on earth.

She should have been with him. He should have died in his own bed, years from now, with her holding his hand. With her ... She got up suddenly and walked over to the small glass-fronted cabinet where they kept their few pieces of good china and two shelves of books and pulled out Thomas's Bible. Its leather cover was worn and the pages had lost almost all their gilt edging. She turned to the Psalms and as she read, imagined herself next to her husband, offering the comfort of her hand and heart and the well-known words. As she read them aloud, she thought, surely Thomas would somehow hear her. Please, God, she implored, let my love reach him wherever he is. "Lo, though I walk through the valley of the shadow of death ..." She could see him walking a dark valley, alone, and she pictured herself running after him, grasping his hand. He looked down and smiled at her and pulled her into his arms. And then he left her. Just before he disappeared, he turned back and smiled, just as he had on that last morning.

She huddled sobbing on the sofa until she had no more tears and then stumbled back to bed.

* * *

The funeral was two days after Thomas Woolcott had been brought in and everyone wondered whether his widow would attend. Word had spread that Mrs. Woolcott had been sick with grief. But early in the morning, Mrs. Gray led Elizabeth out. She was very pale, and her eyes looked bruised from all her crying, but she nodded to all those who approached her with great dignity and whispered her thank-yous as she received the condolences of the officers and their wives.

The service was mercifully short. When the captain read the Twenty-third Psalm, Elizabeth had to dig her fingers into her hands to keep from crying. She would not start. She would not disgrace Thomas by giving in to her grief.

The funeral procession was also brief, for the small cemetery was right inside the stockade. Thomas's flag-covered coffin was carried on a caisson and the colonel and his wife and Elizabeth followed behind. Thomas's company brought up the rear and many of the men had tears in their eyes as they saw his coffin lowered.

Michael's eyes were dry, but his heart was aching for Elizabeth. She looked so small and alone as she stepped forward to toss a handful of red dirt on the coffin. God bless the Grays, he thought as the colonel's wife put an arm around her waist and led her away.

There was food and drink for the officers and noncommissioned officers back at the colonel's quarters, and Michael intended to pay his respects quickly and then leave.

Captain Taggert and Lieutenant Cooper came up the stairs behind him and he heard Cooper mutter something about the "damned mick." His face burned but he wouldn't give them the satisfaction of acknowledging the insult.

"I am glad you came, Sergeant Burke," said Mrs. Gray, greeting him warmly. "Mrs. Woolcott especially wanted to speak with you." Mrs. Gray's voice became chillier and more formal as she turned to greet Captain Taggert and Mr. Cooper. "So good of you to come. Please help yourself to some refreshments."

'Twas a strange, cold thing, this reception, thought Mi-

chael as he nodded and chatted and filled himself a plate.
Elizabeth was surrounded and he stood off to the side, ob-
serving the ritual. Back home, before the famine, there
would have been some *life* in the room. Someone would
have toasted the dead man and someone else told at least
one funny story about him. There was nothing in this
gathering to bring Thomas back to life in their hearts and
no stories to pass down to keep him in their memories.

Cooper was hovering around Elizabeth as though he
had some special right to be there. Michael had to admit
that the man looked genuinely sympathetic, but he wanted
to knock him down anyway. But then the colonel called
Cooper over and people drifted away and Elizabeth was
left alone for a moment.

I'll just be goin' over and offerin' my sympathy and
then I'll be out of here, thought Michael as he approached
her.

"I wanted to tell you how sorry I am, Mrs. Woolcott,"
he said formally.

She looked up at him and this time he could tell she
saw him, because her face softened and her eyes filled.

She offered her hand and he took it. "I have been wanting to thank you, Sergeant, for all you did for Thomas."

" 'Twas very little, ma'am."

"I would like to talk with you more about Thomas's
last moments sometime, Sergeant."

"Are ye sure ye are up to it, ma'am?"

"I promise I will not collapse as I did the other night,
Sergeant. I need to hear it again to take it in better than
I was able the first time. If you don't mind?" Elizabeth
added hesitantly.

"Not at all, ma'am."

"Perhaps you could come by to our . . . my quarters for
a cup of tea when you go off duty tomorrow?"

"I would be happy to."

Mrs. Taggert came up behind him and greeted Elizabeth, and Michael became conscious that he was still
holding her hand in his. "Em, well, good day, Mrs.
Woolcott," he stammered and, bowing to both the ladies,
left Elizabeth to her duties.

"She is holding up very well, don't you think, Sergeant Burke. I am very proud of her," said the colonel's wife, coming over to stand next to him.

"Em, yes, ma'am."

They both watched as Lieutenant Cooper brought Elizabeth a glass of punch and a small plate of food.

"Oh dear," murmured Mrs. Gray.

"I beg your pardon, ma'am?" said Michael, leaning down to catch her words.

"Elizabeth will be moving in with us at the end of the week. I do hope we won't have the lieutenant hovering around. I've always suspected this, but my husband would never believe me. Men!"

"Suspected what, Mrs. Gray?"

"That Mr. Cooper was drawn to Mrs. Woolcott. And now he is hanging around her like a bee over a flower. And when she is at her most vulnerable."

The idea that Cooper would even think of Elizabeth in that way made Michael furious. And what have you been doin', boyo? he thought, being honest with himself.

"Surely he isn't thinking Mrs. Woolcott has anything on her mind but her husband?"

"For today, you are right, Sergeant. But what will she be thinking of tomorrow when it fully sinks in that she must be out of her quarters in a day or so? We are happy to have her with us indefinitely, but living with an old pair like us is no long-term solution for a young and attractive woman, Sergeant."

"*Día,*" murmured Michael. "I had been forgetting that she would have to leave."

"The army is a hard place for women, Sergeant Burke, as I well know." Mrs. Gray patted his arm and said reassuringly, "She will be here for a while, Sergeant, my husband and I will see to that."

"Yes, ma'am. Well, I'll be takin' my leave, Mrs. Gray."

Whatever had the colonel's lady been meaning, reassuring him as though she thought he were an interested party? Elizabeth Woolcott had just lost her beloved husband. She wouldn't be interested in anyone, especially not a poor Irish noncom like himself. She would go home

and he would never see her again. Go home where? he
wondered. Back East? Did she have any family left there?
And if she didn't, how would she survive, with only a
small army pension to support her? A woman in her circumstances had few choices. But, Jesus, she wouldn't
consider Cooper one of them, would she?

Chapter Seventeen

Late the next afternoon, Michael walked over to the Woolcotts' quarters. He stood at the door for a minute before knocking, dreading the task before him. Elizabeth had seemed in control at the funeral, but whatever would he do if she started to try to hurt herself again?

He took off his hat, smoothed back his hair, and knocked twice. He could hear Orion barking in the backyard and smiled to himself.

"Thank you so much for coming, Sergeant Burke," Elizabeth said as she opened the door. As he walked in, she apologized for the state of the parlor.

"I was trying to get some of my packing done this morning. I had a great deal of energy when I started, but after only an hour I am afraid I became overwhelmed."

" 'Tis awful that ye have to be thinking of moving so soon, Mrs. Woolcott."

"It is the army, Sergeant Burke," she replied, shrugging her shoulders. "But please call me Elizabeth."

"Then you must remember to call me Michael."

"Come, sit down. I did make the tea I promised you. And the post ladies have been so busy baking for me that you have three choices of cakes!"

"Ye must eat to keep up yer strength, Elizabeth. Grief is tiring."

"It is exhausting, I have found," she said with a grave smile. She hesitated and then, putting her cup and saucer down, clasped her hands together and looked directly into his eyes.

"Sergeant Burke, I would like to hear the whole story from you. How Thomas died. What he said."

"Are ye sure?"

"Yes," she responded calmly. "And don't worry, I won't lose control this time."

" 'Twas good to let yourself react strongly. It makes the grieving easier in the end. But I must confess it was hard to watch ye in such pain."

Elizabeth put her hands together in her lap. "It is so hard to get through this."

"You survived the loss of your family."

"Yes," she admitted with a catch in her throat. "But that was only because of Thomas. And now that he is gone it is like losing them all over again."

She lowered her face as the tears came and Michael found himself wanting to hold her close and comfort her as she cried.

"I am sorry. It is just that I cannot seem to stop crying," she said, laughing shakily and wiping her eyes. "Now, tell me what happened."

"Em, I wasn't there, as you know. I came back to the rendezvous point and found the lieutenant and half of his men gone."

"*Why* did he go after them? They didn't attack, did they?"

" 'Twas his duty, Elizabeth. He saw one wearing a cavalry cap, another leading army mules and two captive women." Michael paused. "From what Mahoney told me, they followed the Navajo into a small canyon, where they were ambushed. Thomas is a hero, Elizabeth, for he insisted on going in first, to expose an ambush. He saved the others' lives."

"A *dead* hero. Oh, I wouldn't have wanted the others to die, you must not think that. But Thomas was ever the rescuer. Look how he rescued me," she added with some bitterness in her voice.

Michael continued slowly. "Mahoney brought him in."

"He was conscious then? In pain?"

"He was only conscious for a short time before he died, Elizabeth." At least that was the truth, thought Michael.

"But he did speak with you?"

"Yes. First he asked me to commend Mahoney to the colonel."

Elizabeth gave something between a laugh and a sob. "Only Thomas."

"He was a good officer. He thought of his men first, as indeed he should."

"And then me."

"His last thoughts were of you, Elizabeth. Clearly, for him you were the most important."

"What did he say," she whispered.

"He said, 'Tell Elizabeth she made me very happy . . . very happy.' He lost consciousness right afterwards and died almost immediately," continued Michael. *And may God forgive me for the lie.*

The tears poured down Elizabeth's face and she buried her head in her hands. When she finally looked up, there was such pain in her eyes that Michael could hardly bear it and without thinking he ran his hand lightly over her hair, saying, "Whist, now, the lieutenant died thinking of his happiness with you."

"Ah, but you see, Michael, I am trying to understand *how* I made him happy."

"Sure, and you and he would know that best, Elizabeth," murmured Michael. "But 'twas clear to all of us here that the lieutenant was a very lucky man to have such a good wife."

"And what is a good wife, Michael?"

Michael hesitated, puzzled by her question. "Why, one like yerself, who made a good home for him wherever ye were sent."

"I *loved* Thomas," she whispered fiercely.

"Of course ye did," he reassured her.

"What do you want in a wife, Michael, when you marry?"

Michael was taken aback by her question. "Em . . . I suppose what any mans wants: someone who loves me, who welcomes me warmly home at the end of a long day . . ."

"And someone who would welcome you to bed as eagerly as Mrs. Casey does the men?"

Michael sat back from her, his face reddening.

"Now I have embarrassed you and I am sorry. But wouldn't you want a wife to give herself to you passionately? Or is that something men would only expect from . . . laundresses?"

Michael remained silent. Elizabeth apologized again. "I am sorry, Michael. I have gone way beyond what is proper and the only excuse I have is my grief. You see the hardest thing about losing Thomas is that I am only beginning to realize how much I took from him and how little I gave him of myself in return."

"I have been with men when they died, Elizabeth. They don't lie on their deathbeds. Last words are always true words. You made Mr. Woolcott happy, Elizabeth, whatever you did or did not give him. That is the truth."

Elizabeth sobbed. "But that is what is so hard to accept. That I made him happy with what now seems to be so little."

Michael was beginning to understand the source of her grief. He struggled to find some way of relieving it.

"Elizabeth, a person might be capable of loving more and not knowing it until it is too late. But maybe people are also a little like . . ." Michael cast his eyes around as he tried to put clearly what he was only beginning to understand himself. *He* would not have been satisfied with the sort of marriage Elizabeth was describing, which would have been amusing at another time, since he had so envied Thomas Woolcott. But Lieutenant Woolcott had been happy. Michael's eyes came to rest on the crystal glasses and decanter in the cabinet.

"What if one person was like that jug, Elizabeth," he said, pointing to the crystal. "Full of love. And the other was like that glass, waiting to be filled. But there is more love in the jug than the glass can contain, isn't there? The glass would be happy with what it received, even if there was more brandy . . . I mean love . . ." Michael laughed. "I am getting all twisted here and maybe 'tis not the best way to put it, but do you see my meaning?"

Elizabeth sighed deeply. "I do, Michael, I do."

"Do ye see, even if Thomas had lived, he might not have been looking for much more than ye were giving."

"It is so hard, either way," she moaned.

" 'Twill be hard for a while," Michael whispered. "I wish it could be easier. Em, I'd better be going, or I'll be wakin' up a private."

He started to get up, but Elizabeth grasped his hands and pulled him down.

"Thank you, Michael," she said, her eyes lowered in embarrassment, "for letting me speak so frankly. You have become a good friend to me."

Michael squeezed her hands and got up. 'Twas not only her friend he wished to be, he was beginning to realize. "I am happy to offer you my friendship, Elizabeth," he said.

Elizabeth moved in with the Grays a week after Thomas was buried. All her furniture was put into storage except for Thomas's favorite chair, which she squeezed into the small bedroom in order to have something to remind her of their years together.

At first she was too dazed by grief to focus on her situation. The colonel was kind to her in a distracted way and Mrs. Gray treated her like the daughter she had always wanted. For the first few weeks, she spent her time resting and walking Orion.

It was not until the beginning of December that she began to feel in the way. Not that the Grays ever made her feel that way. In fact, when Mrs. Gray told Elizabeth how much she enjoyed the company of another woman, Elizabeth knew she was telling the truth. The colonel was very busy these days in his efforts to keep the fragile peace and his wife would have been alone at supper many nights had it not been for her guest.

But the morning Elizabeth heard the Grays' striker cursing Orion, she began to feel herself an imposition.

"Orion," she said later as they went for their daily walk around the stockade, "how could you repay the colonel's hospitality by stealing a ham?"

The dog only grinned up at her, his tongue hanging out

of his mouth, his eyes dancing as though he were remembering the thrill of getting away with his theft.

"What are we going to do, Orion?" she asked with real despair in her voice. The change in tone made the dog immediately responsive and he pushed his nose into her hand in an effort to comfort her.

"I can't stay with the Grays forever, although I suppose I am there for the winter," she admitted. "And I can't go back to Santa Fe and Nellie. The children are grown and gone and she has no money to support me. I have the pension, but I don't want to live with Nellie, Orion. I must find my own life."

Easily said, she thought. Not so easily done for a woman alone.

She was good with her needle. She supposed she could go to Santa Fe and hire herself out. With the pension and a small income she could eke out a living. But aside from Thomas's sister, she knew no one in the city. And she was used to the army. Despite the moving and the arbitrariness of the service, it had given her security and had been her life for the past six years. But the only way to stay at Fort Defiance was to marry another soldier or move into the laundresses' row, she thought with ironic humor. "Neither option greatly appeals to me, Orion," she told the dog. "Especially since the only offer I'd be likely to get would be from Mr. Cooper," she added with a shudder.

Cooper had made her uncomfortable even when Thomas was alive. He had always sought her out for dancing at a post party, and when they waltzed, his arm always snaked around her waist, pulling her even closer than her husband did. He had seemed sincere in his condolences though, she had to give him that. But he'd been calling too frequently for her comfort, even though his visits were short and respectful. She didn't think he had caused any gossip yet, but if he continued this pattern, soon it would look like his sympathy calls had turned into courting.

Sergeant Burke, on the other hand, had only called once or twice, to see that she was comfortably settled. He had seemed almost distant to her, considering the intimacy of their last conversation, and she was surprised at how much it affected her. He had promised to be her friend, but then had left her to her own devices and to the attentions of Lieutenant Cooper.

"I know it is irrational of me, Orion, to expect more from Sergeant Burke. He probably considers me well taken care of. And why *should* he concern himself with a superior officer's behavior. Or my future, for that matter." The only person really concerned about her future was herself and she had better get used to the idea.

Once Elizabeth had moved into the colonel's quarters, Michael knew he would have to stay away. One or two visits from a concerned acquaintance was appropriate, but he was a noncommissioned officer and not someone who could frequent the post commander's home.

Mr. Cooper was free, of course, to make social calls and Michael was in a helpless fury about it. How dare the oily bastard bother Elizabeth at a time like this? And why did Cooper have the freedom to visit while he did not? There wasn't much gossip yet, but there would be as time went on.

He had returned from a patrol once or twice when she was walking Orion and she had waved to him and he had lifted his hand in a half salute. She looked thin and tired, but he supposed that was only natural. The colonel's lady would make sure she got enough food and rest, of that he was sure.

He went to Mary Ann's occasionally, but her charms didn't work for him the way they had before. His initial attraction to both women had been only physical, but now that he had seen Elizabeth's grief, she was more to him than an attractive woman. She was a fellow human being who had awakened his sympathy and elicited affection. An affection that he had better ignore, he told himself, since he was only a noncommissioned officer and she a lieutenant's widow.

Chapter Eighteen

As Christmas approached, Elizabeth threw herself into Mrs. Gray's preparations to distract herself. The army wives had devised their own rituals for celebrating the holiday far from home and family. At Fort Defiance it was customary for the officers' wives to send fruit cakes to the enlisted men of their husbands' companies. Elizabeth had always made what her mother called a "black cake," dark with molasses and full of brandy-soaked raisins. The rich smells that filled the kitchen the week before Christmas made her grief for Thomas and her family sharper, and yet in some strange way they also comforted her with their familiarity.

She took herself off early for bed in the evenings and would sit in Thomas's chair and crochet gifts for the colonel and Mrs. Gray. She was working a delicate gray shawl for her hostess and a tightly woven dark blue scarf for the colonel. As she felt the wool slip through her fingers, she was reminded of Serena and not for the first time wondered if she would ever see her friend again.

She had received a small package from Thomas's sister and she was glad she had something to put out on the table along with their gifts for the traditional Christmas morning walk along the line. All the wives displayed their gifts from family and friends and walking into each officer's quarters made them all feel that the lovely gifts were for everyone. There was mulled punch to drink, and when the time came to visit the company barracks, Elizabeth, for the first time in weeks, was free for a while of the ever-present sensation of loss.

Michael met the company officers and their wives at the barracks door and led them to see the dining tables, which were laden with roasts and vegetables. On the center table were the cakes glistening with sugar and icing.

"The men wanted me to give you a very special thank you, Mrs. Woolcott," Michael said. "They did not expect anything this year, considering your circumstances."

"Please tell them it was just what I needed to do, Mich . . . Sergeant Burke."

"I'm new to the company, but I understand your cake is always the best, Mrs. Woolcott," he said with a smile.

"It is an old family recipe, Sergeant, which I learned from my mother. It feels good to share it with others."

"Sure, and it is always good to carry over the old traditions into the new ones."

"You must have had some different traditions in Ireland, Sergeant? Although perhaps they were hard to keep up when times got hard," she added, embarrassed that she had forgotten the reason for his emigration.

"We did our best even in hard times. And on the day after Christmas, we always hunted the wren."

"The wren?"

"On St. Stephen's Day. Though I doubt the wren had much to do with St. Stephen. 'Tis likely the custom goes back to pagan times. But we were always good in Ireland at keeping the old while embracing the new. The wren was our 'king' and he was killed and carried by the wren boys, who would beg from door to door."

Elizabeth frowned. "You actually killed a small bird?"

"And decorated him also," said Michael with a smile. "And sang him a song: 'The wren, the wren, the king of all birds, St. Stephen's Day was caught in the furze. Although he was little his honor was great, so come on, boys, and give us a treat.' I think the idea was that though something dies, something else comes back to life. Em, something like Christ, the new King, who died to bring us eternal life."

Elizabeth's eyes filled with tears. "It is hard for me to

believe in resurrection just now. I can't see anything coming out of Thomas's death."

" 'Tis hard in the moment, that I know," said Michael with quiet sympathy. "But I wish you a joyous Christmas, Mrs. Woolcott, and a New Year of coming back to life."

"That is a lovely wish, Sergeant Burke," said the colonel's wife, who came to stand next to them. "Come, Elizabeth, we must be off to our own dinner so the men can eat theirs," she said with a smile.

The Grays' table was almost as laden as the enlisted men's. The colonel always invited his bachelor officers to join them, so Lieutenant Cooper and Captain Lane were present. To her dismay, Elizabeth was seated next to Mr. Cooper and he was so kind and solicitous that she felt suffocated by his presence. He did nothing obvious, but she could feel his attention centered on her, an attention that went beyond sympathy.

They toasted Christmas and the coming year and then sang carols in the parlor. Elizabeth declined to join the chorus, saying she would rather listen, and she sat down next to Captain Lane, who confided in her he was absolutely tone-deaf, so he was sparing their ears.

She had to admit that Mr. Cooper had a fine voice and his tenor solo of "Away in a Manger" almost brought tears to her eyes. Almost, because although it was Thomas's favorite carol, Mr. Cooper kept gazing meaningfully at her as he sang and she could not give herself over to memories of her husband with another man so obviously working himself up to attempting to fill his place. She excused herself early and escaped to her bedroom without having to do more than say a general good night to all. She was afraid if she had stayed the lieutenant would have cornered her and offered her more of his unwanted "sympathy."

"I think Cooper is quite interested in Elizabeth. It would provide her with a neat solution to her problems, wouldn't it, my dear," said the colonel as he and his wife undressed for bed. "I don't like Cooper myself, but he is considered to be a fine-looking man. And Elizabeth would be able to stay with the army. She could do worse."

"If she married a rattlesnake, Charles!"

"Janet!"

"Charles!" his wife exclaimed at the same time. "How can you think that just because a few of the women like Cooper's brand of oily charm, he would be good for Elizabeth?"

"It is only that she cannot stay with us forever, Janet. And what other choice does she have?"

"She can stay with us as long as she needs to, I hope, Charles."

"Of course, my dear," said her husband, getting into bed and patting the space beside him. "You know I am happy for you to have the company. It is only that I don't imagine she will want to stay forever. She will want her own home and for that she must marry. Of course there's Captain Lane, but he's too old, don't you think?"

"And a confirmed bachelor. He'll never marry."

"Lieutenant Falkirk?"

"Too young and he has his eye on the surgeon's daughter."

"Susan? She's a mere child!"

"She's sixteen. Only a year younger than Elizabeth when she married Thomas Woolcott." Mrs. Gray climbed into bed and snuggled next to her husband. "No, I was thinking more of someone like Sergeant Burke."

"Burke? But he's only a noncommissioned officer, Janet. It would be a step down for Elizabeth."

"I think they have formed a friendship of sorts despite the difference in rank. I don't know what Elizabeth feels . . . probably nothing right now. But I have seen how the sergeant looks at her.

"The problem is, there isn't any opportunity for them to socialize . . . I wish I could think of something," she murmured as she drifted off to sleep.

Elizabeth got through the rest of the winter in a daze. It seemed as though some sort of veil hung between her and the rest of the world. She hardly noticed the frequency of Lieutenant Cooper's visits and responded to him the way she responded to everyone: kindly and politely, but with her real self in reserve.

Mrs. Gray was well aware of Elizabeth's benumbed state. She remembered the exhaustion of grief very well, for she had lost two children to the frontier, one from diphtheria, the other from a simple cut that had turned septic. The winter had been a good time for feelings to go underground. But it was time Elizabeth began to come back to life as the spring approached.

"I think it is time for a dance, Charles," Janet Gray told her husband one evening in March. "All of us need a release from wondering whether the peace will hold and what Governor Carleton has in store for the territory."

The colonel looked up from his book and smiled. "You always know just what the situation calls for, Janet. I will announce one for this Saturday evening."

"For noncommissioned officers as well, Charles," said Mrs. Gray innocently as she concentrated on her crewel work.

The colonel cleared his throat and his wife looked up at him, her sparkling eyes belying her matter-of-fact tone. "I so enjoyed my dance with Sergeant Burke, my dear, that I think it is time for another one."

"You think it is time for Elizabeth to have a waltz with him, Janet. You can't fool me. But Cooper has been very steady in his attentions, my dear."

"Much too steady, Charles, although Elizabeth is in such a daze, she hardly notices. Which he, self-centered idiot that he is, probably takes as encouragement."

"Now, Janet."

"Now, Charles. You know it is only in the privacy of our own home that I voice these opinions. I am the perfect post commander's wife in public." She put down her embroidery and pushing her spectacles down her nose, looked over at him. "Seriously, Charles, I am worried about Elizabeth. I know it has not been long since Thomas's death, but who knows what the spring and summer will bring to us? I am sure Michael Burke has some feeling for her, but what time will they have if the peace doesn't hold? In civilian life, Elizabeth would have the luxury of a long mourning period, but the army demands something different from its women."

"Since spring is almost here, I think I will wear my green gown," said the colonel's wife over tea later that week. "Your dark blue would do very well, Elizabeth. It would be only a small step away from black and will not offend anyone's sensibilities."

"I don't think I will be attending the dance, Janet," said Elizabeth calmly.

"No one will think it improper, my dear," said Mrs. Gray. "This is the frontier, after all, and not Boston."

"I'm not worried about gossip," said Elizabeth with a tired smile. "I just don't seem to have very much energy these days."

"Which is quite understandable. It has been a hard winter for all of us, especially you. But all the more reason to get out."

"Well, I will think about it," Elizabeth agreed.

It had been a cloudy week, but Saturday dawned bright and warm and for the first time in months, Elizabeth felt a spark of energy. She slipped out the door before breakfast and, leashing Orion, went for her first walk outside the fort since Thomas's death.

"It is good to see you out and about, Mrs. Woolcott, but don't you go too far," said the sergeant on guard duty.

"I am only going to walk the perimeter of the fort, Sergeant." Which she did three times. Outside she could focus on the sage, which was slowly turning a fresh green again, and the cottonwood trees, which were coming back to life in a haze of tender new leaves. Orion pulled at his leash regularly, looking up at her longingly, waiting for her to release him.

"I *know* you want to be chasing rabbits, Orion, but not today. The colonel wants us all to stay close to the fort and I must be back soon to help Mrs. Gray prepare refreshments for the dance."

The doors were already swinging open when she reached them and the wood detail was on its way out. Michael Burke was in front and merely gave her a quick smile and friendly nod as he rode by, but Corporal Mahoney called a friendly good morning to her, which she returned.

Sergeant Burke might have called out a greeting, she thought. After all, they were supposed to be friends. She felt shivers of anxiety replace her pique as she turned and watched them go. She hated to see anyone leave these days, for now there was always present the fear they might not return.

"You have good color, Elizabeth," said the colonel when she sat down to breakfast.

"Orion and I had a nice long walk and it certainly stimulated my appetite," she said smiling and looking down at her plate, which was heaped with eggs and browned potatoes. "What can I do to help you, Janet?" she asked.

"The baking is well under way in Mrs. Taggert's kitchen, but I would love it if you would make your shortbread cookies to go with the punch."

"I would be happy to," said Elizabeth, surprised to find it was true and not just a polite formula. She had not done much baking since she had moved in with the Grays. She paused for a moment, and surprising herself again, said, "I think that I may go to the dance after all, Janet. Are you sure the blue lawn would be appropriate?"

"I'm glad to hear you've changed your mind," said the colonel's wife matter-of-factly. "And your blue dress will be perfect."

Chapter Nineteen

Aside from the Grays' Sunday dinners, Elizabeth had not socialized since Thomas's death and she was very touched by the quiet expressions of sympathy and welcome that she received upon her arrival. For the first hour, she helped serve the punch, smiled at the compliments on her shortbread, and watched the others dance.

When Colonel Gray approached her and asked her to be his partner in the reel, she felt it would be ungrateful to refuse, after all his kindness, even though she had not intended to dance. She kept her reluctance to herself and, taking his hand, stepped out onto the dance floor. This would be her only dance, she told herself.

But then Captain Taggert came up, and not wishing to offend, she accepted his offer. By her third dance, with Master Sergeant Brimmer, she gave up worrying what people would think and began to enjoy herself for the first time in months.

"I am happy to see you dancing, Mrs. Woolcott," said Lieutenant Cooper, approaching her with two glasses of punch. "I hope I may have the next dance?"

Elizabeth could hardly refuse him, and after sipping their punch and chatting for a few minutes, they moved out onto the floor.

Of course, it would be a waltz, she thought as the lieutenant put his arm around her waist. He was a good dancer, she had to admit, expertly guiding her with just the slightest pressure of his hand on her back. And just as expertly pulling her just a little closer than she was comfortable with. His hand felt hot and she was sure it wasn't only from the heat of the room. But his desire did nothing for her except make her wish the dance was over. When the last strains of the music faded, he led her off the dance floor and into one of the darker corners, where a few chairs had been placed.

"Here, Mrs. Woolcott, rest yourself for a moment," he said as he pulled a chair close to hers and sat down.

She felt trapped by his closeness. The combination of his cologne, hair oil, and male scent was suffocating, and she hoped she wasn't visibly shrinking back from him.

Cooper cleared his throat nervously several times and then reached out and, taking her hand in his, placed it on his knee. It was the first time he had made any physical contact with her and she was mortified. Had she given him any encouragement? She didn't think so. He started stroking her hand and she had to exert every bit of self-control not to jerk her hand away. Yet she couldn't let it stay or he would definitely be getting the wrong idea. She very slowly raised her other hand to the back of her head and loosened a hairpin.

"Oh dear, all this dancing has played havoc with my hair," she exclaimed and, with a little laugh, gently disengaged her hand and fiddled with her hair. The musicians were striking up another waltz. Oh dear, thought Elizabeth, didn't anyone else wish to dance with her!

Michael had danced with the wives and daughters of the noncommissioned officers and then claimed a dance with Mrs. Gray, who smiled and told him that she had planned the dance just for the pleasure of being his partner.

"Sure and ye're as full of blarney as any Irishman," he teased with his most exaggerated brogue.

He had been very aware of Elizabeth the whole evening, watching her smile and serve punch, watching the color come back into her cheeks and the life in her step after the first few dances. He wanted to dance with her, of course, but was almost afraid to. His first dance with her had been when he hardly knew her and he could still re-

Marjorie Farrell

member the feel of her in his arms. Now that they knew one another as friends and now that he was even more aware of his physical response to her, perhaps it would be better to stay away. She was a widow now, to be sure, but an officer's widow and a recent one to boot.

Then he saw Cooper lead her off the floor and over to the corner. Surely she wouldn't go with him if they didn't have some sort of understanding? And why wouldn't they have by now after three months of the man having Sunday dinners with her! When he saw Cooper place her hand on his knee, he thought, There it is, boyo. And why should it be bothering you, after all? She's one of the prettiest women you know, 'tis true, and ye like her, but that's all. If she ends up marrying Cooper, it solves all her problems. She'll have rank and a home again and stay with the army.

He didn't know why he kept watching. Maybe to punish himself or convince himself he had no chance. Not that he really wanted one, mind you ... And then he saw her slip her hand out of Cooper's and start fooling with her hair. At the same time the band struck up another waltz.

He was in front of her before he knew what he was doing. He bowed very stiffly and formally and begged for the honor of the dance. She looked up at him with such a look of relief in her eyes and Cooper looked at him with such fury that he almost laughed out loud.

"I hope I wasn't interrupting anything between you and Mr. Cooper," he said after a few times around the floor. "But I haven't seen you for a while, Mrs. Woolcott, and I didn't want to let the music go to waste."

Of course, he had interrupted something, and she had been so relieved to see someone and happy that the someone was Michael Burke, but for him to mention it annoyed her.

"There was nothing to interrupt, Sergeant Burke," she said very coolly. "And if you haven't seen me, surely that was a matter of your choice." She didn't know where it had come from, this sudden anger. She should be angry at Lieutenant Cooper. She *was* angry at Lieutenant Cooper.

But what business was it of Michael Burke's what she did or didn't do with the lieutenant. Especially since he had been remarkably absent from her life and after she had thought they were friends!

"There is a greater demand for wood in winter, as ye know, Mrs. Woolcott. Our detail has been out early and back late," Michael answered just as coolly, stung by her response. He had thought they had reached a level of friendly intimacy, but perhaps that had only been due to her grief over her husband's death. And a noncommissioned officer could hardly come calling at the colonel's quarters, which she should know very well!

Elizabeth was immediately ashamed of herself. She was furious at Cooper and afraid to tell him, so here she was, taking it out on Sergeant Burke. She relaxed a little in his arms and, looking up at him, said, "I am sorry, Sergeant Burke. There was no need to take my bad mood out on you."

"I should not have pried into what is not my business," he apologized. "And I thought you had already called me Michael, Mrs. Woolcott," he added.

"I will continue if you call me Elizabeth."

"'Tis lovely to see you dancing again, Elizabeth." He wanted to say, 'tis lovely to be dancing with you, for it was. She smelled of rosewater and French soap and she moved so sweetly under the soft pressure of his hand. Under that Boston stiffness, she was a soft woman, Elizabeth Woolcott. And a desirable one.

"I was not going to come," Elizabeth admitted. "I thought it would not be respectful to Thomas's memory."

"I am sure the lieutenant would have wanted you to be enjoying life again."

"I am sure he would," she agreed, ducking her head so that he could not see the tears that had sprung to her eyes. But would he have wanted her to be enjoying this waltz so much, Elizabeth wondered. The pressure of Mr. Cooper's hand had only made her feel hot and sticky. The warmth emanating from Michael's hand felt different, felt as though she were being held with some tenderness, not just the hard wanting she had always sensed in Cooper.

The icy cold of winter was gone. The veil of nonfeeling seemed to have lifted. She was very much awake again and aware of how good it felt to be held in Michael Burke's arms.

When the music ended, they stepped back from one another quickly and Michael stammered out a thank you.

"It was good to see you again, Michael," Elizabeth said shyly.

"I'll be keepin' my eye out for you and the mighty Orion now that it is good weather," he said with a smile, and leading her over to the Grays, he left her without a backward glance.

What had she expected? That he would ask to call on her? Did she want anyone to come calling? Not as a lover. She wasn't ready to love again. She was beginning to wonder if she had ever been ready to love a man as completely as a woman loves. But he would have been very welcome as a friend.

Michael had tried very hard the week after the dance to keep his mind on his duties and off Mrs. Elizabeth Woolcott. He had visited Mary Ann in the hope that a night in her arms would help distract him. But in the end, he had left early, feeling guilty both for being there and causing the disappointed look in Mary Ann's eyes.

When he was out with his men, he found it easier to keep his mind from wandering back to his waltz with Elizabeth and how lovely it had been to have her in his arms.

The peace was holding, but the renegade attack on the supply train had made everyone more vigilant. A few days after the dance, while out on duty, he noticed the small band of Navajo approaching at the same time as his men.

"Spratt, you be sure to keep yer hand off yer revolver this time," he said calmly as they all watched the approaching riders.

"Yes, sir."

Michael breathed a sigh of relief when he recognized

Antonio's bay, and kicking up Lightning Jack, rode out to meet him.

"It is good to see you, my friend," he said as he pulled the mule to a halt. "What brings you this close to the fort?"

"My wife has sent me on an errand. Her niece will be celebrating her *kinaalda* in two days' time and my wife promised to invite Mrs. Woolcott. I've had my men watch for you so that I could deliver the message."

Michael hesitated. "You heard of the attack on the supply train a few months ago?"

Antonio frowned. "One of those fools tried to take refuge with my uncle and we drove him away. We don't need any *ladrones* around us now."

"There was an officer killed, you know." Antonio nodded. "It was Lieutenant Woolcott, Elizabeth's husband."

"I am sorry to hear that."

"So, while I am sure she will be honored by the invitation," he continued respectfully, "she may not feel up to attending."

"My wife would be disappointed but would also understand. We are lucky to have Colonel Gray in charge," he added after a short pause.

"And Manuelito," said Michael. "They have both worked hard not to respond to isolated acts of foolishness."

"The ceremony is four days long," said Antonio, "and the family has agreed to a guest on the last day. If Mrs. Woolcott wishes to come, she can meet me at the mouth of the canyon five days from now. I will wait until noon."

"The colonel will never allow her to go without an escort, you know."

Antonio frowned. "It was hard to get some people to agree to having a *bilagaana* present at all. We can't have a troop of soldiers come riding in!"

"She can't come alone."

"I know *that, bilagaana*. You must escort her."

"That may work. If I got permission from the colonel and was released from wood detail."

"It is a good half day's ride from the canyon. You will have to stay overnight."

"All right. I'll talk to Mrs. Woolcott and if she wishes to go, I'll ask the colonel."

"What is the news from the south," asked Antonio.

"You know the Mescaleros have been subdued?"

"Yes, we heard that our cousins had given in."

"I have heard nothing official, you understand," Michael continued, "but the rumor is that Carleton has Bosque Redondo in mind for more than the Apache."

"My uncle is afraid of that too. We will never go there, *bilagaana*. Tell the colonel that."

"I think he already knows," said Michael with an ironic smile.

They sat quietly facing one another for a moment and then Michael turned his mule. "If ye don't see us by noon five days from now, then ye'll know we won't be coming," he said and waved as he rode off.

That evening the colonel was drinking his after-dinner glass of port and Elizabeth and Mrs. Gray were sipping coffee when a knock sounded on their door.

They could hear voices and then their striker came into the parlor.

"Begging your pardon, sir. Master Sergeant Burke is at the door, asking to see the colonel."

Colonel Gray looked over at his wife and raised his eyebrows.

"Please send the sergeant in, Corporal," said Mrs. Gray.

"Yes, ma'am."

Michael turned his hat in his hand nervously as he stood in the entrance to the parlor. He felt very much out of place as he took in the cozy scene.

"I am very sorry to have disturbed you at home, sir," he said. "But it is a matter concerning Mrs. Woolcott."

"Come in, Sergeant, come in." The colonel motioned Michael over to an armchair and Michael sat down on the edge.

"Would you like a sip of port, Sergeant Burke?"

"No, sir. Thank you, sir."

"You may relax, Burke," said the colonel with a smile. "Now what is this business that concerns Mrs. Woolcott?"

Michael looked over at Elizabeth. "Em, I met Antonio today a few miles from the fort. He wanted me to deliver an invitation to you, Mrs. Woolcott."

"An invitation?" said Mrs. Gray.

"It seems his wife had invited Mrs. Woolcott to a family celebration, ma'am. He didn't know about the lieutenant's death. After I told him, he said his wife would understand if Mrs. Woolcott didn't come."

"What kind of celebration is this, Elizabeth?" asked Mrs. Gray with great curiosity.

"It is to celebrate a young girl's coming of age. I am very touched that Serena remembered." She hesitated.

"It is quite an honor to be invited, Elizabeth. Would you wish to go?" asked the colonel.

"I had completely forgotten it in all that has happened. But I did very much want to, weeks ago."

The colonel took another sip of his port. "You would need an escort, of course," he said thoughtfully, "should you accept."

Michael cleared his throat nervously. "Antonio said it would be impossible for her to attend with a troop of soldiers, sir. He suggested that I would be an acceptable escort. To the Navajo, at least. It would be for the last day of the ceremony and we would have to stay overnight, Mrs. Woolcott," he added, looking over at her.

"What do you think, Janet?" the colonel asked his wife.

"It does seem a little risky, Charles. Although Antonio and his wife are utterly trustworthy, of course, who knows who else is out there. On the other hand, it would be a demonstration of trust on your part and could help strengthen the peace." She turned to Elizabeth. "What do you think, my dear? Do you still wish to go?"

Elizabeth hesitated. "So much has changed," she murmured. "But Thomas had thought it a good thing . . ." She lifted her eyes to Michael's face. "I agree with Antonio:

I can't bring a troop with me. I trust that Sergeant Burke can keep me safe."

"I wouldn't even be suggesting it if I didn't think it was safe," Michael assured them.

The colonel nodded. "Then it is settled," he said. "I'll ask Lieutenant Cooper to release you from duty for a few days."

"Thank you, sir." Michael stood up and bowed to the ladies.

"Good night, Sergeant Burke," said Mrs. Gray.

"Good night, ma'am. Sorry to be disturbing yer evening."

"Not at all, man, not at all," said the colonel. "I'll walk you to the door."

"You are sure of her safety, then, Burke?" he asked as soon as they were out of earshot.

"Absolutely, sir. And I think it important that we learn a little of each other's ways. I've noticed we do a lot of teaching of ours and very little learning of theirs," he added with a wry smile.

"You're a good man, Burke. I only wish more men thought like you." Colonel Gray watched Michael walk down the line and added to himself, "Especially our fine governor."

Chapter Twenty

Three days later, Elizabeth was up before the bugler blew reveille. She had packed her paints and brushes, in case she had the opportunity to record anything. She had also packed her best linen blouse, so that she could change into it to when they arrived. She didn't want it to be thought that she lacked respect. She wanted to bring a gift for Serena, something that would express her gratitude for their friendship. And a gift for her niece. She had so little and there had been nothing in the sutler's store besides the obvious sugar and coffee. She looked through her jewelry box. There were a few pieces of her mother's that the Comancheros had not found and somehow it felt right to wear her mother's amethyst earrings to this special occasion. She unwrapped a small cameo brooch, admiring the white profile carved out of pink shell. It was very . . . *bilagaana,* she supposed, with a smile. But the colors were the colors of the country around them and it was precious to her so it would make an appropriate gift for her friend. For her niece, she chose a soft paisley shawl. She wrapped the cameo and placed it in her buckskin bag, and the shawl she folded with her blouse.

"It will be cold at night, Elizabeth," said Mrs. Gray when she joined her for breakfast. "You had better take a jacket with you. I hear the ceremonies go on all night."

"I think my riding jacket will be fine, Janet. It is wool."

"I hope so."

They were just finishing their tea when Michael was admitted.

"Good morning, ladies. I am sorry to disturb ye, but I'll be ready to leave within the half hour."

"I just have to feed Orion. I will meet you down at the stables in twenty minutes, Sergeant."

"Very good, ma'am."

Sergeant Burke was riding Frost, and Elizabeth, who had only seen him on muleback, aside from his racing, had to admit that he looked quite different on his mare than he did on a shavetail.

"So, Antonio's men will be waiting at the box canyon, Sergeant?"

"We agreed that they would wait until noon. If we haven't arrived by then, they'll understand you weren't able to come."

Elizabeth turned in her saddle and said, "I very much appreciate your willingness to do this, Michael."

"'Tis my willingness to follow orders, Elizabeth. Though I must confess I am grateful to have a rest from wood detail," he added with a grin. "Now what is this celebration we are going to?"

"It is called a *kinaalda* and it is being held to celebrate Serena's niece's coming of age."

"She must think a lot of you to have offered the invitation."

"We have become friends. As I think you have with her husband?"

"So here we are, the two of us, off to a heathen ceremony in the eyes of all at Fort Defiance."

"I can't think of Antonio or Serena as heathen, can you, Sergeant?"

"Sure and *I* don't, but I am surprised that a proper eastern lady like yerself doesn't."

"I am from Boston, Michael, which I assure you is a very enlightened place. There is strong feeling against slavery there, and much concern for the American Indian, I'll have you know. There is a tradition of freedom that goes back to the Puritans."

"And what do Bostonians think of the Mass, then, Elizabeth?"

Elizabeth blushed. She had been brought up to believe that Catholic ritual was superstitious barbarism.

"I have already admitted to you, Michael, that there is some intolerance to certain groups in Boston."

Michael snorted.

"Oh, all right. I confess that to me, going to this ceremony feels not very different from choosing to go to a Catholic ritual. They both would seem strange to me. But I hope I am open enough not to fear things once I have come to know them."

"Like Irishmen and Navajo?" Michael said teasingly.

"At least Navajo," Elizabeth responded, the twinkle in her eye belying her words. "Perhaps some Irishmen," she added.

"Ah, 'tis relieved I am to hear it, darlin'."

Elizabeth touched the sides of her horse with her heels and guided her into a smooth canter. Sergeant Michael Burke was an uncomfortable man to be around. He would not let her old frameworks go unchallenged and his easy intimacy left her both embarrassed and wanting something from him that she could not even name.

Frost caught up easily and they cantered for a mile or so until they caught sight of the canyon, when Michael pulled his mare down to a walk. As Elizabeth fell in beside him, he pointed out the small group of men waiting at the canyon's mouth.

"There they are."

"I am so glad," she said spontaneously. "I was a little afraid they might have forgotten. Or changed their minds about letting a *bilagaana* come to such a special occasion."

"I see you know a Navajo word or two, Elizabeth. The Diné will appreciate that."

"As do you, Michael."

"Only a few, I am afraid. 'Tis a hard language to learn."

As they drew near, Antonio rode up to meet them. He greeted Elizabeth first and then Michael. "It will take us a few hours to get there so I am glad you are here early," he said. "Today is the Biji ... the Special Day, and I don't want to miss much."

Antonio's men rode up and fell in behind them as he turned west.

"What does that mean," asked Elizabeth. "The 'Special Day'?"

"*Kinaalda* is four days and nights long. On the Biji, the fourth day, the *kinaalda* runs, as she has every day. But she also helps make the *aalkan,* the corn cake. And on the fourth night there is singing till dawn. You are lucky to be coming to this *kinaalda,* for Blue Mule is the singer and he is a great singer. He is my wife's grandfather's brother," he added proudly.

"So the ceremony has already been going on three nights and days," said Michael. "Jesus, and I thought a High Mass was long!"

"It is how it must be done, as the Holy People told us. Before there were even human beings, there were the Holy People. And *Asdzaa nadleehe.* Changing Woman. Though in some stories she is also White Shell Woman." Antonio fell silent. Elizabeth wanted to ask him questions, but his silence seemed to indicate he was finished with explanations, at least for a time.

When he spoke again, it was only to say, "I could say a lot more, but I will leave that for my wife."

The ride was long and by the time they reached the family hogan, Elizabeth was hot, tired, and almost dizzy from the hours in the sun. As they got closer, she was relieved to see that they were not the only ones arriving late. Several families were just dismounting and two young men were unloading stacks of firewood from two small burros.

"My wife's niece is inside the hogan, mixing the *aalkan,*" said Antonio, leading Elizabeth over to the shade of a small cottonwood. "Why don't you sit out here and I will get you some food and water." Elizabeth was very grateful to him, for she had felt almost like fainting on first dismounting. It was wonderful to be out of the sun and the mention of water made her realize how thirsty she was despite the fact that she had had some several times during their journey. Food, she wasn't sure of, since her stomach felt a little queasy, but when Antonio returned with what looked like tortillas and a pottery jar full of water, she smiled at him gratefully.

"This is just what I needed. Thank you."

"There is a lot of food cooking, but you looked like you weren't so hungry," he said with a sympathetic smile.

"The sun was too much for me," Elizabeth admitted, "even though I did have a hat. But that reminds me, Antonio," she added shyly. "I brought a clean blouse to wear. I don't want to be here all hot and dusty."

"I'll bring your bag over, Elizabeth," said Michael, who had just joined them. "But first get some of that water into ye. Ye're too red-faced and hot-looking for my liking."

"Yes, *sir*," said Elizabeth.

"Sure, and I am only a sergeant, ma'am," he said with mock humility. "But I don't want ye to be getting heat stroke," he added seriously.

The water and bread made her feel better, but when she closed her eyes for a few minutes after eating and drinking, she drifted off to the sound of soft, guttural Navajo.

When she awoke a half hour later, she was revived and sat up and looked around curiously. The hogan was like others she had seen, except perhaps a bit larger. The women were just coming out and she was about to wave to Serena when she realized that they were part of the ceremony, for they were followed by a young girl.

In front of the hogan, a little to the side, she noticed a round, shallow pit which had been lined with corn husks. The women carried large containers and each one poured what looked like corn meal mush into the pit. When they were finished, Serena covered the batter with more corn husks, ending with a cross made out of four husks woven together. Then she stepped back and the young girl took corn meal from a basket and sprinkled it on top. Then it was all covered with husks and earth and live coals. Elizabeth was startled when only a few minutes later Serena's niece gave a loud, sudden shout and, heading east, ran off followed by girls and boys and several adults. This must be the running she had heard about.

"I am happy to see you, my friend," said Serena as she came over to where Elizabeth was sitting.

Elizabeth stood up and smiled. "I am honored to be here. Are you busy, or do you have time to explain some things to a very confused *bilagaana?*"

"I am ready to sit and rest," said her friend with a tired smile and she sat down, gesturing to Elizabeth to sit beside her. "I have to tell you that while I am happy you are here and so are my family, some Diné are not so pleased. They don't like the idea of a *bilagaana* at a Diné ceremony."

"I can understand that. Are you sure it is all right with your family?"

"Of course. We all think it is important to have friends close by at such a time."

"Thank you," said Elizabeth softly. She reached over and pulled her saddlebags in front of her. "I need to change my blouse at some point, Serena," she said, "but first, I brought a few gifts. Something for you and something for your niece."

Serena sat quietly while Elizabeth pulled out the paisley shawl. "This is for the *kinaalda.*" Serena smiled at the accented Navajo. She fingered the shawl and admired the fineness of the wool and the jewel-like colors. Elizabeth pulled out her buckskin bag and, opening it, shook the tissue-wrapped cameo into her lap. She unwrapped it carefully, and laying it in her open hand, held it out to her friend. "This was my mother's brooch. I would like you to have it, Serena. It seemed like the right thing to bring to this ceremony."

Serena had never seen such a piece of jewelry. Instead of the suggestion of something, there was a head of a woman carved very realistically.

"It is a cameo. They are very popular among *bilagaana* women," said Elizabeth shyly. "It is carved out of shell."

The Navajo woman's eyes lit up. "You could not have brought anything better, my friend. White and coral: good colors for a *kinaalda*. And it is doubly special because it was your mother's. Would you like it to be part of the ceremony?"

Suddenly Elizabeth knew that this was absolutely the right place for her to be, the right time, and the right gift. For her mother's brooch to be a part of this meant something, although she could not explain her feeling.

"Yes, I would."

"I will put it with the other jewelry and my niece will wear it tomorrow when she races."

"But I meant for you to have it."

"Oh, don't worry, I'll get it back. The women only loan their jewelry to the *kinaalda*. Things that are rich and special. I have already put a turquoise necklace my husband gave me in the basket. But this is also special to me."

"Biji?"

Serena laughed. "Yes, the Special Day. Antonio must have told you."

"Yes, but not nearly enough."

Serena scooted her bottom back against the tree. "Come, I will tell you the story."

Chapter Twenty-one

"A long, long time ago, *Altse hastin* ... you would call him First Man, saw a dark cloud covering Ch'ool'i'i, the Giant Spruce Mountain. That cloud covered it to the very bottom and he decided he'd better go and find out what was happening. He set out singing, he surrounded himself with song, and when he got to Ch'ool'i'i, he still sang. And as he climbed, he sang."

Elizabeth rested against the tree. Serena's voice was beginning to "sing," she thought as she fell into the story's rhythm.

"When he reached the place where the peak of the mountain met the sky, lightning was flashing everywhere and he heard a baby crying. He could not see because of the dark cloud and the lightning and the bright colors of a huge rainbow which showered the peak, but he kept walking toward the baby's cry. When he got to where it seemed to be coming from, the rain stopped, the clouds blew away, and the rainbow became softer. And at his feet was a small turquoise figure, no bigger than a baby, but carved like a woman. He carried it back to his wife, *Altse asdzaa,* First Woman, and asked her to take care of it."

Elizabeth wanted to know how a turquoise figure could cry, and if it could, why did it sound like a baby, but look like a woman? But she did not want to interrupt the flow of her friend's story.

"A few days later, First Man and First Woman heard the "wu'hu'huhu" of *Haashch'eeltii*—Talking God, the *bilagaana* would call him. He told them to come to Chool'i'i twelve nights from then. And so twelve nights later they went and climbed by way of a holy trail until they almost reached the top. There they found Growling God and . . ." Serena hesitated. One should tell the story true, she thought, but how could she explain all the others to her friend. For this time, she would try to make it easier for her friend. "Nilchi, the wind. And the Daylight People, who also had a figure of white shell. Talking God laid a buckskin down with the head facing west and on it they laid those two figures with their heads facing west and then he placed a buckskin over them with its head facing east and all the Holy People formed a circle and began to sing." Serena turned to Elizabeth. "The song they sang is the same song the *hataali*, the singer, will sing tonight. They are very holy songs. You are lucky to have a chance to hear them."

Elizabeth nodded. If she thought at all about what Serena was saying, the story was too different from anything she knew. Anything familiar. It sounded like the Holy People were gods, but maybe not. After all, there was someone *called* Talking God. It was better not to think, but just to listen.

"The Talking God and the Growling God lifted the buckskin so Nilchi could blow through it three times. And when they lifted the buckskins, the figure of turquoise was *Asdzaa nadleehe* and the figure in white shell was *Yool gai asdzaa*. Changing Woman and White Shell Woman."

"So the wind brought them to life," said Elizabeth.

"Yes, the same wind that comes out of us when we breathe and speak. When it stops blowing through us, we die."

Elizabeth's face lit up. "Serena, we have this wind too. We call it the Holy Spirit. Although," she continued thoughtfully, "someone could be alive in his body and not have the spirit moving through him."

Serena said matter-of-factly, "Nilchi blows through everyone when they are alive."

"Well, then, I suppose there are differences." Elizabeth

was disappointed, for she wanted to find something familiar, something the same in what they believed.

"You look troubled, Elizabeth. Isn't it all right that we believe differently?"

"Yes," she answered slowly. But the idea was hard for her. Her whole life had been based on the belief that only those who thought as she did were right or good. Yet clearly Serena was a good woman, as was her husband. As was Sergeant Burke. She had never been directly unkind to anyone different from her. For the most part, she had treated people the same, even if she had thought them ignorant. She had never looked down on Indians. She had sympathized with their plight, as she had heard her parents talk about it with friends. But she had not really understood that they had heartfelt beliefs about the divinity. Maybe divinity was not the right word, she thought, but the Divine.

"This is a beautiful story, Serena," she said finally. "But I still don't quite understand its connection to the ceremony."

"It is a *much* longer story," said the Navajo woman with a grin, "and I don't have the time to tell it all now. Changing Woman became the mother of Hero Twins, who made the earth safe for the five-fingered people to arrive. And before she left for her hogan in the west, she had a ceremony which she gave us to perform for a maiden when she becomes a woman. A ceremony which brings Changing Woman to us through the *kinaalda*."

"How do you know exactly when it is time for this ceremony?"

Serena looked at Elizabeth in surprise. "Why, isn't it the same with all women? With her *kenasha,* her first . . ." Serena didn't know the word for it in English. "It happens every month. Her first blood."

Elizabeth blushed and turned away.

"Isn't it the same with the *bilagaana* then? That this time is important? That the *kenasha* is a thing to be proud of?"

"No, Serena. I have always thought it something to be ashamed of."

"Why, what happened when you had your first blood?"

What happened? thought Elizabeth. It was two months after her father and mother had been killed. She had been with Nellie Woolcott for six weeks and when she woke up one morning with her thighs streaked with blood, she was terrified. She had been huddled under the covers and when Nellie came in all she could do was sob and shake. Perhaps her mother had been bleeding like this before the Comancheros had ... If she went on bleeding like this, would men know? Would they then attack her in the same way? Nellie had finally gotten it out of her and had been very kind. She had patted Elizabeth's shoulder and showed where there were rags she could use. But Elizabeth could tell that she didn't want to speak of it again. That it was something to be hidden, something not talked about. Certainly not something to be *celebrated.*

What could she tell Serena? She cleared her throat nervously. "When I had my first, um, monthly, it was right after my parents were killed. My mother ... she was raped. I saw her private parts ... they were all bloody ..." Elizabeth was trembling violently. "We *bilagaana* women, we don't talk about these things," she was finally able to get out.

Elizabeth was crying and when Serena saw this she put her arm around her. It must have been awful to see a mother like that. And to have no mother on her own *kinaalda.* But even if her mother had lived, it didn't sound like *bilagaana* women had much pride in their womanhood. No wonder Elizabeth always felt like a young girl to her.

"I am very sorry that was such a bad time for you, my friend. I think it was very good you have come here. It was right that I wanted you to. I think Changing Woman wants you here."

Elizabeth let herself relax in Serena's arms. She had no idea what she believed about Changing Woman, but it felt very good to have this woman friend hear her story and hold her close.

* * *

By the time Serena's niece and all those running with her returned, it was time for supper. Serena went down to help the other women and Elizabeth sat by the tree, watching with great curiosity all the activity.

Sergeant Burke, who had been over with Antonio, came over to where she was sitting, carrying two bowls full of stew.

"We can eat here, Elizabeth. But Antonio has invited us to eat with them."

"I feel such an outsider," Elizabeth confessed. "The more Serena tells me of the ceremony, the more I wonder if I should have come."

"She invited you, so of course you should have come. But I understand yer feelings completely, since I feel even more of an intruder, being a man. And a few of the people aren't very happy to have us here. They may as well be wearing signs, 'No *bilagaana* welcome!' " said Michael with a smile. "And I can't blame 'em. But Antonio and his wife know that things are changing. The *bilagaana* won't go away, so surely it is good to have some of them here who want to understand."

Elizabeth stood up and brushed off her skirt. "Well, Sergeant Burke, give me your arm and we'll go join Antonio."

"That's me girl," said Michael.

Elizabeth sat next to Serena, and Michael joined Antonio. No eyes were lifted to her face, but she felt as though all attention was on her.

The stew was delicious, as was the tortillalike bread she dipped into it.

"This is delicious, Serena," she said, trying to pretend she was at someone's dinner table.

Her friend said something quickly in Navajo to the other women. One raised her eyes shyly, nodded her head, and then dropped her gaze to her own bowl before Elizabeth could even smile at her.

"Could you tell your sister that I am very grateful to be here."

Serena spoke again in Navajo, this time to the woman next to her.

Her sister replied, looking first at Serena and then giving an appreciative nod to Elizabeth.

"What did she say?"

"That it was a good sign that a *bilagaana* woman appreciates the importance of this ceremony."

"Tell her that she has a lovely daughter, who is also very strong if she can run that long."

Serena's sister smiled when Elizabeth's compliments were translated and then said something quickly.

"She wonders if *bilagaana* women are strong enough to run like that?"

Elizabeth grinned. "Some of us, perhaps."

There was more back-and-forth conversation between the sisters and then Serena turned to Elizabeth. "What about you? Could you run like that?"

"Why, I don't know. I do a lot of walking, but run for a half hour or more?"

"My sister invites you to join the runners in the morning for the *kinaalda's* last race."

"Me!"

Her friend's sister spoke again and although Elizabeth couldn't understand the words, she could the tone: kind, but challenging.

"It is a big thing for her to do, to invite you," said Serena. "Some of the women don't approve."

Elizabeth could tell that from the muttering going on around her.

"Tell her I am honored by her invitation. I will run."

When Serena repeated the words in Navajo, most of the women nodded their heads approvingly.

"I must tell you, Elizabeth," said Serena with a teasing smile on her face, "that most of us do not think a *bilagaana* woman can do this."

"They are probably right! Especially in my riding boots," exclaimed Elizabeth.

"Don't worry, we'll find a pair of moccasins for you."

One of the women gathered up all the bowls, and Elizabeth saw that as the men finished they were beginning to build up the fire over the pit.

Serena came over to her and said apologetically, "I will

be busy with the women and inside the hogan for the singing. But here is a blanket for you to put under you. Get some rest, my friend. You will need it for tomorrow."

"What happens now?"

"Now, many of us will go inside. The *hataali* will lead the singing, though some of the songs only he can sing. He begins with the Hogan Songs, which were first sung by Talking God."

Elizabeth looked over at the hogan and noticed that a blanket had been hung from the door. Serena patted her shoulder and said, "Good luck on your running tomorrow, Elizabeth," and turned to go.

"Wait, Serena. How will I know what to do?"

"You'll hear the shout, like this afternoon. Then all you have to do is follow the runners. Unless you are going to try to beat them all," she added teasingly.

"I will be very happy just to keep up with them!"

"Then I will see you at dawn."

Elizabeth took the blanket and carried it back to the cottonwood. She wasn't tired yet, and so she sat up, arms wrapped around her knees as she watched the stars come out. She heard a step beside her and looked up. It was Sergeant Burke.

"Sit down, Michael. I am trying to find Orion," she added with a smile.

"And how is the mighty hunter's namesake?"

"Behaving quite well, thanks to your advice."

Michael sat down next to her. Her face was lifted to scan the sky and he was struck by the purity of her profile.

"I hear you'll be getting a little exercise in the morning, Elizabeth."

Elizabeth looked over at him. "I think I must be crazy to try, but it didn't seem right to turn down the invitation."

"Ye were right. 'Tis a great privilege for both of us to be here and I'm glad to see you becoming part of it." Michael hesitated. "Ye lost yer mother early, I've heard. And in a terrible way."

Elizabeth nodded, and face set, continued to stargaze.

"I can sympathize with ye. I lost me own ma when I was ten."

"How did she die, Michael?" Elizabeth asked softly.

Michael hesitated. He had never talked of this to anyone before, not since he had left Ireland. "She died of a fever." Elizabeth started to murmur a word of sympathy, when he continued. "Brought on by starvation, ye see."

Elizabeth drew in an audible breath. "Starvation?"

"Aye. Ye were too young to know of it, but there was a great famine in Ireland when I was a boy. Me ma died and me baby sister, and over a million of us."

"A million!"

"Oh yes. We didn't all come over here, we dirty Irish," said Michael bitterly. "Most of us died."

"It is hard to comprehend so much death, Michael."

"Well, it is years past now."

"And the rest of your family? Did they come to America too?"

"No, they just sent me, so that at least one Burke would survive."

"Did they all die then?" Elizabeth asked, almost not wanting to hear the answer.

"No," answered Michael with a heavy sigh. "Me sister Caitlin lived. But she's never married or had the children she wanted. And me da's still alive, though getting on in years." Michael paused. "I keep saying to meself that one day, I'll go home, at least for a visit, but the army keeps me too busy and too poor," he added with a bitter laugh.

Elizabeth wanted to say something comforting, anything, but not one word came to mind. It was one thing to watch your family die, but quite another to be surrounded by the death of all your people. She couldn't imagine it.

"I am sorry, Michael," she finally said. "It is a poor thing to say, isn't it?" she added, turning to him with tears in her eyes.

"Now, I didn't mean to make ye cry, Elizabeth."

"You didn't. I have been close to tears all afternoon."

Michael wanted to put his arm around her and draw her

close, but he resisted and pointed up. "There he is, the aould Irishman himself."

Elizabeth followed his pointing finger and imitated his brogue. "O'Royan?"

"Indeed. See his belt?"

"Yes, yes, I see it. But with all these stars how does anyone find the constellations!"

It was getting cold, and Elizabeth wrapped her arms around herself to keep from shivering.

Michael took his own blanket and shook it out. "Here, Elizabeth, ye'd better have this around ye."

"I can't take your blanket, Michael."

"Don't be silly. I have another in me pack. I'll be fine. 'Tis you who doesn't want to be cold and stiff in the morning." He placed the blanket around her shoulders, and as she pulled it closed he realized that more than anything in the world he wanted to pull her close to his heart. She was a small woman, but there was a hidden strength in her that he admired. And at the same time a young girl that needed comforting.

He stood up and said, "Well, I'd best be getting settled meself. Though when the singing starts, we may not get much sleep anyway."

Elizabeth watched as he disappeared into the darkness and she shivered again, this time not from cold, but from the feeling that something had happened between them, something she was afraid to name. She spread the blanket underneath her and lay down on her back admiring the starry sky above her and trying not to think of anything else.

Chapter Twenty-two

Elizabeth had drifted off under her blankets when the singing started and she was jerked awake.

It was unlike anything she had ever heard. She would not, in fact, have called it singing. Perhaps chanting was a better description. It was repetitive and to her ears, she was forced to admit, monotonous. She had expected to hear drums, but there was no accompaniment. It was one voice she heard at first and she assumed it must be the *hataali*. The song he was singing seemed to go on and on and although there was repetition, it was hard to follow.

She lifted herself up on one elbow to hear better, but finally she just lay back, and giving up her effort to understand the song, she let it wash over her. She finally fell into a fitful sleep. She would wake out of a dream from time to time and listen to the singing, then fall back into nowhere. At one point, close to dawn, she awoke from a dream in which a woman dressed in a soft blanket dress bound with a rainbow-colored sash approached her with a kind look on her face. As the woman got closer, Elizabeth noticed that she was wearing loops of turquoise and in the center of one of the necklaces hung her mother's cameo. She was filled with the most intense longing, wanting this woman to enfold her in her arms. She reached out as they approached one another and realized that the woman she had thought young and beautiful was gray-haired and feeble. Elizabeth wanted to hold *her* in her own arms and cried out when the woman turned away again, in a circle from east to west. As she approached again, she was once more the beautiful young woman. But she never got close enough to Elizabeth to hold her, and Elizabeth awoke, her chest aching with unshed tears.

She could not go back to sleep and so she sat up against the cottonwood and wrapped the blanket around her. The stars were fading as dawn approached and she was gradually able to make out the hogan. The singing was still going on, but by now she was used to it. She looked to her left and there was Sergeant Burke's long, lean form, under a blanket, his head pillowed on his saddle. Her eyes fell and she saw a pair of moccasins next to her. Serena had not forgotten. And, oh dear, she was going to have to run, very soon. She quickly slipped the moccasins on and walked around in a little circle to get used to them. They were an almost perfect fit, although the left one seemed a little big for her foot. But they were certainly better than her riding boots.

She became conscious of a foreign sound—a slow, rhythmic rumbling. At first she thought the singers had added some strange variation, and then she giggled. It was Sergeant Burke, snoring.

She tiptoed over to him. He was lying on his back, his mouth hanging open, snoring gently and steadily. Her Thomas snored occasionally, but when he did, it was with great loud gasps. Michael Burke's snores were quite refined, thought Elizabeth as she suppressed a laugh.

Refined or not, it did not seem very ceremonial to her. Perhaps she could get him to turn over in his sleep, the way she sometimes did with her husband. She knelt down next to him and gently pushed his right shoulder. The snoring stopped for a moment and then started again, but he didn't move.

"Michael," she whispered as she pushed again. "Turn over."

Michael's eyes fluttered and the snoring stopped but he was clearly half asleep when he muttered something like, "Ah, Mary Ann, are ye wanting more from me this morning."

Elizabeth blushed. Clearly Sergeant Burke thought he

was back in bed with his laundress. As he reached out and grabbed her hand, she gasped and stood up.

"Where are ye, darlin?" he grumbled, his eyes squinting open.

"I am not your 'darlin,' " Elizabeth said in a loud, fierce whisper. "It is Elizabeth and I was merely attempting to stop you from snoring, Michael. It did not seem respectful."

Michael pulled himself up and rubbed his eyes. " 'Snoring,' was I? How embarrassing."

What was embarrassing, thought Elizabeth, was to be mistaken for his laundress lover, but she wasn't about to refer to Mary Ann again.

Michael looked at Elizabeth's moccasined feet and then up at her face. Flushed with embarrassment, Mrs. Woolcott was even prettier. A stiffening in his groin made him wish that she were flushed with desire and he drew his legs up to hide the sign of his arousal. He said a quick "Hail, Mary," hoping that the Queen of Heaven would drive all the sinful thoughts out of his head. He had never wanted a woman so much before and now it seemed there was nothing else he wanted. She was an occasion of sin for him, was Elizabeth Woolcott, and for now, there was nothing he could do about it.

He glanced at the horizon, where a thin band of light was beginning to change the sky from black to rose and orange. Just at that moment, the singing, which had become part of the background, stopped and the blanket over the hogan was pushed open. "I think your moment has come, Elizabeth," he said, pointing down at the hogan. And thank God for it, he thought as she turned and started to walk toward the hogan.

Serena's niece came out, gave her shout, and started her final race. There were at least ten who followed her and Elizabeth stood frozen in place as she watched them run east into the dawn. Then she scrambled the rest of the way down the little hill and followed them.

Two of the girls in the back of the group looked at her and frowned as she caught up with them and she almost turned back. But then Serena's niece looked over her shoulder and gave her a look which seemed to hold both goodwill and a challenge. She seemed to be saying, "We've let you join us, *bilagaana*. You are welcome. Now let us see what you can endure."

After what seemed only minutes, Elizabeth was gasping for breath. She realized part of it was from nervousness and she began to pay attention only to her steps and her breath, trying to find a rhythm that would enable her to finish. It was lucky she began to pay attention to her feet, for she missed a wicked-looking cactus by inches. The soles of her moccasins were hardened rawhide, but the spikes of the cactus would have pierced them easily.

At least it was not midday in summer, she thought gratefully as she began to sweat. This *bilagaana* would at least not collapse from sunstroke!

Two young boys had fallen behind her and she realized that she was now in the back of the middle of the runners. And this is where I'll stay. If I can!

It seemed as if they were running out forever, further and further away from the hogan into the rising sun. And then at last, with another shout, they turned and the runners followed, strung out behind her.

For the first ten minutes after they turned, Elizabeth felt she was holding her own. She had found a rhythm and she could finally see the cluster of trees not too far in front of them. But nothing seemed to be getting closer and she felt she was running in place. She became aware that her left heel hurt where the moccasin was rubbing against it. The two young boys had caught up with her and passed her and now there was only one woman behind her. Serena's niece was far ahead, running strongly and proudly, her head and shoulders back, her arms pumping easily at her sides. She looked strong and free and Elizabeth was amazed at her ability to end these strenuous days and a sleepless night with such a run.

"I can't do it," she thought, slowing down so that she was next to the last runner. The two girls who had given her angry looks saw how she had fallen back and crowed out their satisfaction.

She felt a sudden surge of anger. She had been *invited*, after all. She hadn't pushed herself into either the ceremony or the race. The *kinaalda's* mother had asked her and she'd be damned if she would give them the weak *bilagaana* woman they expected. The anger was what carried her for the last five minutes of the race. Digging deep within herself, she found the strength to pull ahead of the last woman and the two boys. As they approached the hogan, she realized that she was just behind one of the mocking girls and she forced herself to ignore the pain in her heels and the aching in her lungs and the feeling that there was no more air in the world, and as Serena's niece reached the hogan, ending her race, Elizabeth pulled next to and then just ahead and finished between her two tormentors. To her surprise, instead of reacting with hostility, they looked at her approvingly and with respect. All she wanted to do was collapse, but she made herself nod to them and walked away on shaking legs. She was aware of no one, only her desire to sit down and gulp air and then water. And look at her heel, which she could tell had been rubbed raw.

She felt an arm under her arm, supporting her, and looked up gratefully. Sergeant Burke was smiling down at her and suddenly she was aware of how she must look. She, the former Miss Elizabeth Jane Rush, one of Mrs. Compton's young ladies, was soaked in sweat, having made a four-mile run across the desert. Her linen blouse was wet and clinging and she was afraid to look down and see what it revealed.

"That was a fine run for a *bilagaana*," said Serena.

Elizabeth looked over and smiled at her friend. "This *bilagaana* woman almost didn't make it back running."

"It is good that you did this, Mrs. Woolcott," said Antonio, who had joined them. "You have won much respect."

"Believe me, that is nothing compared to the respect I feel for your niece. She looked so strong and beautiful out there."

Serena smiled proudly. "My sister's daughter has done very well. She will make a fine woman."

"You are limping, Elizabeth," said Michael with concern in his voice.

"I tried to ignore it, but I think my heel is blistered."

"Sit down here and I'll look at it for you."

Michael knelt in front of her and gently drew off her moccasin. He lifted her foot to examine the heel and Elizabeth felt a small thrill go through her until he touched the blister. Then she flinched and grimaced.

"Indeed, and I'm sure it must hurt," crooned Michael. Then, realizing how he must sound, he cleared his throat and looked up at Antonio. "Do ye have any salve of any sort?"

"I'll ask the *hataali*," said Antonio. He returned with a small pot of greasy salve which Michael smeared on Elizabeth's heel.

"Where is yer riding blouse, Elizabeth?"

Elizabeth looked at him questioningly.

"I need something to bind your foot with or your boot will make it worse."

"I have a chemise in my pack, Michael," she said, red-faced.

Michael jumped up and after rummaging through the pack, found a small cotton chemise. He hated to tear it, but her heel had to be protected or she would risk infection.

He tied the strips gently. "I'd keep the moccasins on for a bit, for yer boots will feel too stiff for a while."

"Thank you, Michael."

Elizabeth stood up and took a few steps. Her heel still hurt but the bandaging protected it. As she turned back, Michael Burke took a step toward her and before she realized what was happening, she found herself enfolded in his arms, his hand gently holding her head against his chest. "I am so proud of you," he whispered into her hair.

He was holding her the way she had wanted her dream woman to hold her. He was saying what she would have wanted her father or mother to say to her: that they admired and respected who she had become. She could have stayed there forever, listening to the steady beat of his heart, smelling the cumin scent of him, feeling both strong and protected at the same time.

When he finally let go, neither could look at the other. Elizabeth started babbling to Serena, and Michael ignored Antonio's questioning look and went over to feed their horses.

Chapter Twenty-three

There had been singing when they returned from the race, and Elizabeth assumed it had been going on the whole time they were gone. But there had been silence for a minute or two now and then Serena's niece and the men and women inside the hogan emerged and gathered around the smoking pit. The coals and dirt were brushed off and the corn husks removed and Serena's sister began to cut the cake. Elizabeth stood by while others were given their pieces but then Serena pulled her into the circle and she took a piece, shyly nodding her thanks. She noticed that the *kinaalda* had not had any yet and whispered a question to her friend.

"The *kinaalda* doesn't eat her own *aalkan,* my friend."

Cutting the cake was the signal for breakfast, it seemed, and all sat down to a meal of tortillas and corn mush, the men separate from the women. At one point, Elizabeth noticed one of the older women pointing to her and then to the two girls who had not wanted to run with them, and laughing.

"What is she saying?"

"She is teasing them about being beaten by a *bilagaana,*" whispered her friend.

"They didn't look too happy that I was part of the race," said Elizabeth. "I am sure the teasing doesn't make them like me any more!"

"Oh, no, they don't mind the teasing. One of them beat you. And you gained their respect by pulling ahead of the

other. Most of us feel good that you respected the ceremony enough to take a small part."

"I had an interesting dream last night," said Elizabeth,
softly. "There was a woman in it, dressed in white with a
rainbow sash. She was wearing turquoise, but also my
mother's cameo."

Serena looked at her inquiringly. "Go on."

"She looked at me with such kindness. But it was very
strange . . . of course, dreams are always strange, but at
first she appeared young and beautiful and then old and
wrinkled and then young again."

Serena was silent for a moment and then turned away
and said something to one of the old women. Elizabeth
felt that she had just shared something special with her
friend and had been ignored. Perhaps it wasn't polite to
tell your dreams?

Serena turned back to her. "Can you tell me all the details of the dream, Elizabeth?"

Elizabeth repeated what she could remember, while her
friend simultaneously translated for the older woman.

The old woman gave a deep sigh and said something to
Serena. Serena nodded.

"We think you are very lucky, Elizabeth. It could be
that your heart was open to her. That you needed to see
her. But we think that you have seen *Asdzaa nadleehe,* the
Changing Woman, in your dream."

"But it wasn't anything like your story, Serena."

"No, and that is why we think it is real. I didn't tell
you everything about her. I didn't tell you how she turns
and walks to the east and then to the south and then the
west and each time comes back different. But that is what
you saw, so it must have been she."

The women were all looking over at her curiously and
Elizabeth dropped her eyes.

"It was a wonderful dream, but it doesn't seem right
that I had it. Surely, *Asdzaa nadleehe*"—Elizabeth struggled over the pronunciation—"should have been visiting
the *kinaalda.*"

"Oh, I am sure she did," said Serena with a smile. "But
she also visited you because you needed her." Serena

spoke again to the other women in Navajo and they all murmured sympathetically.

"I told them part of your story, my friend. I hope you don't mind. We all agree: you had a sad time for your *kenasha*. You lost your mother in a terrible way. And you *bilagaana* women have no sense of the power of your womanhood. So you needed something to help you."

Serena spoke to the whole circle of women again and then to Elizabeth. "You brought an open heart with you. And a gift, something that had belonged to your mother. Something made of white shell. We all think it is not a—what do you call it when something unexpected happens?"

"A coincidence."

"Yes. You brought a gift and you were given one."

Elizabeth looked around at all the women. Some were young and attractive. Others had old, deeply wrinkled faces. Their faces were harder to read than the women's at the fort. But in their eyes she could see respect and feel a warmth emanating from some of them. She felt a strength coming from them to her, and she said to Serena, her voice trembling, "Will you thank them for me. Thank them for their welcome and for sharing the *Biji* with me."

The women all nodded approvingly when she spoke and then began to get up, shaking out their skirts.

"We must go back to the hogan, Elizabeth. My niece will be having her hair combed. After that the *hataali* will sing the White Clay Song and she will be painted. But she will come outside for the final molding."

The singing started again and by this time it was beginning to sound familiar. After a while, everyone came out of the hogan and Serena's sister began to pile blankets and deerskins in front of the hogan door. Her daughter emerged and lay down, her arms stretched out, and one of the women began to "mold" her.

Elizabeth stood there, imagining herself in the *kinaalda's* place, a young Diné girl who was being pressed and formed into the shape of a divinity. She will be Changing Woman for us, Serena had told her. Her celebration would strengthen all the people. Elizabeth could almost feel hands on her own shoulders and neck and when the girl stood up, Elizabeth looked into her face and cried. Serena's niece, who had lain down a girl, had stood up a woman. It was there in the way she held herself, in the expression on her face, the careful and respectful way she began to give back all the blankets and other gifts that had been loaned to her. After she had finished, she turned and walked back with quiet dignity into the hogan.

Serena came over and stood next to Elizabeth. "She will stay here for four more days."

Elizabeth only nodded. She couldn't speak; she had many questions, but somehow didn't need to ask them. She felt deep inside her a feeling of great loss and emptiness. Yet, at the same time, something had changed for her. It was as though when the Navajo girl had lain down, the girl Elizabeth had also. Now that girl was gone and a new Elizabeth had taken her place. She couldn't speak about it; she had no words to explain it. But something had happened to change her that she knew would change her life.

After the *kinaalda* returned to the hogan, a few of the women began cutting the remainder of the *aalkan* and handing out pieces. Michael came over to her and handed her a piece.

"You had better eat some of this, Elizabeth. We have a long ride ahead of us."

Michael Burke was speaking to her in normal tones, a fact for which she was grateful. She did not want to think about, she *could* not think about being held in his arms. It was a moment out of time. One she would treasure, but one that would not likely be repeated. She nibbled at the cake and watched as people began to gather their things and make their preparations for departure.

When she realized she still had on Serena's moccasins, she walked up to where she had left her pack and boots and took them off. Her boots felt stiff and the left one put pressure on her sore heel, but the strips of makeshift bandage held and she was able to walk in them without too much difficulty. She picked up her pack and the moccasins and went down to where Sergeant Burke was holding the horses. Antonio and Serena were with him and Elizabeth held the moccasins out with a smile.

"Thank you, Serena. I could never have finished that race in my boots."

Serena put one hand up in a quick gesture of protest. "You keep the moccasins, my friend. If you don't race in them, they won't rub your heel that much," she added with a smile.

Elizabeth opened her mouth for a ritual protest and then just said a simple thank you.

Serena looked as though she had something else to say but didn't quite know how. Finally she said, "I just want to tell you I am sorry for how your life has changed, my friend." It was the only reference anyone had made to Thomas. Given how he died, Elizabeth had not wanted to make her friends uncomfortable, but at the same time had wondered why they had expressed no sympathy. Antonio saw the puzzled look on her face. "The Diné do not talk about the dead, but this does not mean we do not understand your pain."

They said their good-byes and Sergeant Burke gave her a leg up and then mounted Frost in one easy movement.

"There will be racing next week. I hope ye're coming, Antonio, so Frost can beat your bay!"

"Don't be too sure, Sergeant!"

Michael brushed Frost with his heels and they moved off, both looking back and waving to the Navajo couple. Antonio and Serena watched them go and then Serena turned to her husband.

"What do you think, husband?"

"About what?"

"About Sergeant Burke and Mrs. Woolcott, of course."

"Why, they have become our good friends, I think."

Serena gave her husband a disgusted look and then he smiled.

"Do you mean what do I think about Sergeant Burke holding Mrs. Woolcott in his arms?"

"Yes, husband," his wife replied with exaggerated patience.

"I think I feel sorry for them both. The *bilagaana* soldiers feel very strongly about the difference between their officers and other men."

"The *bilagaana* feel strongly about all differences," said Serena caustically. "But I am not so sure that Elizabeth does. And she needs someone like Sergeant Burke."

"She might need a new husband, but I doubt she is ready for one," said Antonio thoughtfully. "I suspect Michael will suffer more from this feeling that might be between them."

"Trust me, there is this feeling between them!"

Chapter Twenty-four

Michael and Elizabeth rode in silence for the first few hours. Neither had gotten much sleep the night before and they were too tired to talk, as well as preoccupied with their own thoughts. Michael was trying to conjure up memories of passionate moments with Mary Ann and failing miserably. Elizabeth was trying to understand what had happened when Michael held her.

They had reached the valley and were only an hour or so from the fort when Michael looked over at her and saw that she was swaying in her saddle.

"Elizabeth," he said sharply.

Elizabeth's head jerked up. "I just dozed off for a minute, Michael. I am fine."

But a few minutes later she was swaying again and Michael reached out for her mare's reins and pulled both horses up.

"Elizabeth, I'm afraid I can't let ye stop to catch up on yer sleep. I want to make the fort by sundown. And I have no coffee left to boil. I gave it all to Antonio. Ye're going to have to ride with me or I'm afraid ye'll drop right off yer horse."

Elizabeth wasn't awake enough to protest. She slipped off her mare and let Michael lift her up on Frost. He swung up behind her.

"There now, at least ye can't fall," he said as he reached around her to hold the reins in both his hands.

She tried to sit forward, but she soon found herself

drifting off and then jerking awake again from her uncomfortable position.

"If ye'll just lean back against me, Elizabeth, ye can
sleep and be more comfortable."

I know I will be, she thought, so drunk with exhaustion
that she nearly said it aloud. And that is what I am afraid
of. It would feel so good . . . it *did* feel so good when she
let herself lean against his broad chest and let herself feel
his arms around her.

"There ye go," he whispered.

She was asleep in minutes and Michael kept the horses
down to a brisk walk. At this pace, they would just make
the fort before dark, but Elizabeth was not up to a trot or
canter in her state, so what could he do?

It was sweet torture, this closeness. He could feel her
hair against his cheek when he bent to look down at her.
Nestled against him like a child, she was. Except she was
no child. She was an officer's widow, for sweet Jesus'
sake, and he had better remember it. The trouble was, his
mind could remember it, but his body . . . well, that was
another thing entirely.

He could smell a combination of cologne and her own
scent and it made him want to lean down and nuzzle her
neck and drink it in. She was turned a little against him
and he could feel the curve of her breast. He wanted to
drop one rein and cup his hand tenderly around it.

Thank God the saddle was between them, he thought.
His prick was as stiff as Moses' rod and God knows what
would happen if they were rubbing against one another.
He thought of the priest at home, thundering from the
pulpit about the sins of the flesh. He tried to picture the
fires of hell, but the only fire he had in his mind was that
of his own fierce desire.

He remembered how she had looked as she was running back to camp with Serena's niece. Her hair had been
windblown, her cheeks flushed, and her eyes shining with
a sense of her own accomplishment.

He had fallen in love with her in that moment. He had
found her attractive all along, of course, even though he
had disliked her at first, the prim and proper Boston lady.

Then he had gotten to know her better and had enjoyed
her company. His liking had turned to admiration and
sympathy and respect. And now, God help him, love.

He loved an officer's widow. A woman who had suffered a recent terrible loss. The bittersweet realization
was almost more than he could bear. He had found the
one woman for him and she was not for him, could never
be for him.

And it was ridiculous to feel this way to boot. Elizabeth had been a happily married woman. She would be
missing her husband terribly. She might have lost her distaste for Sergeant Michael Burke. She might even consider him a friend. But she most certainly did not want
him or love him.

Michael had never imagined himself to be this sort of
man: the kind that loved hopelessly and forever. He had
thought he would one day find a sweet woman to settle
down with, one he could love calmly and peacefully. Mrs.
Elizabeth Woolcott had destroyed that possibility for him,
damn her. She wasn't the static, sweet dream of a woman
he had had in mind. She was someone who had grown
and changed, even since he'd known her. She had opened
her heart to Serena, to the Diné, and to her own possibil-
ities. He couldn't help himself. Dear God, but he loved
her.

They reached the fort just as dark was falling and Michael rode straight to the Grays' quarters. Elizabeth, who
was still asleep against him, stirred a little when Frost's
regular motion stopped. Michael was just trying to figure
out how to dismount without her falling when the door to
the colonel's quarters opened and a black-and-white bundle of fur ran out, wriggling and barking, and almost
somersaulted over the railing to get to his mistress. The
noise awoke Elizabeth and she opened her eyes and
looked dazedly around her.

God bless the wee bugger, thought Michael as Colonel
Gray tried to calm the dog down. At least he had directed
the colonel's attention away from Elizabeth's arrival in
Michael's arms.

"Michael," Elizabeth murmured without thinking. Michael hoped he was the only one to hear her. It was a natural, really, since they had been together for over thirty-six hours, but the colonel might not understand that.

When Colonel Gray lifted her down from the horse, Elizabeth stumbled and put her hand against Frost's shoulder to steady herself.

"You look exhausted, Elizabeth," said Mrs. Gray, who had come out behind her husband.

"I am, Janet, although evidently I slept all the way home." As she said it, she seemed to realize just where she had slept and with a little embarrassment she said quickly, "Thanks to Sergeant Burke, I didn't fall off my mare."

Orion was alternating between groveling at her feet and planting his paws in her lap to reach up and lick her face.

"I'd better get you inside before he knocks you over," said the colonel, pushing the dog away. "Thanks for taking such good care of Mrs. Woolcott, Sergeant Burke," he called over his shoulder to Michael. "We'll be looking forward to hearing about your adventures."

Michael lifted his hand to acknowledge the thank you and then let it fall again. Elizabeth was not conscious of him. And why should she be, boyo, he told himself. I am just the mick sergeant who did the job the army ordered.

He dismounted and led Frost to the stables, where he brushed her down and watered her. The mare drank slowly but steadily, lifting her head occasionally and turning her dripping muzzle toward Michael and blowing a contented sound out her nostrils.

Michael was almost asleep himself, leaning against her, when Elwell came up behind him.

"Welcome back, Sergeant. I imagine escort duty was more pleasant than gathering wood? You brought the lady back safely, I see."

"Sure and ye startled me, Josh," said Michael. "I'm dead on me feet. I'll be glad to be back to collecting wood tomorrow."

"You disappoint me, Michael. I'd have thought escorting a lady much more your style," Elwell teased. "Mary

Ann missed you last night, by the way. She'll be looking forward to tonight."

Michael groaned. "Not a chance, Josh. All I'm able to do is get meself to mess and then to bed. Will ye tell her that?"

Elwell slapped Michael on his back. "Indeed I will, Michael, but she'll miss you."

Any other time, he would have wanted a woman. Not just for sex, not as tired as he was tonight. But for the feeling of coming home to someone, even a whore. That wasn't fair, he knew. Mary Ann was not really a whore. Her profession was laundering, not dance hall girl. She gave her favors selectively, even though she accepted money for them. But tonight it would have made him feel even lonelier to be with someone else. Mary Ann opening her door to him, inviting him in to a warm, lantern-lit room would only have reminded him of the woman he wanted and couldn't have.

Chapter Twenty-five

Elizabeth slept through most of the next morning. When she finally awoke, it was almost noon and she could hear Orion barking from the line she had put up in the back of the Grays' quarters. She threw her flannel wrapper around her and rushed out, afraid that her neighbors were ready to descend on her for the dog's noise.

"Hush, Orion, hush." The dog dropped back on his haunches and looked up at her with such an expression of idiotic delight on his face that she laughed out loud.

"I was only gone for one night, you foolish dog," she scolded as she untied him. Once again, he was down and squirming at her feet one moment and trying to lick her face the next.

"Come inside with me. Heel, sir," she said firmly, and he followed her into the kitchen.

When the dog whimpered, she said with mock sympathy, "Poor Orion. No one here to see that you were properly fed!" She crumbled some bread into a bowl and added milk and an egg and put it down for the hungry dog. "That will have to hold you for now."

She made herself a cup of tea and sliced a piece of bread for herself. Mrs. Gray must be on an errand somewhere, she thought. And although she was eager to tell the story of her adventures, she was happy to have some privacy. As she drew her legs underneath her, her left heel hit the chair rung and the pain brought back everything from the last two days. She sat there, hands around her mug, kaleidoscopic images not at all in sequence taking

her back to the ceremony. She relived her race and her
dream. She had experienced something profound, but had
no name for it. She only knew that she felt different:
more herself, Elizabeth Jane Woolcott, than she ever had.
That felt very satisfying. At the same time, she felt a deep
longing for something, she wasn't sure what. A part of
her longed for the woman in her dream. For Changing
Woman, if it had indeed been she. For something that was
missing in her life. Something . . . she could only call it
something holy. She had thought holiness was only found
in churches. A church was a holy place. A minister was
a holy person. God was holy. At least that is what she had
been taught. Yet she had also felt holiness approaching
her in that dream in the guise of a woman. If she told that
to anyone, he would think her sacrilegious. Divinity in a
woman's form? Yet that had been her experience. And
that is what the Navajo believed.

As she sat and drank her tea she wanted more than anything in the world to have her mother sitting opposite her.
They would drink tea together and Elizabeth would tell
her everything and ask her if she thought God could take
a woman's form. Then she would pull out her drawings
and unroll them at the table and show her mother how
much she had come to love this country. "I know I was
a terrible traveler, Mother," she would say. "I resisted every step of the way. But now it feels like home." Her
mother would smile and praise her drawings and tell her
what a fine woman she had become.

Elizabeth was crying. Except when Thomas died, she
hadn't cried for years for her mother or her father or herself. She had shut herself off from all memories until today, when somehow her mother had felt very present. She
cried until she drained herself and when she finally
stopped, she realized that opening to the old pain had finally brought her a sense of peace.

Her eyes were swollen and her face sticky and salt-
streaked. She filled the washbasin with water and as she
washed, she glanced up into the oval mirror above the
washstand. She had almost expected to see a fourteen-
year-old girl, she realized as she calmly surveyed the

woman's face looking back at her. How had she remained fourteen for all these years? She wasn't a girl anymore. She was a twenty-three-year-old woman.

What had Thomas seen when he looked at her, she wondered. Had he seen the young Elizabeth whom he had rescued? Or the woman? Whom had he loved? And who had loved him these past six years?

As she sat there, something her mother had once said came back to her: "What a terrible thing it is not to become a woman when one ceases to be a girl." For the first time, she felt like a woman, and she cried again that she had not been able to give Thomas Woolcott what he so deserved.

She had worked hard to make every posting a home. She never complained about the hardships. She was a good hostess and kept the light of friendship burning in their home. And she had never turned away from him in their bed. Why did it all of a sudden not seem very much?

She had given him a happy marriage. She had given him Miss Elizabeth Jane Rush. She had given him her mother's daughter, who had learned what a wife's role was. But she had never given him herself or her own desire. She had loved him with a grateful love. He had rescued her twice: once from Comancheros and then from a single woman's existence, and she had loved him for that. And she had, as he had said, "let him love her." Oh, but what an ungenerous love that seemed to her now.

She told the Grays her story over dinner, and all during that next week the other officers' wives approached her and asked for details. With the exception of the colonel's wife, they all were both curious and resentful. They wanted to know everything about "heathen practices," but after she gave them a very abbreviated account, they looked at her as though she were an oddity.

"Imagine cooking in the dirt!" Mrs. Taggert said when Elizabeth told of the *aalkan*. "I surely hope you didn't eat any of it, Mrs. Woolcott."

"It would have been impolite not to," she answered in her best Boston manner. She wanted to slap the woman's sanctimonious face and was very glad she had shared only a few details of the ceremony.

She found herself wanting to talk to Michael. He had understood what an important experience it had been. He respected the Diné. And her. She wanted to complain about the post women, with their narrow-mindedness.

But he was very elusive that week, Sergeant Burke. She couldn't have sought him out directly, but she had tried to be at the stable with a treat for her mare at the time when he should have been returning with his men, and she missed him by a few minutes each time.

Probably he had forgotten all about their shared experience, she thought. Probably he was spending his spare time with Mary Ann! Not that it was any of her business!

"This is the first time you've come to see me this week, Michael," said Mary Ann.

Michael forced a big smile. "Sure and I have been busy, darlin'. It is only that I'm tired. Mr. Cooper is workin' me hard to make up for the time I was away."

"I can't understand why you don't just request another detail."

"From whom? Mr. Cooper? He'd just love me to come beggin' to him. And ye know ye can't go over your commanding officer, Mary Ann."

"I know. It just seems such a shame to waste you."

"I'm just thankful it has been peaceful."

"Are you going to be racing this week?"

"I think I'll be giving Frost a rest and just be watching this time."

"I have put a week's wages down, and on an Indian, no less," Mary Ann told him.

"Oh, so ye think Manuelito can beat Cooper and his quarterhorse?"

"To tell you the truth, I haven't any idea, Michael," she confessed with a giggle. "I just *want* the lieutenant to lose."

"If he is up against Manuelito, he probably will."

"Let's have our own race, Michael," she teased, pulling

him on top of her. "You are an expert rider, or so I've been told."

Michael groaned and collapsed in mock exhaustion, his head on her ample breasts. "Oh, darlin', I don't think I'm up for any ridin' tonight." Or any other night, he realized. He said his good-bye, knowing that it was the last time he would be visiting Mary Ann alone. Desire and love, which had been two separate streams, were at last united in one river, which flowed only toward Elizabeth Woolcott.

Chapter Twenty-six

By Sunday, it seemed everyone, white and Navajo, had heard about the big race at noon and men were betting everything they had, money or trade goods.

Cooper's strutting like the cock of the walk, thought Michael as he watched the man move back and forth between clusters of officers and their wives. His horse had been brushed until he shone and his mane braided with red ribbon. To tell the truth, he was a sweet mount, thought Michael, and in any other contest would likely run away with the race. But against Manuelito? The man rode like most of the Diné, as though he and the horse were one creature.

Michael made his way around the crowd to where he could see the headman and Antonio giving his pony one last going over.

"So, do ye think I'll win on ye today?" Michael asked. He didn't know Manuelito that well, but the headman smiled at the question.

"I thought most of the *bilagaana* would put their money on the yellow-haired lieutenant."

"I expect they did."

"I think your money is safe, my friend," said Antonio with a smile. "This is the pony he saves for the shorter races."

"Sure, and he looks fresh and eager," said Michael, stepping back as the pony turned to nip him.

"I apologize, Sergeant Burke," said Manuelito with exaggerated obsequiousness belied by the glint in his eye.

"This horse of mine, he has never liked the *bilagaana* blue uniforms . . . !"

"Well, ye'd better hope he doesn't stop to take a chink out of Cooper."

"Manuelito can handle him," said Antonio.

"I am sure he can. So sure in fact that I'm off to put down a wee bit more."

As Michael moved off, Manuelito turned to Antonio and said, "I like your friend. Too bad more of them aren't like Sergeant Burke."

Antonio nodded.

Elizabeth was disappointed that she only had a few minutes to say a quick hello to Serena before the races started, but she arranged to meet with her afterward. She was standing on the viewing platform with the colonel's wife to keep her company since the colonel had been summoned to Fort Wingate.

"Have you been placing any bets, Captain Taggert?" Mrs. Gray asked.

"I have, ma'am."

"On whom?"

"Why on Mr. Cooper, ma'am. That quarterhorse of his loves the short-distance race. And Manuelito is too tall and heavy not to get in his horse's way."

"Is Sergeant Burke racing today?"

"I don't think so, ma'am. I haven't seen his horse out with the others."

"Oh, there he is, over there next to Private Elwell." The colonel's wife pointed him out and Elizabeth couldn't stop herself from looking. But why shouldn't she look? He was a friend now. They had gotten to know one another better. She couldn't help it if she thought him handsome. She couldn't help remembering how it felt to fall asleep against him, or be held in his arms.

"The quarter mile is just starting," said Taggert, and the ladies pulled their eyes from Sergeant Burke.

The first few races went well and the winners were balanced between Navajo and cavalry. Antonio, who was riding his blood bay, won his race easily, and when Elizabeth glanced in Michael's direction, she saw that he was shouting and clapping his friend over the finish line.

It was only a few minutes before the last race of the day, the one between Manuelito and Mr. Cooper. The sun was strong, but the air was crisp and cool and as Elizabeth looked around, everyone and everything stood out vividly: the blue of the uniforms, the winking brass buttons, the bright reds of the Navajo blankets, the shiny conchos on their leggings and belts. Even Mr. Cooper's hair had looked wheat gold in the sun as he had ridden out, she thought with a smile. What a wonderful morning.

There were three others in this race, but they might as well have been invisible. Everyone knew where the real contest lay: between Cooper's chestnut and the Navajo's black.

When the mirror flashed, Elizabeth could only see a cloud of dust and then the chestnut and black emerged from it, running neck and neck. There would be no hanging back and then last-minute bursts of speed: they were neck and neck all the way.

All of a sudden, Manuelito's black veered off the track and Elizabeth could see that he was stretched over the horse's neck. She couldn't understand what had happened: had the horse been spooked by something? Even though his rival was no longer next to him, Cooper kept his horse at a full gallop and when he crossed the finish line, he was surrounded by soldiers clapping him and each other on the back. All of them had bet heavily and had expected a close race. The anticlimactic finish was too good to be believed.

Once Elizabeth had seen that Cooper had won, she turned her eyes to Manuelito. He pulled his horse around to the right in a tighter and tighter circle and at last had him under control. He came in at a canter and as he drew closer, a loud muttering began among the Navajo. Manuelito was only holding one rein, the right one. What remained of the left rein was hanging from his horse's bridle. Luckily it wasn't long enough for the gelding to trip, but it was slapping at his neck and Elizabeth could now understand how the headman had lost control.

"How could leather just snap like that," wondered Mrs. Gray aloud.

Captain Taggert frowned. "I am afraid it must have been cut, ma'am."

"Cut! But who would be stupid enough to do something like that?"

Elizabeth's first thought was of Lieutenant Cooper. He already had a grudge against Manuelito and his vanity was beyond reason. But for a cavalry officer to cheat? It was unheard of.

Manuelito dismounted and his face grim, he examined the rein. He held it out to several of the men who had surrounded him and then led his horse over to the judges, followed by a large group of Navajo. It was clear that they were asking for another race and it was even clearer that the judges were denying it. Mr. Cooper finally climbed the platform and was declared the winner. When he came down and pushed his way past the gathered tribesmen, not even acknowledging Manuelito with a glance, Elizabeth thought she had never disliked anyone so much.

"The man is a fool," said Mrs. Gray, "although I admit I shouldn't be saying so. The least he could do is offer his sympathy to Manuelito. And the judges are acting even greater fools," she added.

Cooper's whole company gathered around him and then two of his men lifted him up on their shoulders, starting a victory parade into the fort. It took the Navajo spectators a moment to realize what had happened: *their* rider's bridle had been cut, the *bilagaana* judges had refused a rematch, and all of them had lost heavily, having bet everything on their headman.

It all happened so quickly that afterward Elizabeth could hardly remember the sequence. Cooper and his men had almost disappeared into the stockade when the Navajo men rushed after them, determined to recover their money. When he became aware of the commotion behind him, and without a thought to who was left outside, Cooper ordered the gates shut. As they swung closed, a few Navajo almost squeezed through. A shot rang out, and one of them fell.

The captain pulled Elizabeth and the colonel's wife down as the gates swung open again and more shots were fired. Elizabeth watched in horror as Navajo men, women, and children scattered, some of them falling as they ran.

"My God, what are they doing," Mrs. Gray moaned. "Everything Charles worked for is being ruined."

Cooper had lost his mind, Elizabeth decided. Then she heard someone shouting orders, not to cease firing, but to bring out the howitzers.

The sequence of events was just as confusing to Michael. One minute he was watching Manuelito come in with a flapping rein and the next that foolish bastard Cooper was being paraded by his even more foolish men and then all was chaos. He and Private Elwell were ordered into the fort by Captain Taggert, who had left the women and suddenly appeared in front of them.

Christ, they were in danger of being killed by their own men, he thought as they ran. The Navajo had not recovered from their shock at the sudden attack and were still running in all directions. The gates swung open again, and just as he and Elwell got inside the stockade, Cooper spotted them.

"Major Wheeler wants the howitzers brought out, Burke. The sergeant in charge is nowhere to be found so you are to bring them."

Michael's mouth fell open. Howitzers? They were turning it into a bloody massacre!

"Don't just stand there like the dumb Irish ape you are, Burke. Get the goddamned howitzers."

Elwell pulled at him and Michael followed. Followed his private and followed his orders. He had been following orders all his adult life. This was only another order. A criminal order. But the criminal was Cooper, not Michael Burke, he kept telling himself as he dragged the gun carriage. He was intent on getting them into position, not on anything else and then he heard Cooper's voice again.

"Aim and fire, Sergeant."

The gun was pointing out the gate. The Navajo hadn't a prayer against a howitzer, thought Michael, paralyzed by the sight of two children off to the left whose wounded mother lay over them, too late to save them.

"I gave you an order, Sergeant. *Fire.*"

"I can't, sir," Michael stammered.

"Can't!"

"I can't fire on innocent women and children, sir. 'Tis criminal."

"You know the consequences for disobeying a direct order, Sergeant."

Michael stood there, silent and unmoving, when Elwell grabbed his arm. "Michael, whether you like it or not, you must obey him. He's our commanding officer."

Michael stepped back from the gun.

"Elwell, aim the gun and fire," shouted Cooper. Elwell gave Michael a pleading, desperate look. He didn't like the order any more than Burke did, damn it. But an order was an order. He turned back to the gun and fired into the crowd.

"I'll deal with you later, Sergeant Burke," Cooper snarled.

Chapter Twenty-seven

It was over very quickly. The Navajo scattered across the valley, attacking the cavalry herd as they ran. The dead were dragged off and dumped unceremoniously into a ditch against the fort.

It seemed a long time before anyone remembered them, but in reality, as soon as the shooting stopped, the women were escorted back into the fort. One of them, Mrs. Taggert, had a slight graze on her arm from an ill-aimed army rifle.

"It is a wonder we're not all dead, Major Wheeler," said the indignant Mrs. Gray. "You have succeeded in one quarter hour in destroying the peace my husband spent months tending."

"I had no choice, Mrs. Gray," he answered stiffly. "They were charging the fort."

"Charging the fort! They had just been cheated out of their money by the stupidity of our judges, of whom you were one, I might add."

"Mr. Cooper won the race fairly, ma'am."

"Fairly? With Manuelito's bridle slashed?"

"There was no proof of that, Mrs. Gray."

"It looked clean-cut to me," said Captain Taggert, who had come over to be with his wife. "A rematch would have satisfied them."

"A rematch wouldn't have satisfied our soldiers, with Mr. Cooper riding a spent horse, Captain," said the major with a look that would have quelled anyone. "I will take care of the women, Captain. And you will convey Sergeant Burke to the stockade."

"Sergeant Burke!" Elizabeth exclaimed.

"Sergeant Burke disobeyed a direct order from Mr. Cooper."

Good for you, Michael. Whatever the order was, thought Elizabeth.

"What order was that, Captain?" asked Mrs. Gray.

"I ordered the howitzers brought out and the lieutenant told him to fire into the crowd. Sergeant Burke just stood there."

"I see," said Mrs. Gray calmly.

Elizabeth grabbed Mrs. Gray's arm. "Janet, can't you do anything? Surely that was a criminal order, to fire on women and children?"

"Captain Taggert, you have a duty to carry out," the major said harshly.

"Yes, sir. Mrs. Gray, will you take care of my wife?"

"Of course, Captain. Come, Mrs. Taggert, we will have the surgeon look at your arm."

Michael had been tempted to push Elwell away from the gun, but what would that have accomplished? Cooper had orders from the major to use the big guns and use them he would, if he had to pull in a raw recruit or fire them himself. He couldn't stop the insanity, but at least he wasn't part of it.

He was unable to watch, and as he turned away in despair, Cooper saw him moving and called over two of his men. "Sit Sergeant Burke down over there," he said, pointing to the guardroom steps, "and keep your rifles on him."

"Yes, sir."

Michael sat, ignoring the two men and their weapons, helplessly watching Cooper direct the attack. He was too far from the gate to see what was happening and could only pray that most of the Navajo had escaped. Please God, Antonio and his wife were safe.

"Sergeant Burke."

Michael looked up. It was Captain Taggert standing in front of him, looking almost apologetic.

"I have been ordered to escort you to the stockade."

Michael stood at attention and Taggert motioned his guards to walk ahead of them.

When they reached the stockade, Taggert dismissed the other men. As he opened the door, he rested his hand on Michael's shoulder for a moment. "I am sorry, Sergeant. It was a stupid order. I would have had a hard time following it myself."

"It was a sinful order, Captain," said Michael. "And thank you for sayin' that."

There were only two other men in the dark enclosure and they were the post drunks, there to dry out. The smell of stale vomit and unwashed bodies made Michael gag and he sat down on a wooden bench as far from the others as he could.

He was only now realizing the gravity of his situation. Disobeying a direct order in battle could lead to court martial, dishonorable discharge, even death. Except it wasn't a battle, he thought, dropping his head in his hands. Most of the men who had rushed the gates hadn't even been armed. And the women and children most certainly weren't. It was murder they'd been wanting him to commit. If he were back there again, he'd do the same thing, may God help him for it.

After taking care of Mrs. Taggert, Elizabeth and the colonel's wife returned home for an early tea. Elizabeth's hands had been shaking enough to spill her tea into her saucer. Mrs. Gray took one look at her white face and pulled a crystal decanter of brandy from her sideboard. She poured a generous amount into Elizabeth's teacup.

"Here, this will make you feel better, Elizabeth. I am going to have mine straight," she added, pouring a glass for herself.

The brandy and tea warmed Elizabeth and finally stopped her shivering.

"Thank you, Janet. I have always admired you for your calmness, but today even more."

"I may look calm on the outside, my dear, but inside I am raving. I can only imagine what Charles will feel when he gets back. Everything we have worked for here is gone up in smoke."

"All I can see is the children," said Elizabeth with tears in her eyes. "And it was all so stupid and senseless."

"Such things always are, Elizabeth. It is usually something stupid and small that starts wars. If Charles had been here, this never would have happened."

"What do you think will become of Sergeant Burke," Elizabeth asked apprehensively.

"He'd get a medal, if I had anything to say about it!" Elizabeth smiled.

"Of course, I don't have any say in the matter. But you can be sure I will tell Charles the whole story and plead extenuating circumstances."

"He couldn't be ... executed, could he?"

"Not in peacetime. And it *is* peacetime. Or was," she added bitterly.

When the shooting started, Antonio had stood paralyzed. All the Diné around him stood like statues, unable to believe what had happened. Then the people ran: men to their horses, women to their children. At first the men wheeled their horses around, as if contemplating an attack on the fort, but when the gates opened again, with the soldiers firing indiscriminately into the crowd, men sought out their wives and children and scooped them up. Antonio, his paralysis broken by the sight of one of the murdered women, ran for his bay. How he found Serena in all the chaos, he would never know, but he boosted her up in the saddle and took off across the valley. He saw the small group of men attacking the cavalry herd, but furious as he was, he was much more interested in getting himself and his wife to safety than exacting revenge. There would be time enough for revenge later.

Several miles down the valley, Manuelito caught up with them and gestured his nephew to halt.

"There is no need to wear out our horses. No one is following."

Antonio was glad to pull the bay back to a walk. They had only recently realized Serena was pregnant and he was concerned for his wife and her unborn child.

They were all silent for a while and then Antonio said bitterly, "You have told us not to trust them, uncle. You were right."

"I have dealt with them a long time, nephew. Maybe if the agent we called Red Sleeves had lived, the peace would have lasted. He spent time with us and understood our ways better than any other of the *bilagaana*."

"What happened today?" Serena asked. "Why did you lose control over your horse?"

"The rein snapped right at the beginning. It was cut."

"That Stringy Ass Cooper," said Antonio, cursing him thoroughly in Spanish and Navajo.

"Maybe. He denied it. And he may be an asshole, nephew, but I don't think he is a liar," said Manuelito with a quick smile.

"Then who?"

"Some stupid *bilagaana* soldier who bet heavily on the lieutenant. It always starts that way, with a stupid, greedy man, white or Diné. But they always expect us to turn *our ladrones*, our stupid young men. They are never willing to punish their own. Can you imagine if we asked for this soldier to be found?"

"What will happen now?" asked Serena softly.

"They have broken their own treaty," said Manuelito. "I am no longer going to hold young men back from raiding. It has been a hard winter and we've lost some sheep. We need to eat. We'll take what we need, and the hell with the *bilagaana*!" He was silent for a moment and then turned to Antonio. "Your friend, Sergeant Burke?"

"Yes?"

"He was the soldier who pulled out the big guns."

Antonio said nothing, merely nodded his head.

"I liked him too, nephew, but a soldier is a soldier. His loyalty will always be to the army."

Antonio still said nothing, merely nodded his head again.

Later, when they had made camp and Antonio had pulled his wife to him, he buried his face in her hair.

"I could have lost you today," he groaned.

Serena wrapped one leg around him to pull him even closer. "But you didn't. I am fine and our child is fine. For now," she added bleakly. "What do you think is going to happen?"

"Manuelito is right. The young men will go back to raiding. It was a short peace this time."

"And will you ride with them?"

"I don't know, wife. Not with the young hotheads, anyway. But with my uncle? I will follow him now, not those who trust too easily. How far west do they have to push us before we turn and face them? We have already lost our sacred mountains and the salt flat at Zuni. Each piece of paper we sign takes more away from us. Maybe our headmen don't always succeed, but they've tried very hard over the past three winters to keep our side of the agreement. And then the *bilagaana* tell us that no one in Washington has agreed to it."

"I had hoped this time . . ."

"As did I, wife. In the end, there are too many of them and we have to find a way of dealing with them in order to survive. But there are some things a man cannot take."

"I will miss Elizabeth," she murmured.

Antonio sighed.

"And you, husband, what of your friend?"

"He turned on us. He was willing to shoot Diné women and children."

"Did he have a choice?" Serena queried gently.

"All men have choices," replied Antonio.

Chapter Twenty-eight

Michael spent a miserable week in the stockade. Cooper had been by twice to torment him with the threat of court martial and hanging. As soon as they sobered up, his two companions were released, leaving him alone to worry about his fate. They had smelled, it was true, but at least they had been some sort of distraction.

He went over and over the events of the race day and each time came to the same conclusion: he could have done nothing differently. It was wrong to fire on women and children even in wartime. And they were not at war. Or had not been then, he thought bitterly. Cooper's order had been a criminal one and he was right not to have followed it. But, sweet Savior, he didn't want to hang for his righteousness.

He wondered how many had been killed and if Antonio and his wife had gotten away.

He was a soldier. He had killed men before, because they were trying to kill him. He had admired the fierce warriors of the plains. But he had never come to know any of them as well as he had come to know Antonio and Serena.

If they didn't hang him, if they only gave him a dishonorable discharge, maybe it would be all to the good. He was getting tired of watching proud and independent people reduced to beggars. It was going to happen here, with him or without him, of course. That was what he had always told himself. And it was true. One man couldn't hold back the greed of many. But if they threw him out, he might just welcome it.

He was summoned to the colonel's headquarters the afternoon of the colonel's return. Michael, who had always been so careful of his appearance, looked like a drunken private after a week without shaving and bathing. He brushed his uniform off as best he could and rubbed the toe of his boots on the back of his legs in a useless attempt to shine them.

When he was led into headquarters he saw that both Major Wheeler and Mr. Cooper were there. *Día*, wasn't he just living up to the lieutenant's opinion of him as a dirty mick, he thought with an inward groan, knowing he smelled as bad as he looked. But he stood at attention as proudly as though he were in his best uniform.

"At ease, Master Sergeant Burke," said the colonel. "I have just heard of the events of last Sunday from several sources and I wanted to hear your account."

"Begging your pardon, Colonel," said Lieutenant Cooper, "but the account of a traitor will hardly be helpful."

"Begging *your* pardon, Mr. Cooper, but before I make any decisions about your recommendation for court martial, I wish to hear all sides. Sergeant Burke?"

"Well, sir . . . I only know bits and pieces, ye see. It all happened so quickly. Em, I was watching the race between Manuelito and Mr. Cooper. We all were, of course, because the betting had been so heavy."

"Did you place a bet, Sergeant?"

"Em, yes, sir."

"On whom?"

"On Manuelito, sir."

The colonel had a hard time keeping a straight face, and he had to raise his hand to silence the major, who had immediately burst out with "You see, sir, a traitor."

"It is hardly treason to bet on what you think is the winning horse, Major Wheeler," Colonel Gray said dryly. "Go on, Sergeant Burke."

"Em . . . well . . . we all saw that the lieutenant and

Manuelito were in front when all of a sudden, and ye couldn't tell why, ye understand, sir, Manuelito seemed to lose control of his horse."

"Yes?"

"The lieutenant came in first, of course. And when Manuelito finally got in, well, we could see that his rein had been cut."

"And how did you know that, Sergeant."

"I was close enough to see that it was a fairly new bridle, sir. And it wasn't frayed, but sliced cleanly."

"Then what?"

"The judges, they gave the race to the lieutenant, even though the Navajo protested. They only wanted a rematch, sir, not to be given the race by default."

"The race was won fairly by Mr. Cooper, sir," the major interjected. "The other judges and I were convinced a rematch would have caused a riot, for our soldiers had bet so heavily."

"Was the rein cut, Major?"

"It would seem to be a possibility, sir."

"Mr. Cooper."

"Yes, sir."

"Did you have anything to do with Manuelito's rein being cut?"

Cooper turned red, then white. His voice was shaking as he tried to answer calmly. "Sir, I give you my word as an officer and a gentleman that I had nothing to do with such a disgraceful act."

Michael believed him. Much as he disliked the man, he knew that Cooper's pride would have kept him from such an act.

"I apologize, Mr. Cooper," said the colonel, "but I had to ask. Who do you guess to be responsible?"

"All of the men bet heavily on me, sir. Manuelito's horse was rumored to be very fast. Probably one of the enlisted men wanted to ensure his wager."

The colonel turned back to Michael. "Please go on, Sergeant."

"Em, the soldiers had hoisted Mr. Cooper on their shoulders, sir, and were going into the fort and closing the gate behind them. Some Navajo tried to follow and was shot."

"Was the man armed?"

"I don't know, sir. The doors opened again and the women and children were being fired upon. It was then Captain Taggert ordered me into the stockade."

"And *I* ordered you to get the howitzers," Cooper interjected. "Following the major's orders, you understand, Colonel," Cooper added obsequiously.

"And I *got* the howitzers. Me and Private Elwell," continued Michael. "It was when I was ordered to open fire that I refused, sir."

"And why did you refuse to obey a direct order, Sergeant?"

"Sir," protested the major, "what difference does it make why. He has admitted his refusal. He should be court-martialed."

"He should be hanged," added Cooper.

"Lieutenant!" barked the colonel.

"Yes, sir. Sorry, sir."

"I did disobey a direct order, sir. It seemed a criminal order, sir, to fire on men, women, and children who were not firing on us."

"Yes, Sergeant. Major Wheeler, why did you order the howitzers brought out?"

"Why? I think it would be obvious, sir. To subdue the hostiles."

"But they hadn't *been* hostiles until one of your men fired on them. Isn't that true, Major? It was a peaceful gathering like all the race days have been. Warriors don't bring their women and children with them if they intend to attack, do they, Major?"

"No, sir . . . b-but things had progressed in such a way . . ." stammered the major.

"Progressed! Progressed, sir! Things had deteriorated in such a way that you overreacted. In twenty minutes or less, Major, you managed to destroy the peace we have had these past months. A fragile one, I grant you, but all the more reason to take care of it." The colonel fell silent for a moment, collecting himself. "But you were, after all, in charge and made the best decision you were capable of. So did Lieutenant Cooper. And so did Master Sergeant Burke."

Both officers sputtered a protest.

"There will be no court-martial over this, I assure you. It was not an order given in war, but in peacetime." The colonel turned to Michael. "Nevertheless, it *was* an order, Sergeant Burke."

"Yes, sir."

"I could discharge you, you know."

"Yes, sir."

"But I think that would be foolish, don't you agree, Major? Sergeant Burke is an experienced Indian fighter and we will need all of those we can get, it would seem," the colonel said bitterly. "However, I am formally reprimanding you, and demoting you from master sergeant to sergeant, Burke."

"Yes, sir."

"And reassigning you to Mr. Lanier's company. Mr. Cooper, you will strip Sergeant Burke of his stripes."

"With the greatest pleasure, sir," said Cooper as he ripped them off Michael's sleeve.

"You are dismissed, Major Wheeler, Mr. Cooper."

"Yes, sir." The two men saluted sharply and left red-faced and furious.

"At ease, Sergeant Burke."

"Thank you, sir," said Michael with fervent gratitude. "For everything."

"Don't thank me, Burke. Thank my wife. And Mrs. Woolcott. They were very observant witnesses and eloquent advocates for you. In this instance, there were extenuating circumstances. I hope you understand that. I am not a man who tolerates insubordination."

"No, sir."

"I've watched you, Burke. You've acted very professionally in a difficult situation. I know you worked hard for your master sergeant stripes and I know you are an excellent noncommissioned officer, but there was no choice but to demote you."

"I understand, sir."

"You are dismissed, Sergeant Burke."

Michael saluted and turned sharply on his heels. At least he was walking out a free man. And still a cavalryman. Eight years it took to master sergeant, he thought, and all wiped out in an instant. Well, he would make the best of it. It was better than hanging!

When he got back to his quarters, he stripped for a much-needed bath. It was wonderful to get out of his filthy uniform, but it was very hard, after he was bathed and clean, to rip the stripes off his clean one. When he walked out to report to his new assignment, Private Elwell was on the front steps waiting for him.

"Well, Burke, I see they decided not to hang you," said Josh jokingly, but with a questioning look in his eyes.

"Thanks be to God," said Michael with a wry smile. "But I am surprised they didn't promote you."

"As a matter of fact, they did," Elwell admitted sheepishly. "To corporal."

"And I'm back to sergeant meself. But sure, I'm lucky not to be taking orders from you!"

"It was a lousy order, Michael," Elwell said vehemently. "I admire you for not obeying it. I wish I had had the courage."

"I don't know that it was courage, Josh, or just that I'm a rebellious, bloody-minded mick. And I doubt you'd be admiring me for it if I were to be swinging from a rope. I'd likely be cursing meself for a fool in that case."

Josh smiled. "Still friends, then?"

"Good friends are hard to find, Josh." Michael smiled and put out his hand. Elwell took it and clapped him on the shoulder.

"Well, I'm off wood detail, Josh, and out from under Cooper at least. I've been assigned to Mr. Lanier's company."

"He's a good officer. Not brilliant, but with a lot of experience in the territory."

"God spare me brilliance and brilliantine, Josh!" said Michael with a twinkle in his eye.

Elwell laughed. "You'll like serving under the lieutenant."

"I'm sure I will," said Michael, "but believe it or not, I'll be missing me men and me mules, Josh!"

Chapter Twenty-nine

Two days after Michael's release, Elizabeth and Janet Gray were again enjoying their afternoon tea.

"I am glad we can have a more relaxed cup of tea this afternoon. But I am sorry there's no excuse for brandy today," Mrs. Gray added with a mischievous smile. "I hear Mr. Lanier has a new sergeant," she added, nodding her satisfaction.

"Yes, Mrs. Taggert told me Master Sergeant Burke had been reassigned."

"*Sergeant* Burke now, my dear."

"Yes. Though I think he should have gotten a promotion for what he did."

"The colonel cannot reward disobedience, Elizabeth."

"I know," Elizabeth admitted, ashamed of her outburst. "I didn't mean to criticize the colonel. And I am thankful we were able to give him the truth about Sunday. But it still doesn't seem fair that Major Wheeler and Mr. Cooper get off scot-free for their bad judgment."

"The army is rarely fair, Elizabeth, as we both know," Mrs. Gray commented dryly. "And the lieutenant and the major . . . indeed, all of us will suffer from their mistakes."

"Do you think it means all-out war?"

"Oh, not like that going on back East, my dear. And not the hordes of savages you read about in dime novels. The Navajo do not fight like that. No, it will mean the raiding begins again. And when it does, it gives Governor

Carleton and all the New Mexicans who want this country an excuse to finally move in and take it."

"Surely the colonel can get word to Manuelito and the other headmen? Bring them in and convince them it was an isolated incident."

"The colonel will be lucky if none of our details are attacked, my dear."

Elizabeth paled.

Mrs. Gray patted her hand. "I didn't mean to distress you, dear. The usual target is not the cavalry, but horses and sheep."

Mrs. Gray's words had brought back the horror of Thomas's death to Elizabeth. And at the same time it had made her realize that it was not all troopers in general that she worried about, but one in particular. She sat there, remembering her first sight of Michael Burke. And her first opinion of him. Her disdain for the Irishman had disappeared, to be replaced by a growing sense of intimacy. She had first despised him and been annoyed by him. She had been attracted to him. One thing she had never been was indifferent. She was beginning to realize that his absence from her life would mean a great deal to her.

"Are you all right, Elizabeth?" asked Mrs. Gray. "You've been gazing into your cup like a fortune teller."

Elizabeth shoook her head a little as if to clear it and smiled sadly. "I wish I could tell what the future holds, Janet. For all of us."

What the future held for the colonel and his wife was revealed sooner than Elizabeth or Janet Gray expected or desired. Several weeks into April orders arrived, reassigning Colonel Gray to Fort Lyon in Colorado. Lieutenant Colonel Chavez was to take over Fort Defiance.

"What do you think, Burke?" asked Josh Elwell.

"I think it is a damned shame to be removin' the one man who might have a chance at making peace with the Navajo. But then, I don't think it is peace Carleton is wanting, but land."

"The fort will be full of New Mexican volunteers,"

said Josh, disdainfully spitting tobacco on the ground in front of them. "I wonder what Mrs. Woolcott will do," he added thoughtfully. "Cooper's been making his intentions known for months, but I can't say I've seen any interest on her part. Her husband had a sister in Sante Fe, I've heard . . ."

Michael had been wondering the same thing himself. From her behavior at the dance, he didn't think Elizabeth would consider Cooper. But she didn't have many choices, did she? Unless the Grays invited her to go with them. Which they would, he was sure, now that he thought of it. And what would be worse, her married to Cooper or gone forever? Seeing her as Mrs. Cooper would be sweet torture, but never seeing her again at all? He didn't know if he could stand it.

"You know that you are welcome to come with us, Elizabeth," Mrs. Gray told her.

They were at the breakfast table, drinking a second cup of coffee together, something that had become a habit after the colonel left for headquarters. The new orders had only come the day before and neither woman had had time to absorb the major changes this would bring to their lives.

"I hope you know that I am not making the offer out of pity, my dear," continued Mrs. Gray. "The colonel and I have truly enjoyed having you with us."

Elizabeth covered Mrs. Gray's hand with her own. "And I appreciate your offer of hospitality more than I can say. But . . ."

"But what? You are filled with ambition to become the best seamstress in Santa Fe?" the colonel's wife said tartly. "You've discovered a great talent in laundering? Or have you fallen desperately in love with Mr. Cooper?"

Elizabeth's laugh was hollow. "I *could* go to Santa Fe, you know. Thomas's sister is still there and while I would not live with her again, I would have an acquaintance. Perhaps I could stretch my pension by offering myself as a drawing teacher."

"Santa Fe is hardly Boston, my dear. There may be a

family or two interested in educating their daughters like young ladies, but that will not keep you in firewood."

"Other army widows have become laundresses," mused Elizabeth.

"Yes, at age forty-five. The younger laundresses, like Mary Ann . . ." Mrs. Gray caught herself.

Elizabeth blushed. She had occasionally wondered whether Michael Burke still visited the buxom Mary Ann.

"An older enlisted man's widow with children to support might stay with her husband's regiment and still be respected," Mrs. Gray continued more gently. "But a young woman like yourself, attractive and an officer's widow? No, Elizabeth, that is not a real possibility. Which leaves us Mr. Cooper. And you will never convince me that you are even considering such a fate."

"Well, I *have* thought about it," said Elizabeth somewhat defiantly.

"My dear, just think, you would be washing your pillowslips daily! You may as well become a laundress!" said Mrs. Gray with a wicked gleam in her eye. They both had to laugh at the thought of the lieutenant's oiled hair.

"Maybe I have misjudged him," said Elizabeth, trying to convince herself as much as her friend. "He has been most kind to me these past months."

"Why shouldn't he be, looking over at your lovely face and enjoying our good food! How could you overlook his conduct at the horse race?"

"I can't," Elizabeth admitted. "You are fortunately or unfortunately correct. I cannot marry Mr. Cooper. Which leaves me . . ."

"With us," said Mrs. Gray, getting up from the table. "I will brook no argument, Elizabeth," she added, patting her guest on the shoulder before she was off to begin packing.

Elizabeth sat there, looking out the window but seeing nothing. She knew Mrs. Gray was being sincere. The colonel and his wife did like her and had enjoyed her presence, though God alone knew why, she thought. I have been poor company even for myself. She poured herself a little more coffee. It was dark and bitter, having sat there for a while. Like my future. Or lack of one. I suppose I will have to go with them. And I suppose at Fort Lyon there may be some nice lieutenant or captain that Mrs. Gray will determine perfect for me. Who *will* be perfect for me.

She heard a demanding bark from the kitchen and stimulated by the coffee and her own restless desire to get out of the house, to get out of the morass that was her life, she quickly pulled on her wool jacket and taking Orion's leash, went to get him for a run.

The day was glorious. The sky was a brilliant blue and the sage and clumps of grass scattered around the fort had turned a fresh green. Orion pulled at his lead, whining and turning back to her as though to say, "Can't we get out of here?"

"All right, Orion, we will," she promised and turned toward the stables.

She had her mare saddled, reassuring the private that she had the colonel's permission to go for a short ride. The gates were open and Elizabeth gave a blithe wave to the soldier in charge as she trotted out. At first she kept close by the fort, but then Orion caught sight of a jackrabbit and took off after him and she kicked her horse into a gallop.

It felt so good to have the wind against her face. She felt awake for the first time since Thomas's death. The canyon walls ahead of her were sharp and clear in the morning light and the air was redolent with sage. She was so intent on what was before her that she didn't hear the hoofbeats behind her until they were almost upon her. For a moment she was terrified: Orion was out of sight and she was by now some distance from the fort. She kicked her mare, but before her horse could respond, a hand reached out and grabbed her reins. It took them a few hundred yards to come to a complete halt and by that time Elizabeth knew it was a soldier who had come after her.

"Are ye mad, woman!" Michael's voice was low and harsh with anger. "Ye know that the colonel has forbidden anyone to go more than fifty yards from the fort without an escort."

Elizabeth was angry too. What was he doing here, the interfering Irishman? She had just spent a most horrible winter, she felt her life was closing in on her; surely grabbing a few minutes of freedom was not such a crime.

"Let go of my horse, Sergeant Burke."

"Sure and I will not."

"I have the colonel's permission," lied Elizabeth.

"Ye do not. 'Twas the colonel himself sent me after ye."

"I . . . I only went after Orion. He took off after a jackrabbit and disappeared. I was afraid . . ."

"Ye were not afraid enough, Elizabeth. We are now in the middle of a war and we cannot have foolish women endangering themselves or the men sent after them."

"Well, you can just take yourself back to the fort and out of danger, Sergeant Burke!" Elizabeth said wildly. She knew she was in the wrong, but she could not bring herself to admit it. "And Orion *did* take after a rabbit," she added defiantly.

"I am sure he did. And where is the mighty hunter now?"

"He was heading toward the canyon."

Michael started to turn their horses around.

"Wait, Michael, we can't leave him," Elizabeth protested.

"He'll find his own way back."

"What if he were injured . . . or attacked?"

"So now ye're finally a little fearful!"

"Please, Michael," Elizabeth pleaded.

"Ye stay right here. I'll go ahead a little ways. If I am not back in fifteen minutes, ye are to head right back to the fort," he added in the tone of voice in which he gave orders to his men.

"Yes, sir, Sergeant Burke," said Elizabeth.

"I am not jesting, Elizabeth. There have been several bands of Navajo spotted close to the fort these last few weeks." Elizabeth was suddenly ashamed of herself. Michael was right and she was wrong. "I will do as you say, Michael," she said quietly.

Michael only nodded and rode ahead slowly, his field glasses in his hand.

Suddenly he descended into a small arroyo and was out of sight. Elizabeth sat as patiently as she could, hoping she had not put them both in danger.

It was a full eight minutes by Thomas's watch, which she kept pinned to her blouse, when Orion came loping along, his tongue hanging out, his jaws bloody and rabbit fur clinging to them. Michael Burke was right behind.

Elizabeth dismounted and attached the lead to the dog's collar. Orion looked ecstatic from his run and successful hunt and she did not have the heart to scold him. And why should she? He hadn't done anything wrong; she had.

"Ye won't have to feed him tonight, Elizabeth. He made a good meal of that rabbit," said Michael in gentler tones than he had been using.

Elizabeth's legs started to shake and she reached out and clung to her stirrup. The enormity of what she had done came home to her and also the memory of why she had done it.

Her voice shaking, she said, "You were right, Michael. I did not have permission and it was very foolish of me to ride out. I am . . . or was an officer's wife and should know better."

Michael could see how distraught she was and dismounted immediately.

"Now then, Elizabeth, I shouldn't have yelled at ye."

"Oh, yes you should have. Thomas wouldn't have done so," she added with an attempt at a smile. "He just would have been very disappointed in me. I wasn't thinking, really. I just had to get out of the fort. Out of my life," she added, almost in a whisper. "Did the colonel really send you?"

Michael nodded.

"Oh dear, and they have been so kind to me. I am ashamed to have caused him to lose his temper."

"He was more worried than angry, Elizabeth."

Michael had been furious with her, but when he caught up with her he was struck by how much more alive she looked than at any time since Thomas Woolcott's death. Now it was like the light had gone out inside her again.

"The news of the Grays' transfer must have come as a shock?"

Elizabeth nodded. She was quiet for a minute and then said, "They have invited me to go with them to Fort Lyon."

Michael thought he had resigned himself to the eventual loss, either to Cooper or to Santa Fe. But he had hoped she would be a few more months with the Grays. Now she would, but not at Fort Defiance. Having her married to Cooper would have been sweet torture, but at least he would have seen her occasionally. This way she was just . . . gone.

"And ye'll be goin' with them, then?"

"I don't have much choice," she replied bitterly.

"Em, I thought that . . . em, well, Mr. Cooper seems very attentive."

"He is. But I dislike him too much to marry him, even for the security it would give me. Of course, I *could* become a laundress," she continued. "Would you come and visit me the way you visited Mary Ann, Michael," she added wildly, hardly knowing what she was saying. She was just so tired and so lonely. Once again she was alone. Why hadn't life given her someone who wanted her, just for herself, not as someone to take care of or rescue.

"Ye should not be talkin' of things like that, Elizabeth," said Michael, putting his hand gently on her shoulder. "You are an officer's widow, someone to be respected. Ye'll make a good home with the Grays and maybe find a fine officer to love at Fort Lyon." He tried to make his tone light. But sweet Mary, it was hard to be so close to her.

She stood there, the tears finally coming and running down her face, and he loved her so much 'twas killin' him. He couldn't help it. He reached out and, pulling her to him, crushed her against his chest.

She stayed there willingly, relaxed against him, and then pulled back.

"Ouch." A strand of hair had caught in one of his brass buttons. He held her in close again while he worked her hair free.

"You are a good friend to me, Michael," she whispered after he let her go.

He didn't think about it. If he had, he wouldn't have had the courage to say it.

"Elizabeth, would ye ever consider marrying me?"

She looked up at him, eyes wide with surprise.

"Em ... forget I even asked," he stammered. "I know 'twould be a comedown from bein' an officer's wife and if ye go with the Grays ..."

"If I go with the Grays I will be dependent upon them until I find some imaginary officer. If I ever did. Oh, Michael, why are you asking me this?" She wanted him to say, Because I love you and cannot bear life without you near me. Because *I* need *you*. Because I cannot let you go.

"Ye don't have many choices, Elizabeth. I wanted to offer ye one more. We are good friends, I think?"

Elizabeth nodded.

"Ye would have yer own home again, although non-commissioned quarters are not as fine," he added apologetically. "Of course, I am not only a sergeant but a mick to boot," he added teasingly. But she could feel the vulnerability behind the attempt at humor.

"I hope I am a little different than I was a year ago, Michael. I would rather an Irishman than skinny-arsed Cooper any day," she added tartly.

"What are ye saying then, Elizabeth?"

What *was* she saying? It was clear that life wasn't going to give her what she wanted. But it was offering her what she needed: a good man who cared about her the way Thomas had. One she liked and respected. One she desired. She had to admit that to herself. It was hard, for he had never given her any sign he felt anything but affection for her.

"I think I am saying I accept your offer, Michael. But

I will give you a chance to rescind it," she added with a twinkle in her eye.

Michael couldn't believe it. A few minutes ago she was lost to him and now she was going to be his wife. He felt the strangest combination of incredible happiness and awful disappointment. What he had so desired was now his. But the reason was not a love that matched his own or even mutual passion, but need. She needed him, Elizabeth did. She was backed into a corner and he had offered her a way out and she had taken it. She had taken him because he was the way out, the only way that gave her some measure of the freedom she'd lost. And they *were* friends and surely that was something to build on. He would not expect desire in a woman newly widowed, but perhaps desire could come later.

"*Do* you want to take your offer back," Elizabeth said in a strained voice, for she realized Michael had said nothing in response.

He pulled her back in his arms and kissed the top of her head. Suddenly, Orion was pushing between them. They both looked down at him and each other and laughed.

"I hope you don't mind that Orion comes with me, Michael?"

"Not atall, Elizabeth. 'Twill be a fine thing to have another Irishman in the house."

"I must confess something to you, Michael," said Elizabeth, sounding serious again.

"Yes?" Michael didn't know what she was thinking, but was afraid she would say something like "I don't feel I'll ever love you as more than a friend."

"The only reason I didn't consider Mr. Cooper as an option is that he would never take a mongrel into his household!" Michael let out a relieved laugh and Orion barked happily.

" 'Tis lucky ye are, ye devil, to be having me and not Cooper then," said Michael to the dog.

And lucky I am too, thought Elizabeth as they rode back to the fort to share their news.

Chapter Thirty

"I have never tried to plan a wedding *and* pack all in the same week," grumbled Mrs. Gray to the colonel that night after they went to bed.

"You love it, Janet. Admit it."

His wife laughed. "You know me too well, Charles. I do! And I am so happy for Elizabeth."

"She might have done better at Fort Lyon."

"Better a bird in the hand, Charles. Though I might indeed have been able to find her someone in Colorado. But never one as handsome as Sergeant Burke."

"He is a good man, and that's the important thing, Janet," the colonel answered with teasing sternness. "But she'll be living on less than she did with Woolcott."

"I don't think the material things are that important to Elizabeth. I just hope . . ."

"What?"

"I hope she didn't accept him just to keep from being a burden to us, Charles. He deserves better than that."

"Cooper will be furious," said the colonel with a smile of satisfaction on his face.

"Ah, yes, Mr. Cooper. To be beaten by a mere sergeant, when he didn't even know he had a rival."

"Do you mind leaving here, Janet?"

"You know I mind very much, Charles. But mainly for your sake and the Navajo. With Chavez and Carson they'll never have a chance."

"I would have had to follow Carleton's orders, though,

and so I am just as glad not to be here and be part of their destruction."

"Will it be that bad?"

"I am afraid so, my dear, I am afraid so. But come now and get some sleep. After all, you have a wedding to plan tomorrow!"

The ceremony was small and private because Elizabeth was going straight from mourning to marriage. She wore her best dress, a dark green silk, which was very appropriate, said Mrs. Gray, quieting her fears. "It is a return to color, but not too bright, my dear, and you look lovely in it."

Elizabeth's hands were shaking as she fastened the small mother-of-pearl buttons that ran up the front of the gown. "Oh no," she cried, almost in tears, as one of the top ones popped off.

"There, there. You can take my brooch," said Mrs. Gray unpinning a circlet of pearls from her own gown and pinning it just under Elizabeth's throat.

"Do you think I am doing the right thing, Janet?" Elizabeth whispered as she fingered the brooch.

"Wearing my pin? I think you must, for we have no time to search for that wretched button," the colonel's wife teased.

Elizabeth's smile was fleeting. "You know what I mean. Marrying Sergeant Burke. I mean Michael."

"It matters little what I think, my dear. It is you who will be living with him after all." Mrs. Gray did not intend to put the weight of her opinion either way.

"I do like him and we have become good friends, you know."

Mrs. Gray nodded encouragingly.

"But . . ."

"But what, dear?"

"It feels so disloyal to Thomas."

"To marry so soon? Yes, I imagine it must. But the army has given you no choice, has it? No one would understand that better than a career soldier like Thomas Woolcott."

"It is also something else," continued Elizabeth, her voice so low that Mrs. Gray had to strain to hear. "I . . ." She cleared her throat. She had never spoken of such things before. "I find Sergeant Burke . . . not unattractive."

There's a fine way of putting it, thought Mrs. Gray, struggling not to smile.

"Surely that will be a helpful thing in your marriage, Elizabeth."

"But I didn't feel exactly the same way about Thomas, although I loved him very much."

"Thomas was a number of years older than you, Elizabeth," said Mrs. Gray matter-of-factly, for although she knew that the pain in Elizabeth's voice was very real, she did not want her to make too much of her feelings. "Your desire for him would be bound to be different from what you felt for Thomas. Michael is young and handsome and even though I am happily married I find him 'not unattractive' also!"

"Then you don't think I am terrible?"

"Not at all," said the older woman briskly. "If you bring friendship and desire to your marriage, then love has a good chance to develop, don't you think?"

Love was already present on Michael's side, of that the colonel's wife was sure, after seeing him with Elizabeth for the past two days. She also suspected that Elizabeth was close to being in love with him, but would hold back out of loyalty to Thomas. In time, things would sort themselves out, for if any two people were perfect for each other, it was these two, she was convinced.

"Come, my dear, they are only waiting for us."

Michael had asked Joshua Elwell to be his best man. "But before ye stand up with me, would ye play a tune for us, Josh?" So Elizabeth walked into the parlor to the sweet strains of Elwell's fiddle. Mrs. Gray had her by one arm and the colonel took the other, for she had asked both of them to give her away.

It was a short walk to where Michael was waiting, looking pale and nervous. His blue eyes fairly burned through her as she took her place by his side and her legs trembled as the chaplain began to read the marriage service.

Michael said a short prayer to himself, asking for forgiveness for not being married by a priest. Surely God would understand. There were no priests closer than Albuquerque and even if there had been, he didn't know if he could have convinced Elizabeth into a papist ceremony. Perhaps someday, for his sake, they could have one of the Spanish friars marry them. For now, well, many a young couple in Mayo had had to wait weeks for a priest to sanctify their union.

They said their vows very quietly and Michael slipped a plain silver ring set with a green turquoise that he had traded a Navajo for months ago. It had had to be cut down by the blacksmith to fit Elizabeth's finger. She looked up at him with shy pleasure. Clearly she had not expected him to produce a ring in such short notice.

"I hope you like it, *muirneach*," he whispered.

"Oh, I do, Michael."

They turned and made the short walk to the other side of the parlor, where Mrs. Gray had set up her good crystal and china. There was a light lunch, a small wedding cake, and even a bottle of champagne that the Grays had kept for a special occasion.

Joshua offered the toast. "Here is to Michael and Elizabeth. We wish them a long and happy union and many children!"

"Hear, hear," said the Grays as they lifted their glasses.

Elizabeth was blushing furiously. Children. She hadn't even thought of that. Of course Michael would want them. Did she? And could she give them to him? Had it been Thomas's age or was it she who had been unable to conceive?

The colonel and his lady offered them their good wishes. Mrs. Gray joked that they must finish every last bit of food, and quickly too, for it must all be packed by this evening!

They all laughed. But it was true: the colonel and his wife were leaving the next day and Mrs. Gray had kept out her dishes just for the ceremony.

When they finally took their leave to walk to Michael's quarters, they were showered with rice by Mahoney and one of his friends.

"Corporal *Ma*honey!" Michael exclaimed.

"Congratulations, Sergeant Burke, Mrs. Burke, ma'am," said Mahoney with a grin.

Elizabeth laughed and thanked him. "Now I feel like a real bride."

When they got to Michael's quarters, Michael took his hat off and a handful of rice fell out.

"Damn the boy," he said with a rueful laugh.

"Oh no, Michael, it was very sweet of him," Elizabeth said, but she could tell by the way Michael's eyes were twinkling that he really wasn't annoyed at all.

Elizabeth surveyed her new quarters.

"I'm afraid it isn't what you're used to," said Michael apologetically. "Sure and it isn't what I'm used to, but I am the one who's moved up in the world!"

"So that is why you married me, Sergeant Burke!" said Elizabeth with mock indignation. "Just to get out of bachelor quarters?"

"And away from all that snoring," he joked.

"Ah, but what if *I* snore," she teased.

"Em, but ye don't, do ye, Mrs. Burke?"

"I am not the one who snores, Sergeant. It seems to me that I remember you snoring at the *kinaalda*. Had I only remembered this earlier," she said sadly, "I might have reconsidered your proposal."

They laughed together, and Michael thanked God for their shared sense of the ridiculous. 'Twould make the first night a little easier.

"Em, there is only this one room, the kitchen, and our bedroom," he said. "I furnished it as best I could in the time I had. But we can choose things together."

Elizabeth nodded, suddenly quiet.

"Shall I be showing you the bedroom?"

She nodded again and reached out for his hand. Hers was freezing cold and his heart sank. *Día*, what if she didn't want him that way? Should he even be asking her for this tonight? But it *was* their wedding night.

The bedroom was so small that to Elizabeth's eyes it was all bed.

"Em, there is a rod to hang your clothes on over there." Michael pointed. "And I hung a curtain so that you would have some privacy."

The "curtain" consisted of two old paisley shawls sewn together, and Elizabeth's carpetbag stood beside it.

"Thank you, Michael," she said, letting go of his hand. "I'll get ready for bed now, shall I?" She slipped behind the curtain before he could answer. She had no special night rail for tonight, only her best cotton one. But Mrs. Gray had given her a beautiful silk shawl in a green that brought out the green in her eyes. As she slipped it over her shoulders, she could feel the delicate fringe brushing her arms.

When she stepped out from behind the improvised curtain, Michael wasn't there. It felt anticlimactic to have thrown the luxurious shawl on to please him and not have him there to see, but as she slipped under the covers, she was mostly grateful that she did not have to face his eyes.

He returned only a minute later. "I wanted to make sure the dog was settled in for the night, Elizabeth. Em, I didn't want him to disturb our evening." Michael started undressing right there in the bedroom, although he kept his back turned. Just as he got down to his drawers, without thinking she blew out the lamp, leaving them in semidarkness.

It was the night before the full moon and light was pouring in the bedroom windows. Elizabeth could see Michael's outline as he stripped off his underwear. He turned and walked quickly over to his side of the bed and she lifted the covers to welcome him. Did he always sleep naked, she wondered, or was he naked because he intended to make love to her? It was a cool evening but for some reason she was feeling very warm and she let the shawl slip from her shoulders. She was sitting against the pillows. Should she keep sitting there? Should she turn to him? Away from him? She had never felt so flustered or so aware of any man's presence before.

Michael sat next to her and, sliding his arm around her, pulled her against him.

"Em . . . we do not need to be doing anything tonight, *muirneach*. If you are feeling it is too soon after Thomas, I would understand."

"Thank you, Michael," she whispered, breathing a soft sigh of relief. Maybe they would never need to do "anything," she thought, and she would never have to face her wild desire.

Michael's hand was resting just above her breast and she felt a pleasant tingling in her nipple. Her own hands were folded in her lap, fingers plaited. She was conscious of his thighs, hairy and muscular, through the thin lawn of her night rail.

Michael loosened his arm and, lifting her chin toward him, ran his finger down her cheek and across her lips. Then he leaned down to give her a gentle kiss.

"Good night, Elizabeth," he whispered.

She should have just whispered good night back and turned away and gone to sleep. It was all he seemed to expect, a good-night kiss. It would be foolish to reveal her desire to a man who had married her only out of friendship. And she didn't love him. She couldn't, not so soon after Thomas. But the light kiss wasn't enough for her. She opened her lips under his and nibbled hungrily at the edges of his mouth.

It was as though they went up in flames at the same time. Michael made his kiss deeper and she answered with a hunger that she had hardly known was there, a hunger that must have been hidden in some dark corner of herself when she was with Thomas. As though she had shut it away years ago when she realized Thomas's love sprang from satisfaction, not need.

"Elizabeth," Michael whispered, pulling away for one agonizing moment, "if we go on like this I can't promise to stop. I didn't want to push you too soon."

Her answer was to slide down and pull him with her.

His mouth soon wanted more and he started to massage her breast as he kissed her and then, opening the buttons of her nightgown, he lowered his head and began to tease her nipple with his tongue. Elizabeth gave a little moan and slid further under him, rubbing herself against him as he drew her breast into his mouth.

She could feel his hardness through her night rail, but she wanted to feel flesh against flesh, and she started to pull the gown up.

"Just a minute, *mo muirneach*," he said, and letting go of her breast, he gently drew her gown off and settled on top of her.

She could feel his manhood resting on her belly and started to move against it. It felt so silky and soft and yet hard at the same time, and she wanted to keep rubbing against it. Except she also wanted him to rub against her, against that part of her that she was only now becoming aware of, and so she opened her legs and moved herself up so that the tip of him was caught just where she wanted it. Michael lifted himself up a little. "Ah, so that's what you want, darlin'. Sure and I don't know how long I can give it to ye, but I'll try."

He moved himself in circles, exerting only a little pressure, and Elizabeth thought she had never felt such exquisite pleasure. Then he groaned, and whispering "Sorry," slipped down to enter her.

His entry was gentle, as his every move in this love-making had been, but once he was in her, the two of them began to move together in satisfying rhythm, faster and faster, until Michael gave a cry and collapsed upon her.

The pleasure had been so great that it took Elizabeth a minute to realize that she still wanted something, that she was still hungry. It was different than it had been with Thomas, but now it felt the same. Some part of her was alive and wanting more and that was the part she had shut away. But how could she shut it away again?

And then Michael shifted his body just a little, not withdrawing, but giving himself enough room to stroke her and she knew that she would not go hungry tonight, as she had so many nights with Thomas and never even known it. His fingers were like his cock, circling slowly and then quickly. But he was still in her. She pushed herself back into the mattress and up and up as though he were pushing her higher and higher. Which he was, until she was so high that all she could do was come down, down, into his arms, flowing over him as he had flowed into her.

She heard sounds she had never heard before and realized they were her own cries, involuntary and wordless. She clung to him, burying her face in his shoulder, dying of pleasure and embarrassment. Dear God, whatever would he say, whatever would he think of her? Her husband dead only a few months and here she was totally abandoned, opening her deepest desire to Michael when she had never done it with Thomas. She started to cry, from the release of it and the confusion of it, very softly, trying to stop, but unable.

"There, there," murmured Michael.

Elizabeth wanted to say . . . what? Thank you, I'm sorry, I'll never do that again, I've died from pleasure, I am so ashamed . . . But all that came out was "Oh, Thomas . . ."

She could feel Michael pull back, although it was not physical distance that came between them. He took a deep breath and said, "Sure and ye would miss him now, when ye're feeling what ye must have only felt with him."

She wanted to say, No, that isn't it at all, I never felt like this with Thomas. I was just thinking how sad it was we never had this. And how good it is that you and I have this, especially since we don't have love. But he didn't give her a chance. He pulled her close and they spooned together, his chin resting on the top of her head. But for all that you couldn't have fit a feather between them, Elizabeth knew that the distance between them was greater than when they had begun to make love.

Chapter Thirty-one

The next morning, Michael awoke first. He was lying on his back and Elizabeth was on his chest, her head cradled by his right hand. He stroked her hair gently and felt himself getting hard.

Día, what was he to do? She had been so wonderfully responsive last night and then that crying out for her dead husband. He couldn't put her through that again. Or himself, he added honestly. He had taken her in love, but he couldn't tell her that. Someday, perhaps, but not now, when she was so newly widowed. And he didn't want her remembering Woolcott, God forgive him. He wanted her thinking only of himself.

And yerself better relax, boyo, because ye won't be doin' anything this morning. Or any time soon, unless she wants it too.

It took a few minutes, but by the time Elizabeth stirred, he was limp again. Or almost.

She moved her fingers slowly through the black curly hair on his chest and when she lifted her head to look at him, he could see her expression shift from puzzled wonder to recognition. He wondered how long it would take for her to get used to waking up to him and not Thomas Woolcott.

"Good morning, *muirneach*," he whispered.

"Good morning, Michael. Have you been awake long?"

"Oh, I've been lying here thinking for a few minutes. I'm wondering something, Elizabeth."

"Yes?"

"I'm wondering if it wouldn't be better to wait a wee while before . . ." *Día*, he didn't have the words for it. "Em, before being like husband and wife as we were last night. I'm thinking maybe when you are ready and not missing Thomas so much, ye can let me know." He paused and then pushed on. "What I'm tryin' to say is I won't be bothering ye until ye want me to."

"I see, Michael." She hesitated. "Perhaps you are right." Oh God, she was so ashamed of herself. She had been afraid he would think her completely abandoned, but it was even worse. He thought her lost in memories of her husband's lovemaking. And here she was, her hand resting on his flat belly, wanting to slide it down to his thigh and then up again, wanting to feel him lift under her fingers. What if she said, I want you now? He would think her utterly unfeeling, which was what she must be. How *could* she be wanting him so when Thomas was only gone a short time?

Michael had never been so grateful for reveille in his life when the bugle sounded a minute later.

"Don't get up, then, Elizabeth. I'll get meself a cup of coffee."

"No, I always got up for Thomas," she said without thinking and then stopped. "I am sorry, Michael," she whispered.

"Don't be, Elizabeth. 'Tis only natural for you to be remembering. We'll work out our own ways, but for today, why don't you rest a little longer."

He was dressed and gone quickly and Elizabeth lay there until she heard him clatter down the front steps. Then she pulled her wrapper around her and went into the kitchen to let Orion in. At least that was a familiar ritual, something constant in her life, she thought as the dog gave her his usual ecstatic greeting.

"You can't fool me, dog. You just want to be fed," she told him as she did every morning. She put down a bowl of scraps and then warmed a biscuit for herself.

After breakfast, she didn't take the time to wash the dishes, for it was the morning of the Grays' departure and she wanted to help Mrs. Gray with last-minute packing and have some time to say a private good-bye.

"I hope your first night in your new home was a . . . comfortable one." The colonel's wife gave Elizabeth a teasing glance and the younger woman blushed and then busied herself with folding kid gloves and silk scarves into tissue paper.

"I know I shouldn't be meddling, Elizabeth, but I care about you and I like Sergeant Burke. You did not feel physically repulsed by him, I hope?"

Elizabeth gave a short laugh. "On the contrary," she admitted. "He is a very attractive man and that is the problem."

"Surely not a problem, my dear?"

"Not in the . . . emotion of the moment, no . . . but I felt so disloyal to Thomas . . ."

"Of course you would," said Mrs. Gray as she continued to place the tissue-wrapped packets in the top drawer of her trunk. "Thomas has only been gone a short time and if you experienced certain feelings with Sergeant Burke you had had with Thomas, well, then . . ."

"But I didn't."

"Yet you found him attractive?" said Mrs. Gray in a puzzled voice.

"No, no, I mean I didn't with Thomas. Feel the same." Elizabeth was twisting a pair of gloves into a knot and Mrs. Gray gently removed them, sat down on the bed, and pulled Elizabeth down next to her.

"So you desire your new husband in a way you didn't Thomas Woolcott?"

Elizabeth nodded. "I feel so ashamed."

"Nonsense, my dear. It is natural that Sergeant Burke should awaken these feelings in you."

"But I *loved* Thomas."

"Of course you did. And sometimes, when we are lucky, love and desire go hand in hand. The colonel and I have been lucky that way. But it is not disloyal to Thomas to feel differently about Michael Burke."

"But Thomas was so loving to me, so good, and I couldn't give him this," protested Elizabeth.

Mrs. Gray patted her hands. "Yes, he took care of you very well, my dear. And you were grateful and gave him your love in return. And were an affectionate wife, I am sure?"

Elizabeth nodded and whispered, "But that was all I was."

"Well, perhaps that was all Thomas Woolcott wanted. And perhaps," she added gently, "he did not know how to awaken your desire."

"He was a wonderful husband," Elizabeth started to say, and then remembered the nights that Thomas would roll over and leave her there, wanting something. Something Michael had known exactly how to give her.

"It is hard when someone has gone, to remember what he was lacking. Thomas may not have been looking for a passionate response from you, but I would think Sergeant Burke is very different."

"I thought so last night, but this morning he told me that he would not . . . uh, initiate anything. He didn't want to rush me, and he feared he had last night because I cried for Thomas afterward."

"A sweet, chivalrous response, my dear," said Mrs. Gray with a smile. "A bit foolish, but then he is young," she added, getting up. "So you will wait, of course. I can see that. Well, perhaps it will give you both time to get to know one another better."

Elizabeth stood up and Mrs. Gray's tone became more serious. "But you'd better not wait too long, Elizabeth. The new commandant, Colonel Chavez, is a New Mexican. He and Christopher Carson are not going to give the Navajo much time. Your husband will soon be very busy and quite possibly in danger. Things are different in the army, Elizabeth, you know that. In civilian life, you would have had a year of mourning and perhaps a year of courting. But you are not a civilian, and you don't have that kind of time," she said, closing her trunk. "There, I'm ready."

"Oh, Janet, I don't know what I'll do without you," Elizabeth cried.

The colonel's wife opened her arms. "I will miss you too, dear. You have been like a daughter to me."

When they separated, the colonel's wife dabbed at her eyes with a crumpled handkerchief and then gently patted Elizabeth's cheeks dry. "I've been crying off and on all morning, so this is all wet and almost useless." She laughed. "I *hate* leaving," she added fiercely. "Charles has worked so hard and Carleton is out to ruin everything."

"What do you think will happen?"

"They want this country, my dear, and they are going to get it. In all my time with the army, I have yet to see a tribe keep their land. The Navajo will end up at Bosque Redondo."

All of a sudden, Elizabeth's troubles seemed quite small. What were her problems compared with what was happening around her? She had not been able to imagine going back East when Thomas died, for the red rock country had claimed her. And she was only a newcomer to this land. What must it feel like to be Antonio or Serena? How could they even think of leaving?

"Do you think some will try to stay?"

Mrs. Gray nodded. "I am sure Manuelito will never give in."

"He'll fight?"

"And be overcome. I am glad, at least, that if we couldn't stop it, we won't be a part of it."

The post band played "Garry Owen" softly as the colonel bade good-bye to his troops and officers, and then a more rousing rendition of the "The Girl I Left Behind Me" as he and his wife rode through the gates.

"Sure, and they are happy enough to use an Irish tune and Irish men for their killing, aren't they, *Ma*honey."

"Ma*hon*ey, sir," said the boy with a grin.

"But 'No Irish need apply' when a man is looking for work," Michael continued bitterly.

Mahoney looked over at Michael curiously. He had

never heard his sergeant be anything but spit-and-polish army.

"Are you disappointed that the colonel has been transferred, Sergeant Burke?"

"He is a man who acts humanely, whatever his orders, Corporal. And he is a career soldier. Our new commanding officer, Colonel Chavez, is only from the New Mexico Volunteers and so are the troops he is bringing. All any of them is interested in is removing the Navajo from their land."

"But this is all United States land now, Sergeant," said Mahoney. It was a statement, not an argument.

"And isn't that just what the English were saying when they came to Ireland, lad? Pushing us all off the land we had lived on for centuries. When a people have been in a place for so long, when the very dirt and air and water of it are in your cells, then you belong to the land, not the land to you." Michael looked over at Mahoney, who looked like he was trying to understand. "Ah, you were born in the great city of New York and you don't know what I am talking about, do ye? All I know, lad," said Michael, more calmly, "is I have been doing this too long."

It was his first night coming home to Elizabeth after a day of regular duty and only his second in a real house and not the barracks. The lamps were lit, the stove was hot, and Elizabeth had prepared a delicious meal, if the smells coming from the kitchen were to be trusted.

" 'Tis lovely," said Michael as he scraped his boots and hung up his coat.

"Is that you, Michael?" Elizabeth called from the kitchen.

He almost answered "Yes, my love" but caught himself just in time. " 'Tis indeed."

Elizabeth emerged carrying a bowl of stew and a plate of homemade bread.

"Let me just wash up, Elizabeth," he said, thinking how lovely she looked, her cheeks flushed from the heat of the kitchen stove.

When he came back, hands clean and hair slicked back, she was sitting at the table.

"How was your day, Elizabeth," he asked politely as he sat down.

"I helped Mrs. Gray finish her packing, Michael. I will *miss* her,"she added, her eyes filling up.

"She was a great friend to you, I know. And we will all miss the two of them."

"I think underneath her sadness, she was almost glad to be leaving, Michael. She said if they couldn't prevent what will happen, they are happy not to be part of it."

"I think the colonel and his lady are surely the lucky ones. The Ute and the New Mexicans have been trying to get rid of the Navajo for years and now Carleton is going to give them their chance."

"And there is no hope of making one more attempt at a peaceful settlement?"

"They don't *want* a peaceful settlement, Elizabeth, if they ever did."

"I have always loved the army, Michael. It has been my home for eight years. The only home I have had as a grown woman. I never questioned much before now. I saw Thomas's job as keeping the peace. But Serena and Antonio are my friends . . . our friends," she added shyly. "How can we stand by and let them be driven off their land?"

"I don't like it any better than you do, Elizabeth."

"And the army is even more of a home to you, Michael."

"It has given me a job I am good at, and home and friends. I've been lucky up until now. I've been in skirmishes, Elizabeth, but I have not had to be part of a full-scale war before."

"Will there be much fighting?" she asked, suddenly remembering Mrs. Gray's words to her.

"In a fight, Elizabeth, you forget your moral qualms, if ye ever had any," he said with a sad smile. "You get caught up in it, you can't do anything but react to whatever is coming at you. I'd hate to be fighting Manuelito and his people, but 'tis what I'm trained to do. What I fear, *muirneach,* is that this will be a very different kind of war. If Carson is as smart as they say he is, he won't be doin' what all the others have done: seeking a fight and wondering where all the Indians disappeared to. He'll go after their fields and stock, if he's anything like they say he is. He'll starve them out, is what I am afraid of."

Elizabeth reached out her hand and put it on top of his. "We are husband and wife now, Michael. And we are friends. We must try to be each other's home," she said softly, afraid to lift her eyes to his.

Elizabeth's words went straight to his heart and Michael turned his hand over and grasped hers.

"Thank you, Elizabeth," he whispered, stroking her fingers with his thumb.

They finished their dinner in silence and after Elizabeth finished the washing up, spent an hour in the parlor, Elizabeth knitting and Michael trying to read.

"Em, have ye ever read Mr. Dickens, Elizabeth?" he asked, looking up from his battered copy of *Nicholas Nickleby.*"

Elizabeth lifted her eyebrows. "Why, yes, I have. Is that whom you are reading?"

"Ye sound surprised."

Elizabeth blushed. "Why, no." She paused. "Well, yes, I confess I am. I suppose I didn't expect an enlisted man . . ."

"Ye mean an uneducated Irishman . . ."

"Truly, I didn't mean that, Michael."

"I am only teasing ye, Elizabeth. Not all enlisted men or Irishmen are illiterate, ye know. Anyhow," he said, putting the book down, "I've read this one so many times and I never get any further . . ."

"Why, which one is it, Michael?"

"*Nicholas Nickleby.* Em, ye see, I've only got the first volume to read and I know it by heart. There are not too many booksellers on the plains, I am afraid!"

Elizabeth looked over at Michael's book. The leather cover was worn, exposing the cardboard underneath, and the pages looked soft, almost tissue thin. She thought back to her own school days, when she had never heard anything but "Watch out for the dirty Irish children," and was once again ashamed of herself. Michael's book was obviously a treasured possession and his hunger for the written word almost palpable to her.

"Not everything of mine was destroyed by the Comancheros, Michael. My father brought his books with him and I saved a few. I haven't unpacked completely, but I think I have the three volumes of that book." She hesitated. "Thomas wasn't fond of reading, but my father used to read aloud to us in the evenings. It would be nice to do that again. That is, if you would enjoy it?"

" 'Twould be heaven," said Michael with a smile that lit up his face.

Elizabeth set her knitting down. "Tomorrow night, then." She cleared her throat. "Today was a long day, and I think I am ready for bed."

"I'll be joining ye soon. After I bank the fire."

She was in bed by the time he had finished with the stove, her back turned away from him. He crawled in and gave her a soft kiss on the cheek and then turned away himself. "Good night, *muirneach*," he whispered.

Elizabeth lay awake for a while. She could feel the warmth of his body and hear his breathing, which became soft and regular after a few minutes. Obviously he wasn't suffering from thwarted desire, the way she was. She wanted him. But she couldn't, for the life of her, show it so soon again. At the same time, she could hear Mrs. Gray's words, "Don't wait too long, Elizabeth. Don't wait too long."

Chapter Thirty-two

The hostilities started slowly and gathered momentum. Kit Carson, who had acted as agent for the Ute, hired the best warriors and Mexican guides from Abiquiu and by early June raids on Dinetah were being led out of Cubero and Cebolleta as well. Slave traders, claiming to be part of "volunteer" companies, captured and sold several hundred Navajo women and children. One of them was Serena's niece.

"What will happen to her, husband?" Serena's throat was hoarse from crying and she was exhausted from the night she had spent attempting to comfort her sister and brother-in-law.

"She will become someone's servant. If she is lucky, the family will treat her well. If she is *very* lucky, someday they will release her. Perhaps someday someone will even marry her."

"But she was to have married the son of Left Hand this spring!"

"I know."

"I don't know if I can bear it. It reminds me too much of our own daughter."

Antonio sat beside her and pulled her into his arms. "You must rest," he said, putting his hand on her belly. "You can't do any more for your sister. She will have to live with this the way we have. What is important now is our new child."

"And where will he or she be born, husband? At Bosque Redondo?" Serena asked bitterly.

"Never. I promise you that. Our daughter will open her eyes upon Dinetah."

"So you think it will be a daughter?"

"I hope so. Not to replace our lost one," he added.

"No, I understand you. And I feel the same. I hope for a daughter too. May Changing Woman give my niece strength," she murmured.

"May Changing Woman bring us all strength, wife. Chavez has given us until July twentieth to come in. After that, any Diné who is not willing to go to Bosque will be considered hostile."

"You can tell that Colonel Chavez and Rope Thrower that I am already hostile," said Serena, her anger taking over from her grief.

"That is what I have always loved about you, wife. Your spirit. You would have made a fine warrior," he teased. "Like the women of the Indeh."

"I will fight next to you if need be, husband, you know that."

"For right now, why don't you lie here next to me, and get some sleep," he said, drawing her down against him.

They lay there quietly, Antonio's hand resting on her slightly swollen belly. "Our daughter must be tired too," he whispered. "She is being quiet."

Serena nodded.

Antonio reached under his wife's dress and stroked the soft skin of her belly. "You are as round and tight as a little drum," he whispered.

"Soon I will be more like a giant melon," she joked. "Too big to lie with." It felt good to have him stroke her and she gave a little sigh of pleasure. Antonio brought his other hand around her and cupped her belly, pressing her close against him. Then his left hand wandered between her legs and he began to stroke her there too.

Serena could feel him hard against her buttocks and started to turn toward him.

"No, no," he murmured into her ear. "Let me pleasure you."

So she let herself relax against him as he gently brought her to climax. He was her husband and all male and she could feel him stiff against her. But as much as he was husbanding her he was also mothering her, holding her and their unborn child in his hand as she sobbed out her release against him.

"Go to sleep, wife," he finally whispered, and after a few minutes of blessed peace, she did.

But Antonio lay awake, considering their options. A few Diné had begun to surrender, reasoning that there were too many *bilagaana* to fight. They would be pushed onto the reservation anyway, so why not go of their own free will?

"But you are not free," Manuelito and Barboncito had told them. "How can you be free away from Dinetah?"

But the words of the headmen could not overcome the hopeless resignation of those first to go.

Antonio knew that soon more and more would join them. He would not. He could not. He would follow his uncle. Disappear into the red rock canyons with his wife. They had never been defeated before, they would not be now.

Antonio's optimism was well founded: the army had always come after the Diné with full troops, supply wagons, and large guns. Time after time they had entered Dinetah only to find their enemies had disappeared into the remote canyons of the Chuska mountains. But this time, Carleton was determined to fight differently and the soldiers were sent out in small groups carrying their own supplies with them. And they were not so much hunting Navajo as Navajo sheep, horses, and mules. There was a bounty on all livestock and money was a great motivator for the ill-paid soldiers.

The troops at Fort Defiance were drawn in slowly. At first they only watched as Carson's volunteers brought in Navajo livestock.

"I wish we were out there, making money hand over fist like Carson's men are," said Elwell one day as they were unsaddling their horses.

"Do ye now, Josh?" replied Michael.

"Why, couldn't you use a twenty-dollar bonus for a few horses, Michael?"

"Sure and I'd love a few dollars more a month, Joshua," he said easily. "But no use grousing about the army. We both know it too well."

These days Michael felt he was becoming the walking effigy of a soldier. The only place he was able to speak his mind was to Elizabeth. Despite their lack of physical intimacy, he felt closer and closer to his wife. It was a new and wonderful thing for him: to have someone of his own to come home to. To have someone who greeted him with warmth, who was truly interested in his thoughts, in his day's work. He would sit down at the dinner table facing his wife and the cares of the day would fall away for a bit. Then later, over coffee, he would pour out his concerns. With Elizabeth to share them, he didn't feel quite so isolated. And somehow she always knew just when they had both had enough of problems they couldn't resolve and, opening Dickens, they would read for half an hour before bedtime.

The first few weeks of their marriage, Elizabeth had half expected Thomas to walk through the door at night and had to hide her surprise and guilty pleasure at seeing Michael. Their routine was very familiar and yet different. Thomas would talk about his men and the other officers, it was true, but he took his orders for granted and had never questioned what the army asked him to do. As the summer wore on, Michael was becoming more and more concerned about Carleton's policy, especially as more and more Navajo arrived at the fort on their way to Bosque Redondo.

"Another herd of horses and mules today, Elizabeth, and Joshua grumbling about the bounty," Michael said with an ironic smile as they drank their coffee that night. " 'Tis foolish, I know, but I keep looking for Antonio's bay whenever they bring in horses."

They both sat in silence, each feeling helpless, when Elizabeth got up and went to the bookshelf.

"Come, let us see what Mr. Dickens has in store for us tonight, Michael."

They had finished *Nicholas Nickleby* and had moved on to *Bleak House* and agreed it was a more powerful book, even though they would both sometimes find themselves annoyed at Esther's narrative. "She is just *too* good," Elizabeth had complained one night, dropping the book in her lap. Michael had smiled at her reaction. "Sure and I agree with you, but by having her tell a part of it, he keeps the story going."

They were coming close to the end of the book and Elizabeth had begun the chapter entitled "Jo's Will." As she was pulled further and further into the scene of the little crossing sweeper's death, she forgot Michael, herself, and everything in the power of Dickens's words. Her voice was trembling as she read:

"Art in heaven—is the light a-comin, sir?"
    "It is close at hand. 'Hallowed be Thy name.' "
    " 'Hallowed-be-Thy ...' "
    The light is come upon the dark benighted way. Dead! Dead, Your Majesty. Dead, my lords and gentlemen. Dead, Right Reverends and Wrong Reverends of every order. Dead, men and women, born with heavenly compassion in your hearts. And dying all around us every day.

Michael's eyes had been half closed and his head had been resting on the back of his chair, but when Elizabeth finished reading Dickens's words, he dropped his head into his hands. When he lifted it to look at her, his pupils were so black and large, his gaze so haunted and intent that she felt as if he were drawing her into his soul so that she could see what he was seeing: the faces of his family and friends who had been victims, like Jo, of a heartless world. For a moment, she stopped breathing. For a moment—for an eternity—everything stopped for her: her own heart was drawn into his, felt his pain and also the universal pain that Dickens evoked. When she came to herself again, when she could feel her own individual heartbeat, she knew. She loved Michael Burke. She had probably, without knowing it, loved him for some time.

It was strange. The words were the same. "I love you, Thomas," she had said many times. And it had been true. She had loved Thomas Woolcott. I love you, Michael, she said to herself, and oh, the difference. All of herself was open to him. The love went beyond the gratitude and affection she had felt for Thomas. There was no safety in *this* love. In that moment, she felt she could die from it, yet was only fully alive because of it.

She could say nothing, of course. He had married her out of friendship, not love. But there was desire between them, which they had kept banked like the fire at night. "I will only make love to you again when you ask me, Elizabeth," he had said. "Don't wait too long," Mrs. Gray had told her.

She stood up and placed a trembling hand on his shoulder.

"Michael, come to bed," she murmured.

He looked up at her, a question in his eyes. They both knew what he was asking.

She couldn't say it. Not here, not like this, so she only nodded slightly and leaned down to kiss his cheek.

He quickly turned down the lamps and followed her into the bedroom. The moon was full and she had not drawn the curtains but stood in a river of silver light. Her hair was around her shoulders and here and there a golden strand glinted in the moonlight.

"You look like a *bean sighe*," said Michael hoarsely.

"A what?"

"A woman of the *sighe*. A faery woman." He moved close to her and touched her hair gently. " 'Tis beautiful you are, *mo muirneach*."

She shook her head. "No, it is only the moonlight, Michael."

He reached out and began to unbutton her blouse, feeling her tremble as his hand brushed her breast.

In a minute she stood there, her clothes in a pile around her feet.

"Now you," she said and started on his blouse.

"First me boots, darlin', or we'll be in trouble," he said, smiling.

His legs and feet were swollen a little from the heat of the day and he thought he would never get his boots off.

"So much for us enjoying the sight of each other in the moonlight, Elizabeth." He laughed. "Get into bed, for this may take all night." But she didn't move.

Finally, he got them off and he stood in front of her again. He was dying, but he let her unbutton him and unbuckle his belt and undress him. It seemed like forever, but at last they were facing each other, bodies bathed in the gentle light of the moon. He put his hands on her shoulders and let them slide down her arms, then he cupped her breasts in both hands. "*Día*, but you are lovely."

"And you, Michael." She let one finger trace down his chest, brushing the black curls lightly, then she stopped at his belly.

Michael let his hands move downward slowly as though measuring her waist with them, and her hips. He bent his head then and teased one of her nipples with his tongue and she arched a little against him. His hand reached down and parted her with his fingers. Then, before she realized what he was doing, he knelt down in front of her and was seeking her out with his tongue. Her legs opened to welcome him without her even thinking, and she rested her hands on his shoulders. Elizabeth had never imagined anything like this before. She was embarrassed and frightened but the agonizing pleasure it brought her took her beyond any everyday feeling, and as he stroked her with his tongue, she buried her hands in his hair.

Elizabeth couldn't stand. She sank slowly down to her knees and he followed her down. When he lifted his head for a moment, she moaned in disappointment.

"I want to make you comfortable, *muirneach*," he whispered. "Come, lay back over here." He pillowed her head on her own skirt and petticoats and crouched over her. She reached down and felt his satiny shaft poised over her and pulled herself up so she was positioned beneath him.

"Now?"

"Please, Michael."

He entered her gently and cradled her head with his hands as he moved slowly. *Día,* but he loved this woman, he thought. He wanted to tell her, to cry out his feeling for her. But he couldn't burden her with that and so he concentrated on telling her another way. The way of bodies moving together as one, of hearts racing, seed spilling into her just at the moment when she let her whole self flow down on him.

They both uttered wordless cries, nuzzling one another, nibbling one another as though they were horses.

"Oh, Michael, I love"—Elizabeth stopped herself—"the way you make me feel."

"And how is that?" he whispered.

"Like I am not myself," she answered. "But I don't know who I am."

I know who you are, he thought. *Mo muirneach.* My beloved. He lay there, holding her close for a few minutes and then said, " 'Tis chilly down here on the floor, Elizabeth. Let's get into bed."

Elizabeth nodded but didn't move. She couldn't bear the thought of not having him inside her. She wanted him there all night. No, forever.

"Elizabeth," he said again.

"Yes, Michael. All right."

They quickly pulled down the covers and climbed in and he pulled her close. "Go to sleep."

He could feel her nod her head, which was against his chest, and in a few minutes she was relaxed and asleep in his arms.

Michael lay there feeling both a great joy and a great sadness. There had been no crying tonight or memories of Thomas Woolcott. In fact, it had felt like their real wedding night. They had come to know one another better over the past few weeks and Elizabeth had come to care for him. Michael was sure of that. But affectionate friendship wasn't love. He needed more than what they had and he didn't know if it was hers to give or if her capacity for that kind of love had been buried with her husband.

On the other hand, Michael Joseph Burke, don't be lying here feeling sorry for yerself, he scolded silently.

Ye're the lucky one who is alive and in her bed. And I hope ye can forgive me for rejoicing in that, Thomas Woolcott.

When they awoke, Elizabeth was flooded with memories of the night before. She wasn't sure she could even look Michael in the eye, she was so embarrassed. But oh, how wonderful he had made her feel. With Thomas, it was as though she had been a river, partly dammed, with only some of her allowed to flow freely. Last night she had run strongly and full force, as though racing to meet the sea, to meet her source. It had been wonderful. Yet today she realized there was still a barrier: she didn't only desire Michael, she loved him, and not to be able to tell him that was painful.

But they had time, she reassured herself. They were good friends who desired one another. All the ingredients for love were there and in time, love would grow.

Chapter Thirty-three

By August, the Rope Thrower had succeeded in destroying thousands of pounds of grain and driven away or stolen most of the Diné livestock. Manuelito and Barboncito had withdrawn further into Dinetah and had managed to keep their horses and enough sheep so that their followers were not starving.

Serena's child was due in September and Antonio made sure that she received extra food despite her protests that all should share equally.

"You are eating for yourself and our child, wife," he would gently insist.

"I know, but everyone has so little."

This was true enough. They were living on corn and herbs and whatever squash and other vegetables they could harvest. They would butcher a sheep occasionally but the headmen knew how hard the winter was going to be and encouraged families to dry the meat and save their livestock.

Despite hunger and a constant state of vigilance, Serena was happy. She knew her child was healthy for he or she was moving a lot now. Sometimes she would wake up in the middle of the night from a sudden, hard kick.

"What is it, wife?" Antonio would ask.

"Your child doesn't seem to be able to tell the difference between night and day, husband."

"Oh, already it is beginning," he would tease. "I can see this will be my child when he disobeys!"

Serena struggled to her feet.

"Are you all right?"

"Oh, yes. I just need to relieve myself. Even if the baby isn't kicking, I am up three times a night anyway. I'd forgotten what it is like," she grumbled, pressing her hand into her back and pushing the hogan blanket door aside.

"Do you want me to come with you?"

Serena snorted. "I think this is something I can do for myself," she responded sharply.

"Ouch! I'd forgotten what this is like too. Sometimes I think I've taken a scorpion to bed."

When she came back, Antonio was on his side, facing the hogan wall. She crawled in next to him and pinched his buttock. "Your scorpion is back," she said, her voice dripping sweetness.

Antonio laughed and, rolling over, pulled her down next to him. "This is the only way I can hug you anymore," he complained as they lay together, her back against his chest.

"It is not so long now," she whispered.

"I know. Go back to sleep."

Perhaps it was the lack of food or the strain and tension they were all under, but Serena's baby did not wait for the end of September. One morning in the first week of the month, she felt the pains starting and by suppertime, after only seven hours, their daughter was born. She was a small, scrawny thing and when Antonio first saw her, he was worried.

"Didn't you hear her first cries, husband," Serena reassured him. "She has strong lungs and a strong heart. And she found the breast right away," she said proudly, running her finger down the satiny cheek of her newborn. The baby, who was half asleep, automatically turned and rooted at her mother.

"See!"

All the families in their small band made sure that Serena got a little extra something to eat those first few weeks. The women would bring a pouch of dried peaches or the men small rabbits, saying, "This is a little something we didn't need tonight. We're all pretty full."

Everyone's belly was drawn tight and aching with hunger, but Serena and Antonio would accept the gift gratefully. Their child needed to put on some flesh before what promised to be a hard winter, and they would have done the same thing, had the situation been reversed.

Those first few weeks of their daughter's life were peaceful and happy for them, despite the circumstances. Serena's milk was coming in strong and although she was thin, their baby was thriving.

"She is a great gift," Antonio said one day as he felt his daughter's hand curl around one of his fingers. "We were lucky to have another daughter."

His wife nodded, but her eyes filled with tears.

"What is it," asked Antonio with concern.

"I know I should be happy. I *am* happy, you know that. It is just that it brings back all the old memories."

Antonio put his arm around his wife and drew her close. "We will never forget our first daughter. We all continue asking Asdzaa nadleehe to keep her safe. And we will tell the little one when she is old enough to understand, that somewhere she had an older sister."

"But will this little one live to hear the story," Serena said with a sob, holding her daughter close to her.

"I swear to you, wife," Antonio answered fiercely, "that this child will grow beautiful and strong. Will run fast for her *kinaalda* and will take care of her old parents when she is a woman grown. We *will* survive this."

By October, so many of the fields had been burned and sheep driven away that the headmen had gathered together to discuss the situation. The Diné were going into the winter with very little to sustain them and with the knowledge that Rope Thrower would continue his siege of Dinetah.

Antonio had accompanied Manuelito to the council and when they returned after four days, Serena asked them what had occurred.

"Delgadito and Barboncito are gathering some of their people together and going in to Fort Defiance, where they will ask for peace," Antonio told her. "I will go with them, to see for myself what this new colonel is like."

"And you, uncle," she asked, turning to Manuelito.

"It is too late for peace, if this *bilagaana* ever really wanted it! I know what their answer will be: Bosque Redondo or war."

When Antonio and the headmen reached the fort, they found Colonel Chavez waiting for them in front of his quarters. The headmen were coldly summoned inside and Antonio was left with a few men to watch the horses. While he was standing there, several of the troopers passed by, giving him hostile looks and muttering insults in English and Spanish. Antonio could feel the men stirring restlessly next to him.

"The Diné did not come to start trouble," he said sharply. But he felt himself stiffen with anger when he saw Sergeant Michael Burke approaching with a broad smile on his face.

"Antonio! I heard that Delgadito and Barboncito were coming in today, but I didn't expect your uncle or you."

"For good reason, *bilagaana*."

Michael was not surprised by the hostility in Antonio's voice, but at the fact that it seemed personally directed at himself.

"I am glad to see you, my friend," he said, "and hope you know that Governor Carleton's policies are not mine."

"Why should I know that, when you helped point the big guns at Navajo women and children."

Michael's face blanched and then reddened, as though he had been slapped.

"It may have looked that way, Antonio," he said slowly, "but I was not the one firing."

Antonio only stood there, distrust still on his face.

"He's telling the truth," said a voice behind them. "He lost his master sergeant's rank because of it."

"This is Corporal Mahoney," said Michael, red now from embarrassment.

"He disobeyed a direct order and risked a court-martial," Mahoney continued.

Antonio's face relaxed and finally he broke his silence. "Then I have done you an injustice in my mind, my friend."

Michael said nothing and Antonio continued. "I knew, of course, that in your army you must obey the orders given to you. But I blamed you anyway . . ."

"I couldn't have taken part in any massacre, but don't make me out to be any kind of hero, Antonio. I will fight Diné when it is necessary. Though I will not like it," he added.

"Of course." Antonio nodded. "And I'll fight the *bilagaana* soldiers if they invade Dinetah. We are both warriors."

"And friends, nevertheless?" Michael said hopefully.

"And friends."

" 'Tis a hell of a world when one friend may have to fight the other. Manuelito did not come in then, to see Chavez?"

"No, he means to hold out."

"And you, Antonio? Will you hold out with him?"

"I haven't decided."

"Carleton is out to destroy you all. You know that?" said Michael, his voice heavy with despair and anger.

"We know. But the Diné will not be destroyed."

"Elizabeth and I pray that this is so."

"And how is Mrs. Woolcott? My wife will be eager to know."

Michael blushed again and Mahoney laughed and broke in, "She is Mrs. Burke now."

Antonio's whole face lightened. "My wife will be very interested to hear that, *bilagaana*. And happy," he added with a smile.

"Your bay looks too thin, Antonio," said Michael with concern. "As do you."

"You know the Diné way, my friend. We take care of one another, but this time has been hard on all of us."

"I know," said Michael. "I . . . oh, damn it all to hell, man. I wish you all well." His eyes filled with tears and he grabbed Antonio to him in a fierce embrace. *"Slainte,"* he murmured. "That means 'Good health.' God keep ye till we meet again."

If we meet again, they both thought but did not say.

Chapter Thirty-four

For most of the fall, it was the New Mexico volunteers who did most of the raiding and burning, and Michael was relieved that he had no part in it. His duties were closer to the fort, with the exception of two escort assignments.

Then Christmas was upon them before they knew it. It was very different for Elizabeth that year. She was no longer an officer's wife, so she had no walk down the officers' line to view the presents, nor role as official gift bringer to her husband's troops. She made her Christmas cake anyway and gave it to Michael to bring to his platoon on Christmas Eve.

"The men were surprised, Elizabeth," he said when he returned. "And very pleased."

"Well, why should officers' wives be the only ones playing Lady Bountiful," she responded.

After the New Year celebrations, it became clear that volunteers were not sufficient for what Carson and Carleton had in mind and Michael came home on January third with such a black look on his face that Elizabeth was sure he was ill.

"What is it, Michael," she asked before they even sat down to supper.

"In three days we are setting off to Canyon de Chelly."

" 'We'? But I thought Carson had his own troops?"

"Not enough for what they are wanting to do, Elizabeth. The only good news is that Mr. Cooper goes with Carson and I have been assigned to Lieutenant McLaoghlin."

Elizabeth sat very still. She did not think she could bear it if she lost Michael also. But a soldier's wife never protested or cried. She just got busy making sure her husband's uniform and equipment were clean and in good condition. So she only said, "I'd better make sure you have enough long underwear and stockings, hadn't I?"

She said it so calmly, with neither worry nor agonizing in her voice, that all the hopes that Michael had had for their marriage seemed to die in that moment. They were friends and lovers, true—but she could let him go easily, it seemed.

That night they did not make love, but lay apart from each other after a cool good night. Elizabeth knew she could not have trusted herself not to cry out her love and fear for him and she couldn't send him off with that burden. He had enough to carry. And Michael knew that seeing her passionate arousal so separate from her feelings for him would be too painful.

Elizabeth busied herself with her mending and laundering and Michael with his careful cleaning and repairing of his gear for the next two days. They had quiet meals and no reading, for as Elizabeth said, gesturing to the stockings in her lap, Mr. Dickens would not keep his feet warm in this weather. She would go to bed first and Michael would stay up awhile to give her time to get to sleep. Their good-night kisses were cool and both made sure not to have any lingering physical contact in bed or out of it.

The morning of the sixth was crisp and cold and Elizabeth awakened before reveille. The water in the pitcher had frozen overnight and she was almost glad to feel the sting of the icy water as she splashed her face. It made her pay attention to something besides the pain in her heart.

Breakfast was quick and silent and Michael was dressed in his wool greatcoat and ready to go before she had even finished clearing the table. She handed him a small package. "Here is some fruit bread I made with the last of the dried peaches, Michael. It is not a Twelfth Night cake, but it will have to do."

"Thank you, *muirneach*."

It was the first time in days he had used the endearment and she had to turn to the stove so he wouldn't see the tears in her eyes.

She walked him to the door and wondered if he would kiss her good-bye. When he turned toward her she reached her hands up to his shoulders, but he only dropped a kiss on her head and she pretended to be retying his wool scarf so that he wouldn't think she had been waiting for a more loving good-bye.

"Shut the door after me, Elizabeth. 'Tis freezing out." As she closed the door and began to slide the bolt she heard his boots clattering down the steps. Dear God, what if she never heard them coming back? What if the next steps she heard were his lieutenant's, calling to tell her he had been killed in action? She opened the door and stepped out. "Michael!"

He turned, and forgetting everything, she ran down the stairs and flung herself into his arms.

"Be careful, Michael. Please be careful," she sobbed. It wasn't all she wanted to say. She wanted to tell him she would die without him, that she loved him more than her own life, that she ...

He was murmuring in her ear in Irish. She couldn't understand a word. She didn't need to. The words were full of comfort and care and that would have to be enough for her. For now. Please God, he would return and then, she vowed to herself, she would tell him she loved him with all her heart and soul, whatever the cost.

Michael had mustered and inspected his men automatically. His mind was on his duty, but his heart was with his wife. Thank God she had called after him. He had so wanted to hold her, but had been afraid to break through the barrier that had been between them these past few days. Maybe she was afraid of being left alone again, but surely some of it had been her care for him. It was hard to leave without knowing. And harder still to be going on such a duty.

As the troops moved through the gates, the band struck

up a tune. It was an old Irish tune, but the men sang new words to it:

"Come dress your ranks, my gallant souls,
  a standing in a row,
Kit Carson he is waiting to march against the foe.
Although we march to moqui o'er lofty hills of snow
To meet and crush the savage foe, bold Johnny Navajo,
Johnny Navajo! O, Johnny Navajo."

" 'Tis no 'lofty hills of snow' we've been climbing," Michael muttered on their third day out as he heard Mahoney humming the tune next to him. "There's nothing lofty about this atall."

They were two of the fifteen men Captain Pheiffer had assigned to break trail, and as he wielded his pick, Michael was reminded of the crews of men and women he had seen as a boy, building the famine roads of Ireland.

It took them five days of making their way through deep snow to reach the entrance to Canyon de Chelly. The men who had been hacking out the trail were kept with the advance troops under McLaoghlin, and they were to march from east to west, meeting Colonel Carson at the west entrance.

A creek ran through the canyon and every few minutes a mule or horse would break through the ice and Michael would have to talk the animal to safety. A few times, one went down completely and he and Mahoney would run to unpack the supplies and push the animal up.

Almost immediately after they entered the canyon, the Navajo appeared on the rim above them, hurling sticks and cursing the troops in Navajo and Spanish. Several troopers fell back to kneel and fire up at them, but they only managed to wound a few trees.

They camped halfway, and huddled together for warmth.

"Whatever are we doing here, Sergeant Burke," Mahoney asked as they drank their coffee and chewed on the last of Elizabeth's fruit bread. "We can't get up at them. They're not even living down here in the winter. What's the point of it all?"

"The point of it all, boyo, is that we're showing them that they can't stop us from invading the very heart of their country. That's what this canyon is and even if we never kill or capture any of them, Colonel Carson will have made his point."

"So I'm freezing my balls off to make a point!" protested Mahoney.

"Be thankful they're just freezin', lad, and that ye're not dead and some warrior relieving you of them."

"They are terrible savages," said Mahoney, automatically rubbing at his groin as if to reassure himself he was still intact.

"All men are fearful savages, Mahoney. Did ye never hear of being hung, drawn, and quartered? The British have been cutting out a man's guts and cooking them before his living eyes for centuries."

Mahoney gagged.

"And I've seen cavalrymen carrying pouches made of a woman's . . . em . . . private parts, so don't talk to me of savage, boyo," Michael said bitterly.

"Then why are you in the army, Sergeant?"

" 'Twas a good job, I told meself. Better than shoveling manure in a livery stable. And I wanted to see Indians." He was silent for a moment, gazing into the coals of their small fire. "And so I did, lad, so I did."

It was too cold to rest against the rocks, and so Michael and Mahoney dozed off back to back.

It took them two more days, but they finally reached the main camp at Chinle, where they were at last able to rest while awaiting Carson and his men. Two nights later, three Navajo came in, wanting to surrender, and before the troops started their return march to the fort, almost sixty starving Indians had arrived, saying they were now willing to go to the Bosque.

Michael was lucky to have been in the advance detail. Seventy-five men under Captain Pheiffer had been left to burn any hogans they could find. And to destroy the peach trees. But his troop was to return to the fort with Carson. Had he been with Pheiffer's men he was not sure what he would have done. Followed orders, he supposed, for this time following orders didn't mean directly killing women and children. But he was glad he didn't have to make a choice, for Carson's policy was designed to destroy the hearts and souls of the Navajo.

Chapter Thirty-five

Elizabeth had spent an agonizing week and when the returning troops were finally spotted, she joined the other wives who were lined up waiting to see if their husbands had come home safe and well. The men looked exhausted as they came through the gates. They weren't marching proudly, but limping in on frostbitten feet. It seemed to Elizabeth it took forever for the unfamiliar faces of the volunteers to file past before she recognized the men of Michael's troop.

Tired as they looked, none seemed to be injured and by the time she saw Michael's face, her heart was beating at close to its normal rate. He looked as worn out as the others, but he was back, whole and alive, and she offered up a silent prayer of thanksgiving before turning away. She could go home now and prepare supper and dream a little of what it would be like to have his arms around her again.

When he walked through the door she was appalled at how thin and drawn he looked. She helped him take off his coat and scarf and hung them up while he was pulling off his boots.

"Here, let me help you," she said, kneeling down and pulling. The boots were stiff and hard and when she got the second one off, she was upset to see that his socks were bloody from where his feet had been rubbed raw.

"Thank God, 'twas only blisters I got and not frostbite," he said reassuringly when he saw the look of horror on her face.

"Thank God, even if it was frostbite. You are safe and whole and that's all I care about," she said as he pulled her up and into his arms.

" 'Tis so good to be home, *muirneach*," he whispered.

"Your poor face, Michael," she cried as she reached up to stroke his cheek. "It is almost as red and raw as your feet."

They both smelled something burning at the same time.

"The soup!" said Elizabeth, pulling herself away.

Michael wanted to say, Damn the soup, but the truth was he was as hungry for food as he was for her and so he let her go.

He ate three bowlfuls despite the slightly burned flavor.

"You look like you lost almost ten pounds, Michael."

"I am sure we all did. 'Twas hard going and I was one of the ones breaking through the snow and ice," he told her, leaning back in his chair.

"Was there any fighting?"

"Only some firing at those who were foolish enough not to pull out of sight after dumping rocks on top of our heads."

"What was the point, then, of such a march in the middle of winter?"

"The point was to show the 'Johnny Navajo' that even in the deep snow we can reach their strongholds," said Michael with some bitterness. "Surrender or be burned out. 'Tis what Pheiffer and his men are doing now, burning every hogan and destroying the peach orchards."

"The peach trees Serena told us about?"

Michael nodded. "Almost one hundred Navajo surrendered to us while we were there. After Carson is finished with them, they will have nothing left to stay for."

After dinner, Michael excused himself to have a "decent wash," and Elizabeth cleared the table. She didn't want to read tonight, she wanted her husband. But he was exhausted. Much too tired to make love to her, she was sure.

When she went into the bedroom, she found him asleep in the copper tub they kept in the corner of the room, leaning back against the rim, his mouth open and gently snoring.

Elizabeth smiled at the sound and shook his shoulder. "Michael, the water is getting cold. You must come to bed."

He awoke instantly. "*Día*, I didn't realize how tired I was," he said sleepily as she handed him a towel.

"I've hung your nightshirt by the stove to warm it. Let me get it for you."

When she came back, he was sitting on the end of the bed, half asleep again, and she slipped the flannel over his head as though he were a child.

"Lift your arms, Michael. Now get up so I can pull the covers back."

As soon as she did, he crawled into bed and was out like a light.

She stood there, amused and disappointed. However was she to tell him she loved him when he fell asleep on her! She slipped on her own nightgown and crawled in next to him.

They were standing there, sunken-eyed, just looking at him. Their clothes hung from their skeletal frames. They said nothing, just looked at him. There was no expression on their faces, no appeal in their eyes. They were the living dead and he thought he had left them long behind.

Elizabeth was not sure what woke her but she was immediately aware that Michael was no longer next to her. He could have gotten up to relieve himself, she thought. But she lit the kerosene lamp next to their bed and went into the parlor.

He was sitting in the chair, his head in his hands.

"Michael," she called softly, "are you all right?"

When he didn't lift his head, she put the lamp down on the table next to him and rested her hand gently on his shoulder.

"Come to bed, my dear, my dear. You'll get a chill."

He lifted his head and she reached down and took his hand. When he didn't immediately respond, she said again, "Come back to bed with me, Michael. Please."

He could hear the concern in her voice. He would go back with her, he thought. Pull the covers over him. Pull her to him. Fall asleep and forget his dream.

But when they were under the covers, she wouldn't let him.

"What was it, Michael? A bad dream?"

Just nod, he thought. Just reassure her that he was fine. Just cling to her and he would forget.

But he could still see the faces, so it wasn't just a bad dream. He needed her to think he was all right, though. So he tried to say, Yes, it was just a dream, but he choked on the words. He was choking on grief and rage that seemed to have come out of nowhere and he started to turn away to hide it. He needed to protect Elizabeth ... he needed ... *Día,* he needed her arms around him, he thought, and he turned back as she pulled his head down and murmured his name. Then he was in her arms and sobbing and she was comforting him.

"Hush, Michael, hush, I am here and I love you," she murmured over and over.

She didn't realize what she had been saying until his crying stopped. She wasn't sure whether she wanted him to have heard it or not.

When he pulled away abruptly, her heart stopped. He didn't love her and didn't want her to love him. But she had no choice in the matter. She had said the words without thought, right from her heart.

He sat up against the wall and she lay very still. It seemed like an eternity before he said anything.

"Elizabeth?"

She could say nothing. He slid down again and pulled her against him. "Did ye mean what ye were saying, Elizabeth?"

She nodded against his chest. And now it was her turn to cry, hard enough so that she couldn't hide it from him.

" 'Tis all right, *muirneach,*" he said comfortingly.

"It is not all right for me to have told you," she cried. "Not when you don't love me."

"Don't love you? Don't love you? Haven't I been loving you for a long year or more? Haven't I been hazarding my immortal soul for the love of you, Elizabeth? Why in the name of God do you think I married you?"

"Because we were friends, Michael. That's what you said."

"And what else could I have said to a newly widowed woman? That I was dying for love of her? You didn't need to be feeling responsible for my feelings, Elizabeth. You needed a quiet place to be mourning your husband. You needed a home and a husband's protection."

Elizabeth was quiet. He was right. She had needed him as a friend, first and always. But now she also needed him as a lover.

"Do you really love me, Elizabeth. As much as you loved Thomas?" Michael was ashamed of himself for even asking that question.

"So much more than I loved him, Michael. So much more," she sobbed, turning and burrowing into his shoulder. "I have felt so ashamed of myself that I wanted you the way I did. I never wanted Thomas like that and I felt so disloyal to his memory."

"I love you, Elizabeth. With all my heart and soul. I always will."

She could feel him getting hard through his nightshirt. "I didn't want to make love tonight, Michael."

"Then we won't," he reassured her.

"Because I thought you'd be too tired," she added.

"Sure and since I fell asleep immediately, why wouldn't you think that," he said with a soft laugh.

She reached up and stroked his face. "Do you want to tell me what woke you, Michael?"

He groaned and clung to her. "I can't speak about it now. Not even to you. Maybe one day . . ."

Elizabeth pulled herself out of his arms, and unbuttoning her nightgown, pulled it over her head. When he realized what she was doing, Michael took his own nightshirt off. Her body was warm and welcoming and he buried himself in it, taking her slowly and gently. Or maybe she took him. He couldn't tell and neither could she. When they climaxed, it was together and for the first time the release was as emotional as physical, for they both cried out words of love as they shuddered in each other's arms.

Her uncle's hogan was burned and the peach trees destroyed. Antonio had told Serena twice, but she still couldn't take it in. She could close her eyes and almost smell the scent of peach blossoms that filled the canyon in the spring. She could remember how the fuzz of the peach skin felt against her lips when she bit into a ripe one and the sweet juice ran down her throat. Serena had spent all the summers of her childhood visiting her mother's brother and had expected to bring her children there and watch them climb trees and play in the warm, wet sand of the creek. And they would have brought *their* children. Something more than the orchards had been destroyed, she realized. The trees were important for something beyond the fruit they bore: they had been there for so many years that they held the memories of past generations and promises for the generations to come.

"So many are going in to Fort Defiance. What will we do, husband?" she asked Antonio that night as they huddled together for warmth. They had taken refuge in a small cave, once the home of the Ancient Ones. It was early to go to sleep, but it was so cold that they had crawled under the few blankets they had and kept the baby warm between them. They had scattered their fire after cooking the last of their food. Firewood was scarce and smoke might have led the *bilagaana* to them.

"Manuelito will not surrender," said Antonio.

"I admire him for that. I don't want to leave Dinetah either. But I do want to eat," she added sharply. "Manuelito is not the mother of a new baby."

"Your milk is still coming in strong. We can gather piñon nuts and wild potatoes to keep us going."

"I feel cowardly, husband. But a new baby makes you feel that way. What I would do if I were alone is different. The soldiers have promised food and clothing at the Bosque."

"I will leave it up to you, wife," said Antonio after a heavy silence.

Serena sighed. "Let us see how the winter goes. If we do not have to travel too much and if we can forage enough food so that I can feed her," she said, stroking their sleeping daughter's head with trembling fingers, "then we will stay."

"You are an amazing woman," said Antonio, holding her close.

"No," she said tartly, "I am Diné, and no more than you or your uncle do I think it right to leave this land. But I am also a woman who has lost one child. I don't think I can survive the loss of another."

"Nor I," Antonio whispered.

Chapter Thirty-six

By the middle of February, Elizabeth had become used to the sight of hundreds of campfires around the fort. Colonel Chavez had estimated that there were already over a thousand Navajo there, with more arriving every day.

They were coming in because Rope Thrower had won. He had chosen to fight a different kind of war, one in which a warrior could not fight directly. The enemy in this war was hunger and cold, and against these foes the Diné could not win. And so they surrendered, starving and suffering from exposure.

A few times a week, Elizabeth would collect as much leftover food and scraps as she could and bring it out to the families closest to the fort. Some of the women at the fort just laughed at her. "Whyever would you want to feed them, Mrs. Burke?" they would say. "We have them right where we want them, weak and starving." But most were touched by the plight of their former enemies and would give her an old skirt or worn-out army blouse to bring with her.

It was nothing, what she was doing. More families came in every day, gaunt and exhausted. They joined the others who were just waiting, for food, for clothing that never came. And for the army to bring them to their new home.

"Except it *can't* be home to them, Michael. This is their home and leaving it is making them as ill as hunger and cold," she cried one night at the table. She pushed her half-eaten food away. "How can I eat when I know that others are starving almost at my door. All I can think of is Antonio and Serena. They may be out there; one of those fires could be theirs and I'd never know."

Michael reached over and gently pushed her plate back in front of her. "Eat, *a ghra*. Your not eating won't help anyone."

Elizabeth wanted to cry out, But you are not eating either, Michael. Or sleeping! But she couldn't. Unless Michael chose to share his troubles with her, she could not force him. But it was hard to wake in the middle of the night and realize he was gone, driven from sleep by whatever nightmares plagued him.

By March, more than two thousand Navajo were camped at the fort and Chavez sent them on their way to Fort Sumner at Bosque Redondo with a company of his volunteer troops.

"Día," muttered Michael as he watched the ragged groups of Indians start on their more than three-hundred-mile walk.

Sergeant Elwell came up behind him. "What do you think, Burke?"

"I think it will be a miracle if any of them make it."

"You know I am no Indian lover like you, Michael, but even I am appalled. And even more are coming in as these leave."

Within a few days the number of campfires was increasing again and Elizabeth, who had not been outside the fort for over a week, gathered up some leftovers and, leashing Orion, went out for a walk.

She didn't recognize them and would have passed them by had she not out of the corner of her eye seen Antonio's bay. Her first thought was, That bay gelding looks like Antonio's, but he's too old. The horse looked almost like a skeleton, his coat dull and his eyes lifeless. But there was something about his face that was so familiar that she turned back to have another look. And then she saw them.

At first, she just wanted to turn and run. Here she was, healthy and well fed, leading a dog who probably had more to eat today than they had had in the past week. How could she look them in the eye? How could they still call her a friend? She felt guilt and outrage and shame wash over her in great waves. She hadn't seen the ocean in years, but she remembered what it had been like as a child when her parents would take her to the shore. How terrified she had been of the breakers that pushed you and knocked you down and pulled you under. She felt she was facing them again, as she turned and walked slowly over to Antonio and Serena.

"Serena?"

The woman looked up at her, dull-eyed. Her eyes were sunken and the skin stretched over the bones of her face. Her friend had had a round face, thought Elizabeth. Maybe she had made a mistake.

But then the man stood up and said her name. And some light came into the woman's eyes and she smiled and opened the ragged blanket she had clutched around her shoulders to reveal a small, black-haired bundle.

If it hadn't been for the baby, Elizabeth wouldn't have been able to get any words out. But she immediately smiled and began to make the universal crooning noises women make when close to a small human being.

The baby was thin but not gaunt like her parents and looked healthy. Elizabeth was sure that Antonio had sacrificed his own food for his wife and daughter.

"I . . . I am surprised to see you here," Elizabeth was finally able to say. "I had heard that Manuelito refused to surrender."

Antonio nodded. "My uncle will remain in Dinetah. He says he would rather die there than live anywhere else. But I promised my wife and daughter we would survive this. And we cannot out there. At least they have promised us food and shelter at Fort Sumner. This is not what we want to do, but what we have to do."

"Michael and I . . . we have been thinking about you, worrying about you."

"My husband told me you married that handsome sergeant," said Serena with a hint of her old humor.

"Yes," Elizabeth said shyly.

Serena gave her a tired smile. "Didn't I tell you, husband?" Her smile faded quickly, as though she were too weak, too tired to let any feeling surface for very long.

Elizabeth reached out for her friend's hand. "We will do whatever we can for you, Serena. I have been getting food to as many as I can. And old clothes and blankets. I will bring a bundle tomorrow, if you don't mind," she added, suddenly self-conscious. It was one thing to be charitable to strangers, but she hated putting her friends in a humiliating position.

"Why should I mind," asked Serena. Then she smiled. "Oh, it is another strange *bilagaana* notion. The Diné are accustomed to both giving and receiving. Sometimes one is the giver, another time, the receiver. It just depends on the times. And *this* is a bad time for the Diné," she added ironically.

"I will come back the first thing in the morning. And every day," added Elizabeth. "You will need all your strength to make it to the Bosque." That was all she could say to them. She would not undermine their determination to survive by telling them any of the news that had reached the fort of the ones who had died of starvation and exposure along the way. Maybe they would be able to stay at Fort Defiance until the weather became warmer.

Whenever she could, Elizabeth would visit Antonio and Serena. She started cooking twice as much as she usually did and would bring what she called the "leftovers" to the makeshift shelter Antonio had set up. She had originally imagined that in a week or so Serena's cheeks would fill out and some of the sparkle return to her eyes.

Her friend did look better, it was true, but Elizabeth soon realized that whatever she shared with her friends, they were sharing with their people.

Michael was not able to get out as often, but when he did, he tried to bring grain he had shaved off Frost's rations and soon the bay had filled out a little.

"So now he only looks half starved," he told Elizabeth

bitterly one night after supper. "*Día,* but I feel so helpless."

He was feeling more than that, Elizabeth knew. His nightmares were becoming more frequent and his eyes were shadowed by lack of sleep. But he had not opened up to her and she could not make herself invade his privacy. He would tell her in his own time. Or so she made herself believe.

As March turned to April, the number of campfires increased so that the ground around the fort looked like the earth was a mirror reflecting the star-studded sky. Michael knew that very soon the soldiers would have to move this group on. He didn't know whether he should be praying to go or to be left behind.

He was summoned by Lieutenant McLaoghlin in mid-April.

"Sergeant Burke."

"Yes, sir."

"It is no doubt obvious to you that these Indians are ready to be moved on to Fort Sumner."

"Ready" was not the word Michael would have chosen. They would never be ready to leave Dinetah. And physically most of them weren't ready. But it was, he had to admit, necessary to move them soon. Presumably there would be food and shelter at Sumner that wasn't available here.

"I know that you have been friends with some of them."

"Yes, sir."

"I need someone familiar with Navajo ways to be assigned to this escort duty."

"I am happy to serve under you, sir." And Michael was. Mr. McLaoghlin was not vindictive. He would do what he had to do without regrets, but at least he wouldn't be enjoying it.

The officer cleared his throat. "I am staying here, Sergeant. Mr. Cooper will be in charge and I am transferring you into his company."

"Yes, sir," said Michael through clenched jaws.

"I understand you have some history with the lieutenant. I hope that won't get in the way?"

"No, sir."

"Good. You leave the day after tomorrow."

"I can't do it, Elizabeth," he raged when he got home. "I can't serve under that *amadan. Día,* that they would put him in charge of something like this."

"At least you will be able to help Antonio and Serena, Michael," she offered hesitantly.

He supposed she had a point. But something in him was rising up. Not just the hatred of Cooper, although that was enough, but a stronger combination of rage and grief.

"I don't know if I can do this, Elizabeth," he said in a low voice.

"But you have no choice, Michael. Carleton's policy is not your fault. And surely having someone sympathetic along will help the Diné?"

"No one can help them now, Elizabeth," he said despairingly. "No one in New Mexico cares how many die along the way. The fewer Indians, the better. All they want is the land and the minerals it holds. And I am playing a part in it, whether I want to or not."

"Maybe it is time for you to think about leaving the army, Michael?" Elizabeth suggested hesitantly.

Michael looked at her in surprise. "Would ye want me to do that?"

"I want you to be able to live with yourself."

It was as though Elizabeth had put words to a conviction that had been growing stronger for months, perhaps years. But it was a huge step. And whatever would he do then to support them?

"Let me think about it, *a ghra.* When I come back, we will see how I feel."

It was spring, but you would never know it, thought Elizabeth as she watched the troops line up inside the fort. The sky was gray and threatened snow and the temperatures had been close to freezing for a week.

The troops were mounted and ready, their faces buried

in wool scarves. Outside the fort, twenty-four hundred Navajo waited. Some would ride the wagons, some their own horses, but most of them would walk.

Thank God Antonio's bay had regained some weight and strength, thought Elizabeth. At least Serena and the baby could ride.

It was too cold for the usual band send-off. "I miss the music," said Mrs. Taggert, who was standing next to Elizabeth.

"I think the trumpeters' lips would have stuck to their instruments" was all Elizabeth said in reply. It would have been awful to have lively music starting off this march.

Michael lifted his hand as he rode by and Elizabeth waved in response. She hated to see him go. She wasn't afraid for his physical safety this time, although perhaps she should be, given the weather. But she did worry about how he would cope with his duty. Would his nightmares keep him from sleep? Would he be able to take orders from Cooper and keep still?

Chapter Thirty-seven

It started snowing the first afternoon of the journey and by evening heavy winds were beginning to drift the snow across the road. By early morning when they started off again, the drifts were almost impossible to move through and so Michael and a few other men rode ahead, their horses breaking a trail.

Most of the Navajo were poorly clothed even for mild weather and some were actually half naked. The people clung to each other for warmth as they struggled through the snow, but by the end of the second day, Michael knew many of them must be suffering from frostbite as well as near starvation.

"*Día*, he is keeping us at a forced march," Michael said in a furious voice as he sat down next to Joshua Elwell at camp that night.

"That is exactly what he considers it, Michael. These are prisoners of war."

"Prisoners! They came in of their own free will, Joshua."

"That doesn't matter to Cooper. He wants to get them out of the territory and onto that reservation as quickly as possible."

"Well, half of them will be dead before we get there."

"Do you think he cares?"

"I know he doesn't." Michael spilled the rest of his coffee out without thinking. Damn it, boyo, he scolded himself as he realized what he was doing. Save whatever you can for Antonio and Serena.

The next day before they started, Cooper had the soldiers distribute flour to the Navajo. Michael was in front again, breaking trail, and he didn't realize until the next day that the people who were unfamiliar with it had been eating the flour raw or mixed with water. Their stomachs couldn't take it and they were crawling off the side of the road, doubled over by the cramps of dysentery.

Cooper kept his men after them, dragging them to their feet, forcing them to continue walking. That evening Michael dreamed again of the silent faces frozen in anguish. But this time, they were not the faces of his family and friends and neighbors. They were Navajo faces. He woke in a cold sweat and lay there shivering under his coat and blanket. It seemed to him that time and reality had shattered and shifted in some way. He didn't know where he was: in Ireland, where people had been sent Indian corn from America and doubled over and died because they didn't know how to prepare it and ate it raw, or in New Mexico, where Indians doubled over and died trying to eat European flour. Had any time passed since he was eleven? Had anything changed? How could it all be happening again? How could a troop of healthy, well-fed men drive starving people like cattle?

Something in him had split, but he knew he had to hold himself together, at least until he got back to Elizabeth. And so he prayed for sleep, which came for a few hours at least.

They had moved through the worst of the snow and Cooper sent the trailbreakers back to their platoons and pushed on even harder than before.

Michael had looked for Antonio but had not been able to find him. But the next day, he saw his distinctive bay and rode Frost over to him. He pulled several small bundles out of his saddlebags. "Here, take them quickly, Antonio, before old Stringy Arse comes breathing down our necks."

Antonio flashed him a quick smile and nodded his head gratefully.

"Are you and your family all right?" Christ, what a stupid thing to ask, thought Michael. How could they be all right, leaving their home behind and being driven across New Mexico like sheep. But what else was there to say? "I am sorry"? *Día,* he was sorry. He was in agony, not knowing who he was or what he could do about anything. He couldn't have saved his mother; his uncle had died. . . . He shook his head to clear it. He was *here,* not there. Oh, but here was so much like *there.* . . .

Serena had turned to him with such a look of gratitude in her eyes that he was ashamed and ducked his head. Then he saw her hands on the reins: they were wrapped in scraps of blanket but her fingers weren't covered and were looking almost white. She followed his glance and shrugged. "My husband and I think maybe I am turning *bilagaana,*" she joked. "Do you think they would let us go if that happened?"

Michael stripped off his gauntlets. "Here, put these on."

Serena protested. "But your hands will freeze."

"Take them, *please,*" he said, his voice breaking. " 'Tis little enough I can be doing for you except praying."

Serena reached up and grasped Michael's bare hand. "Whatever happens to us, my friend, I am glad to have known you. I think it will be important to remember your kindness to keep our hearts open in the days to come."

On the fourth day of the walk, more people began to drop by the side of the road. Their relatives surrounded them, encouraged them. Some families even carried the fallen ones, taking turns with an old grandmother or grandfather.

The soldiers were prodding them with bayonets, but some were so far gone that even that couldn't get them on their feet again.

"Put her in the nearest wagon," ordered Michael when he came up to three troopers pushing at an old woman's body with their boots. The men were halfway there with their burden when Lieutenant Cooper came riding up.

"What is going on here, Sergeant Burke?"

"We are moving this woman into a wagon, sir."

"The wagons are overloaded as it is, Sergeant. We'll be

lucky if the mules make it. Take her to the side of the road and shoot her, Corporal."

Michael started to move forward, his mouth open to protest.

"Is there anything you wanted to say, mick?" Cooper said with deceptive mildness. "Some order you wanted to refuse? You are lucky I am not asking you to do it." Cooper wheeled his horse and rode back to the beginning of the line.

Michael couldn't watch. He kept saying to himself, She was old, she wouldn't have made it anyway. Perhaps this was a merciful end.

The next day, it happened again. Only this time it was a young woman who had just given birth. Her husband was beside her, carrying their baby, and she was stumbling along when a woman behind them saw the snow becoming bright red in front of her as she walked. "Your wife . . . she bleeds!" the woman told the young husband. "Let me take the baby."

The man lifted his wife into his arms. She was only semiconscious and he could feel her few garments soak with blood and then freeze stiff. "Put me down," his wife whispered as he stumbled along.

"Never." But after a few minutes, he realized he was too weak to carry her and he moved off to the side, laying her down gently and brushing her hair back from her face with his blood-soaked hand.

Michael saw them and spurred Frost. "Get going, man," he said urgently, "or they'll shoot you."

"My wife is bleeding," the man whispered.

"*Día*," exclaimed Michael when he saw her. The woman who had taken the baby was standing next to the couple and he motioned her back to the march. Before he could think of what to do, troopers ran by him, their rifles ready.

"*No*, ye cannot," said Michael, starting to dismount. He didn't hear Elwell come up beside him and almost kicked him in the face as he swung his leg over Frost.

Elwell grabbed him by the collar of his coat and pulled him backward, nearly choking him.

"You dumb mick! Do you think Cooper will let you get away with insubordination a second time? He'll have you hanged, you fool!"

Michael fought only for a minute and then sagged against his mare. One shot rang out and then the two men moved by. The third was prodding the young woman's husband, saying, not unkindly, "Come on, man, get back to the march. I don't want to have to shoot you, too." Finally, the woman who was carrying the baby pulled the father up and led him along.

"Mount up, Burke, before Cooper sees you over here."

Michael mounted up and rode on. One more Navajo, an old man, was shot just before they stopped to make camp. And he was sure it would get worse the further they went, for the people had started out weak and hungry and were now dying from exposure as well as hunger.

He was fumbling with the coffeepot, trying to pour his coffee with his frozen fingers when Elwell squatted down beside him.

"What the hell is wrong with your hands, Burke? Are your gloves worn through?"

"I gave them away," Michael muttered.

"You *are* a madman, Michael," said Elwell.

"I am keeping them wrapped in my scarf. They'll be fine."

"Better be careful or you'll have yourself a case of frostbite," Elwell warned him. "What is it with you and these Indians, Burke? You've fought the Sioux. You've been Indian fighting for years."

"Maybe I've done too much fighting, Joshua. Maybe I'm just tired of seeing the same thing happen again and again. Maybe I'm wondering what the hell an Irishman is doing to others what was done to him."

"You're a damned idealist, Michael, and you'd better keep out of Cooper's way or you'll be a dead one."

"Thanks for grabbing me today, Joshua," Michael said, smiling ruefully at Elwell.

"Just keep that Irish temper of yours under control for now, man," said his friend, spitting out the dregs of his coffee onto the ground. "Save it to keep yourself warm!"

Michael made it through the rest of the walk by blocking out as well as he could the sights and sounds around him. He did not forget Antonio, however, and whenever he could speak to him and Serena without drawing attention to himself, he would. The soldiers were on reduced rations themselves by now, but he saved whatever he could and passed it on.

Chapter Thirty-eight

Michael had expected that when they at last reached Fort Sumner there would at least be food and shelter. But with their arrival, the number of Indians doubled and there were almost five thousand Navajo gathered on the edge of the Llano Estacado, the Staked Plain, one of the bleakest regions in the territory. Makeshift hogans and tattered tents provided shelter for some, but most were exposed to the freezing winds blowing out of the Staked Plain. The troops at the fort were on half rations so that the Navajo might receive at least subsistence level.

If he had seen the march as hell, thought Michael, then he had been mistaken. It had only been the approach to hell. Sumner itself was Hades.

By the time they arrived, two of his fingers were frost-bitten and he sought permission to find the camp doctor.

"Damn it, Burke, I can't spare anyone," yelled Cooper. "Only a dumb mick would let his fingers get frostbitten. Where the hell were your gloves?"

"Em, I lost them, sir."

"All right, all right. Get over to the infirmary."

The doctor kept Michael overnight. "Lucky I can save them, soldier," he said, clucking over him sympathetically and giving him whiskey laced with laudanum. "But they'll be painful as you regain feeling."

He was in the infirmary for another day and night, drifting in and out of his laudanum haze. He had a vague memory of Mr. Cooper standing at the foot of his bed, looking down at him in disgust. And of Elwell, sitting next to his bed, saying, "I told you so," and then, "Good-bye."

By the third day, however, the pain was at a manageable level. When the doctor unwrapped Michael's hand, he nodded, a smile of satisfaction on his face at his own good work.

"We've saved them, Sergeant. You'll be able to leave the infirmary today."

"Thank you, Doctor. I am grateful to have me fingers, I can tell you."

"Yes, well, your friend Elwell told me what you did. It was a stupid gesture, but a good-hearted one and I am glad to send you home so well. I understand you have a wife back at Fort Defiance?"

Michael laid his head back on his pillow, nodded, and closed his eyes. He couldn't, for the life of him, summon up Elizabeth at all.

"She'll be happy to have you safe at home then. But you'll be traveling by yourself."

Michael remembered Elwell's good-bye. "The troop has left?"

"Yesterday. I asked for another day for you to recuperate."

The next day, Michael dressed himself, fumbling awkwardly at the buttons on his blouse and grimacing with pain as he pushed them through with his healing fingers.

First he visited Frost at the stables with a couple of dried apples in his good hand. The mare approached him slowly as if to say, "Well, you've taken your time, haven't you?" She took the apples from Michael's outstretched hand and chewed slowly as though she were considering whether she should forgive her neglectful master. Then, with a low whicker, she pushed her head into Michael's chest in her usual gesture of greeting.

"So ye forgive me, do you," he whispered. "It looks like they've been taking good care of you. I'm glad, for we have a long ride back and we leave tomorrow."

He picked up a curry comb and after a few awkward minutes of adjusting his grip, got into a good rhythm of

brushing. The familiar activity relaxed him, and by the
time he finished, he was feeling better than he had since
he arrived at Sumner.

"I've got to find your old friend, the bay," he told the
mare. "But I'll be seeing you tomorrow."

It took two hours and Michael was almost dizzy from
the effort of keeping his emotions in check as he walked
through the camp looking for Antonio and his small family. Finally he found them huddled together with two
other families. When he greeted them and squatted down
beside them, they only looked at him with dull eyes as
though they had never seen him before. They were the
eyes of his dream, and he had a moment of terror when
he wanted to jump up and run away. He made himself
stay and keep quiet. The terror subsided, leaving a very
real fear for their chances of survival. He had never seen
faces so expressionless, eyes dead, with no light or spark
of determination behind them. If they had given up, then
what would happen to them?

At last, Antonio spoke. "We thought you had left with
Cooper."

"Em . . . no . . . I had some orders to carry out before
I left. You know old Stringy Arse," he added with a
smile.

There was no response from either Antonio or his wife.

"Em, how is the baby?"

"She is alive," said Serena quietly, as though speaking
took a great effort.

They all sat silently for a while and Michael feared he
was going to lose them. They would give up here and die
away from Dinétah. And why not? What reason was there
to live in this godforsaken place. And what use to them
was his anger and his grief and his guilt at what his
adopted country had done to them.

Finally he pulled out a small pouch. It was why he had
come, to give them this. He would do it quietly and leave.

"Antonio, I have a little money that I brought with me.
I am thinking that it will be a while before the crops come

in here. And there is always someone willing to sell if you've got the means to buy."

Antonio said nothing. Did nothing.

"Antonio"—Michael's voice was harsh—"ye must take this."

"Why must I, *bilagaana*? So that we will live a few extra weeks? Why would we want to live anyway, so far from Dinétah?"

Michael was twelve again. Saying to his da, "Da, I'd rather be here, starving with you. I can't leave ye, Da." Meaning he couldn't leave the green hills and rocky hills and pearl white strands of Ireland. He might die if he stayed, but surely would die if he left. But he hadn't died. He had taken the chance his da had given him. Some small group of Indians far away had given him. It was all one, it seemed to him: his grief, Antonio's grief. What was between them but an ocean of salt tears for all those who had died before them, victims of mankind's greed. He had to close the circle. He had to give back what had been given.

"Antonio, look at me." The passion in his voice made Antonio look up, although the Diné never looked anyone directly in the eye. It was torturous, but Michael's eyes held him.

"Antonio, I am here. I survived. Some of my family and some of my neighbors survived. So many of us had to leave our homeland," said Michael, his voice breaking. "I *know* what that is like."

Antonio's eyes changed. Only a little, but Michael could see some life come back to them.

" 'Tis my heart speaking to your heart, Antonio. You will take this money. Sure and 'tis little enough. But it will get you through this, you and your family. I *promise* you."

Antonio nodded and reached out his hand. "Thank you," he whispered. The Diné rarely said thank you, but this was a time to break that custom, if any was.

"I must go, my friends. I will be praying to the mother of my God for you. I will be keeping you in my heart and I will be hoping we will meet again." He said something softly in Irish, and then repeated it in English, "Deep peace of the son of Peace to you," and as he got up to leave, Antonio stood too. The two men were silent for a moment and between them was all the pain and unassuageable grief of parting: their own, which might be final, and the sorrow of losing one's own place and becoming a stranger in a strange land. It felt to Michael that the world's heart was breaking between them. And as it broke open, what it revealed at its core was the essential spark of the universe: love. Despite greed, despite cruelty, it was love that had kept him alive. And that love, which was not his to give or to claim as his own but only to experience, had flowed through him today and would give strength to Antonio and his family.

"I *will* see you again, Antonio," he said softly. "And if God and his Holy Mother are kind, it will be in Dinetah." Michael turned and walked away quickly. He could not look back.

Holy Mother of God, who am I to promise anything, he thought. He was suddenly drained of all energy and whatever had filled him for those few minutes had left him empty. Maybe it would have been better to offer no hope at all.

He left early the next morning, having said his goodbye and thanks to the doctor the night before. Frost was fed and rested and eager to get home, but he made the journey slowly.

No one had picked up the bodies of those who had died along the way and as Michael retraced the route, he saw their bones, already picked clean by buzzards. He felt like he was moving in darkness and the only thing that kept him going was that occasionally the dark curtain lifted and he would have a glimpse of Elizabeth's face.

Elizabeth had been frantic when the troop returned without Michael. She had received a short note from Lieutenant Cooper, which only informed her that her husband had been left behind in the Fort Sumner infirmary, which sent her running to the barracks to look for Joshua Elwell.

When she handed him the note, her face was white and her hands shaking. Elwell looked up after reading it. "He is a stupid bastard. Or a meaner one than I thought. There is no need to worry, Mrs. Burke. It was only a touch of frostbite that kept the sergeant behind."

"You are sure it wasn't something worse than that?"

"I swear to you, it was only a couple of fingers that were affected."

"Oh, thank God."

"He'll probably be back within a week," Elwell reassured her.

It was ten days. Ten days of walking Orion near the fort. And around and around the fort. Ten days of scanning the southeast with field glasses. Ten days of worrying if he had become lost, if not in the desert, then in one of his nightmares.

Elizabeth knew she was being foolish, but she couldn't help it. Her anxiety took her over completely and by the end of the tenth day she had almost stopped eating.

She was sitting in the dark in their parlor when she heard footsteps on the stairs. She was frozen in place. What if it was someone else, come to tell her he had been found dead. The door opened and there he was, his pale face shining through the shadows.

"Elizabeth?" He sounded disappointed as he called into the darkness.

She willed her fingers to be steady as she struck a match and lit the lamp next to her.

Michael was fumbling with the buttons on his coat and looked up like a startled deer.

"You *are* here."

Elizabeth walked slowly over to her husband. She looked up at him and her eyes held all the worry and all the love that had tortured her these past few weeks, and with a little sob she put her arms around him and collapsed against him.

"*Día, a ghra.* 'Tis all right. I am home."

He held her to him the way he had at the *kinaalda,* his

hand pressing her head against his chest. They stood there awhile and then Elizabeth released her hold on him and pulled herself out of his arms.

"Let me help you with your coat, Michael." She finished unbuttoning it for him and then he drew off his gauntlets. It was only then that she realized it hadn't been only exhaustion that had caused his awkwardness.

"Your hand, Michael?"

"Sure, 'tis fine now, Elizabeth," he said lightly.

"Sergeant Elwell told me they'd been frostbitten." Her voice was strained. "They look barely healed."

Michael flexed his fingers. "They are feeling very good, as a matter of fact. I'm lucky the doctor was so good," he said, shaking his head in disbelief.

"Come and sit down, Michael. You look exhausted."

They sat on the sofa and she curled her feet up under her and held his left hand in her lap, stroking it gently as though that might speed the healing.

His arm was around her shoulder. It felt so good, so right to have him home, and for him to *be* home that they just sat there quietly. Finally Michael broke the silence.

" 'Twas an awful march, Elizabeth. I didn't disobey any orders, but only because Josh kept me from it. I don't think I can stay in the army any longer."

"Leave the army, Michael? I know we have spoken of it, but it has been your life for so long. What would you do?"

"It has been your life too, Elizabeth. Could you stand to leave it?"

Elizabeth was silent for a moment. "Oh, Michael, it was my life because of Thomas. It became a home for both of us. It stayed my home because of you. But you"—her voice was so low that he had to lean down to hear her—"*you* are my home, Michael."

Michael drew her head against him. "And you mine, *muirneach*. I will be sad to leave. But I don't think I could stay under these circumstances, Elizabeth. I can't bear being part of this destruction any longer." He paused. "I was thinking . . . em, what would you think of being a rancher's wife?"

"Cattle?"

"I was thinking maybe sheep with a little horse breeding on the side. Frost is a fine mare."

"I think that is a wonderful idea."

"We'll not have much while we are getting started," he warned her. "It will be hard times for a while."

"I can take hard times as long as we are together, Michael."

He leaned down to kiss her and they lost themselves in each other's arms until Michael's stomach interrupted them with a loud grumble and Elizabeth realized that she was hungry for the first time in days.

"Let me get up and make us some cocoa and toast some bread, Michael."

They sat in companionable silence over their cups of cocoa, dipping toast slathered with butter and honey.

Elizabeth drained her cup and looked over at her husband. Michael's eyes were half closed and she got up and shook his shoulder.

"Michael, come to bed."

Chapter Thirty-nine

He had fallen asleep instantly, on his stomach, his arms thrown out. Elizabeth tucked herself under one of them and very shortly was asleep herself.

Sometime just before dawn, she realized that he was gone. She got up and sleepily made her way into the parlor. There he was, seated on the sofa again, his head buried in his hands.

"What is it, Michael? Another dream?"

He raised his head and looked at her and the torment in his eyes was unbearable.

"*Día*, I wish it was a dream." He began to cry, great wracking sobs, and Elizabeth knelt down in front of him.

"You must tell me, Michael."

" 'Tis their faces I cannot stand, Elizabeth. The eyes . . . they are death in life."

"Who, Michael? Are they dream people?"

Michael's laugh was ugly. "Dream people? No. They are me friend Kevin and me cousin Tom and the neighbor down the road."

"Why would they come to torment you, Michael, if they are people you know and love?"

"Because I am alive and well fed and damned to hell for leaving."

"Michael, you have never told me the whole story about how you left Ireland."

"I left because me da made me. Because the praties were blighted again and the fever was taking anyone who hadn't already starved to death. He wanted one of us to live."

"But your sister and father are still alive?"

"Yes. But so many of the others died. And God knows what kind of living they can be scraping out of the fields now"—Michael groaned—"and then this . . ."

"The Navajo. Yes, I see," said Elizabeth. "You are seeing the same faces, the same hunger . . ." It had been terrible enough for her, thought Elizabeth, seeing the emaciated bodies, passing the outstretched hands when she brought food to Antonio. But her family had never starved to death before her eyes. They had been slaughtered, yes. But her mother and father's suffering had been short, compared to the Navajo. And Michael's people.

" 'Twas an awful march, Elizabeth. Old and young were dying by the wayside. From Ballina to Llano Estacado." He shook his head and smiled a bitter smile. "Ye see, 'tis crazy I am. I can't keep it straight. The only difference is that Cooper ordered them shot, the ones who couldn't keep up. Even the English didn't do that."

"What about Serena, Antonio, and the baby, Michael?" Elizabeth was almost afraid to ask.

"Still alive, by some miracle. They made it to Sumner, God help them. Maybe 'twould have been better to let them die. There is nothing there, nothing. Even the soldiers have had their rations cut in half. Over six thousand Indians, no shelter, no food, and the water hardly drinkable. And *nothing* I could have done. I keep thinking there might have been something, if I'd stayed," he said despairingly.

"Michael," said Elizabeth, taking his head in her hands and looking into his eyes, "your family wanted you to survive. To live a fuller life. Somewhere where famine wasn't a danger. They wanted you to keep the Burke family strong and alive. It was good to leave, although it was so painful." She paused. "And there is nothing more either of us could have done to save the Diné." All of her own grief and anger surfaced as she said passionately, "I hate it, I hate what is happening. I could kill Carleton my-

self. I would if it would change anything. But this is
something that started before we even got here."

Elizabeth stroked Michael's cheek. "Come back to bed,
my dear. It is too cold out here." She stood up and took
him by the hand and led him back to bed as though he
were the eleven-year-old boy she had never known.

They heard the bugle call reveille only a few hours
later, but only stirred in each other's arms and went back
to sleep.

When Michael finally opened his eyes the sun was
streaming in under their bedroom curtains. Elizabeth was
asleep still. He took a deep breath and realized that the
pall of darkness had lifted. The grief was still there,
would always be there, but not the despair. He was here
in his own bed with his beloved wife. He was alive. He
had a future ahead of him and he owed it to everyone in
his family and to all of his people to live that future. He
couldn't give their lives back to the dead and he couldn't
change the lives of his da and his sister. But he could give
them his own life by living it. And by living on through
his children.

He turned toward Elizabeth. He was so lucky to have
found her, his beloved. He traced her eyebrows and her
cheek and then her lips. Her eyes flew open and she
looked at him questioningly.

"Thank you, Elizabeth, for holding me last night," he
whispered.

Elizabeth reached up to his face. When her thumb
touched the corner of his mouth, he bent down to kiss her
gently.

Her mouth opened hungrily and she heard his sharp intake of breath as he deepened his kiss. When he finally
pulled away she slipped out of her nightgown and helped
him pull his nightshirt over his head. Then her hand
found him and both were surprised at how quickly desire
had overtaken them.

"Easy," Michael groaned as she stroked him. He drew
his hand between her legs and felt that she was already
wet.

Elizabeth loved the usual slow, considerate way Michael aroused her before he entered her. But this morning, she didn't need it. Didn't want it. She wanted him inside her right away and as though he could read her mind, before she guided him with her hands, he was on top of her and in her.

It was as though all the released anger and grief had freed them for an altogether different release. Their hunger could only be satisfied by one another and at the same time both felt it could never be satisfied. Michael tried to get deeper and deeper, into her very self, her soul, and Elizabeth drew him in, arching up, opening herself to him even more than she had ever done before. When he climaxed, Elizabeth was close to her own and only a few strokes of his finger brought her up and up and then down all the way to meet him. And in the moment he flooded her, she knew, because she wanted him so much and because she wanted his child, that this morning's lovemaking would bring them a son or a daughter.

Between the time it took to process Michael's discharge and the time it took to pack, they had a week at Fort Defiance.

Elizabeth had been setting aside some of her housekeeping money and between that and Michael's pay, he was able to purchase an old wagon and two mules to carry their furniture and belongings. They both spent the week packing and saying their farewells, Elizabeth to the officers' wives she felt close to and Michael to his men.

"What are your plans, Michael," Joshua Elwell asked him the night before they were to leave.

"Raising sheep and horses, Josh. I know a little about sheep and a lot about horses," said Michael with a laugh. " 'Twould be better the other way around, to be sure, for the sheep will be the moneymakers. But I've always wanted to breed Frost and see what kind of foal she produces."

"Are you staying in the territory or heading north?"

"South. Not too far south from here. I've heard of some good land near Zuni. They're running cattle there, but there is room enough for sheep."

"If the cattle ranchers agree with you," Josh warned him.

"Well, 'tis hardly crowded there."

"So, you'll be meeting more Indians."

"Em, I suppose I will. The pueblo isn't more than thirty miles from where I'm thinking of."

"Maybe I'll come down and visit you someday."

"There'd be a place for you, Josh. I could always use a good hand with horses."

"And sheep!" Elwell gave him a mocking look of distaste. "Well, I'm not that far away from retirement, Burke. I may take you up on it. And bring Mrs. Casey with me!"

"She'd be welcome too. As long as you married her, boyo!"

"Should I say good-bye to Mary Ann for you?" Elwell asked slyly.

Michael blushed. "Em, yes. Indeed, and I was going to ask you to anyway. Tell her . . . em, tell her I appreciate her . . . kindness."

"Anything else you appreciated?"

Michael jabbed him with his elbow. "Begone with ye now. I am a happily married man."

"I can see that, Burke. You are a lucky man."

"I am that, Josh, I am," said Michael fervently. He gave Elwell a pound on the back, shook his hand, and said, "Don't forget your promise, Joshua. Good-bye then till we see ye."

"And you deserve your happiness, Burke," said his friend when Michael was gone. "You are not just a lucky man, but a damned good one."

It was almost as hard to say good-bye to Mahoney.

"Will ye be staying in the army, lad?" Michael asked him.

Mahoney's eyes lit up. "I am hoping to make sergeant in three years, sir." He paused. "I only hope I'll be as good with my men as you were with us, Sergeant Burke."

"Michael to ye now, Mahoney. And you weren't thinking that the first week I had ye!"

Mahoney kicked the dirt with his toe, watching the pebbles fly as though their trajectory were very important to him. When he lifted his face, Michael could see the tears glistening in his eyes. "I was a stupid young git, wasn't I, Sergeant? I've learned a lot since then. I hate to see you leave."

"And a part of me hates to leave, lad. But you have a fine career ahead of you. And if ye're ever in need of a place to work, ye'll always be welcome."

"Thank you, Serg . . . I mean, Mr. Burke . . . Michael."

Michael drew the boy into his arms and gave him a quick hug, after which both men became very busy, one with his neckerchief and the other turning and slapping his hat against his leg to get the dust off.

"Good-bye then, *Ma*honey," said Michael, turning away quickly.

"That's Ma*ho*ney, Mr. Burke," the boy called after him. "I'm an American!"

Michael smiled when he heard the boy's protest. "An American, eh. Now what in the world is that, boyo?"

Chapter Forty

They left early the next morning, Elizabeth driving the wagon with her mare tied behind and Orion sitting next to her, just barely able to restrain himself from jumping out. Michael was on Frost. He was wearing his cavalry boots and a relatively new pair of uniform trousers from which Elizabeth had carefully pulled off the yellow stripes. But his shirt was an off-white linen one and his hat was stripped of its insignia. It was strange to see him out of uniform in the daytime, thought Elizabeth as she slapped the reins on the mules' backs and they started off.

The big gates swung open and then closed behind them for the last time. Elizabeth wondered if Michael felt the same pang she did, leaving the army behind.

When they were about a half mile from the fort, Michael, who had been riding a little ahead, came back and motioned to her to stop the mules.

"I'd like to make a little detour if ye don't mind, Elizabeth."

Elizabeth tilted her head questioningly and Michael dropped a quick kiss on her lips.

" 'Tis the little canyon north of here. I want to leave something there. Maybe even camp there tonight? 'Tis a lovely place and I'd like to say a proper good-bye to the red rock country."

"Yes, Michael, I would like that."

So they turned north. When they reached the entrance of the canyon, Michael kept his eye out for the spring he had seen the day he had arrived at Fort Defiance two years ago. There were still a few prayer sticks and feathers, but nothing recent, for the people were long gone from here. He dismounted and pulled his old wallet out of his pocket. Elizabeth watched him as he dug deep and pulled out a small metal disk.

"What is that, Michael?"

"Well, Elizabeth, 'tis what ye would have called a papist superstition before ye met me!"

Elizabeth blushed and Michael came up to the wagon and held his hand out. " 'Tis a medal, Elizabeth, with a picture of Mary, the Mother of God."

Elizabeth ran her fingers lightly over the portrayal of a woman hammered into the silver.

"Caitlin had it from me mother and then gave it to me."

"And you would leave it here, Michael? After treasuring it for so long?"

"It seems to me me mother would think it a good thing to do. To leave it here as a thank you for you and all I've been lucky to find in this country. And as a prayer with the other prayers . . . that someday the people will be able to come home."

He attached the medal to a small stick and planted it a little ways up from the spring. "I don't want to disturb anything, you see," he explained. "I don't think anyone would mind, but out of respect . . ."

Michael rode ahead and Elizabeth followed. She didn't know what she thought about such images; her Protestant soul recoiled from the idea of elevating the Mother of God . . . And yet, there had been Changing Woman . . . She knew what she felt about her husband, though: she loved him with all her heart.

They tied the mules where the canyon began to narrow and then walked a little further to make camp, Frost carrying what they needed.

Orion had been tied to the wagon and was ecstatic at being finally released. He ran in circles and then took off downstream.

"I hope he doesn't disappear, Michael."

"He'll be back."

They set up camp and then Michael peeled his boots

off and put his feet in the water. "The sun will be going down soon, Elizabeth. But the water is warm here, where 'tis shallow. Do ye want to wash the dust off ye?"

Elizabeth giggled. Michael was standing almost in the spot where she had first seen him washing the dust off of him.

"Ye like the idea, do ye?" Michael quickly stripped off his shirt, exposing the white skin under his brown neck. His trousers followed and he waded in, his back to her.

This time, she could look to her heart's content. This time she could quickly strip off her own clothes and join him. This time, she could run her hands down that white back and over his muscled buttocks.

Michael shivered when he felt her hands slide downward and when he turned to face her, he was fully erect.

Elizabeth laughed.

"Ye think it is funny then," he said with mock outrage. "Ye weren't laughing the other night, me darlin'."

"Oh, Michael, it is only that you still look like a pie-bald."

"Still?"

Elizabeth ducked her head and he pulled her chin up. "I have a confession to make."

"Sure and I thought 'twas only papists who went to confession," he teased, reaching down to the water and splashing her lightly.

"Do you remember the first day we met?"

"I remember the first day I saw ye, standing on the porch and looking at me with great disdain!"

"Well, earlier that day I had come sketching to this canyon ..." Elizabeth felt her whole body grow warm with the memory. "I was walking downstream and I came upon this naked man."

"*Día*, ye were there watching me!"

"Not for long. I could hardly avoid it, could I? I turned around and left immediately. Well, almost immediately," she added with a shy smile.

"So ye'd seen me naked bum before I even knew you existed?"

"I did. And it was hard not to keep looking at it again,

in your blue trousers. You filled them so much more satisfyingly than Mr. Cooper."

"Old Bony Arse. I should hope so!"

"Serena agreed with me. As did Mrs. Gray," Elizabeth added demurely.

"And here I am thinking that respectable women only discussed recipes and embroidery and ye're comparing men's bums!"

"Only occasionally. You can't tell me men don't talk about women's . . . bosoms!" she said, aghast at her own boldness.

Michael's hand reached out and cupped her breast. "I have never discussed your bosom with anyone, *a ghra.* 'Tis too lovely to describe."

Elizabeth held her breath as he cupped the other one and then pulled her into him.

"Michael, we can't. Not in broad daylight!"

"*Día,* Elizabeth, how else do we do it at home but naked?"

"But that is in our bed . . . under the covers."

The sun was going down over the canyon wall and Elizabeth shivered.

Michael released her. "Get yourself washed, darlin', and quickly, for I have more than bathing on me mind."

They splashed at each other, laughing like children, and then came out and stood in the last puddle of sunshine as they rubbed themselves dry with a linen sack.

Michael had spread out the blankets and he pulled Elizabeth down on them.

The sun was more than halfway over the canyon's rim and they lay there watching the light leave and the canyon become veiled in twilight.

Elizabeth shivered and Michael pulled her closer and wrapped the blankets around them. The dying of the light had darkened both their moods and neither made a move toward the other.

"What are ye thinking, Elizabeth," Michael asked after a few minutes of silence.

"I am thinking of all the Diné who have come to the canyon over the years and who will never come again. I am ashamed of myself for forgetting and just enjoying myself in the sun and the water." She paused and then continued, almost harshly. "We are so lucky to be alive and together, Michael. I can't help wondering why it is that we are so happy and Antonio and Serena are suffering so ... if they are even still alive ..."

Michael stroked her hair gently. "Oh, *muirneach,* if anyone knew the answer to that question ..."

"I am so happy, Michael," she said, ending on a sob, "but then I think of all that has happened, is still going on. We have no right to this."

Michael hesitated. "I don't have any answers for you, Elizabeth. But I am thinking that our happiness is not an everyday happiness, born from easy times. We are together now because everything in our lives brought us together to this place. We have been living and walking toward one another for years, *a ghra.* And those years were filled with much sadness. 'Tis that very sadness that made us who we are, Elizabeth. It formed our hearts for one another."

Elizabeth sighed a long sigh, as though releasing some of her grief.

Michael continued. "I'm thinking that there is no happy-ever-after. We cannot just ride away from what happened here."

"Oh, Michael, and I would not want to."

"But there is *ever-after,* my beloved," he whispered, leaning down and gently touching her lips with his. "We will find a way to live through both joy and sorrow."

His cheek was wet. She could feel it as he kissed her and she licked at the tears after her mouth was free.

"Lie back, Michael," she whispered. He lay back on the blankets, the tears still slipping down, and she licked his cheeks clean and then moved her mouth down. This time, it was her tongue circling his nipples and following the track of black hair down to his navel.

"*Día,*" he groaned.

She slid back up along his body and then slipped herself down on him, sheathing him in her warmth and wetness. She moved very slowly at first, as he did, as though they were struggling for words, trying to find a way for their bodies to speak to one another.

It was slow and sweet and exquisitely pleasant torture, to be on the edge between great joy and great sorrow. Both knew instinctively what the other wanted: to go as deep as the heart, to reach to one another's core. Not to heal each other's heartbreak, but to draw from it, as a well. As they sought one another's hearts, they found the world's: a heart that had been broken over and over and over again and yet was still an inexhaustible source of joy.

They reached their climax together, for one had disappeared into the other. The pleasure was greater than either had ever known, but neither could tell whose it was. It was all pleasure, all sorrow, coming up to them from the red earth that held them and shining down upon them from the stars.

Afterward, they lay there in each other's arms. It was a moonless night and as the blackness grew deeper and more stars were revealed, Elizabeth could no longer find the patterns of the constellations, only the broad swath of the Milky Way. Suddenly she saw a star blaze up and fall swiftly in an arc and Michael heard her sharp intake of breath.

"A shooting star, my darlin'. A good luck sign for us. We will be needing it, I am thinking, for there will be some hard years ahead."

Elizabeth nestled more closely against him. "Nothing will be so difficult that we can't help each other through it, Michael."

They fell asleep in one another's arms and when Orion returned just before dawn, he settled himself next to Elizabeth and all three slept, cradled by the canyon and watched over by the last handful of stars.

Epilogue

"A package for you, Antonio. From Ramah. You must have a good friend there," commented the Fort Sumner postmaster as he handed over the parcel.

Antonio only nodded in agreement and turned away. Never since their long walk had he really talked with a *bilagaana*, soldier or otherwise. He kept his face still and his eyes expressionless. Not one of these men would ever come to know him. Not like his friend Michael Burke had.

He wondered whether he and Serena and their daughter would have survived without these packages from the Burkes. Many of the Diné had, of course. But almost a quarter of the people had died: of fever, dysentery, starvation. And many more of them had been almost constantly sick. And some of the young women ... He frowned when he thought about how many had sold themselves to the soldiers for extra ration tickets and were now suffering from those diseases caused by bad relations between men and women.

His frown turned to a smile when he saw his wife sitting outside their shelter with their daughter. The little girl was four now and when she saw her father approaching, she jumped up and ran to him, clutching at his legs so it was hard for him to walk.

"You had better come and sit by me, daughter," Serena called out. "I need your help with this yarn."

Perhaps it was their daughter who had helped to keep

them alive, thought Antonio as he watched her run back to sit beside her mother. By some miracle she had survived a difficult first year at Bosque Redondo when both she and her mother had suffered from the dysentery brought on by the alkaline water at the fort. But after that, despite the continuing desperate conditions she had somehow thrived. Well, not thrived, he commented to himself sarcastically. She was thinner and smaller than a four-year-old should be, but she had kept joy and love and hope alive in their hearts.

"Is that from Michael and Elizabeth? Is there a letter from them?" Serena asked eagerly.

"Give me a minute, wife," he grumbled, sitting down next to her. "Let me use your knife." Serena passed her knife over and Antonio sawed at the rough twine that bound the brown paper. Their daughter sat there, her eyes wide and expectant. She knew that there would be something special in that package for her. They came every few months, these packages from Michael and Eliz ... the people with strange *bilagaana* names. She thought she might have met the man when she was very little, for she had a faint memory of waking up at night and seeing a white face with very blue eyes looking down at her. At first she had been scared and whimpered in her fear and the face withdrew, but her father had whispered words of reassurance and she had closed her eyes and gone back to sleep.

She wished her father would just rip the package open, but he never did. He unfolded the paper slowly and carefully.

"Look, wife, a length of flannel and one of wool."

He passed the material over to Serena, who fingered the flannel appreciatively. "I will be able to make you a new shirt and pants," she said with a smile.

"You will make yourself and our daughter something first."

Serena shook her head and said firmly, "No, you are the one whose clothes are falling off."

Antonio grunted and pulled out a packet of sugar and a similar one of coffee.

"Now we won't have to boil and boil the leftover grains, wife," he said with a smile.

At the bottom was a flat brown paper packet and Antonio opened that very carefully. He pulled out two pages, one a lined ledger paper and the other a plain sheet. His daughter saw a very small parcel slip out. She wanted to grab it, for she wondered if her father had even seen it when her mother reached over and picked it up.

"Now I wonder what *this* could be? But read us the letter first," she added, her eyes twinkling.

Antonio unfolded the pages and cleared his throat and started to read. "Dear Friends—"

The little girl squirmed. She couldn't help it.

"Here, daughter," said her mother, handing her the little square of paper. "This is for you, I am sure."

Her fingers trembled as they untwisted the ends of the paper. There were three round red-and-white buttons inside and she slowly turned them over and over in her hand. They were very pretty and she wondered what they were made of. Then she felt her hand becoming sticky and licked her fingers. They tasted sweet!

Her mother and father laughed as they watched her and then looked over her head at each other. It felt so good to laugh. There wasn't much laughter at Fort Sumner, except for the drunken laughter of the troopers on Saturday nights.

She touched her tongue to the red-and-white buttons.

"Go ahead, you can put it in your mouth. It is 'candy.' " Serena used the *bilagaana* word. Her daughter placed a button carefully on her tongue. "Now go ahead and suck it," Antonio encouraged her.

Sweetness ran down her throat and a fresh clean taste filled her whole mouth and her tongue tingled. Her eyes alight, she offered the two candies left in her hand to her mother and father.

"Those are for you," Serena wanted to say. But she didn't. Her daughter was a Diné child and the Diné shared. So all three of them sat there quietly sucking away at the sweet, hard candy, momentarily lost in a few minutes of shared pleasure.

Serena broke the silence. "I haven't tasted mint in such a long time ..." Her voice trailed off as she thought of chewing on the fresh green leaves of the wild mint that grew near the canyon springs at home.

"I know," said Antonio softly.

The little girl looked at her parents. She could feel it again, the heavy sadness that was an almost physical presence at the fort. It had to do with this place called Dinetah that she could not remember. All of the people were weighted down with it. She wondered all the time about "home" and once, when she was very little, she had asked her father why they couldn't just go there. Now she knew better. They had to stay here because of the soldiers.

"What does the letter say, husband?" Antonio began again and Serena listened with great pride as her husband read the *bilagaana* words. It was one thing to speak English; it was quite another to be able to read it. But Antonio had grown tired of having soldiers read to him and had used what little free time he had to learn from one of them.

Dear Friends,

As always, we hope you are well and that this package meets some of your needs. We are sorry that this time we cannot send any money, but things at the ranch have been difficult this year, what with little rain and one promising colt killed by a mountain lion.

Elizabeth includes a small sketch of Caitlin in front of our ranch house. She is a frisky little girl and it is hard to get her to sit still. (Elizabeth says that I mean "lively" not "frisky" and that I've been working too hard with the horses and can't tell the difference between a child and a filly!)

We have found out that General Sherman and Colonel Tappan are the peace commissioners assigned to look into Diné affairs. Please God this effort will finally end your exile. I have great hopes of it and know in my heart that when we next meet it will be in Dinetah.

    May you all be well,

Your friends,
Michael and Elizabeth Burke

"Do you think he is right?" Serena asked, afraid to let any hope into her heart.

Antonio sighed. "Nothing happened when they summoned the headmen three years ago. But surely they will be able to see that we can't endure this much longer. The crops have failed every year, there is no firewood, and the water is poisoning us . . ." His voice trailed off. Of what use was it to catalog their woes. "Yet Dodd has been speaking for us. He is the first agent we have had in a long time who seems to care."

"You need to read this letter to your uncle."

"I will."

That night Antonio arrived late, after Serena and his daughter had gone to sleep. He had met with a gathering of the headmen and told them of the imminent arrival of the commissioners.

"You must speak with them, uncle," he pleaded. "You must make them see that if they let us leave here, we will survive only in our own country."

"How many times must we say it before they will hear it," Manuelito responded bitterly.

Barboncito and Delgadito nodded.

"As many times as it takes to *make* them hear," responded Antonio. "This new agent, Dodd, has listened and learned much since he arrived."

The older men nodded.

"We will try again, nephew," said his uncle with a tired smile. "We will keep saying it until they are so sick of hearing it they will let us go."

A few days later, Antonio waited impatiently outside the adobe officers' quarters where Manuelito and the rest of the headmen were gathered in conference with Sherman and Tappan. The *bilagaana* had been at Sumner for two days, looking into everything at the fort and its surroundings. They had learned of the crop failures, the alkaline water, and the fifteen miles men had to walk for mesquite wood. Now they were letting the headmen speak.

When his uncle and the rest finally emerged, Antonio looked at Manuelito with a question on his face. His uncle only shook his head.

Barboncito spoke first. "Your uncle has always held out the longest," he said with an ironic smile. "He was one of the last to come to the Bosque. He is silent because there is no answer yet. But we made it clear to these men that we will agree to any conditions as long as we can return to Dinetah. And only Dinetah," he added. "I think there was some idea of sending us to the territory in Oklahoma."

Antonio looked at his uncle. Manuelito grudgingly admitted that it was premature to shake his head. "Perhaps," he said sarcastically, "we will be the only people to keep our homeland."

Antonio understood his uncle's cynicism very well. He had had a long, hard experience of the *bilagaana*'s treachery. And he was right. Most nations had been moved from their own lands. Why should the Dine be any different? The most the headmen could accomplish would be to get them out of this death trap.

"And yet . . ."

"And yet?" prodded Serena.

"For some reason, I believe that this time they will allow us to go home." Antonio smiled. "You may laugh at me tomorrow, wife."

"I am not laughing, nor will I be. Dodd has become a good friend to the people. He will add his word. Maybe we will see home again." Serena's voice trailed off and she and Antonio sat there, seeing red rock and clear water, and the clouds gathering over the holy mountains.

* * *

The camp was alive with speculation and hope and when the headmen were summoned again two days later, the people knew that something had been decided and many of them crowded around the adobe building, waiting for the decision that would determine their destiny.

This time, Antonio stayed away. He couldn't bear it, if his uncle came out with the same expression on his face. He would wait with his wife and daughter. And so he sat next to Serena as she spun her wool and he repaired his bridle, which was falling apart in his hands. It seemed to take days, but it was only hours later that a shadow fell over them. Antonio looked up into his uncle's face. There were tears in Manuelito's cheeks and Antonio stood up, letting his awl and bridle fall in the dust.

"Uncle?"

"Nephew."

There was a long silence and then Manuelito whispered, "We are alive. We are going home."

For a moment it seemed to Antonio as though everything stopped, including his heart. So many years of suffering over, just like that. It was almost too much. And then the world started again: he could see the tears running down his uncle's seamed face and they were the streams running down the canyons of Dinetah. He could hear the people all around him, talking again after so long a silence. They were alive, truly alive. Suddenly he was aware that Serena stood next to him and he turned to her and gathered her into his arms.

Ramah, New Mexico, 1868

Elizabeth was making bread and Caitlin was next to her, kneading her own "loaf," a small piece of dough her mother had given her. Elizabeth smiled as she looked down at her daughter's chubby fingers working a rather dirty piece of dough. It had fallen on the floor twice and Caitlin had reached down to pet the cat, which had twined itself around her legs. It would not be the cleanest miniature loaf, thought her mother, but it was for Michael, and

Elizabeth knew he would praise it and eat it eagerly, cat hairs and all, for he adored his daughter.

"Come now, Cait, it is time to let the bread rise and then we will bake it."

Caitlin gave up her lump reluctantly and watched her mother slip it under the edge of the damp towel covering the rest of the dough.

"How does it get bigger, Mama?"

"The yeast makes it rise, and the heat of the kitchen. Yeast likes the warm weather."

"What is yeast, Mama?"

What is yeast, thought Elizabeth. What is yeast? "Oh, it is something that makes little bubbles of air, like you do when you blow through your lips, and the bubbles make the dough stretch and grow." Thank goodness her daughter accepted that explanation. Really, thought Elizabeth, being a mother called upon everything a woman knew!

She heard the sound of their wagon approaching. "Listen, Cait! That's your da."

Caitlin, who had been peeking under the towel waiting to see the bubbles form, turned and ran for the door.

"Just wait a minute, young lady," said Elizabeth with mock sternness. "You have flour and dough all over you."

"Da won't care, Mama," said Caitlin as she streaked out the door.

Your da wouldn't care if you were covered in mud, thought Elizabeth as she pumped water over her hands. She dried them quickly on the bread towel and, untying her apron, went out to the porch.

Michael had lifted Cait up onto the seat beside him and was allowing her to "drive" the team the few remaining yards to the hitching post by the corral.

"I'll tie them and you sit right there, Cait," he said after dropping a kiss on top of her dark brown curls before he climbed down.

After he tied the team he came back and lifted her down and, reaching into the back of the wagon, he pulled out a brown paper package and handed it to her. "Now run and give this to your ma."

Caitlin jumped up and down. "What did you bring me, Da? What did you bring me?"

"Now, what was I telling you to do?"

Caitlin stopped jumping. "Bring this to my ma."

"Well, then . . . are ye going to help me out?"

"Yes, Da," she said and turned and walked to the porch with a sense of great pride as though she had relieved him of one of his heaviest packages.

Elizabeth thanked her for being such a helpful girl and took the package. "Tea, Michael! Oh, thank you." She ran down and flung her arms around his neck. "You don't know how I have been wanting a good cup of tea."

"Sure and I do, *a ghra*. And so have I, truth be told. We had a little extra this month, so I thought I'd treat us both."

Caitlin was standing quietly by and he handed her a small package. "And this is for you, Cait."

She ripped the paper open and squealed when she saw the stick of candy. "Molasses candy, Mama. Look!"

"You can only have a small piece now, Cait, or it will spoil your supper. Now go see how the kittens in the barn are doing. Maybe their eyes are open today."

Elizabeth had seen the folded newspaper on top of the other packages in Michael's arms.

"Is there news, Michael? Has the Peace Commission made a decision? Can they go home?"

Michael dropped everything on the table and picking up the newspaper, read from the front page, "Treaty signed 6/1/68. The Navajo Indians who have suffered for four years at the hands of former governor Carleton are to be returned to their homeland."

"Oh, Michael, is it really over?"

"It is over, Elizabeth. And the same newspaper that four years ago was calling them 'vermix carletonious' is now happy to be seeing them go home. They are on their way by now, Elizabeth, for the newspaper is two weeks old."

Elizabeth was laughing and then crying all at once and Michael drew her close, bending his own tear-streaked face over her hair, and murmuring into her ear, "There, there."

She clung to him and he guided her out of the kitchen and onto the sofa in the adjoining room. There they sat, her head resting on his arm, their fingers intertwined.

"Oh, Michael, it has been a long four years. We've struggled to make a living, but at least we have had a home and shelter. I've been so happy most of the time, but all along I've felt the price of my happiness has been Serena and Antonio's exile."

"I know, Elizabeth. I've felt the same. And helpless to change things. It has seemed such a pitiful gesture each time we have sent them anything."

"I am sure your letters to Washington helped."

"Perhaps, but it is more likely they were buried under all the paperwork," he said with an ironic smile. "I think 'tis that they were *meant* to return home. Of course, from what the article says of the treaty, Dinétah is considerably smaller than it was. And they will have to be supplied with sheep and goats, for their own herds were so reduced."

"Can we go back, Michael?" Elizabeth asked. "I would so love to see the canyon again. To find Antonio and Serena and see how they have survived."

"We will do that someday, Elizabeth."

Dinetah, June 1869

The sun was beating down on their heads as they approached the mouth of the canyon. Although they had tried to travel in the early morning and the late afternoon and rest during the heat of the day, they were all exhausted. Elizabeth looked back under the wagon's canopy and smiled at the sight of their daughter curled up against Orion. The dog raised his head and thumped his tail when he saw Elizabeth's eyes on him.

She touched Michael on his arm and he turned and looked back. "So the wee witch is asleep at last."

"Michael!" said his wife with mock horror.

"Ye have to admit that she was driving ye mad today."

Elizabeth sighed. "She did. But she has been so good the whole trip. And this is the last day."

"Thanks be to God. This has been worse than any cavalry march," he said with a twinkle in his eye.

They had passed the fort half an hour ago. "Do you miss it, Michael?"

"The army or Fort Defiance?"

"Both, I suppose."

"I have fond memories of the old fort, Elizabeth. After all, 'tis where I met a certain snobbish Boston lady," he added. "But no, I am glad to be out of the army. It seems that raising horses is what I was meant to do."

"What about raising sheep," she inquired with a smile.

" 'Tis the wooly brainless buggers that pay for the horses, me darlin'."

"What's a bugger, Da?" said a tired voice from the back. "Is it like a beetle?"

Michael laughed as Elizabeth exclaimed, "Caitlin!"

" 'Tis not a polite word, Cait. Someday when you are older I'll explain it to ye."

"Like *gob-shite*?"

Michael heroically suppressed his laughter and said as seriously as he could, "Yes, Cait, I'll tell you about that one too."

"Michael Burke!"

"Yes, ma'am?"

"Whatever are you teaching our daughter?"

"I'll watch me mouth better, I promise you, Elizabeth."

"Till next time! Now, lie down, Cait. When you have finished your nap, we'll be there."

Now, here they were, almost to the mouth of the small canyon.

"Do you think they will be there, Michael? Would they have gotten our letters?"

"The letters never came back to us, Elizabeth. And if they have not, well, then, we'll spend some of our time looking for them."

As they entered the canyon, Elizabeth kept her eye out for the shrine at the spring.

"There it is, Michael. And look, there are so many prayer sticks and offerings!"

Michael pulled the horses up. "Hold the reins, Elizabeth," he asked and jumped down. He approached the little pool reverently and watched the feathers fluttering in the breeze. He saw the sun winking off a small metal disk. His medal was still there. He bowed his head and said a silent thank you. For the return of the people and for his own blessings. "Thanks be to you, blessed Mother of us all," for surely Mary and Changing Woman were one and the same, Mother to *bilagaana* and Diné alike. "Thanks to you for bringing the people home and thanks to you for bringing me home at last." For this was his home now, this land of red and yellow sandstone, redolent with green sage. This land which had given birth to many peoples over the years. This land where he had found his soul's home. And his heart's, he thought, turning back to Elizabeth.

She was pointing downstream, excitement in her voice. "There they are, Michael, there they are."

He climbed back up and, arm around his wife, drove slowly toward the figures waiting for them. The stream flowed toward them from the heart of the canyon, purling joyfully over the rocks and sparkling in the sunlight, leading Michael and Elizabeth to the people of the red rock whose home it had been for centuries.

The soft glow of candlelight spilled from beneath the doorsill like a guiding beacon. Slowly, Duncan cracked the door, glaring at the hinges as if daring them to make a sound. Hefting his knife, he slid into the room, edging around the pool of moonlight that flowed between the tattered remnants of the draperies. All the while he kept his eye on the mound in the center of the bed, trying to detect any change in the rhythmic rise and fall of the heap of blankets. When he reached the headboard, he doused the guttering candle before pulling the covers aside with a swift motion.

The sudden shock of cold night air was like a slap, bringing Kate to instant wakefulness. Her startled scream froze in her throat as a hand clamped over her mouth and cold steel pressed against her throat. She lay still, barely above to see the edges of an outline limned against the moonlight.

"Dinna cry out," the apparition warned softly.

Kate shook her head in an infinitesimal movement signaling submission. Mindful of her sleeping daughter huddled beneath the covers, she prayed heaven that he would not notice Anne and that the child would stay in slumber.

With deliberate care the intruder eased his grip, but the knife remained steady at her neck. "I will not scream," Kate whispered, trying desperately to think of some way to distract him. "Money . . ." she said. "If it is money you want, I shall lead you to what we have, but first you must let me get up." When the knife was withdrawn in seeming acquiescence, Kate pushed the blankets aside, lumping them into a heap to mask Anne's presence.

Duncan watched as she rose in a fluid movement, the folds of her flannel nightrail falling around the briefly revealed curves of calf and ankle. As cool as moonlight, she was, with a sangfroid that startled him almost as much as her beauty. The beams of light played on her hair, coloring the rich brown with silver tints. Green cat's-eyes glittered in the darkness, fear in their depths, yet her expression did not otherwise betray her. Her carriage was ramrod stiff as she turned to face him. He stepped into the moonlight, revealing his face, and waited for her reaction, the horror, the shrinking that was inevitable when members of the frail sex first beheld his scarred countenance, but she did not recoil.

"Follow me," Kate said quietly, searching the stranger's marred face for some sign of his intent. That single icy grey eye was empty of any clue. The lack of visible emotion was far more disturbing to her than the marks on his skin or the hideous black patch. For a brief moment terror held her in thrall, but she quickly passed the outer boundaries of that initial fear. A minute movement from beneath the covers caught her eye, but the intruder apparently had not seen it because of his blindness on one side. With a cold sense of purpose, she knew what she must do and quickly. Another few seconds and he might notice that she had not been alone in the bed.

It was a dangerous game, one that she would likely lose, but it was her only chance. Kate turned her back to the intruder, moving to the door with calculated provocation, swaying her hips in a manner that needed no interpretation, even masked beneath a thick layer of flannel. She glanced over her shoulder, giving the intruder a smoldering look half-veiled beneath a curtain of thick lashes.

For a moment Duncan was startled. It had been a long time since any woman had looked at him that way, not unless she had been paid well for her glances at any rate. Surprise quickly gave way to cynicism as he followed the temptress in brushed cotton. He moved warily, expecting some trap to spring momentarily. There was not long to wait. They had reached a turn in the hallway when the woman bolted abruptly. She sprinted rapidly out of arm's reach, her hair flying behind her like a fox's tail before the hound's nose. Duncan gave a grin of satisfaction as she disappeared down the kitchen stairs. Trapped between himself and Fred, there was little chance of her escaping. He ran down the staircase, fully expecting to find his man-servant holding her at the bottom, but he reached the final step just in time to see her disappear through a door. *The servants' hall,* he recalled, as he followed, *a room with no exits save the tower. She would not evade him again.*

Kate glanced at her unstrung bow and the quiver beside it. There would be no time to string it, much less nock an arrow, and the door to the tower was kept locked, so there would be no gaining time by hiding up there. She pulled a chair to the wall, standing upon the unstable furnishing as she attempted to pry the ancient blunderbuss from its place above the mantel. Just as she had hoped, he ran in after her without heeding his feet. He trod on one of the geese, and it rose to peck at his legs, a hissing, angry bundle of feathers protesting its disturbed rest. As he backed away, he slipped on some goat droppings, falling into the nesting hens. They began to cackle in agitated chorus, waking the rooster to protest his brood, and he began to crow. William, the goat, roused from his sleep, bleated irritably. Focusing on the source of the disturbance, the billy goat lowered his horns to charge the intruder. The stranger scuttled out of the way just in time, placing a chair between himself and the rampaging animal.

William wheeled and began yet another attack. The intruder raised the legs of the chair, and for a moment Kate dared to hope that he would retreat. He edged toward the kitchen door, brandishing the chair as a shield. William gave a bleating battle cry and dashed toward his opponent, but at the last moment the man slipped out of the way. William was into the kitchen and the man slammed the door shut behind the animal.

Kate pulled the weapon from its mounting with a cry of triumph, scrambling down from her perch upon the chair as the intruder started toward her, a murderous expression on his face. "Do not move," she warned, raising the heavy weapon with effort. The nanny goats bleated nervously as they heard William's frustrated cries from beyond the closed door.

"Madame," Duncan said, his lip curling in a mocking grin. "That weapon has not been fired since a Stuart was upon the throne of England and will likely not discharge again until the Jacobites are restored. I stand more chance of being pecked to death than being wounded by that antiquated piece. Now, who are you and what are you doing here?"

All at once, there was a burst of curses from beyond the door, followed by a retreating bleat. "Roast yer on a spit, I will," Fred roared as he burst into the room, decidedly worse for wear, pushing before him a frazzled-looking Daisy, her hands bound behind her. "Damned goat tried ter turn me into a bleedin' soprano. Found th' woman sleepin' in th' pantry. Damme if she didn't pop me on me noggin with a skillet. A reg'lar tiger this un is."

"A lucky thing your head is so thick," Duncan commented in amusement.

"Don't look ter me like yer was doin' so well either," Fred said, taking in his master's bedraggled appearance. "Cor!" He looked around him wide eyed. "It's Noah's ark, it is."

"Let her go, or I will shoot your compatriot!" Kate threatened in frustration. Was the man mad? For he seemed about to burst out laughing.

Fred looked at Duncan in puzzlement.

" 'Compatriot,' as in companion, Fred. She says that she will shoot me unless you let the woman go."

Fred hesitated, but Duncan shook his head with a chuckle. "There is no need to release your captive. Any hope that she has of firing that antique is merely an exercise in wishful thinking," Duncan said, stepping directly in front of the muzzle. "For even if there is shot in that old blunderbuss, 'tis extremely unlikely that the powder is dry. And even if the powder is dry, I suspect 'tis as likely to blow up in the female's face as into mine. But then, any rearrangement of my visage is bound to be an improvement. However, I would mourn any damage to yours, lovely one.

"Let her go," Kate demanded hoarsely, but neither the stranger nor his cohort made a move. She looked into the intruder's eye, pleading with him. "I *will* pull this trigger," she whispered, trying to convince herself as much as him. "Do not make me kill you."

"Why not, inasmuch as it might be saving the world from villains like myself?" Duncan asked, regarding her steadily as he walked toward her, wondering if she would indeed pull the trigger. He felt a stab of admiration; she had courage aplenty this wee Amazon, for she stood barely to his shoulder. Still, he doubted that her strength of spirit was sufficient to enable her to kill a man. *Who was she? And what was she doing in this hell hole?*

He wants to die. The thought struck her with all the strength of a physical blow as she stared at her advancing nemesis. *Now,* she told herself, as he stood at the mouth of the gun, the rod of metal the only barrier between the two of them. There was something in that grey depth that held her in thrall. Somehow, she could not pull the hammer back. She felt the weight of the gun leaving her hands and felt herself sagging. She was a fool. Now they were defenseless because of her cowardice. His arm came around her, supporting her, keeping her from falling down in utter despair.

"It would not have fired anyway," Duncan said, feeling a strange need to comfort her. She seemed so utterly bereft. Tears were slipping silently down her cheeks. He rested the stock against a nearby chair. It slipped, discharging as it fell with a roar and a flash. As the dust settled, Duncan eyed the blackened hole at his feet with curious detachment. "Then again, I have been known to be occasionally wrong," he said, coughing at the sulphurous smoke.

"I am sorry, Daisy," Kate apologized, looking at the other woman in anguish. "I have failed you."

"Never, milady," Daisy declared stoutly, her eyes glistening.

"Milady?" Duncan asked, his eyebrow arching sardonically.

"I am the late earl's wife," Kate said, seizing upon Daisy's slip of the tongue. "My husband, The MacLean, was killed at Badajoz."

Fred made a strangled sound, and Duncan eyed his manservant, warning him to be silent. "He left you in rather dire circumstances, it seems," he said, looking around the moonlit room at the gobbling, bleating, crowing circus of feathers and fur. "Or are you merely aping the latest fashion? I have heard that the Duchess of Oldenberg lives with a zoological menage."

"T'was the storm what knocked down the henhouse, y'see," Daisy began to explain, bristling at the implied disparagement of her housekeeping abilities. "And the goat's pen was near a wreck . . ." but her voice trailed off beneath the one-eyed man's quelling look.

Her captor's silent gaze sparked Kate's flagging resolution. Time was passing, and Anne might wake to find herself alone in the dark. The child would likely come looking for her. "We have not much," she said rapidly. "But I will give you the little money that we have if you will leave us in peace."

"Money?" Duncan said, feeling strangely distracted. He could feel her heart pounding a drumming tattoo, belying her courageous facade. But it was her eyes that betrayed her. Unlike most women, she was a poor liar. "Ah yes, money . . . But a trifle compared to the other riches that I have found." He raised his free hand to brush Kate's cheek. "MacLean's wife, you say?"

Kate quivered at his touch. "Take the money and go," she said, her voice hoarse as his fingers traced the arch of her throat. "I warn you, sir, the magistrate will deal harshly with a man who trifles with a lord's wife."

"Even a dead lord?" Duncan asked in amusement, pulling her closer to him.

"Especially a dead lord," Kate said, gasping as he brought her up against the hard length of him. There was no softness, only lean sinex, taut beneath his dark clothing. "My husband was a war hero."

"Oh, he was a war hero?" Duncan gave Fred a slow wink. The Cockney grinned.

"Duncan saved his regiment in the battle of Talavera," Kate spoke quickly, fighting against his grip, but it was like a vise holding her fast.

"They decorated him for valor."

That much was true; the wench's story was getting more interestingly by the minute, Duncan thought, enjoying the sensation as she struggled against him. He tightened his grasp, bringing her close and circling her with his arms.

"He was killed while trying to overcome a French artillery position in Badajoz" she said, trying to recall all that she could about her late husband's fallen comrade. "He was blown to pieces, so mangled that there was nearly nothing left for burial."

"Is *that* the story they told?" Duncan asked. "Surely, they could have done far better than that? MacLean was far too intelligent for such foolish heroics, I hear. There was no better man when it came to protecting his hide."

"Not always," Fred said sourly, his comment punctuated by a plaintive bleat from the goats in the corner.

"Aye, true enough," Duncan said, his eye flinty as he recalled his failure. "Every man has his flaws."

"You ought not to not mock, sir," Kate said, conscious of his fingers splayed against the small of her back. She could feel them burning like a brand even through the thick stuff of her nightgown. "My husband was The MacLean of Eilean Kirk. Harm me, sir and I swear his ghost will haunt you."

"A MacLean of Eilean Kirk!" Duncan said, drawing back in a mock display of dismay. "Then it is true what they say of MacLeans?"

"Aye," Daisy pronounced darkly. " 'Tis a pact with the devil they have. The MacLeans come back from the dead, they do, to deal with their enemies."

"How very tiresome," Duncan said, cupping Kate's chin with his hand. He could feel her tremble and felt a twinge of regret, but she deserved all that she got for her ridiculous pretense and more. He might have let her go had she chosen to tell him the truth, but the affront of an outright lie deserved punishment. "Nonetheless, I *have* heard that the MacLeans are cursed with the nine lives of a cat. I have also been told that their taste in women has always been the finest." He brought his lips down upon hers, tasting the sweetness of that lying mouth.

It was a kiss meant to frighten. Duncan crushed her to him, ravaging with calculated lust, storming her as if she were a castle under siege, demanding nothing less than total surrender. But somewhere in the midst of the attack, he lost all constraint. Premeditated passion was replaced by a strange longing to lose himself in her softness; to pretend for a brief interval that this woman truly desired him, to dispel the utter loneliness that had dogged him ever since his face had become a mockery.

It was like nothing Kate had ever experienced, this harsh and demanding assault. She could barely breathe before the bombardment began anew. His hands tangled in her hair, keeping her captive. It was shocking to find that a part of her was responding to his caresses, almost eager to explore these new sensations that shook her to the very marrow. There had only been one man in her life, and her late husband's kisses had been few and perfunctory. Then the intruder's tongue began to plunger, consuming her like a fire raging out of control, and every last trace of curiosity was banished. She was being disloyal, wanton, an empty-headed fool. Terror welled up within her, but she knew that she could not give way to her fear. *Anne,* she reminded herself. *Think of Anne.*

Duncan felt her stiffen, begin to struggle against him, and he knew that he had achieved his aim. Slowly, reluctantly, he released her, expecting to see utter horror in those emerald depths. Instead, there was glittering anger, so strong and feral that he half expected her to hiss.

"Are you quite finished?" Kate asked, wiping her hand across her lips as if to clean them.

"Leave her be, you dirty scum!" Daisy shouted, lunging at Duncan, but Fed held her back.

"Canna a man even steal a simple kiss?" Duncan asked, feeling a touch of grudging admiration. Pluck to the backbone this one; it seemed that stronger measures might be required to force the truth from her. Gathering up a moonlit handful of her hair, Duncan rubbed it against his cheek. "A damned poor homecoming it seems to me, for a man given up for dead when he cannot even get a kiss. But then why settle for a kiss?" He scooped her up in his arms like a rag doll, setting the chickens to squawking as he started for the door.

"Let me go," Kate screamed, beating her fists ineffectually against his chest. If he brought her upstairs, he would surely discover Anne. "They will hang you, I swear they will, and if not, I shall kill you with my own hands, but not before I cut off your—"

"Tsk, tsk!" Duncan said, shaking with suppressed laughter. "I must admit that it is no wonder that I have forgotten marrying you, my lady wife, for you seem something of a shrew. Is that why I went off to war, do you think, Fred? Many a man has found the battlefield a more peaceable place than the marriage bed."

"Aye, 'tis true enough, Major," Fred said, trying in vain to stifle a guffaw. "A real spitfire that 'un. Don't look ter be a female that a man 'ud forget real easy though."

"True enough," Duncan said softly, watching the moonlight cast its alabaster glow on her flawless skin and trace the swollen line of her lips.

"It cannot be," Kate whispered, ceasing her struggles and looking at Duncan in dismay as the meaning of his words finally penetrated.

"Ah, but it is," Duncan said, his smile sardonic and chilling. "Duncan MacLean, at your service, madame. Now who in bloody hell are you?"

From *The Devil's Due*
by Rita Boucher

BREATHTAKING ROMANCES YOU WON'T WANT TO MISS

WE NEED YOUR HELP

To continue to bring you quality romance
that meets your personal expectations,
we at TOPAZ books want to hear from you.
Help us by filling out this questionnaire, and in exchange
we will give you a **free gift** as a token of our gratitude.

- Is this the first TOPAZ book you've purchased? (circle one)

    YES   NO

    The title and author of this book is: _____

- If this was not the first TOPAZ book you've purchased, how many have you bought in the past year?

    a: 0 - 5   b 6 - 10   c: more than 10   d: more than 20

- How many romances in total did you buy in the past year?

    a: 0 - 5   b: 6 - 10   c: more than 10   d: more than 20 ____

- How would you rate your overall satisfaction with this book?

    a: Excellent   b: Good   c: Fair   d: Poor

- What was the main reason you bought this book?

    a: It is a TOPAZ novel, and I know that TOPAZ stands
       for quality romance fiction
    b: I liked the cover
    c: The story-line intrigued me
    d: I love this author
    e: I really liked the setting
    f: I love the cover models
    g: Other: _____

- Where did you buy this TOPAZ novel?

    a: Bookstore   b: Airport   c: Warehouse Club
    d: Department Store   e: Supermarket   f: Drugstore
    g: Other: _____

- Did you pay the full cover price for this TOPAZ novel? (circle one)

    YES   NO

    If you did not, what price did you pay? _____

- Who are your favorite TOPAZ authors? (Please list)

- How did you first hear about TOPAZ books?

    a: I saw the books in a bookstore
    b: I saw the TOPAZ Man on TV or at a signing
    c: A friend told me about TOPAZ
    d: I saw an advertisement in_____magazine
    e: Other: _____

- What type of romance do you generally prefer?

    a: Historical   b: Contemporary
    c: Romantic Suspense   d: Paranormal (time travel,
       futuristic, vampires, ghosts, warlocks, etc.)
    d: Regency   e: Other: _____

- What historical settings do you prefer?

    a: England   b: Regency England   c: Scotland
    e: Ireland   f: America   g: Western Americana
    h: American Indian   i: Other: _____

- What type of story do you prefer?

  a: Very sexy b: Sweet, less explicit
  c: Light and humorous d: More emotionally intense
  e: Dealing with darker issues f: Other

- What kind of covers do you prefer?

  a: Illustrating both hero and heroine b: Hero alone
  c: No people (art only) d: Other_____

- What other genres do you like to read (circle all that apply)

  Mystery Medical Thrillers Science Fiction
  Suspense Fantasy Self-help
  Classics General Fiction Legal Thrillers
  Historical Fiction

- Who is your favorite author, and why?_____

  _____

- What magazines do you like to read? (circle all that apply)

  a: *People* b: *Time/Newsweek*
  c: *Entertainment Weekly* d: *Romantic Times*
  e: *Star* f: *National Enquirer*
  g: *Cosmopolitan* h: *Woman's Day*
  i: *Ladies' Home Journal* j: *Redbook*
  k: Other:_____

- In which region of the United States do you reside?

  a: Northeast b: Midatlantic c: South
  d: Midwest e: Mountain f: Southwest
  g: Pacific Coast

- What is your age group/sex? a: Female b: Male

  a: under 18 b: 19-25 c: 26-30 d: 31-35 e: 56-60
  f: 41-45 g: 46-50 h: 51-55 i: 56-60 j: Over 60

- What is your marital status?

  a: Married b: Single c: No longer married

- What is your current level of education?

  a: High school b: College Degree
  c: Graduate Degree d: Other: _____

- Do you receive the TOPAZ *Romantic Liaisons* newsletter, a quarterly newsletter with the latest information on Topaz books and authors?

  YES NO

  If not, would you like to? YES NO

  Fill in the address where you would like your free gift to be sent:

  Name: _____

  Address: _____

  City:_____Zip Code: _____

  You should receive your free gift in 6 to 8 weeks.
  Please send the completed survey to:

Penguin USA•Mass Market
Dept. TS
375 Hudson St.
New York, NY 10014

APR 26 1996